Mary Baader Kaley

BURROWED

ANGRY ROBOT
An imprint of Watkins Media Ltd

Unit 11, Shepperton House
89 Shepperton Road
London N1 3DF
UK

angryrobotbooks.com
twitter.com/angryrobotbooks
I am but a dullard

An Angry Robot paperback original, 2023

Cover by Apostolos Gkantinas
Edited by Gemma Creffield and Alice Abrams
Set in Meridien

ISBN 978 1 91520 214 7
Ebook ISBN 978 1 91520 215 4

Printed and bound in the United Kingdom by TJ Books Ltd.

9 8 7 6 5 4 3 2 1

FSC
www.fsc.org

MIX
Paper from
responsible sources
FSC® C013056

To my father
who survived polio as a child.
To my daughter
who survived meningitis when
she was only weeks old.
And to the medical workers
who made them well again.

CHAPTER 1

Horrific Thing to Say

Ghosts roam the shadows of our Sublery's walls. Or, at least, that's what some of the younger sublings claim. I don't normally see them – the withering souls reaching from the shadows – but today I do. My mind tells me they're not real, but the icy tendrils of fear reaching through me scream otherwise.

My nurserymaid snaps my travel skirt in the air, sending enormous shadows cascading down the slate walls of the underground room. Even the ceiling lights flicker as if to complain from the sudden breeze as I shiver in my underslip. *They're not real, they're not real,* I chant silently to myself, even as these shadowy ghosts and flames reach for me one last time to claim me as their own before I can leave this place. As nursery lore tells it, they're the spirits of deceased children wailing in the crematorium, screaming for the lives they don't get to live, and cursing the rest of us who remained healthy enough not to die. We believe they want to steal life from the surviving children, not realizing that once a life is separated from a soul it cannot be used by anyone else. Robbing a life only creates another dead child, and the cycle starts again, much like the plague that sent sublings underground in the first place.

"Stop your whining," Na'rm Anetta says as she snaps the skirt again.

I flinch, but neither she nor the ghosts can spook me

much longer. I'm leaving today, I remind myself over and over. I take my deepest breath.

"May I wear a cap?" I try to smooth my wispy hair, but my goggle straps get in the way, and it sticks out in confused directions.

A scowl grows on my nurserymaid's face. "Hats are only for boys, and only because they have no hair," she says to the beat of her up-and-down skirt snapping, and then holds it out for me to step into. She'd taken the hem up and adjusted the waist so that it falls exactly at midcalf-length.

Across the room, another nurserymaid sings a melody while brushing her subling's long, white hair. I begin to hum with her but she's singing at a slower pace, and the usually comforting song now has a hymn-like lilt to it. The subling girl wipes tears from her cheeks, her voice crackling as she tries to sing along for the last time. I'm sad for her, but she'll be okay at the burrows. She's a good size, has never been to the infirmary for longer than a week, and she doesn't wear goggles.

"Pay attention." Na'rm Anetta holds out a starched blouse. Her gaze bounces across the room and back to me. "I don't suppose we'll miss each other as they will."

I straighten my body like she's taught me – as if a giant Omnit is pulling me up by the roots of my hair. "I will always be grateful to you for your dedication in raising me to my seventh year," I say perfunctorily, as I hand her my good-bye gift. The traditional hand-painted bead will be her first ever memento, so I used the finest brush to paint a design that the artmaid *oooh*ed over – she said it reminded her of a mist of water frozen in the air.

My na'rm isn't moved by my masterpiece, though, and drops the bead onto the wheeled dressing cart. It falls with a tinny clank next to the brush that we don't need.

On the other side of the room, my roommate's na'rm kisses the simply striped bead she's been given and strings it onto her necklace – which now has two beads – before replacing it around her neck. The two of them weep, embracing as if they could never be separated by something as slight as Sublery Graduation.

I tilt my head at my na'rm and blink really hard, testing if tears will sprout from my eyes. I'm too excited, though; glad we're leaving a month early. After Common Good sent word that they're clearing all subs from this region, it forced my graduating class to pack for the burrows that much sooner. I was the only one who clapped when the Grand Na'rm announced the news.

"Maybe we'll miss each other in smaller ways," I say to my na'rm, trying to be as grateful as a non-wicked subling should be. But that's the difference between us – she's allowed to tell when I misbehave, but I cannot help her see her own temper. "You're a wonderful seamstress," I add.

Na'rm Anetta's eyes sour, as if everything about me has grown blurry. It's the face she makes most when she looks at me – like she's pretending I'm not really there, like I'm a child-ghost on the wall. She bumps into the dressing cart, and the bead begins to roll. I point as it nears the edge, but then it slows to a stop.

"Don't stare at me like that, subling!" She smacks my hand and sighs. "I never did connect with you. *Give it a few months*, they said. *How can I raise her if I can't see her eyes?* I implored. Somebody had to, though, and I was that unfortunate somebody." She hands me the satchel packed with my book. "Hear me this one last time, girl. Do not allow your temper to slither out of that wicked mouth of yours."

I swallow the redhot words at the tip of my tongue because *unpleasant sentiment isn't to be tolerated.* My thick goggles hide my rage. Besides, I've only pointed out her blunders to help her do better with her next subling, not for the purpose of being wicked. Not the sole purpose, anyway.

"Your medera will not allow you the same cheekiness I have endured all these years. My full report includes pointers on how to manage you."

My face prickles as if she slapped me. "Report?" Sublery Graduation is my chance to start fresh. "You didn't say I'm cheeky–"

"I've relayed the pertinent facts." She steps back to inspect me. "It's up to Medera Gelia Cayan to gauge the degree of your wickedness."

"No." I rub the sweat from my palms into my new skirt. "Fix it, please. Or at the least tell her I'm a model learner, and I coach the younger sublings to read."

"Your medera already has the report, not that I would revise one word." She steps back as if she's completely done with me. Her hand moves in a half-flutter-half-wave as she spins the wheeled table around to walk off. "Good health, girl." Her pleated skirt rustles about in awkward swishes as if it's fighting to free itself from her.

"I do *not* wish you good health!" I call back, tightening my fists. "*You* are wicked."

The other maid gasps, covering her subling's ears.

Na'rm Anetta flies around and stands above me in an instant, yanking my satchel. "Give me the book."

"No!" It's the memento I chose, the one thing that I'm allowed to bring with me – she can't take it back. "I will report you to Common Good." I have no idea if my threat carries any weight, but if our government is serious about their pledge for the good of common people like me, then they might be interested to hear about Na'rm Anetta.

Her face twists as I struggle, but she manages to strong-arm the bag away.

I jump for it as she slaps my hands again.

She rips the book out of the bag and throws the empty satchel at my feet. "This belongs to the Sublery." Her voice turns growly. "You were supposed to choose something of *mine* to take with you, you impudent, shameful child!"

"Anetta!" The other na'rm calls.

Na'rm Anetta's head snaps to her fellow maid, and then

she straightens her back. She tosses my book to the floor: *The Chronicles of Narnia*. "Take it then," she growls. "We'll probably leave the paged books behind when the Sublery transfers to its new location, anyway. And they've all but promised me that my new subling will be normal, thank all that is good." She fixes the cuffs of her blouse and scuttles off.

I slump onto the floor even though my skirt will wrinkle, which will reflect poorly on Na'rm Anetta. But now I want it to wrinkle, so I crumple chunks of my skirt into my fists. I press lightly at first, but nothing happens. So, I squeeze my fists as hard as I can, grinning at the star-shaped creases I make. Something small and hard pokes into my thigh against the cold tile. Sweeping my hand under my leg, I pull out the bead – the one my na'rm should have strung onto her necklace. Something she should have worn to her dying breath, disdained and discarded.

"Come, child," the other nurserymaid stops near me, her subling's arms wrapped around her waist. "Walk with us to the transport tunnel."

"She hated me," I say as I hold up my bead. Perhaps she even wished me dead. My ears begin to ring as the lights flicker around me; the children of the shadows laugh at me from the walls. Their ghostly voices cackle all about me, and I want to flee. The shadows shift around with the flickering, and I'm sure the dead children begin reaching out with their ashy arms to steal my life.

I cover my head and scream.

"Okay, child! It's okay!"

I hiccup to a stop as the ringing ceases. It's the other nurserymaid who has picked me up, not a charred phantom. She holds me tight. Perhaps she got to me just in time.

The walls return to their gloomy slate color – I check each one to be sure. I don't have to squeeze my eyes or blink hard. The tears fall and fall, catching in a pool inside my goggles.

I am alone.

* * *

Hundreds of seven-year-old sublings from the region crowd together at the check-in line by the transport tunnel. All of the girls wear the same blouse and skirt, and all have various shades of albino-light hair grown to the standard shoulder-length. The hatted boys wear pants made with the same tweed material as our skirts, and collared shirts to match our blouses. We make up an army of tiny soldiers, marching off to fulfill our civic duty – to learn as much as possible so that we may embark on a sustainable trade when we graduate from the Burrows at the age of twenty. Or die trying.

The din of children shuffling and buzzing about calms me; I'm able to stay camouflaged in the center of it all. I scan the floor, hoping to discover an errant cap to cover my short, nonstandard hair. The Grand Na'rm told me not to worry, that it would grow by the time I graduated the Sublery. It didn't.

"What's wrong with you?" asks a tall boy with sunken eyes, four people in front of me in the queue. He carries a gallon-sized cage with a mouse in his left hand, and his right arm must be broken as it's covered with a wire-mesh cast.

There are many things wrong with me. Where shall I start? I'm forever unloved. My new medera must certainly already hate me because of the report from my na'rm. I can't possibly blend in because of my goggles and patchy hair. People will always detest me, and maybe I deserve it because I'm wicked whenever I'm angry, and I'm prone to anger whenever someone points out how I'm different. Like now. Always.

Before I can figure out how to respond, a transport tech spins him the other way, mumbling, "You're next."

I flatten the wrinkles in my skirt with my hands. All the other sublings probably know the difference between red and purple and green – no one else wears goggles, and they all have a favorite color.

When it's my turn, a travel tech scans my finger and then reads my identification number from his tablet. A machine begins to hum and whine, inscribing my data onto a shiny bracelet. "Terminal six. Your magnetran leaves in twenty minutes." He affixes the band onto my wrist and hands me a white fabric travelmask to go over my nose and mouth. "Good health."

I'm pushed forward and away. Finding my way to terminal six, I soon discover the perfect spot – just behind a wooden crate with giant letters spelling out *CAUTION*.

The boy with the broken arm and the caged mouse stares at me from the front of the terminal. I tighten my fingers around my satchel as he snakes his way through the crowd of children, edging closer. When he makes it to my side I pretend not to notice, studying the new scuff in my bootstrap. I do notice him, of course. His giant shadow could swallow me whole. *You're this size because you didn't grow when you were supposed to,* Na'rm Anetta exclaimed a year ago.

The boy's eyes continue to scour over me, so I inch my right foot to the side, and then my left, hoping I can shrink further behind the crate.

"You're a curious case," he says a little too loudly, and a few siblings turn our way. He'd never have survived Na'rm Anetta. "It's okay. I'm a scientist." He holds up his mouse as if it proves his claim. "Genetics are surely at the bottom of your – err – uncommon features." He doesn't seem to know when to stop talking.

My cheeks flame and I close my eyes. *He isn't here, he isn't here, he isn't here.*

He jabs two fingers from his casted arm like a sword into my ribs, singing, "*Touché!*"

"Ow!"

He laughs and lunges like he'll do it again, so I jump.

"I'm just playing. You're old enough for the Burrows, then?"

Without lifting my head, I hold up my bracelet. "Seven point seven years old."

He checks his own wristband, which only lists his date of

birth. Seven point nine years if he wants to know, but he doesn't ask. Instead, he smiles like I've divulged the secrets of the universe.

"Ah – intelligence on top of your odd features. That's why you've been sent to Cayan. I'll bet someone messed with your genetic coding. You've barely any hair." He reaches out and flicks a tuft on top of my head.

"Clearly I have some if you can touch it. Please don't."

A girl I've never met turns around, and my muscles tense, ready for her to join in. But instead, she glares at him. "You're a rude, miserable subling. Leave her be." The rims of her eyelids are swollen, and her hair shines like silk. Her nurserymaid probably sang a lullaby too slowly before walking her to the travel tunnel.

"You've got to admit she's an interesting specimen with those glasses." He touches his cleft chin. "I'd bet she's nearly blind."

Wickedness fires up inside me, and I move away from the shelter of the crate. "These aren't glasses, you bumbling chunk of flesh!"

"Okay." He makes the peace-sign with his hand. At first, I think he's apologizing and say nothing. But he continues, "It's an experiment. How many fingers am I holding up?"

As the heat rises to my cheeks, I know without a doubt that I hate-hate-*hate* scientists. I shove him as hard as I can.

He grabs my arm and raises his mouse up high in the air. "Woah, a fast temper, too. You must be more careful before someone breaks."

The girl beside us lets out a screech and karate-chops me free from his grip. I lose my balance from the force of it and topple to the ground. My palms slap onto the cold marble floor. Our commotion has drawn the attention of all the children in our terminal. I want to stay down – to never get up, at least not until everyone stops watching.

A whack resonates over my head, and I pull my shoulders in.

When I finally look up, the girl is standing nose-to-nose with the boy, who is now rubbing his cheek. She presses her fingers into his chest, even though she's a few inches shorter than he is. "Mind your manners, lest you want someone to mind them for you. Is this how your nurserymaid taught you?" Her eyes shimmer like fire, and he shrinks away from her.

For a moment, I consider doing the same.

But she reaches down and yanks me from the ground. Lacing her arm in mine, she holds her head high and walks me to the edge of the platform near the metal grate. "I despise hateful people." She motions to my satchel. "What did you bring?"

"It's the book my na'rm wouldn't allow me to read while I was at the Sublery. She said it would inspire my mischievous side. I plan to read it on the magnetran." I rub my stinging palms together. "He's half right, though. I'm blinded by light, but I can see perfectly fine with these goggles because they block most of the rays. Except I can't make out colors – just white, black, and lots of gray."

She checks my hands, and rubs them for me, keeping one arm wrapped in mine. "It's okay. He's not worth an ounce of his own fuss."

I crane my neck to search for him, but thankfully, he's disappeared into the crowd.

"I'm scheduled on the next tran to the Cayan Burrow," the girl says, showing me the data on her bracelet. She's a month older than I am.

"Why?" I examine her up and down. She's grown to a good height, her hair falls to her shoulders, with no signs of sickness or ailment whatsoever. "I don't see anything wrong with you."

She drops my arm. "That's because there *is* nothing wrong with me." Her voice falls flat as one of her eyebrows arches high on her forehead. I've insulted her without even trying to, but I refuse to give up on having a friend.

"I'm going there, too," I whisper, grabbing the tube of

emergency serum hanging from a chain on my neck, hidden under my blouse. "My na'rm said that Cayan is the poorest of all the burrows and only the sickliest, most disabled children go there. She said even with a full-time medtech, a good portion of Cayan burrowlings die before they graduate."

The girl gasps. "What a horrific thing to say. *My* na'rm said only the kindliest and most intelligent children go there. As in, off-the-charts intelligent." She blinks quickly, like it's settled.

Could Na'rm Anetta have lied to me?

The girl puts her arm in mine again and smiles. She's connecting with me – she doesn't mind the goggles. Even if it turns out I'm not good enough for Medera Gelia, this girl will be with me at Cayan. I smile so hard the muscles in my face hurt from the abnormal stretching, and it makes me want to giggle.

A bell clangs and the lights flicker, warning us to step behind the line. The flash reflects off a chain around the girl's neck, causing a sharp glare. I press my lids shut as a stabbing pain hits in the center of my eyes. The sharpness moves to the center of my head, and I keep them shut until the flickering stops. My new friend's neckchain mirrors mine, which means she has fatal allergies too. I tighten my grip on her arm. For her, I will pretend that the Cayan Burrow is packed with the most promising, intelligent children. After today, it will have at least two.

"I hear we're allowed to name ourselves once we know our calling," she says. "Medera Gelia Cayan may be old with hundreds of hairbeads, but I think that makes her all the cleverer, don't you?"

I nod as if I already knew these things.

Our magnetran blasts its way into the station underneath the grated edge of the platform, and the warm gust makes our bell-shaped skirts fan out. My friend's eyelids flutter and she buries her head into my shoulder. Her hair whips about, stinging my cheeks and forehead, and I can't remember ever being so content.

"My na'rm said that I'd save the world someday," she shouts over the squealing of the magnetran brakes while she pulls her travelmask over her mouth and nose. "I'm glad you'll be there to save it with me."

The next morning, the Cayan burrowmaid calls out, "Time to rise," and I hear bedchamber drawers squealing open. Yesterday's tedious journey feels more like a dream now.

My beddrawer squeals like a tortured banshee as the maid yanks it open from the outside – perhaps I was not fast enough for her. As light smashes into my space, a horrific white pain strikes me. Even Na'rm Anetta knew better.

"My goggles–" I don't sleep with them on because the strap presses into my scalp when I lie down. Frantic, I rake the bottom of the beddrawer until I find them.

"Your eyes–" My friend stands somewhere nearby. "They're a beautiful pink." She helps me affix the strap around my head until the protective goggles are in place. "And your face is an elegant oval shape, now that I've had a proper look."

I smile even though my vision remains foggy, and the entire time the burrowmaid dresses us in uniform, the smile doesn't fade from my lips. I've never been called elegant, and have never thought of my eyes as beautiful. How can I when I haven't seen for myself?

"Do you think," asks my burrowmate as we dress, "that if I already know my calling, Medera Gelia would allow me to choose a name today?"

"You already know what you'd like to be?" I study the faces of the other girls getting ready. Maybe I'm the only one who doesn't know. Even that strange boy with the mouse knew he's a scientist, which is the only thing I can safely rule out.

"A seven-year-old knowing her calling?" The burrowmaid tsks. "Complete folly."

I clench my teeth at our rude ba'rm, adding her career as something to never aspire to be, alongside scientist.

"I want to work where people need the most help," my friend says with a matter-of-fact air. "In humanitarian politics, fighting against things like the subpar treatment of our maids and servicetechs, or perhaps aiding the hungry Omnits in the farmlands." Her eyes shimmer and grow distant, like she's imagining herself after graduation helping faceless masses of people.

The burrowmaid pauses, putting both hands on her hips. Her face opens with the same awe that rumbles inside me. Here I am, battling every second to keep from being wicked, and this girl has chosen to do nothing but good for others as her calling. Somehow, the thought of her wanting to be so compassionate gives me hope. Maybe there are others who, like her, will accept me as I am.

And then the room echoes with two dull but heavy thuds. "On your guard, ladies," a woman's deep voice rings out.

The maid scurries to line up our group of five girls. "Hush up and stand straight for your medera." And then she stands at the end to make a row of six.

My humanitarian comrade slips her hand in mine as the stately woman enters our chamberroom. I wonder if I should drop her hand. There's no reason I should take her down with me. I'm sure her na'rm's report was written with a much kinder pen than mine.

The elder medera – perhaps in her late forties – walks with a straight cane and a bent limp, stopping just a few feet in front of us. She wears a long, dark robe with *Cayan* embroidered on her lapel. She nods at the maid, who then rushes off.

"Hear me now: I am Medera Gelia Cayan." Her thick lips enunciate each word, and her eyes light up as if she's excited. Former students' beads line the front strands of her hair, clicking as they bounce together at her movement. "You will follow me to the first years' lessons gallery now."

We follow her out of our chamberroom in single file, joining a line of boys.

I scarcely make it out to the hallway before I'm face-to-face with the scientist-to-be, the boy who made fun of my goggles.

"Watch it." His eyes bulge with severity. He lifts the mouse out of reach as if to protect it from me. "I must keep my distance from you and your friend. My brittle bones have plagued me since birth, and you're likely to cause them to break."

I frown at the cast on his arm. Brittle bones must be one of his ailments, landing him here at Cayan. He and I had a poor start yesterday, but we are more alike than different. He's as much of a target for bullies as I am. Besides, a new burrow means new beginnings. "What's the mouse for?" I whisper as we march along, extending a possible hand of friendship.

"It's my experiment. I've coded it with some of the same genetic sequencing that's found in my own DNA, and the adverse antibodies that curse me. Specifically, the level-seven or higher allergies, the deadliest."

I cock my head. "So, if you come too close to something that is harmful—"

"I'll know before I get a chance to get close because it will affect the mouse first. I call it a canarymouse." He shrugs one shoulder.

My foot twists beneath me, and I reach out for the wall to steady myself. Somehow, I underestimate the distance between me and the curve in the wall, and I tumble to my knees before I have a chance to catch myself.

"Are you hurt?" The boy puts his mouse cage down. His face is inches from mine, and worry shoots across his eyes, and I almost cry. Not because I'm hurt or embarrassed, but because he seems genuinely concerned for me. Maybe he isn't as bad as I thought.

"Check your bones," he says. His warm hands tremble as they find every long bone in my arms and legs in search of injuries. Despite his seriousness, I smile because I'm sure I've found another friend.

"I'm okay."

He helps me up and he smiles while he searches for my hidden eyes. I try to make my smile even bigger to make up for it, until I realize everyone is watching.

"Pip, pip," Medera Gelia says. "She'll mend." She then leads us into a room and asks us to form a circle with the girls on one side, boys on the other. I take a spot next to the girl who called me elegant.

She curtsies, tugging my hand as a hint. I nod and curtsy too. "Good health, Medera," I add for good measure. Anyways, I have nothing to lose. The other girls amazingly follow our lead, and the boys bow.

"Such manners." Medera taps her tablet and pauses to read. "Surely this nurserymaid's report must be mistaken," she whispers barely loud enough for anyone to hear.

My neck heats like lava. I'm saddened that my friends are about to know me for my former ways once the medera explains. Perhaps she won't. Of course she will. *Please don't look my way.*

"Most of you have been pulled from your nurseries early. I'm sure your na'rms did their best, but what matters to me now is how you do here. My small burrow houses seventy-six members. Each and every day, you will demonstrate your capacity to learn, your mental stamina, and quickness of thought. I expect no less. These skills are crucial in today's workforce. Are you up for the challenge?"

I stretch my body straighter with the help of my imaginary giant Omnit at the notion that she doesn't care about my past. "Yes, Medera," I say with pride. Learning is my specialty. A few burrowlings echo my response, though not with the same fervor.

Medera strikes her cane into the ground and everyone quiets, straightening their bodies like me.

"Our Omniterranean relatives count on you to improve their world. Their healthy bodies afford them a long life of hard labor so that we have desks for research, clothes to wear, and food to eat." She begins to hobble down the line of girls, inspecting each one of us, while I imagine giant people walking above us on the very top of the ground. What would it be like on the surface among all the people and animals? It sounds absolutely chaotic. Maybe the Omnits are so large that I would get trampled if I went up there. Would I be eaten alive by wild animals? I shiver.

"Who can tell me why we Subterraneans live in burrows away from our Omniterranean family?" Medera Gelia asks.

"I can, Medera." My humanitarian friend steps forward from our line. "We live away from our Omniterranean family because of our weaker immune systems."

Our medera smiles. "And why are our immune systems so weak?"

This time, it's the scientist-boy who steps forward. He doesn't speak until Medera Gelia motions to him. "The Genetic Plague caused it, ma'am, generations ago. Before then, we all lived together. But afterwards, humans were born either Omniterranean with extremely robust, healthy bodies, or they were born Subterranean with smaller bodies and various physical ailments and weaker immune systems." He takes a breath as if he might keep going.

"Correct," Medera Gelia says, cutting him off. "Subterraneans have accounted for about ten percent of the human population ever since the Genetic Plague, but we all must remember that we're born from Omniterranean parents. We're all still one species."

I must admit I haven't thought about them much. Why would we? We're not allowed to know where we came from. Rumor has it that the first time Subter children were sent below ground, their Omnit parents tried to visit them which just put all the Subters in danger of catching diseases.

"Interesting point, Medera," the boy says, stepping back into line with a contemplative furrow in his brow.

"So," my friend with beautiful hair steps forward again. Her eyes narrow as if she's finally thinking things through, too. "Our parents sent us here because they love us and wanted us to live."

Medera Gelia nods, walking around the circle of students. "It is a travesty of scientific abuses that started the Genetic Plague and separated us all. As Subters, we are cursed with weaker bodies, but we are also genetically wired to invent, to research, and to solve problems." She stops in front of me and cocks her head. "Beginning today, you may indeed pay your families homage by serving them with the power of your minds."

A family – my family of giant people – lives somewhere up there. Brothers or sisters or maybe both, a blood connection to people I don't even know, who build or farm or manufacture things each and every day for our survival. My stomach twists because Medera Gelia's words hit every sadness I've ever had. Nurserymaids were supposed to be like parents for their sublings, but mine was far from it, at least compared to how the other na'rms were with all the other children. Parents are supposed to love you no matter what, even when you're different. Maybe my na'rm didn't want me, but surely *my real family* would. It's not fair – I would gladly toil by their sides even if it risks my death. My legs weaken, and I grab my friend's arm, but surely her na'rm treated her with affection. I glance across the circle at my mouse-loving friend whose eyes start to glisten with tears, as if he feels the same.

"Pah, pah, sweet burrowling." Medera strokes my fuzzy hair and her voice softens. "Though I can never take the place of your parents, it is my honor to serve them as your medera."

Before I can think about what I'm doing, I wrap my arms around Medera Gelia and squeeze her waist. The face of the kind nurserymaid who embraced me yesterday flashes in my mind, and then that of the nursetech at the old infirmary who fixed my blankets and fed me broth when I was sick, and even the image of a mother I've never met who caresses my face; I see it all as I squeeze my medera tighter.

Medera gently wraps her hands around my wrists, and her enlarged knuckles press into me as she gently pries my arms loose, but holds onto one of my hands. "We will begin your names with an initial."

My group of new burrowlings begin to buzz with excitement.

She looks into my eyes. "You shall be called Z until you know your calling, and then you will name yourself accordingly. Your name will be celebrated from that day forward."

"Z," I breathe outwards. How beautiful it sounds. Because of it, I'm less invisible, less blurry. "Thank you" doesn't seem adequate, so I take the bead out of my pocket. "Please, Medera Gelia Cayan, will you wear my bead?"

The other sublings gasp at my request, but I cannot care about that for now.

"My na'rm –" I drop my voice. "The one who wrote the report – she didn't take my gift."

For a fleeting second, a look of shocked surprise passes on the medera's face, and then she allows me to place the bead into her hand. "These beads," she strokes a few in her hair, "are from my burrowlings who have graduated: researchers, historians, scientists, and even a medera or two – all beautiful and brilliant in their own way. But I will save yours here." She unfastens her necklace and strings my bead onto it. "It will be safe with me until your graduation day."

Energy fizzes in my chest, because I finally know what my calling is.

Staring into Gelia Cayan's eyes, it's clear to me I'm supposed to become a *medera*.

CHAPTER 2

Absolutely No Celebrating
(Present Day, Twelve Years Later)

During my first years at Cayan, even Medera Gelia's love and kindness couldn't reach the cracks in my soul, and I often found myself wondering if I should run away to search for my Omnit family. I would estimate how long I'd last above ground, exposed to every toxin and microscopic bug known to this Earth. Would it be a week before I died? A few days? In my young mind though, I still believed it would be worth it. But that was only if I could find them in that amount of time – my mother, father and any brothers or sisters that I might have. I'd always hoped I'd be able to tell who they were because we'd have similar traits – like, maybe my mother had the same shape to her chin or the same colour as my sister's eyes. I could almost see what they all looked like, and how I would fit in.

Ten years later, that crisp picture I had of my mother has faded away along with my hopes of ever meeting her. But I do occasionally wonder – does she think about me? Does she wonder about the shape of my chin? Does she think I'm already dead?

I'm not dead, not yet. I have four-and-a-half years left according to the Life Expectancy logarithm. But since I don't graduate until I'm twenty, I'm burning seven more weeks off my LE just to make it to my birthday, which rots. In seven weeks, I'll probably be washing someone's dirty socks. Most post-grad professions require a minimum of five LE years, if not ten – that is, except for maidships – but I have my sights set on being a medera. Medera Gelia urged me to apply anyway, insisting that despite my low LE, they couldn't ignore my high scores.

As it turns out, they can.

I have zero job offers so far, while Maddelyn, my old friend from the tran ride, has four job offers to choose from. *Four*.

"Let's go, let's go, my precious queens," Maddelyn calls out to the youngest and newest girls in our burrow, with just a vein of irritation running through her words, not unlike the hairline fissures tracing their way through the chiseled tunnels of our underground burrow. Night has fallen somewhere far above us, so she and I pull the hyperbaric drawers from the wall for each child to climb into for bed, just after they hang their canarymice cages adjacent to their drawer. We all carry our mice with us now for our protection.

A soft chime sounds on Maddelyn's tablet – a job notification, and hopefully this one is for me. I don't have my own tablet since the light messes with my vision, so I'm grateful she's agreed to field my offers. Her gaze flashes in my direction. I know she's also hoping for news for me. But all the previous notifications have been for her, so every new chime sends waves of panic instead of the excitement it used to. She and I look away at the same time. Despite my grim odds, my chest flutters – maybe one of the largest burrows has room for a junior medera?

We can't check the message, though, until after we put our eight-year-olds to bed.

"Would Medera Gelia be angry if I called her 'mother'?" a girl called *C* asks Maddy.

"Of course you can't!" Maddelyn says sharply, and C flinches. I turn to Maddelyn and tilt my head, which helps set her straight. I don't know what it is, but my best friend's patience has thinned lately. Maybe the pressure of graduation is getting to her, but these children are new to our burrow and questions like this are normal. *Everyone* longs for the parents they've never met. "Your real mother loved you enough to send you underground for your health." She sighs. "Don't ever forget."

C frowns as Maddelyn slides the child's beddrawer into the cement wall to tuck her away.

"Good health," I say just before the beddrawer closes. In all reality, Gelia is the closest thing to a parent we have down here. It's Gelia's face I now see when I think of motherhood, and it's because of Gelia that I want to become a medera.

After tucking in our remaining five youngest burrowlings, Maddelyn nods at me as if to say she's not worried about my future. She slides her arm through mine to reassure me, but also to stay warm as we make our way through the cobblestone-walled hallways of this wing. As the oldest underground school for Subterranean burrowlings, Cayan holds a lot of charm. Maddy complains the burrow is too rustic with its candlelit corridors and old-fashioned finishes, but I prefer candles to bulbs since the intensity of electricity forces me to use the strongest setting on my room-darkening goggles.

We each use a long snuffer to extinguish the candles set on iron sconces as we pass by; the ashy scent of smoke follows us like it's sad to see us go. As the flames die, shadows and fleeting smoke dance upon the walls, playing into my childish fear of ghosts. I stiffen. My imagination haunts me with the dark silhouette of chubby phantom arms, or a ghostly face, open-mouthed in a perpetual scream, only silenced because it's trapped inside the stone. I hold my breath as we hurry past the dark corridor that leads to the cremation chamber. It's all very silly now, but I cling to Maddelyn's arm as a *new* panic rises inside my chest. What will happen after she graduates in a few short weeks and I'm left to wander these halls alone?

My friend pulls me into the last room of the corridor and sets her caged canarymouse down on the floor. The small space was originally used for storage but when we were first years, Medera Gelia converted it by installing recycled shelves and collecting donations of paged books, all for my sake. Then she dubbed the space our *library*.

Maddy and I sit down on the burlap pillows set against the rough, rocky wall. I used to think the unfinished room felt more like an abandoned cave, but Maddy and I have spent so much time here over the years that now it's our favorite place in the entire burrow. I breathe in the stale smell of inked pages while trying to calm my nerves about that jetting notification.

"Let's just get this over with," I mumble.

"It's got to be for you." She activates the tablet and I turn away from the brightness, adjusting the setting on my goggles. I set my canarymouse next to hers.

Our elbows remain locked as I wait for her to read the message. The silence between us looms larger and larger as the seconds tick on. My thumping heart stills because she would have told me by now if she had good news for me. It must be another job offer for her. I take a breath, steeling myself.

"Did that offer from Common Good come through for you?" I hope my voice sounds cheery, but inside I'm panicking about being alone like I was before I met Maddy. I wish I could snuff out the memories of how lost I was back then. Maddy changed everything for me and as much as I long to be a medera, nothing will be the same without her.

She gives one tiny nod, like she's sorry, and flips the tablet over. Of all the offers she's received, this is the one she's been dying to hear about. "The next one will be yours," she says. "You have to believe hard, that's all. Hard as diamonds."

"Common Good is selective with its interns." The last thing I want to do is ignore *her* accomplishments, and I *am* happy for her. "It's a huge honor. Congratulations, Maddelyn."

"Absolutely no celebrating." It's one of her rules, but a small smile spreads across her pale lips, anyway. "We'll jinx it. It's only a trial run for six months," she says, "but I'd get to sit in on policy review, elbow-to-elbow with decisionmakers on all aspects of social reform."

"They'll adore you."

She swivels around and holds me by my shoulders, her smile disappearing. "Someone will call on you soon. You'll be the medera of all mederas. Someday, children will weep with joy when they discover they've made it to Medera Zuzan's burrow."

It's easy to hard-as-diamonds believe while looking into Maddelyn's insistent eyes, except believing is too close to hoping, and sometimes hope is scarier than my imaginary ghosts. I manage a smile before she lets me go, and I get up to return my latest book to its shelf. If I'm not offered a permanent position in my chosen field before my birthday, I've no doubt we'll never see each other again after I'm assigned to maidwork. I'll be washing sheets, and she'll be too busy implementing social regulations. What would we talk about, anyway? Our worlds would be too different.

"You still have two months – plenty of time for a burrow to open a slot." Maddelyn calls from two aisles down.

"Seven weeks." I run my fingers over the bumpy spines of the books as I walk toward her. I've read every one we own and when Medera Gelia adds a new title, I celebrate like it's my Name Day all over again. Most burrows use tablets now – even Cayan, except for me with my light-blindness.

Maddelyn rubs her eye with her fist and holds onto a metal bookshelf as if she's trying to steady herself. Her canarymouse squeaks like it's been pinched.

"Are you sick?" I catch her arm as I approach.

"My eyes–" She blinks hard, as if her vision has turned blurry. "They feel funny, but I'm – I'm okay, Zu." She shakes off my hand.

"We can stop at the infirmary." I hold her chin still to check her eyes for inflammation, but this time she slaps my hand away. Maddelyn never complains yet she's a little jittery. Her emergency injection hangs from a chain around her neck; she and I have been lucky enough to never have needed our needles, thank all that's good. I frown at the dark circles forming steadily under her eyes. "Maddy?"

"Stop being ridiculous!" She huffs as if I'm overreacting, but everyone is supposed to go to the infirmary at the onset of even the slightest symptom. She knows that.

She blinks hard several times, like she's confused. "I – I'm sorry. I'm just tired. Everything is irritating me. I'm mad about your job offers. If anyone should get one, it's you. The whole system rots, and it's too focused on Life Expectancy, even though anyone can die at any time."

I'm not sure how to respond, except to turn her back to calmer thoughts from a few minutes ago. "I just have to *believe hard*, right?" I smile, hoping she's just nervous about leaving Cayan, like I am. But there's a tremble in her hand when she flips her hair behind her ear. Something's definitely wrong. "I'm sure the medmaid is awake at the infirmary."

"I said *no*!" Her voice cuts deeply, like I'm her enemy instead of her closest friend. She shakes her head, almost arguing with herself. "I'm sorry. Again. I'm exhausted and I can't stand the sight of these *jetting* books right now."

Her mouse begins to bite the wire bars on its cage, and I swear it's trying to get at my mouse next to it. "You're mad at the books?" I ask, puzzled. She's never complained about our books before. She's always enjoyed the time we spend here together.

She shoots a nervous glance around the room, and then tilts her head apologetically at me. "I'll stop at the infirmary if it'll make you happy."

I smile and nod, which feels like a lie because I'm anything but happy right now. This must be what Medera has been worried about these last few weeks, and why she asked me to keep an eye on Maddy. We're hoping Maddy's unusual moodiness will level off soon, but it's not.

A voice booms in the hallway. "Zuzan? Zu–" Jal's lanky frame appears in the library's doorway as he skip-jogs over to me. Maddy takes the opportunity to pull away. "There's an undertech opening in the *Genomic Center of Excellence*, and guess who they want to interview!" He beams at me, glints in his eyes.

"Can you yell any louder about it?" Maddelyn speaks through her teeth. "You must realize she has yet to hear any news on mederaships, you insensitive slatebrain." She huffs past him without another word, grabbing her mouse's cage too roughly. Maddy's albino-white hair flairs out as she storms into the corridor.

Jal watches after her with pouty eyes, and then he whispers, "Was I that loud?"

I shake my head at Maddy. "You can't be too loud with such amazing news. Congratulations." I bow in an exaggerated way, making him chuckle. But it's hard to be excited through my worry. "Did you notice something off about Maddelyn?"

"She was cranky, but also very right." He shrugs. "I may have aced my placement exam, but I fail miserably in the sensitivity department. You've got the best regional academic stats in the past ten years – you'll hear something soon. Besides, your birthday is almost two months away."

Seven weeks. My face warms and I try to read the titles of the textbooks on the shelf across the aisle from us to keep from crying, both from Maddy's outburst and from my lack of job offers.

"I feel selfish to ask." He takes my hand and leads me to the table and chairs. "Help me with my speech? I mean, just in case I'm accepted. Can you imagine me speaking to a roomful of scientists? I was thinking of using my serious face." He crosses his eyes and makes fish lips, trying to cheer me up.

It's working. "You'll charm the labcoats off of them."

"An undertech can never have enough labcoats." He hands me his paper. "I wrote it down so you can look it over. I'm thinking about dressing like a canarymouse in a cage."

I giggle, imagining him with ears and a tail. "You're joking!"

"Mostly," he shrugs, "but Medera wants me to take credit for developing the canary-mouse method of detecting fatal allergens." Jal is the reason we all carry our own mouse now, and why fatalities due to toxic exposures and allergies at the Cayan Burrow have dropped by seventy percent since implementing the practice. Other burrows have begun requesting them too, and Jal is considered a science prodigy.

I snap my head towards the door. "Her canarymouse was acting funny," I say. "Just like she was."

"Was the canarymouse in respiratory distress, or excessively lethargic?" he asks like he's consulting on a case. "Maddelyn sure wasn't."

"No – her mouse was hyper and aggressive, if anything." These are not behaviors that would suggest her health was about to take a turn, but it's an odd coincidence.

"It wouldn't be hyper if it were undergoing anaphylactic shock." He fidgets in his chair, like all the excitement about his interview is pumping through his veins – it's like his Name Day all over again. "The DNA manipulation done on canary mice really only detects fatal allergens, not behavioral patterns."

I nod, and try to focus on Jal's speech as he asked. He opens it with his obsession for genetics, moving on to an outline of his canarymouse research. "I love how you touch on your experience with human genomes manually, without the proper equipment," I say as I break out into a smile. "Your passion shines through loud and clear."

Then he jumps up, grabbing the paper from my hand before I can finish reading. The page rips. "Read this later. I'll explode if I sit still for another second."

I laugh as he lifts me out of the chair, almost a foot into the air, before plopping me down. I enjoy the sense of weightlessness as he holds me in his hands and the jitters in my stomach. But he's going off to become a scientist, and I'll be a medera, I hope. There's no point in liking him.

"Run with me, Zu?" He touches his forehead to mine, and

he'd be looking right into my eyes if it weren't for my goggles.

"What about your bones?" I glance at the protective mesh brace on his right forearm. "Besides, Medera would bang her cane if we start running around with all the first years sleeping in their beddrawers."

"Number one, I'm invincible tonight. Number two, we'll stay in the north corridors so we don't wake anyone up." He pulls me by my hand, and goes to skip out of the door. "Celebrate with me!"

I barely have a chance to fret about the recent worsening of Maddelyn's condition or even about her warnings about not-celebrating before we're off and running. In our excitement, we leave our canary mice behind as if we could take on the world without such trivial worries. When we come to the first turn, Jal skids to a stop, crashes into the wall, and I crash into him.

"Ow!" He grabs his shoulder, his voice still echoing through the rock tunnels.

"Jal!" I take his arm and search his pained face. He's broken that bone so many times it practically falls apart at a touch. But he can't transfer to the *Genomic Center of Excellence* without medical clearance. All the joy from a few seconds before drains from me immediately. "Can you move it?"

He pulls my body into his, and he pivots his shoulder up and down, grinning. "Just kidding."

I almost collapse with relief. "Don't do that!"

He stares into my face for a moment, our breaths coming fast and mixing together, and he wiggles his eyebrows. "I can't believe I've fooled the world's brainiest human to walk these tunnels alone."

"You didn't trick me, but Jal–"

He squeezes me tighter into him. "I've fallen for you, Zu. Literally. For that insanely brilliant mind of yours, for your passion and kindness – everything." In the twinkling of his eyes, I can see he means it. Maddy always teased me about having a crush on Jal, which stung in ways she could not know because I'd always believed I was too different for him to like me back.

"But – but I'm awkward and goggled and weak, and–" And he's leaving. He'll meet other people at the GCE. Women with higher Life Expectancies who have beautiful, color-seeing eyes.

"Well, then I guess awkward and goggled is my type." He pulls a small, round object from his pocket, dropping it into my palm. "This is for you."

It's a smooth rock about an inch in diameter, still warm from the heat of his body. He's painted a rose on its surface, with the petals wrapping around the curves.

"It's red," he says.

For me, it can't be anything but variations of gray, but I'm glad to know. I flip it over, and in the tiniest, most extraordinary calligraphy, he's painted a message that curves inside itself like a coil.

May good health find you always.

His gaze shifts to my mouth. "May I kiss you, Zuzan Cayan?"

I smile in response, and his lips press into mine. It's soft and close – so real that I don't doubt that awkward-and-goggled must be his type. All the objections I have fly out of my head, and for now I pretend that tomorrow doesn't matter.

When he pulls away, he brushes his fingers down my cheek. The tenderness in his touch almost makes me want to cry. In the next second, he takes my hand again and laughs, pulling me down the next hallway.

CHAPTER 3

Ratgirl

I would definitely be obsessing about Jal and my lack of job offers if it weren't for Maddelyn. She has been alternating between moody-Maddy and normal-Maddy for several days now, but this morning is the worst. She walks two steps ahead of me down the dismal corridor for chore time. If I speed up to keep her pace, she adjusts her speed to stay ahead. If I try to speak, she covers her ears and mumbles to herself. With each day, I lose more and more hope that she'll get better, or that she'll be able to accept that dream internship position at Common Good.

When Maddy was forced to stop at the infirmary, the nursemaid did a routine bloodlab workup, but nothing turned up. Until she improves, Maddy's no longer allowed to tuck in the first years in the evenings, which makes her even angrier. She refuses to take her canarymouse with her anymore, and won't look anyone directly in the eye.

"Wait up, Zu!" Jal calls from behind.

Maddelyn spins around and her eyes narrow into slits. "We have work to do."

"You go ahead," I say, taking another few steps in her direction. "I'll only be a minute."

When I touch her arm, she pulls away like I've burned her. She shrinks away and scurries off to the library like a fiery ghost who's escaped the walls.

Jal catches up to me, and there's an instant electricity between us again. He hooks his pinky in mine with a shy smile, and then his eyes turn science-y.

"She's... *off*," Jal says in a hushed tone. "Way off. I hate that you're alone with her."

"I'm not afraid of Maddy. What did you want?"

His face brightens like a newly lit candle. "I've nearly finished mapping your genome."

Ahh, his pet project. Only Jal would try to take that on without the proper equipment.

"There are several more sequences I'm piecing together," he continues, "but they're not critical." He's got his science-y voice going, and I have bigger worries.

I sigh. "Look, I have to go—" and I turn to catch up with Maddelyn.

"But I might find out more about your Life Expectancy!"

I swivel back to him. LE logarithms are ninety-nine percent accurate, so I've already accepted that my remaining four-and-a-half years might be made as meaningful as possible working as a medera, or even a medera's assistant at a larger burrow. He can't change the facts, yet he's full of hope, as always. It's the hard-as-diamonds kind of hope, enough for the both of us.

"Thank you," is all I manage.

"There's more." He drops his voice. "Don't freak out."

I laugh nervously, but I'm stifled by his stoic expression. "What is it?"

"I – I'm not entirely positive, but–" He steps backwards like he's going to leave. "It's probably nothing."

I grab his meshed arm. "If it's nothing, just tell me."

"I'm not convinced you're... Omnit-born." He shrugs, faking like it's not important.

My lips turn numb as I soak in this wild claim, and I glance up and down the hallways to make sure we're alone. My fingers brush down my sparse hair at the nape of my neck, and smooth over my goggles' strap. *Ratgirl, ratgirl,* the older kids teased when I first came to the Cayan Burrow. I always had to check for loose labmice in my beddrawer before climbing in each night. They never let me forget how different I was, even among Subters. The oldest girl cornered me in the bathroom once, telling me that only humans could use that room. I fell to the ground and cried, desperate to use the toilet, and ended up urinating on the floor. I was mortified. A few days later, Maddy walloped that girl in the hallway and made her apologize to me. The older girls stopped picking on me, but the way they looked at me didn't change. I'd never be considered human in their eyes.

"I... I don't know what you're trying to say."

"Your patterns don't have the typical dominant-recessive markers, like the rest of us with two Omniterranean parents," he explains.

The phrase *the rest of us* echoes round my head, tightening, squeezing. The feelings where I'll never belong rush back. I want to run and cry in the corner, just like I did that day so long ago. After all this time, I'm desperate not to be different.

If he's right, that means I'm almost untouchably different. My theoretical parents and brothers and sisters who live above ground – the Omnit family I've been fantasizing about all my life, the people who look like me, those who prove I've never really been different – would be nonexistent.

Which means, once again, I'm alone.

"You might be the product of two Subterraneans, or perhaps one of each, or some manipulated combination. In fact–" His mouth is moving, but I can't keep listening,

"The product?" *Ratgirl, ratgirl.* "For all good! Everyone is Omnit born. Subters have been sterile for two generations. It's impossible." My fingers grow cold. Even Jal can be wrong sometimes. "You are Omnit born and so am I."

He points to his findings jotted on a piece of parchment. He's been including me in enough genetic analysis to last a lifetime, so he doesn't need to explain the markings.

"It must be possible for you. Just in case, though, I've sent an inquiry to GCE." He smiles like this is a good thing to do. To share me with people I don't know. To hand me over to scientists with as much sympathy and decorum as a dental exam.

He's crazier than Maddelyn if he believes proving I don't fit in will help me. "You never should have shared this with GCE, Jalaz Cayan. What if they find out I'm some wild mix of mutated, wrong, non-Omnit offspring?" I crumple the paper and hurl it at his chest.

"That's not what this means."

"I thought you liked me. Why would you alert GCE?"

"This means you're special, not *wrong*. It explains so much – your extreme albinistic features, your sight, your uncharted intelligence, even for a Subter, and so much more. If anything, you're super-Subterranean, more than any one of us. It might even mean your LE calculation isn't valid, or it may indicate something about Subterranean fertility. It's something to celebrate, not fear."

"No. Whatever you've got here, you've made a mistake. Leave it alone!" I pull away. My mind spins and whispers of taunts creep into my pores like an incurable infection. *Ratgirl, ratgirl.* I just wish he'd shut up. "Don't study me anymore."

He calls after me, but I run away and don't look back.

When I catch up with Maddelyn in the library, shame washes through me. I'd rather keep my measly four-point-five years than allow anyone to discover that I'm *that* abnormal. Especially Maddy, in her sickened, mean state.

I place my canarymouse in its wired cage on the floor next to a bookshelf. The mouse jumps to the middle, stands on its hind legs, and sniffs.

Maddelyn strolls over to the closet and fetches a broom. Instead of getting one for me, like we normally do for each other, she slams the door shut. She looks down at the broom in her hand, the floor she's about to sweep. "We are all going to die."

All my muscles tense. This is something new.

She backs away a bit, blinking hard. "They're coming for us."

I hold my breath. I realize now that I can't keep an eye on her by myself. I am failing in my promise to Gelia. We need a ba'rm – a burrow maid – to keep her safe, preferably a large one.

"Gelia Cayan lies and lies, but I know the truth," Maddy continues, eyes dancing about the room. "Omnits are killing Subter children. The Burrowlings. All of us – it's a mass extermination." Her right shoulder falls unevenly compared to her left.

"I don't think that's accurate," I try to reason.

Magazines cascade to the floor from the shelf in the back, and I jump. They must have been stacked unevenly.

"Don't worry." Maddelyn kicks my mouse's cage. "I won't let them get you." She holds the broom up as if she's thinking about hitting someone with it, but the only person within range is me. "Gelia received a message today about you. Some military academy in the east is looking for burrowmaids."

"I'm not applying to maidship positions."

"Low LE-ers can't be choosers," she laughs. It's a cruel joke since ba'rms basically become the property of the burrow – more like servants than real contributors. Maddy had been wanting this inhumane loophole in the workforce law to change for years – and now she laughs about it? "I heard the headmaid said they would consider an application from someone with an LE lower than five years if accompanied by a very strong recommendation."

My chest tightens. There are no other seniors with such a low LE. The message has to be in reference to me. "How do you even know about this?" I ask a little too defensively. Gelia has always supported me in my choice to become a medera.

She ignores the question. "*Now* do you believe Gelia lies?" Maddy smacks her lips smugly.

"Zuzu?" a small voice calls out.

I spin around, finding C swaying from foot to foot inside the doorway. She holds the long stick used to light the hallway candles each morning. Clearly she's just finished lighting the candle outside the library. Shadows dance across the stone walls as she moves about. But my head snaps immediately back to Maddy. She's not supposed to be around the first years – especially not now.

Maddelyn drops her broom to the floor and stomps out of the library, mumbling about interruptions. C's dejected gaze follows my friend as she leaves, like she misses the real Maddy as much as I do. I need to go after Maddy, but I need to get C safely back to her burrowmaid first.

"May I borrow another book?" C asks. "I already know the one I want." She's the only one in her class who reads any of my paged books.

"Of course, but hurry." I should go to Gelia first, rather than chase Maddy down myself.

C runs to a shelf near the center aisle and slides out the oldest book in the room: *The Chronicles of Narnia*. I wrestled that book from Anetta, my nurserymaid, who, while she never called me *ratgirl* once, made me feel like one every day. She's probably wearing a bead from her next subling by now.

C's gaze shifts to the far wall. "What's that noise, Zu?"

I edge closer to the back of the room until I hear it too, close to the magazines that fell over. *Plop, plop, plop.* An odor wafts from that direction, like a fermenting load of wet laundry, heaped into a pile. I cover my mouth and nose with my sleeve. How did I miss this?

"Get back to your burrowmaid, C. Now."

Startled at my tone, she runs off without question.

I follow the sound to the back corner where we keep the old

journals stacked against a wall that abuts the farthest boundary of the Cayan Burrow.

My feet hit a puddle before anything else. A jagged crevice has made its way down the outer wall. It's been there for years but it's grown since I last checked. Now, water trickles down, saturating the periodicals, with the *Ancient Art of Self-defense* journal Maddelyn and I enjoyed rummaging through, sitting at the very top. Running my hand along the wall, my fingertips bump into wet sections where newer cracks have branched out.

I lift an old textbook from a nearby shelf, and the dampness of its pages makes the binding bend. Shadowy spots have formed on the pages, too dark to be water. *Oh, jet.*

CHAPTER 4

Sterling's Plague

There's only one thing this could be: mold.

I drop it and yank more off the shelves, holding my breath. These are only textbooks, but I'm surrounded by a thousand more novels collected over time – stories that made me imagine colors I've never been able to see with my eyes. These stories raised me up to bask in the warmth of the sun on beaches I'll never visit. Are they all contaminated?

The damp conditions inside this enclosed room make a perfect breeding ground for the mold. I fly across the aisle hoping my favorite bookcase will be spared, but book after book that I tear from the shelves has been exposed.

My eyes well up with tears which then pool inside my goggles with nowhere to go. Like me. I was foolish to believe my LE wouldn't matter. I have no books, no job, and my best friend's madness has altered her beyond recognition. There is no such thing as hard-as-diamonds hope.

Terror takes hold of me, stifling my tears. Little C!

I bolt from the library, slamming the door shut, and head for the new burrowlings' chamberroom. All I can see is C's face and her hands holding *that* book as I speed past the crematorium. There's no way to know how many Cayan burrowlings have hypertoxic reactions to mold. It's safe to assume that I'm not at risk – the mold has been building for several weeks and, after rifling through it all, I'm likely now coated with enough spores to start my own colony.

Pumping my feet as fast as my body will allow, I turn down the corridor and manage to catch up to C, almost knocking her down.

"Zu!" she says.

"The book," I pant, "give – it – to me."

She cocks her head, but hands it over. "You'll read it to me later though, won't you?"

I turn the pages, which look clean, and let out a sigh. Aslan is safe for now. "Go to your ba'rm and tell her you need to be washed. Thoroughly."

"But –"

"Go now, child! Please."

She backs away a few steps, doe-eyed, and then spins to leave.

I let out a breath in relief, then immediately rush back down the hallway. My eyes begin to tear again as I think about the damaged books. I was supposed to take the textbooks with me when I leave so I can use them as a medera. Is this a sign? Should I just give up? I'm walking so fast that I don't notice people passing in an intersecting hallway.

"Zuzan?" calls Medera Gelia.

I twirl around. So many things are at the tip of my tongue: the mold, C's exposure, Maddy's worsening mental state, her mention of the ba'rm inquiry from the Military Academy. But before I can speak, a strange young man standing to Medera's left clears his throat as if he won't be ignored.

Medera bangs her wooden cane. "Perhaps you should slow down."

"Yes, Medera," I say hoarsely. "I'm sorry. But my library–"

"Good health to you, girl." The visitor towering Medera's side interrupts with a terse nod. He wears a mask. An Omnit, then. It protects him from the change in air condition from his home environment to ours. He looks only a few years older than Jal, and his hatless head shines more brightly than candlelight. All males are supposed to wear hats to cover their bald heads.

Shameful, really.

"Likewise, sir. Medera, I have to–"

"What's in your hand?" he asks with a small accent. It's so slight that I can't place it. His vowels sound fatter somehow. His pin-striped suit and long coat mean he's some sort of official. Although most of his features remain hidden behind his travel mask, his lack of manners have me imagining he's hideous underneath.

I hold up Aslan's story. "A book."

"Zuzan," Medera says. "Might I introduce you to–?"

"Isn't a reading tablet standard equipment at Cayan?" He takes the book from my hand, flipping through the pages. He interrupted my medera and now he's demeaning my wonderful tome? I immediately want to snatch it back from him. *Hatless* man.

"Yes, it is. But this is the only format I can read." I look toward the library, my heart hammering wildly in my chest – time is slipping away and Medera should see for herself.

When I turn back to her, the man is staring at me with severe eyes. My cheeks warm.

I put my hand on Medera's arm to guide her. "Medera, there is an urgent matter."

"Certainly." Medera leans into her cane. "*After* Maven Ringol's tour. You are dismissed."

Maven? I scan his uniform again. He surely can't be old enough. And a maven visiting our burrow? "But–"

"Mind my words." One of Medera's eyebrows rises and falls, and that's the end of it.

I bow my head and take a step back, but then stop. I cup my hands around her ear and give her a rushed report. After all, her burrowlings are in danger. Her children.

Medera stiffens against me.

"Maven, you must excuse us," she says. "Zuzan, go directly to the decontamination chamber. We'll close the library and the wings that lead to it until we assess the situation." She stands silent, staring at me. I'm stuck fast to the ground. *"Go! Now!"*

I'm off and running in a heartbeat. She bangs her cane again, this time to direct a ba'rm to check on Maddy and C. Thank all good no one else has been impacted. Mold is a tricky contaminant – a level nine breach for three percent of us. No one knows if they're a poor reactor to mold until they encounter it, so each of our emergency injections contain a minimal treatment for mold poisoning just in case. Thank all good that most Cayan burrowlings read only on tablets.

I strip off my clothing in the decontamination chamber and place it into the hazmat bag, and then begin the cleansing shower and low UV treatment. When I'm done, I change into the only other uniform I own and rush to the cremation wing so my contaminated clothes can be burned. I take a few slow breaths and then make my way to class. Everything will be okay. Medera Gelia knows what she's doing, and she'll fix everything. Maybe my library is lost, but that doesn't mean all is gone. Lessons will start soon, and nothing will stop me from spending time with my fellow seniors before they leave. *At the very least, I will have that.*

As I turn the final corner on the way, I'm met by Jal coming from the boys' corridor. A crazy smile forms on his face and my cheeks turn to fire. We've been friends forever, and we're silly to push our friendship to something more, with only a small amount of time left before we go our separate ways. It's so impractical.

"Zuzan." A tiny circle of light waltzes over his pupil. He bows his head and touches his hat as if to tip it, but only moves it a fraction. He scans the hallway, and then kisses me quickly on my cheek, beaming. He must not have heard about the library, which means Gelia must have everything contained.

"I thought I'd missed you by a wick. I've some pressing news."

But his shoulders slump, like he's afraid to tell me. *What now?*

Maddelyn passes behind him, followed by a watchful ba'rm, and she acts like she doesn't notice us. At the last second, though, she flips her head back and smirks. Her usually bright eyes have dulled like stone, causing me to shiver.

And suddenly it all connects. For all that is good. "The library!"

"What?" Jal's eyebrows go up.

"She's always in there with me. Because of me."

He shakes his head. "So?"

"There's mold on the journals by the far wall. The spores must have contaminated her mind – and somehow they affected her canarymouse, too. *That's* what caused this."

He glances back at her, then leans in to see past the doorway into the Lessons Gallery. "She seems docile at the moment, but what about your books?"

Maddelyn's ba'rm has her sit in a cubicle all the way at the end, something that should irritate her. But Maddy simply complies. Maybe she's turning a corner. Maybe I'm wrong.

"Zuzan." Jal places his fingers under my chin. "I've been officially called." A proud smile pours over his face, but then he reels it in like a subdued child. He should be ecstatic, and I should be ecstatic for him, except this means our impending separation is official. "It's for research, an undertech position at the Genomic Center of Excellence."

GCE, just as he always hoped. He'll be living his dream. He'll give his speech. He'll be happy. So why can't I be pleased for him?

"Maven Ringol says the outside world is a mess, that Omnits believe we're an entirely different species."

"Ringol?" I barely consider what he's said. I thought Maven Camu was in charge of GCE? But, I reason, positions open up all the time. People die. So now *that hatless guy* will be the maven who supervises our brilliant Jal?

He nods. "But that belief is about to end, with Ringol's work. In fact, he believes we can end the separation of Omnits and Subters altogether. He's working closely with the Immunology Center of Excellence, and they're testing theories. Amazing theories. Can you imagine that, Zu? Getting healthy, living above ground, united once again? Because I can."

I take his good hand. "That's outstanding news." He'll turn twenty in a week. I trace the vein from his wrist to his knuckle with my thumb and his warm pulse jumps under my touch. He feels too real to disappear from my life in seven days. Losing my books is nothing compared to losing Jal.

"Maven Ringol agreed that I should pursue LE research. Don't you see? The sooner I get started –"

But I don't hear any more, too occupied by my own impending sadness. Once he leaves, I'll be left with a red-yet-gray rock to fiddle with. When I die in less than five years – I still round up to five to make myself feel better – he'll forget about me. Why should I hold him back now? I can pretend to be happy for him for a week. I owe him that much.

"You're flushed," he says. "Zu?"

Medera Gelia Cayan bangs her cane at the door of the Lessons Gallery. "On your guard, ladies and gentlemen. Study Session shall begin momentarily." Her steps grow weary, like moving each foot is a heavy task.

Jal, never letting go of my hand, leads me through the gallery to my desk.

Maddelyn watches as I take my seat all the way at the back wall where the lights are dimmed to accommodate my vision challenges. Half-walls of darkly painted burlap surround my table to further block the light.

Maddelyn jumps at every sound. She's *not* better; it's troubling to watch. This brilliant girl whom everyone wants to employ, and who every younger burrowling wants to emulate, reduced to twitches and anxious fidgeting. The mold has done this to her, I'm certain.

Medera Gelia eyes her with concern, but then limps her way to her podium and begins the Omnit v-clip. She has a set of about thirty videos that she rotates, playing one each morning: Omnits working the fields to bring us the food we eat, Omnit children toiling to sew the clothes we wear, Omnit parents crying as their baby – born Subter – is taken away underground for its safety. Today's v-clip is how Omnits built the underground structures we use as burrows.

I grab the pictures from underneath my workstation, the only thing I can look at. The light used from the holograms is too much for my eyes. I focus on one photo: a man who transports a large load of dirt with a bulldozer. Not only does this man have a full head of hair, but according to the pictures in my bound album, Omnit women grow their hair all the way down to their waists. Aside from Gelia, who's braided strands of string into her hair to hold all of her beads, Maddelyn has the longest hair at Cayan, and it only grows to her shoulders.

When the v-clip stops and shuts off, Medera nods to us all, her cue for us to speak. *"Thank all that is good for our Omnit brothers and sisters who care for us."*

Medera Gelia glances at me with a strange expression, stands, and starts to hobble in my direction. When she reaches me, she's winded. "Maybe you should take a day at the infirmary, and we can run your bloodlabs."

I shake my head. "I have a theory about Maddelyn–"

Maven Ringol enters the gallery. Hatless man. He squares his shoulders and nods at Jal. I can't help but hate him more now for taking my Jal from me.

"Let me worry about Maddelyn. We've rerun her bloodlabs and we have more tests planned. In the meantime, one day of rest would benef–"

"I'm fine, Medera. Zero symptomatology. Please send word to the medtech that we need Maddy tested for mold toxicity." Maven Ringol waves at me from the front, and I ignore him. "I'm staying here."

She sighs. "You'll need to use a tablet until I can requisition new textbooks. I've turned the brightness to the lowest setting. I cannot even see the words, so you might well manage it. If it vexes your eyes, I recommend you use the text-to-language mode."

Text-to-language is much slower than I'm accustomed to reading, but my options are limited. "I'll make it work."

"It's a science placement exam," Medera explains. "You've taken most of the other placement exams for your mederaship prep, but you've avoided this one for some reason."

I shrug. It's Jal's subject, not mine, although I've helped him study for it as if it were.

Medera raises her voice as she turns. "On your guard, Cayan ladies and gentlemen." Each member of our burrow turns toward his or her workstation. "Study session has now begun."

I stare at my tablet, my eyes straining to force each letter into submission. After only a few minutes, I know the backlight is just too much. Each word blooms into a shiny blob. The symbols curl and twist, jumping left and right. Medera glances at me and points to her ear. I shake my head – I hate listening to the drone-ish reading.

When I'm about to give up, the bolded words at the top of my lesson untangle, becoming clear enough to interpret: *Viral and Biotoxic Effects on Human Genomes.*

I put the tablet face down to give my eyes a break, but the lesson's title sticks in my line of sight. The words stain everything in the Lessons Gallery as I blink. The letters appear on Medera's desk, they cover each of the paneled columns throughout the room, and every student's face.

BIOTOXIC EFFECTS.

BIOTOXIC EFFECTS.

As the burning words slowly fade and the gallery settles again before my eyes, one person shifts and crosses his arms, as if trying to get my attention. Maven Ringol nods at me, leaning against the iron support beam at the side of the gallery.

He might be the youngest maven I've ever heard of. Shiny-headed fool. Why is he here? It's irresponsible for a scientist to waste an entire day watching burrowlings study lessons. What information would that give him? He's interviewed Jal and hired him, so end of story.

I give up trying to read from the tablet, so I dislodge the remote auditory device from its side and nestle it into my ear. It beeps and counts down in a low voice made to sound like a sleepy woman.

Ten seconds to your lesson. Nine. Eight.

The sluggish pace of it makes me groan. Maddelyn will beat me today, of course – that part of her brain remains sound. In fact, most of the faster readers should beat me. I watch them all, heads bent, writing furiously.

Five. Four.

It's okay, though.

Two.

I don't have to finish first *all* the time.

One. Your lesson will now commence. I sigh in relief, close my eyelids and listen.

The first section of my lesson focuses on review topics, like Mendel's discovery of recessive and dominant traits. I'm well-versed on these thanks to many hours spent poring over textbooks with Jal, so I skip to the subexamination section. Unfortunately, the drone has to read the entirety of each question, not to mention each one of the ten multiple choices, *before* I can enter a response. The pace tenses every muscle in my body.

Next, I listen to a few sentences about Punnett squares and alleles, but quickly skip to the subexamination for this part, as well. This is no challenge, either. I skip to the questions for most of the sections without listening to the text. One addresses how viruses invade healthy cells and take over DNA. Another, how certain viruses can infect gametes, the ova and sperm cells so that all offspring are automatically impacted for generations. Maven Salas Sterling had identified numerous strings of defective DNA and bioengineered corrective code, fusing it with a pro-virus and using it to treat previously untreatable medical conditions.

And, of course, there's the section on how Maven Sterling's discoveries were stolen, and re-engineered as a biological weapon – a highly contagious virus coded to weaken one's DNA. When it was accidentally released – or on purpose according to conspiracy theories – it led to the weakening of the population, now known as Subterraneans. Us. Ultimately, it drove us to live underground to protect the fragile state of our health. *I highly doubt*, I remember Jal saying during one study session, *that Maven Sterling would approve us calling it Sterling's Plague.*

The answers to all previous questions line up like a chart in my mind, making it possible for me to figure out the common pattern used in the answer key. These old answer keys are one of the first things I'll change, I think, when I become a medera.

That is, *if* I ever do.

Maddelyn turns and glares at me with her stony eyes. Then she looks back to poking at exam responses on her tablet, picking up her pace like she's trying to beat me. My text-to-speech drone yammers questions and potential responses at a turtle's pace. I figure out that I can press the screen *after* I hear the correct response, rather than listening to all options, which speeds things up incrementally.

True or false? My tablet mutters in her soporific tone. *The members of the dominant human phenotype commonly known as Omniterranean are immune to viruses and antigens of any kind.* Pause. *True.* Pause. *False.* I press false. While Omniterraneans have the body chemistry to kill nearly any antigen, they are still plagued by a few. The quicker true-false questions are my favorite.

Correct. A celebratory trumpeting horn sounds.

Next question. The average adult weight of the dominant human phenotype, commonly known as Omniterranean, is what percentage larger than the adult weight of the recessive phenotype commonly known as Subterranean? Pause. *Five percent larger.* Pause. *Ten percent larger.* Pause. At this rate, I'll have to hold on until the last answer. The Subterranean phenotype – my phenotype – has an average weight of a hundred and ten pounds, and rarely grow more than five feet two. Omniterraneans weigh in at an average of one-sixty-five and average almost six feet tall.

The answer key still follows a pattern, and I know what the last answer should be before the question is even broadcast. I press the screen when she finally says fifty.

Correct. Another celebratory trumpeting horn sounds.

Your final question is true or false. Maven Salas Sterling volunteered his DNA coding data for use in the most notorious weapon of mass biogenetic alteration because he believed in the Human Virus Theory. Pause. *True.* Pause *False.*

I don't respond. Any first-year burrowling could answer this. Like Jal, Salas Sterling never would have bought into a theory positing the human race as a virus infecting the earth. What a rotting waste of time.

But the correct response does not follow the jetted answer-key pattern – the one I'm sure they've been using on this entire test. Is it a trick? Of course, Medera has instructed me in the past not to rely on the answer-key patterns I may or may not imagine to have uncovered. There were only a hundred patterns until I told her about them, and then someone came up with a hundred more. It was fun for a while.

Maddelyn bangs her fist on the metal table, causing the younger members around her to jump. She must have responded incorrectly. It will set her back another five or so questions until the program accepts that she's conquered the material.

True. Pause. *False.* Pause. *Would you like me to repeat the statement, Zuzan?*

The drone pronounces my name *zuh-ZHAHN* and I snort.

I'd named myself after Susan Geoffries, the first medera. Jal named himself after Maven Salas Sterling, his hero. He actually asked Medera to assign him the letter S his first day here so that he could name himself Salas, but Medera Gelia forbade it. Subter superstition believes that S is bad luck. Some even blame the letter for Maven Salas's murder. However, Medera agreed to give Jal the letter J, if he was okay with modifying Salas's name. They settled on *Jalaz*.

Still a very bold move, Medera had said at his Name Day ceremony. *Gutsy.*

Stay away from jets, Maddelyn added sheepishly. Jet travel was unsafe once the plague hit, and Salas was murdered on a plane.

This question wasn't in Jalaz's study material. I'm sure of it. Maven Sterling was a good man, a wonderful scientist. There's no way he gave credence to HVT. But the answer key says differently. What am I missing?

Jal shifts in his seat, glancing up at Ringol. But Ringol continues to stare at me. His eyes widen and he holds out his hands, as if he knows I'm delaying my answer. How could he? For a fleeting second, I suspect he's the one who has designed this test, right down to the broken answer-key pattern.

But no. There's no way he could do all that.

Ringol points to me, and then rolls his hand, as if I should hurry up, like I'm delaying *him* in some way. Jal glances up and notices Ringol's irritation. He follows Ringol's gaze to me as Ringol throws up his hands.

I look to Medera questioningly, but she's keeping an eye on Maddelyn. Maddelyn slaps the table with both hands as if infuriated with her lesson. Soon, though, lessons will be over and she'll get the help she needs.

Jal nods at me, like I should keep going, so I place the auditory chip into my ear again.

Kindly respond "true" or "false" to the following statement, Zuzan. Salas Sterling volunteered his DNA coding data for use in the most notorious weapon of mass biogenetic alteration because he believed in the Human Virus Theory. Pause. *True.* Pause.

This time, as soon as the drone says *false,* I press the screen and hold my breath. According to all historical accounts, Maven Sterling was taken hostage and meant no harm. As soon as the mutineers forced Sterling to give them what they needed, they slaughtered him and his entire staff. However, once the virus was released, his killers perished along with ninety percent of the human population, and the separation of Omnits and Subters began.

So, no one won.

A bulb blinks at Medera Gelia's station, signaling that one of her members has completed the challenge. She half smiles and raises her eyes to Maddelyn who is still working feverishly on her lesson.

Maddelyn jabs a final tap on her screen and then spins toward Medera.

"Congratulations, Zuzan." The chairs squeak as all members turn to face Medera. The many beads in Medera Gelia's hair make a clattering sound as she moves about. Each one, the memory of a former student who has graduated her burrow.

Maddelyn's mouth twitches and pulls. Her head begins to shake. Her crazy anger is returning, and I hate it. Maybe I should have let her finish first – not that I could have guessed what would trigger her. The mold is playing havoc with her mind. Guilt washes over me again.

"Likewise, congratulations to Maddelyn." Medera brightens her voice. "Our runner up."

Before Medera finishes, Maddelyn knocks over her stool as she stands. Its metal spine bounces against the stone floor with an ear-piercing clang, and she storms out of the gallery. This outburst must be a direct result of those toxins. I slump in my chair.

My library, my mold, my fault.

CHAPTER 5

Page Sixty-One

Maven Ringol claps quietly like he's giving me a standing ovation, even as Maddelyn rushes by him. I roll my eyes behind my dark goggles, and fold my arms across the stainless-steel table. Pressing my forehead into them, I try to blink away the after-burn in my eyes from using the tablet. My hot breath fogs the metal in a dull circle. I wait for it to dissipate, and then I breathe another warm circle. For a few moments, I want to stay in my dark cubicle forever. Breathing, waiting, breathing. But then someone taps the wall and I jump.

"Medera, I didn't mean to –"

"Hear me now. I've just heard that a first year has fallen ill." Her bottom lip quivers.

"C?" I stand.

"Her burrowmaid brought her to the infirmary in a horrible state, even after she'd gone through decontamination. Her breathing is labored, and she's severely rashed." Medera Gelia glances around, then drops her voice and leans in closer to me. Perspiration speckles her creased forehead. "We've already administered her personalized emergency injection to no avail. They're running bloodlabs now."

I rub my forehead at my hairline, and my hands start to shake as I picture little C in such a state. "I should have stayed with her. It's my fault. She was in the library this morning."

"She's asking for you."

"Has the medtech come back from his hiatus?"

Medera shakes her head. "I've contacted the ambulatory medtech division, though. They will be here within a day. Our medmaid tends to her now. You… you should hurry."

"I'll meet you there." I motion to Jal. "Walk Medera to the infirmary, please."

I speed past Maven Ringol without the courtesy of a nod. The infirmary is in the centermost point of the burrow, a five-minute walk through the meandering halls, at least eight minutes for Gelia with her limp. I'll make it in three if I run. As I picture C lying on the cold metal table gasping for air, my feet can't move fast enough.

I pass Medera's administrative office, and a masked man stands and holds up his hand. "Miss!" He holds up a package. I recognize him as the black-market procurer. Not a good visitor to have while a maven is in the burrow. "Your medera?"

"Not now," I say as I fly past. My soft-soled boots slap across the floor, sending echoes against the walls.

When I turn the corner to the final stretch of the infirmary, someone growls and tackles me to the floor. The back of my head whacks against the stone tiles and my vision blurs. Maddelyn, at least fifteen pounds heavier than I am, pins me down with her body. She yanks on my emergency shot, trying to detach it from the metal chain by force. She can't seem to figure out how to unclip it.

"Maddy! C is sick." I swat her hands away. "Leave my injection alone!"

"Perishing before they come is key, that's what the mederas think!" Her voice is flat and low. She spouts the same nonsense as before.

"Maddy?" I say, still struggling beneath her. "I barely recognize you."

"No words." She punches me in the center of my chest, and I groan in pain. "I shall euthanize you." *Bam*. A punch to my stomach. "Only the dead belong underground." *Bam*. She strikes my jaw. She's truly gone mad.

I try to turn over while dodging her blows but it's no use. She spits, hitting my goggles.

"I know all of it!" The tightened muscles in her biceps shake from strain, and for a second, she looks like she'll cry. She grabs the hair at each of my temples and her nails dig into my skin. She pulls my head up and then bangs it into the floor.

"Why are you doing this?" My voice falters in my anguish. It's as if my dear friend has left her body and someone else has moved in. I would take a thousand beatings if it would bring her back to me. "Maddy!" I plead, but the deadness in her eyes tell me she's no longer there.

I never thought I'd need to use any of the self-defense from that moldy old journal we once laughed about, especially not on Maddelyn. But I grab hold of her hands, using my palms to crush her bent knuckles into the hardness of my skull. *Page forty-two*. Her grip loosens, and I push harder until she screams in pain. Her fists recoil, so I shove her knees away and roll over. *Page nineteen*.

I'm up for a split second before she charges me again, but I duck away and trip her with a low kick. *Page sixty-one*, her favorite. She lands on her face, then rolls onto her back, and covers her bleeding nose with her hand. I shake, hoping she'll stop but waiting for her next move nonetheless. No sign of shame or pain registers across her face, but she stumbles as she tries to stand up.

My chest heaves up and down and my skull throbs. I want to cry and scream at her at the same time, try and bring back the old Maddy. But C needs me. *Now*. "If you're planning to kill me, you'll have to *wait* until after I check on C. I have to go!" It's no longer Maddelyn, but the mold monster that's taken over. After she's treated, once we figure out how, she'll be good as new. Off to her internship even. I have to believe that's true.

Maven Ringol steps forward. He's panting like he's been running, wide-mouthed, hands on his knees.

"Good health," he sighs. I glare at the bubbled image of him through the spittle stains on my goggles, tucking the loose hem of my blouse inside my skirt. Maddelyn's nose still drips blood. She startles at the sight of him, and scurries away like a mouse escaping its cage.

Ringol must think we're both jetting crazy. He looks after Maddy like he intends to go after her. But I don't have time to worry about her – or him – so I dart down the opposite hall towards the infirmary. The corridor spins a bit with each step, and my stomach churns a little, but I ignore it and carry on.

When I reach C's bed in the infirmary, she's clutching her blouse like she wants to rip it off. She gouges scratches in her arms with her nails. Her breath clips too shallowly – hissing against the air caught in her throat. Her eyes protrude and her face flushes a darker shade. *Oh, my poor C.*

When I was five years old, I was horribly sick at the central nursery before coming to Cayan. I contracted a bronchial infection and I was sent into soft quarantine. I eventually overcame it, but it took its toll on my LE before I recovered. While the other children's nurserymaids came to the central infirmary dressed in full-body scrubs and masks, risking their health just to visit their subling, mine never came. Na'rm Anetta stayed away from me for three weeks. While I was struggling to breathe during the worst part of my illness, another subling in the next cot over, sick with the same bronchial condition, died in her na'rm's arms. All I can remember thinking was, *I will die alone.*

"You're not alone," I say to C. "I'm here with you."

The gloved-and-masked medmaid presses a cloth to C's cheek. She's doing what she's supposed to, but C needs so much more.

"Move away."

The medmaid obeys me, all too happy for the help. She rattles off C's vitals and advises the treatment steps she's taken, following protocol.

"Bring me the preparation for another anti-inflammatory injection, preferably a steroid. Go!" She nods and flies off. It's a tad early for another dose, but Maven Buckner-Wheeler's pharmacokinetics study showed that Subters could withstand more frequent dosing for acute cases with close monitoring. "And bring our strongest antihistamine!" I shout after her.

When I take a seat on the bed next to C, she grabs my arm, pulling me closer like she's drowning and I can pull her up, her fingers digging into my flesh. Tears stream over her temples as she wheezes through her next breath.

I wish it were me, not her. Why couldn't it be me?

"You're going to be okay, my girl. I promise. Try not to cry, not now. It's harder to breathe."

She slaps her hand over her windpipe, and her eyes widen.

"We will fix this." My hand shakes as I take her fingers in mine, speaking softly, the way I needed my absent na'rm to do for me when I was five. "Do you believe me?"

She nods, fixing her eyes on mine.

"Perfect. Take in as much air as you can before you release it. You're reacting to that nasty mold from the library, and those tiny spores can linger and transfer onto your clothing if your ba'rm made any errors during decontamination. This is a war, just like *Narnia*. We'll read it together soon, but for now, it's us against the toxic spores, and we intend to win."

While I pull off her boots, a shadow crosses over my shoulder. "Hand me the needle." I demand. "And search for a hazbag."

"Needle?" Maven Ringol asks. "From where?"

My eyes snap to Ringol; the one taking Jal away. I'm about to tell him where he can stick the longest needle if he finds one. Unless… The words die on my tongue and I ask him something different: "Do you have any direct medical training?"

His helpful expression fades. "Academic, not clinical." For a moment, my vision doubles and I see two overlapping images of Ringol. I close my eyes, my head dizzy, until my sight clears again.

"Step away, then. I have to undress this patient."

He nods. "Of course. I noticed some biohazard containers on my way in. I'll leave one outside the door."

Once he's out of the room, I peel off her skirt and strip her bare. Her rash-scaled body shivers and shakes. "The first battle is recognizing the enemy, and we've already won this battle, soldier."

Another tear slides down her cheek. Her breathing becomes more labored.

The medmaid brings over the glass syringe. Estimating C's body mass, I load it as the library's medtext prescribes. I'd studied it nearly a year ago with last year's senior classmates. My vision doubles again, and my movements slow down. But then I imagine the tablet's not-quite-human voice urging me. *Move, Zuh-ZAHN, move.*

Pressing in the crook of C's arm, I find a tiny vein and insert the needle, releasing the steroid. "You're going to be all right, C," I say, trying to focus on her treatment instead of the awful hissing in her throat. "This is our second battle now – neutralizing their stronghold. We need perseverance. Do you hear?" She nods as I prepare the other syringe for the antihistamines.

I refuse to look at the walls, though I swear they have started to cry out in an eerie, hushed manner. Waiting. Those blasted child-ghosts will not come for my C. Not today. *They aren't real.*

From the hallway, the maven's voice echoes as he instructs our only medmaid to dispose of C's clothing, and to change her own garments when she's through. He further directs her to bring medsmocks for everyone. "Prepare the decontamination chamber and bring me antifungal ointment and steroid cream for a topical salve."

I'd be annoyed if it weren't for the fact that he's instructed her exactly as I would have.

After a few minutes, C's breathing still hasn't improved. I'm not sure if it's worsened, or if it's just harder to watch her struggling the longer I'm here.

"Zuzan?" Ringol shouts from the hallway while the medmaid is gone. "You might have to consider tracheal bypass."

I shake my head, and the room spins. That was a mistake. I steady myself against the bed. "No. The steroids haven't kicked in yet. They will." C's eyes flutter. "Do you hear me, C? Perseverance. Now it's our third battle. The rest will be downhill." I begin to slip off my clothing. My second and *last* set of clothes has been contaminated.

"But if it doesn't," he continues, "you must prepare for any circumstance. I can secure the equipment."

Hasn't he heard of the healing effects of positive thinking? I could rattle off numerous studies by world-renown scientists. I blow a frustrated breath and steady my words. "With all customary respect, *Maven*, the inflammation has likely settled into her lungs. A tracheotomy won't bypass that. We simply need to demonstrate patience and a tiny bit of faith."

"What dosing model did you follow when administering the steroids?" His muffled voice carries through.

I clench my teeth. "The correct one!"

The medmaid brings our medsmocks, thankfully cutting off our discussion. She drapes one over C's quivering arms as I slide mine over my shoulders and snap the side. "They are decent now," she calls to Ringol. "You may come in."

"No, he may not," I say, spinning around but it's too late. Medera enters, Jal holding onto her arm with Ringol behind. Ringol still has his travelmask, and Jal and Medera now have cloth masks over their mouths and noses. The open shock crossing Medera's eyes as she approaches her smallest student subdues me.

"How is our C-bear?" she asks gently, handing me a mask. I tuck it into my medsmock pocket. I don't need it – if I were in danger of reacting to the mold, I'd be dead by now. The medmaid slides the metal stool close to C's bedside, and Medera sits down. Her thick fingers cover C's hand. I stand like a sandbag at the foot of the bed, waiting the storm out.

"How much antidote for mold does our injection typically contain?" I ask, but everyone stares at me blank-faced. "The exposure was too much. I don't know if a single injection is enough."

Jal pulls out his tablet, and Ringol turns on the bright light of his chip projector, the image appearing in the air right in front of him like magic. As I shade my eyes from them, I take off my emergency shot.

"Zu, what are you thinking?" Jal asks.

I stare at the liquid contents of my injection. "Nothing in it can harm C, and maybe the additional mold treatment would help –" But before I can finish, Jal rips off his own emergency needle and injects it into C's neck. I stare at him, open mouthed.

Not more than a minute passes when the hissing sound loosens and C's breathing steadies.

"C-bear?" Medera says. Our girl takes a shaky breath and smiles. "Pah, pah," Medera coos. "Well battled."

And then C holds her other hand out to me. I move to the far side of the bed, taking her hold of her. I kiss her wet temple and whisper in her ear. "You won, my Narnia soldier."

Medera touches my arm. "Thank you, Zuzan. And thank you, Jalaz."

She should blame me because I didn't notice the mold in my library sooner, she shouldn't thank me. I want to tell her as much, but the thoughts in my head start to swirl together. The adrenaline is finally fleeing my body, much like my senses. The throbbing at the base of my skull picks up where it left off and my stomach jitters with nausea.

"Wall crack – water leak…" I'm mumbling. I know I must be. I can tell they don't understand me – not even Medera. My words become staccato beats, like the throbbing in my head. "Find – cause."

"Zuzan?" Medera's voice grows fuzzy.

Ringol makes it to my side in two steps. "She took a few blows from your eldest female." His breath hits my face but his voice echoes like he's far away. He smells of coffee and spices.

"Have to – rest." My knees begin to bend, when Maven Ringol flips me into his arms and carries me to an empty bed in the adjacent room. I want to tell him I can walk on my own. I want to tell him to put me down. I want to say a lot, but I'm too dizzy and I can't see much of anything anymore. I tell him to "go fly" instead, but he probably doesn't understand that either.

CHAPTER 6

Keep Up, Girl

The medmaid rises from her seat when I wake, and hustles away. A moment later, Medera knocks with her cane on the floor and shuffles inside.

I try to sit up, but the room spins.

"Pah, Zuzan. Don't unsettle on my account. I've come to check on your concussion."

I adjust my goggles, closing my eyes as she lights a candle. "How is C?"

"She'll recover fully. But we've not found Maddelyn yet. No one has seen her since she attacked you, going on four hours."

"It's not her fault."

"Maven Ringol witnessed the whole incident. We have his statement. Central Forces will arrive on the next magnetran to escort her to the psychiatric clinic. I hate it Zu, but –"

"No!" I try to sit up, but instantly fail. "Hear me, Medera: the leak must have been there for a while, and is only just noticeable now. It must have caused Maddy to endure repeated exposure to the mold, weakening her mind." The words come with some effort. "We treated C because her reaction manifested immediately, and it was contained to a physical reaction. Maddelyn's symptoms deserve the same consideration. We must find a cure. Is it antifungals? Some type of full-system cleansing?"

Medera nods. "You might be digging in the right tunnel in

this case, Zu, but she needs help we can't give her here. Let us all hope that it isn't too late to recover our Maddelyn."

My mind ticks through a hundred thoughts a minute, and I can't seem to spell them all out quickly enough. "Please see to it that mold is listed as a level-nine reactor on C's list, and the best fungal antidote included in her emergency injection? Maven Ringol's group should perform genetic analysis and determine where the mold sensitivity exists on C and Maddelyn so we can forewarn other burrows of the danger. And our maintenance tech should call in a specialist, and perhaps a duct inspector to ensure the mold hasn't traveled."

"Of course. It will be done as you say. Save your energy now."

"What were the findings on the leak in the library?"

She pulls the sheet over my legs. "The leak is the result of a broken pipeline."

I shake my head. "Our service techs wouldn't miss anything so huge."

She sighs. "Someone damaged the pipes near ground level. We're not sure when, but it appears... purposeful."

"Maddelyn said Omnits are after us! Is she right? Have Central Forces stopped them from doing further damage? How long will it take to repair?" I look into Medera's puzzled face, and I slow down. I'm spinning myself into hysterics, and she's clearly worried.

"I'm sorry Medera..."

"Pah, my girl." Medera shifts to rise. "Hear now. Maven Ringol intends to talk with you."

Me? Again? What could he want? "My head aches, and he'll only make it worse."

Medera gasps. "Pip on you, Zu. Where has he displayed such egregious behavior before?"

"He's a bit of a know-it-all." Really, it's because he's stealing Jal away. Although if Ringol didn't, some other maven would have, instead. But the smirking, and interrupting – it's rude. He's too much. "And he's bull-headed–"

Maven Ringol steps into the room and I clamp my mouth shut. His face is no longer covered by a travelmask now that he's adjusted to our air system. The full view of him is not as grotesque as I had pictured. His youth strikes me again.

"I thought that we had a bonding moment, Zuzan," he says with a smirk.

A realization hits me as all the blood from my body rushes to my face. In this light, it appears that Maven Ringol isn't ugly, he isn't even plain-looking. Some might even call him handsome. I almost feel cheated.

Medera taps the top of her cane. "I must pardon myself – and Zuzan's manners." Medera purses her lips. "Maven trumps medera. I will, however, call the medtech and ask about mold toxicity. If he agrees, once we hunt down Maddelyn we'll administer treatment, even under screams of duress. Which I imagine will be inevitable."

The maven bows reverently to Medera, and my insides curl. She pauses as if she might say something to him, but she decides against it.

When she is out of ear shot, I speak. "On how much of our conversation did you eavesdrop?"

He clears his throat, stepping forward. "Are you referring to the part where you barked orders at your medera, or the part where you insulted a visiting official?" He points to his nose, as if he's some important figure, which makes my insides burn. Mostly because he is.

"*Bark* orders?" I have never barked at Medera Gelia. "I adore and respect her."

"Did I say bark? My bumble. You were merely stating your opinion in an insistent manner until she acquiesced."

My jaw tightens. "I wasn't–"

"Yet you admit to insulting a visiting official?" His intense eyes curl into playful crescents, and I clench the bedsheets in my fists.

"Where is Maven Camu, the greatest mind in all of genomics? I thought she was in charge."

He blinks in a crazy-slow way that I just now realize I despise. "Nope."

"What do you mean by no, Maven Ringol? You, a person who holds such a high position with no publishing credits that I've ever read. What do you want with me?"

Maven Ringol's full lips part into a faultless smile, with faultless teeth. He has a neckline that curves favorably into his jaw, and a squared chin that sets off his smile. Even the shape of his hatless, bald head arches in an infuriatingly likeable manner. No matter how much I try to find a flaw, something tangible that reveals his evilness, I turn up empty.

"Surely you're aware that I've called Jalaz to a position in genome research?" he says.

I fold my hands and nod, squeezing until there is no air between my fingers.

"He mentioned you during his interview." He pauses, as if he wants me to ask him about it.

I press my mouth shut. I agreed to listen, not to speak. And definitely not to play his games.

"You're not even curious about what he said?"

I maintain my silence.

"He urged me to consider calling you for employment at my facility."

"What?"

"Truly. I told him that I might have a labmaid opening in the short future – almost the same bit of time it will take for you to turn twenty, but we usually require at least five full years remaining of your LE." The rapid tempo at which he speaks makes my ears ring. "FFR put these rules in place to disqualify low LE-ers who, well, whose costs outweigh their benefits. Most are better suited for busy work, anyway. Jalaz wouldn't let it go, however, so I promised I'd review your abilities firsthand with no guarantees. The boy is clearly smitten, and I was confident he'd overestimated your talents."

"Labmaid?" My mouth falls open. "No. I'm going to be a medera!"

"Not with your visual impairment," he retorts simply. He presses the chip at his temple, and a projection of light fills the space in front of him. It causes a shock of pain behind my eyes and I turn away. "This is the newest virtual textbook library – it's all accessed through chip projectors. All burrows are supposed to transition to this model within the next eighteen months. How can you be a successful medera when you can't review your students' study materials?"

"Just turn it off," I mumble. I didn't know. It's no wonder that no one has called me for mederaships. "So," I look into his face, "you want me to scrub droppings from animal cages and boil germ-infested beakers instead?"

He pulls his finger to his lips and waits for me to stop talking. "Imagine my surprise to discover that the object of my bright new recruit's affection was a nothing but a mouthy waif, with little hair and wearing the thickest goggles, no less." He leans in and flicks the leather strap of my goggles with his finger.

"Please. Leave." I growl through clenched teeth. Self-absorbed. Hatless. Shameful. I point to the door. "I *will* be a medera," I say, defiantly, but it sounds so ridiculous when I say it aloud now.

He puts his finger to his lips again. "You might also imagine my astonishment when the said-waif's academic performance smashes all reasonable expectations on the relevant subject matter. Even on the extra questions I'd added, somehow you deduced correctly. You must realize not everyone catches the answer key patterns."

I blink at him. How could he know? "Wait. *You* asked Medera Gelia to test me in Genomics?" Why hadn't she mentioned it?

"Only someone who figured out the pattern would have hesitated on the easiest question." He smirks. "Outstanding sequencing skills."

I can't tell if he's trying to get me to admit I cheated by

following an answer key pattern. I didn't, of course. Just because I understand the pattern, doesn't mean I follow it. I always answer with what I think is right. But clearly he knows that.

I scowl. "I prefer 'expectation smasher' to 'mouthy waif.'"

"A perfect score," he says, ignoring my comment. "And with a time that few could dream of, even using the text-to-language mode." He grins as if he's made a rare scientific discovery. "When I checked your session history for the past two years – a messy task indeed," he holds up his charcoal-stained fingers from my pencil-and-paper exams. "I couldn't find a single question you'd missed. Tell me. When is the last time you were marked wrong on an item?" He says *wrong* as if there's something wrong with being right all the time.

He's mocking me. My eyebrows pull down on the top seal of my goggles, and I turn away. It's not shame that washes over me, exactly, except something that once made me proud has now mutated.

"I see," he says. "You never have. Which explains why no one questions you, and why the great Medera Gelia takes orders as if you were in charge. Well, that legacy will not carry over. Each GCE staff member builds a reputation as they prove themselves on the job."

My mouth falls open. He's offering me a job? I shake my head. My first offer of employment is – for all good – from this foolish maven? No. "I will not work for you."

"Will not work...?" He sits straight. "There's a two-year waitlist full of people who would die for this opportunity."

I don't respond.

"Besides," he continues, "I've already sent the request to Fundamental Force Recruits. As long as this is your only offer–" He eyes me suspiciously, a slight curve to his lips. "Or have you another?"

No one has called me, and he knows it. Either I take his offer, or I risk being assigned to maidwork. Could I be happy as a burrowmaid at a military academy?

No, I couldn't.

"Hear me," he implores. "I know how hard it is to start over in a place where no one knows you."

He's relentless, and he's hit me at my very heart. Tears pool in my eyes that he cannot see. I look away. I can't speak without my voice cracking, so I don't.

"Fine." His voice is clipped. "Once FFR registers my request, you'll have to file a grievance with them if you are compelled to have it overturned. Even then, there's no guarantee."

I take a deep breath. I can't keep fooling myself. No one wants me – except him. I clear my throat to disguise my tears. "What are the typical job duties for labmaids at GCE?"

"Pardon?" His face turns puzzled. "No. Well, yes. I did tell Jalaz that I'd consider you for a labmaid position. But that's changed."

"I'm confused. If you're not making a job offer, then what are you requesting through FFR?"

"Keep up, girl, will you? I've completed my recruitment report. I've witnessed this waif – er, *expectation smasher* – display intelligence that breaks the scales, top-notch managerial skills, bravery under attack, coolness under pressure even after sustaining physical injury, not to mention the keenest of problem-solving abilities. I'll dare to add after my *accidental* eavesdropping, concern for her fellow members, highly observant diagnostic assessments, and follow-through with ideas for future improvements. For the sake of a clean report, I'd left out your brashness, temper, and tendency to ignore authority. In all, though, I'm forced to conclude that if anything, Jalaz's praise of you pales in comparison to the real you. Of course, we'll have to wait until you've reached majority age for graduation."

"And so, you've called me to…?"

"Do research, of course, just like Jalaz. Genomics. We have a full laboratory for the Genomic Center of Excellence, a staff of a hundred or so members, and slightly better-than-meager funds for study." He glances around the room with a sour expression, as if our burrow holds no comparison. "How does *Undertech Zuzan* sound to you? You'd be able to work side-by-side with Undertech Jalaz." His smile returns, beaming like he's the grand granter-of-favors.

My heart slows. I want to be a medera; I want to help people. But if there's no possibility of that, then GCE research is, as much as I hate to agree with Ringol, an unimaginably good alternative.

"What about my LE? How is *that* exception supposed to pass through FFR?"

"Once they see my data, there will be no issue. I've committed a position for you regardless of the time you have left to offer."

As much as I want to see the maven as a villain, I don't think I can anymore. He's the only one calling me for a meaningful job, and I'd get to work with Jal. But it is a complete change from everything I've been working towards. I was supposed to establish a burrow where my students felt like they were gaining a family, and give them all the love they need and deserve. I was never meant to work in a cold, fact-driven lab environment.

Still, if I'm honest with myself, maybe my hopes and dreams were always unattainable. Impractical. I can't read the material my students would, or design lectures, or even grade them properly. Medera Gelia realized this before I did, and so did Jal. I've been blind to facts as well as light.

"I – I accept." I reach into my pocket for Jal's stone, and frown. I'm wearing the medsmock, not my uniform skirt, and all I find is the face mask Medera had given me.

Before I have a chance to figure out what's happened to the stone, a medmaid screams from somewhere down the hallway, and a crashing of metal rings out. Both the Maven and I jump, turning toward the closed door as if it will fly open.

"C," I say, struggling to my feet. But the room sways and my head aches. I find I can't move an inch without falling. *Jet, jet, jet.* I slump over the bed.

"You've lost your senses." Maven Ringol grabs my arm and guides me back into bed, covering my feet with the sheet. He averts his eyes as if he's uncomfortable. "I'm sure it's our medmaid being clumsy, but I'll check on the sick girl. In the meantime, Undertech Jalaz promised to stay nearby. Might I send him in?"

I nod, and try to smooth my wispy hair.

But when Maven Ringol slides the door open, Maddelyn stands on the other side hugging something under her arm. Before he can react, she jumps up with a growl and clocks Ringol in his temple with the hard object. The clunk of it hitting his skull makes me flinch.

He collapses to the floor. A hat, had he worn one, might have buffered the blow.

"You've hurt him!" I shout, but then I stop. Maddelyn's skirt runs crookedly across her waist and her blouse hangs untucked. She's carrying a lidded, pint-sized jar filled with a dry powder. The bridge of her nose bends, swollen from when I tripped her earlier. "Stop this. It's the mold, Maddelyn. You're not yourself. We can treat you."

"Now you've done it!" she says in a voice not quite her own, hoarse and low. "You've put it to Gelia that I'm crazy in the noggin." Her head jerks twice and she pants as if she's been running.

"I've not said anything to Gelia. Please Maddelyn..." I implore.

With her chin to her chest, she looks up through her lashes with empty, stony eyes.

"What?" She jerks her chin sideways. "Did you think a dull ba'rm could find me?" She never uses that term "*dull.*" She considers the slang term used by cruel Subters for Omnits too derogatory. At least, she used to.

Maven Ringol murmurs from the floor, and his hand goes to his temple. I breathe a quick sigh; at least he's moving.

"We just want to help you Maddy."

Something moves behind her in the hallway, but she doesn't notice. Then Jal appears, creeping, edging silently toward us, with a finger to his lips.

"This is over now, girl," Maven Ringol says as he struggles to his feet, and steps in front of me. "Zuzan wants to help you, although I can't understand why. Regardless, you won't get past me, so surrender yourself and there's no harm done." The maven's towering frame must be close to six feet. He's the tallest Subter I've ever seen.

Even with his height, Maddelyn doesn't seem the least afraid. Her lips curl back from her teeth, and she sways energetically. "Step away, maven, or perish." She raises the jar, similar to the kind that I've seen brought in from the black market. The pale powder inside shifts and bumps against the glass. I can't wrap my mind around the fact that my best friend is threatening a *maven*.

Ringol stays put. "What is that, girl?"

She moves the mask hanging around her neck over her mouth and nose. "On your guard, ladies and gentlemen." She uses a voice that kind of sounds like Medera, but creepier. Her hand cups the jar's lid, and shakes as she opens it. "Your demise has now begun."

Just before she's about to throw the contents into my room, Jal wraps his arm around her and she lets out a guttural scream. He pulls her backwards into the hallway. The fine powdery contents of the jar clouds around them, coating their faces. When they hit the floor, Maddelyn's mask slides to the side so it covers her ear instead of her nose and mouth. Jal moans in pain.

Ringol rushes for the sink. He dampens two washcloths, placing one over his mouth and hands another to me to do the same. "Where are the reinforcements in this rotten hole?"

Maddelyn fights to face me, even as Jal bear-hugs her and clamps his legs around her torso. He begins to cough, and she punches at his calves.

"Jal!" She'll crack one of his soft bones if she keeps at it. Somehow Jal's grip remains tight and he keeps her in the hallway. I swing my feet over the side of my bed to help him, but dizziness wins and I tumble to the floor.

The jar rolls forward and into my room, crackling over the peanut dust on the marble tile. Ringol squints at its label. "Jet blasts! It's peanut flour! Stand away."

Any form of peanut is an illegal substance; it is most lethal in powder form. Almost instantly so.

Jal's eyes begin to swell.

"Help him!" I cry. But Maven Ringol lifts me up and moves me to the farthest corner of the room. I try to crawl away, but Ringol blocks my path, holding me back.

Maddelyn starts to wheeze as she pounds her fist continually into Jal's thigh. The she lurches upwards and bites into his hand.

Jal doesn't scream, but I do. In fact, he doesn't move at all, and the flesh around his neck billows into hives.

"Jal?" I scramble against Maven get to him, my heartbeat pounds in my throat. "Jal, talk to me! I – I'm going to GCE with you."

Maddelyn's movements weaken and she collapses backward, knocking Jal off balance. He finally releases her and rolls onto his back, his arms stretching outward. His eyes stare at the ceiling. In a scratchy whisper, almost lost in the confusion, he utters, "I – love you – Zu." And then his body begins to shake with seizure, kicking up the powder all around him.

"Jal!" I inch forward, but Maven Ringol still won't allow me through. He holds the washcloth to my mouth along with me.

"Stay put!" Ringol rips the sheet from the bed and wraps it over his face.

Maddelyn lies prone, wheezing as C did earlier. My rock from Jal, the one that I'd left in my skirt, slips from her fingers and clinks onto the tile beside her. It must have fallen out of my pocket when she attacked me earlier.

I grab Ringol's arm and remove my emergency injection from around my neck. "Use this on him. Hurry!" Everyone's emergency injection is loaded with a level-ten peanut antidote, but it only works if administered immediately. "Directly into his heart. Now!" I shake his arm and push him toward Jal

Ringol narrows his eyes as if to question my logic, but then nods. When he turns, he hastily grabs some medsupply gloves and squats next to Jal. His seizure has quieted and Ringol lifts Jal's good arm to feel for a pulse. My heart skips when he moves to the artery in Jal's neck. I hold my breath. Ringol's hand moves up, down, searching, searching...

No, no, no.

"Jal?" I beg.

Ringol turns to me, but his eyes remain downcast. He shakes his head. "I'm sorry."

"What are you waiting for?" I scream. "Do it!"

"He's gone, Zuzan. It would only work if his heart were still pumping."

His words ring in my ears. "You're not even trying. Save him!"

The maven walks over and places his hand on my shoulder. "I am truly sorry."

I smack him away and kick at his legs until he steps back. "Give me the needle."

"Not before I check on C," he replies, stern. "You know they've used her syringe already. Or would you have her die, too?"

My pulse beats in my head like a painful drum and the room spins cruelly, but I keep my eyes on Jal. And then they come, announcing themselves with piercing screams: the child-ghosts. Their achy cries turn into growls, the shadows masking their arms extend from the floor. I see it. I cover my ears but I see it *all* as infant ghosts come to claw at his chest.

"You're not real," I whisper to them.

Ringol takes one of my arms at a time and slides medgloves

over my hands. "I've sent a warning to Medera Gelia. I'm going to check on little C," he shouts. C is screaming from a nearby room. She must have heard everything that's happened.

Maddelyn slaps the floor with her palm as her eyes begin to swell. It's too much. I can't watch both my friends die.

Ringol yanks my hands away from my ears, and pulls my chin up to his face. "Now, hear me: stay put. The powder cannot reach any of your pores, your mouth, your nose, nothing, if you stay where you are. Leave everything as it is so we do not spread the contaminant." He shakes me a little. "Do you understand?" And he hurries off.

"No," I say over and over as I crawl over to Jal. I hardly think about the consequences because he's Jal, *my* Jal, and I can't believe he's gone. I watch his chest for breathing, but no, there's nothing. They scratched out his life, and he is dead. Gone. I hiccup a sob, and cough from the powder lingering in the air. I use the ends of my smock to wipe the dust from his beautiful face. A whimpering sound gurgles in my throat.

This can't be. It isn't right, none of it.

Lacing Jal's fingers into my gloved hand, my body trembles with sobs. My gaze shifts over to the half-empty vessel of peanut flour. The powder crescents along the jar's round bottom like a sweet smile, as if it couldn't possibly be poison.

Maddelyn wheezes like C had earlier. She wanted to kill *me*, not Jal. That's why she was trying to take my injection before – she wanted to take it away from me before attacking me with the peanut powder.

Her neck begins to swell like Jal's had, and her breathing comes in shorter gasps. Her emergency syringe slides to her shoulder, close to her face mask – two things that are supposed to protect her. I play everything over in my mind, trying to make sense of what just happened, but my brain isn't quite letting me. This can't be real. My thoughts slow to a crawl.

I scramble toward the jar, lifting it slowly so I do not lose any more of its contents. Reaching for the lid, I replace it onto the jar and set it down. When I do, it bumps Jal's rock flipping the stone over. *May good health find you always.*

Maddelyn's eyes follow my movements. A small tear trickles down her temple, washing a clean path through the dust on her skin.

My forearms break out with a webbed rash. Within minutes, it will bubble into hives and the antigen will overtake my blood stream. When Maddelyn's hand brushes my knee, I jump. She's begun to seize. She hasn't got long. Jal and Maddelyn are my oldest friends. Are we all lost?

No. We will not all die. I won't let that happen.

I grip the emergency injection from Maddelyn's neck and pull it off. If the maven uses my needle on C, this is the last one nearby. But I don't care. My neck begins to feel thick and itchy.

Maven Ringol's hard shoes echo with each step as he approaches. "What are you doing? Back away!" He's wearing a full hazmask, and begins to run toward me.

Maddelyn's body contorts under her seizure. I unlatch the lid from her emergency injection and wrap my fingers around its tube.

"Zuzan, wait!" Ringol rushes toward me, but he is too late.

I raise the injection above my head and plunge it into Maddelyn's chest, directly into her heart.

"May good health find you," I whisper, and thumb the tear off her cheek. The skin on my arms start to feel like they've caught on fire, and now I know what C felt earlier. I cough as I struggle to breath while my throat swells.

When I fall to the floor beside Maddy, Ringol stands over me. "Fool."

And yet, he opens my own emergency needle – which C evidently didn't need – thank all good. C is okay. And then he jabs it into my chest.

"Now who's the bull-headed one?"

"Hatless maven," I say hoarsely.

"This," he says, while taking out another shot and stabbing it into a vein in my neck, "is a bonus. It will knock you out, so bonus for me too. I'll explain the rest later. Rest up, my greenest and most foolhardy undertech."

Pah. Jal is gone, and I won't work for Ringol without him. Everything I'm thinking slows to a stop. All except for one thought that definitely pushes through. I want to tell this patronizing young maven to rot with the vermin, but luckily for him, his face blurs out of sight.

CHAPTER 7

Nothing More Than a Canarymouse

I wake up chilled to my core in a room lined with stainless steel – one of four large decontamination chambers in the burrow. When we toured these rooms back when I was a first year, the ba'rm took us down a central hallway that separates the rooms. Two cubicle chambers sit on each side of the hallway. Inside my cell, the lights have been left off, probably to protect my eyes which are goggle-free. My skin tingles, and I'm guessing it's from some sort of cleansing spray from the overhead sprinkler heads. Alone and wearing only a thin, sleeveless and legless leotard, I sit up. Although my goggles are gone, the room is dark enough that I can see.

Someone lets out a piercing scream and then wails in one of the cells across the hallway. I recognize her voice: Maddelyn. She bangs on something every ten seconds without fail. Her screams penetrate my pores, settle into my icy bones, and I almost believe they will shatter.

Darkened bruises spot the skin under my collarbone – several spots from where Maddy punched me, and the one where Ringol injected the emergency shot. I run my fingers over it and wince.

Memories of all the horrifying events flood back. The peanut powder, Maddelyn turned monster, and... Jal. Jal is gone. He'll never charm the labcoats off a roomful of scientists. He'll never do the work he was destined to do.

My breathing quickens, and even though I have enough air, I feel like it's not enough.

Maybe I'm wrong – *maybe* Jal was saved after I lost consciousness? But snapshots of his swollen face flash through my mind, and I know I can't be wrong. He's gone.

I turn away from the door and my hand goes to my head. Stubble from my shaven scalp scratches my palm. My bare legs stick to the metal surface of the bedtable, much different from the comfortable infirmary beds. I roll onto my side and curl into a tight ball.

A light mist begins to prickle my skin. The droplets give off the faint scent of the chemical sanitizer used to detox contaminated areas. As the mist coats my body a stinging sensation sets in.

Maddelyn shrieks again like she's burning alive.

My body shakes. I squeeze my legs to my chest, and press my eyes together. I open my mouth to scream with her, until someone touches me. I flip over and the silhouette jumps back. A papery material has been placed on me.

"Ah," Ringol says. His deep voice resonates below Maddelyn's screeching. "You've returned to your flesh." He steps away awkwardly and holds out disposable towels. I can't look in his direction, not with him in those mesh briefs. My cheeks burn despite the chill.

I don't move except to cover myself with my arms. The mesh of my leotard merely acts as an extra layer of skin over my girl-like figure, hardly more developed than C's. I know he can't see me like I do him, yet I feel exposed.

"Cover up and turn around," I say. "Were you born without a sense of dignity?"

He snorts. "I can't see a thing in this darkness. Besides, who do you think has cared for you these past two days?"

Two days? Him? *No.*

I spring up to my feet, suddenly finding the will to move and duck behind the table. "Does Medera Gelia know?" She'd never allow a stranger to *handle* me.

"Does Gelia know that I've been tending to her most prized pupil? That I had to shave your head without light so I wouldn't further harm your vision? Change that leotard? Or dry your body after every cleansing—" He waves around his hand in the darkness, and he swallows. "Of course she knows and, I might add, she is grateful. She also realizes how tedious this trip has been for me, and how it has taxed my entire research center in my absence." He pauses his rapid speech while he feels for the edge of my bedtable and sets the towels down. "When you have changed, you might consider visiting C." He points to a closed door. "She's been quarantined with us as she was in the same wing when..." He does not continue.

When Jal died. My throat thickens and my knees want to give out.

"Zuzan," he continues in a softer tone now. Some might even consider it soothing if they didn't already know him. "You and I are people of science. One human form is the same as any other." This time, he takes a deep breath. "Preservation of dignity isn't practical when facing a life-and-death situation. Besides, the cleansing mist only comes every eight hours now. We will be released in another day and a half."

I frown at my plain, bony body. Of course he sees no dignity in it – I'm waif-like, after all. I'm *ratgirl*. But no. Maddelyn convinced me that I'm not.

"You, Maven, may be full of nothing but science, but I am a human being. Jal was the one obsessed with genomics, and I can't work for you without him. The genomic institute can rot for all I care. Now, get out!" I throw the scrunched-up paper towel at him, hitting him squarely in the chest.

He catches it blindly and his face tightens. The darkness hides nothing from me. He steps over to me and gently replaces it on my bedtable. "You will find a change of wrapping in the chute next to the door. Your old wrap and the towels should be placed into the hazmat chute on the opposite side when you are finished." Before I can register what he's said, he exits the chamber on my side of the cell and the door slides closed.

As I shiver behind the bedtable, the tears I wanted to shut out flow down my cheeks, over my lips, and dampen the mesh wrap. Maddelyn has stopped shrieking from the cleansing mist, only to scream-sob with more force than before.

Although I want to curl up in a corner and cry for the loss of my friend, I can't. C needs me; she is the only thing that keeps me moving. If she's going through this with no one but Ringol for comfort, she's probably terrified.

I peel off my leotard and find the new one just as Ringol described. I walk over to the door Ringol indicated was hers, and knock.

"C?" Her name comes out breathy. "Can you turn off your light?"

"Oh, Zu!" she answers, and it winks out in seconds.

I pass through to the connecting cell and take her in my arms. She cries into my ribcage and I cry with her.

Our fingers remain laced the entire day and night, while Maddelyn's screaming eventually dies down, turning into quiet, defeated sobs. Oddly enough, C also holds Ringol's hand for long stretches. His tenderness is more than I'd have bargained for. They're blind in the dark, so I wonder if Ringol knows that I can see this. He surely doesn't notice the silent tears I shed for my friends.

"I'm sorry," Maddelyn says every so often from the cell over. Waiting her out has been the only other thing to distract me. I'm relieved to hear her true personality return bit by bit, even though she now sounds broken and desperate. "I'm so sorry," she repeats.

According to Ringol, she is locked in the nearby quarantine room across the hall, pacing her metallic cell in a square pattern. Once she hits the corner, or rather crashes into it, she turns and crashes into the next. I'd grown accustomed to the banging. Only now, that too has stopped.

I saved her life with the hopes that she would recover. But as soon as she does, then what? She killed Jal, her other best friend in our unbreakable trio. Jal's death has formed a crater-sized hole in my heart so deep that I fear I might crack on the inside. I can't imagine what it does to *her* when she realizes that she is the one took him away from us. She wouldn't have done any of it without the mold poisoning, I know that, but I don't know how much that will matter to her. Can she ever be the same? No. I don't think so. It's impossible.

The next day, as our quarantine runs into its final minutes, we wait by the steel exit doors in C's cell. I tremble, and can't wait to see my medera's face again. I need her comfort now more than ever.

"I've so much work to do." Ringol bounces up and down on his feet like he'll sprint out of the burrow as soon as the doors open. I avoid looking in his direction. C and Ringol have been understanding about keeping the room dark since I am still without my goggles. Maybe he can't see me, but I see way too much of him through his mesh suit.

"You were right. Maddelyn's bloodlab results came back positive for mold poisoning," he says. As if it matters now. If I'd made the connection sooner, Jal would still be alive. "I suspect her immune response triggered microglial activation in the brain," Ringol rattles on, in the same science-y way that Jal had, "but once the inflammation subsides, she has a good probability of regaining her former personality."

"If she remembers everything, it'll be impossible for her to return to her former self." I kiss the tiny whiskers beginning to grow on top of C's shaven head.

"I hope Medera ships her away." C clenches her teeth. "She doesn't deserve to return at all after what she did to us."

"Did you want to stop breathing when you were exposed to the mold?" I say a little too harshly, so I lower my voice. "Maddelyn's reaction was the same – unwanted. Only, instead of her lungs sustaining the damage, it was her mind."

C's eyes blink, full of remorse. "Sorry."

Maybe I'm just trying to convince myself, though. Here I am trying to persuade C it wasn't Maddelyn's fault, but I'm not even sure I'll be able to forgive her. Jal's body was cremated within hours of his death to contain the peanut exposure. I never got to say good-bye.

A metal latch sounds on the other side of the door. My fingers curl and uncurl. When the door slides open, I clamp my eyes closed and turn my face from the light.

"Your goggles," the medmaid says from the other side of the door.

I reach out, feeling for and finding the goggles in her hand. I slide them onto my face – ah, they're my older pair. They probably burned the newer ones. This ancient set fits too snugly, and I'd forgotten about the hairline fracture in the left lens. These goggles don't have the adjustable lenses either – only one setting no matter what the degree of light.

"Where's Medera?" A cloud of disappointment passes over C's eyes.

"I'm sure she's on her way," I say, my eyes roving for her too.

"She's not on her way," the medmaid answers, handing each of us a set of clean clothes. "She's busy clearing everyone out."

"What's happened?" My head snaps to Ringol, and he shifts anxiously. *He already knew.* I close the space between us, forgetting my mesh suit. "Tell me, Maven."

C takes my hand from behind me. "We weren't supposed to tell you… An entire wall in the library wing collapsed while you were unconscious. It was from the crack and the water pressure. Then our burrow flooded in the connecting corridors. The infirmary shut down after the peanut powder. It was all too much."

"But what about our burrowlings?" I look to the medmaid.

"Common Good has issued a condemnation order." She says it like it's old news, but her words shock me so much I'm not even sure my heart will beat its next.

The Cayan Burrow will be shut down? *Impossible.*

"The evacuation is underway," the medmaid continues. "Our good Medera of Cayan has been seeing her children off at the magnetran platform over the past few days."

"No." The word sits on my tongue. "No, no, no."

I hurry into my clothes as C pulls on my arm. Ringol dresses himself right over his mesh suit and ignores all this conversation.

"Promise you'll come with me to my new burrow, Zuzu? Wherever it is."

"C–" I start.

"Good health to you both," Ringol interrupts after squeezing into his too-short replacement clothes. He looks like a schoolboy who just went through a growth spurt.

C runs up to hug him, and his eyes soften. He genuinely seems to care for C. The oddity of it irks me. But in this moment, the thing that bothers me most is something I haven't seen from him before.

His silence.

What more don't I know?

Over the next few days after being released from quarantine, I try to make it a point to send off students departing for their new burrows not only for our sad good-byes, but also to ask them what they saw while I was locked away. The hazmat crew who came in – the ones who cremated Jal – cleaned up after the peanut contamination. A fifth-year burrowling told me how large the crewmembers, all Omnits, had been. Monstrous, she claimed. They had to duck to walk down the hallways with lower ceilings – all dressed in head-to-toe white suits, completely covered. Not for their safety – none of the mold or peanut powder could harm them – but so they wouldn't leave behind any form of infection. They'd only been here for two days before the burrow flooded and Common Good condemned the entire structure.

As the students depart Cayan each day, for forever, they buzz with whispers about the terror they felt while the Omnits were here, telling tales of how the giants now despise us. C and I stay the longest, needing to wait until we're strong enough to travel. Maddelyn's departure is likewise delayed, but she's been kept out of sight.

On my last day at Cayan, Medera and I huddle on a bench located on our meager magnetran platform with C sitting between us. My mind keeps replaying a simple image: Medera Gelia had Jal's name engraved in the cobblestone above her bedchamber alongside the names of the other Cayan students who died before they graduated. "In death and in life, my children are my heart," she had said.

I can't rid myself of the image, and I don't know that I want to. Jal, at least, gets to stay in Cayan forever. I'm leaving the only true home I've ever had. Back at my nursery, where I was raised to age seven, where Na'rm Anetta hated me – that was *never* home. Home is love. Medera taught me that.

The only other time I'd seen the magnetran platform was when I first came to Cayan, with Maddelyn and Jal. It's nothing like the large station at the nursery. Instead of marble floors, we have nothing more than rough flintstone. Instead of iron grates above the boarding pit, we have aging wood beams and a make-shift hatch.

C and I will bring little more than the clothes on our backs to the Zamption Burrow. I haven't heard much about it but if Medera Zamption is half as good a teacher as Gelia, we should be fine. According to Common Good's reference material on burrows, Zamption has three times as many students as Cayan, though, and the burrow has produced some of the highest ranking Subters in multiple fields of study. Luckily, Medera Gelia will escort us on her way to Fundamental Force Recruits for reassignment. It will be a tedious sixteen-hour ride for us, but Gelia's ride to FFR will be a total of twenty hours.

Maddelyn stands on the other end of the platform, about ten feet away, with a medmaid on one side of her and our sole remaining burrowmaid on the other. They will travel with her to the psychiatric clinic. Maddelyn's hands are bound in a tight-fitting jacket like she's still a threat, but anyone can see that she's not. She's my dearest friend again, and I ache for her loss, for *our* loss. I swallow hard, waiting for her to look my way. I even wave, trying to get her attention. How can we leave each other like this? Like we're just strangers who've never met?

Medera Gelia catches my arm, motioning for me to sit down. "If we upset her," she says in a shaky voice, "the traveltechs will not be gentle in subduing her for the trip."

Instead of sitting though, I pace closer to the tracks. Maddy's tran arrives first, stopping on the tracks below the platform and sending a gush of wind upward. She glances over before she boards, and I wave again.

Thanks to her broken nose, deep circles have formed around her beautiful eyes, making it look like she's wearing goggles herself. She blinks heavily, and for a moment, I see my Maddelyn in her expression again, but a grieved, drained, and defeated Maddelyn. She mouths *I'm forever sorry* before the medmaid pulls a travelmask over her face and they climb down the ladder and into the magnetran car, along with a piece of my heart.

C spins around and buries her face in my arm when the wind from the departing tran whips upward toward us. Her hair lashes about and pelts the skin on my arm.

"Zu," the girl says. "I'm so glad we get to stay together."

I smile at C, but my thoughts are with Maddy. She wanders off, searching for any sign of the tran.

"Stand back, girl," Medera says in a sharp tone. These past few days have taken a toll on her, too. Especially her patience. Her eyes soften again. "You're too close to the edge, C."

C leaves my side, obediently sitting where Medera points, while I watch the dark tunnel where my Maddy disappeared.

Within twenty minutes, a horn blows in the distance, and we line up together. C squeezes my hand. Medera kisses C's almost-bald head. "Be brave, and good health."

Tears form in her eyes as she looks to me. I've only seen her cry once before. My heart races, because I know every minute expression on my medera's face. Though she tries to hide her emotions from me, she can't. Something's wrong – there's something beyond her tears.

"I am sorry, Zuzan," Medera says. "Zamption refused your enrollment because you're too close to aging out, and old enough to draft into maidship. This isn't the tran for you."

C tightens her fist around my hand. The tran's magnet hisses as it releases, and the levitating car clanks to a rest on the lower platform. The techs begin to open the hatch above the magnetran for boarding.

C shakes her head. "No! You promised, Zuzu!" Her eyes well up, and she pulls my arm downward so she can grab hold of my shoulders.

I open my mouth to say something, but I have no words. How could Medera wait until *now* to tell us?

"You promised you'd come with me!" C melts into sobs.

The only words I can think to say are, *Yes, yes. Of course I'm coming.* But I'm not.

Medera slams her cane into the stony platform. "On your guard." Her voice cracks, but she raises her head high.

We both snap to attention.

"Hear now," Medera says. "Zuzan had no idea of this arrangement."

Tears fill my eyes.

"Be brave, my bear," Medera says, her voice softening. "Perhaps this is for the best."

C crashes into me, her arms stretching around my waist, and I lean down to kiss her shorn head. "What if something else happens to me? I will die without you, Zuzu. Do you hear? How can I go on without you or Mother Gelia?" I don't correct her. Neither does Medera. How could she do this to us?

I bend down in front of C, offering her the only strength I have left. "Today is a hard day, my little C. Very hard, and I'm so sorry." I sniff, but I have to be brave for her. No crying. "I know where you'll be, and I *will* find you as soon as I can." She's got the same pouty mouth that Maddelyn had at her age. "A piece of my heart will travel with you for always." I kiss her cheek. Right now, she is my entire Cayan family.

An official-looking transport tech makes his way over.

C puts her hands on either side of my face and kisses my forehead. "Me too, Zuzu. For always." Her hands are torn away from me, and she screams.

The tech has snatched her off, carrying her to the hatch as she sobs. "I'm not ready!"

"How dare you?" I shout.

But Medera catches my arm. "They must keep their schedule."

"Good health!" I cry out, but C is carried down the hatch before she can answer. Her small hands reaching for me is her only goodbye.

The engine hums as the car begins to levitate on the magnetic track. As it picks up enough energy, the tran blasts away, pulling every thread of my clothing in its direction, and I wish I could disappear into the vacuum of its wake.

Anger bubbles within my chest, along with fear. "Where am I going, Gelia?"

She startles when I address her without formality, and I'm immediately sorry. Maybe she should have told me sooner, but she's also a victim. She's lost her entire burrow.

All of her children, all at once.

"You are called, Zu," she says, taking a seat on the steel bench. "I am so sorry. I contested the Zamption Burrow's rejection of your placement but there were a great many transfers and they claimed you would be a hardship since you're so close to majority age. Your magnetran will arrive within the hour. You are going to the Woynauld Military Academy as a burrowmaid for their first-year burrowlings. It's a newer establishment, and the best I could do on such short notice."

"Maddy told me you had been working on a ba'rm placement at a military academy for me days ago. Before the library incident." I speak almost in a whisper. "She must have broken into your message center."

Medera's hairbeads click as her gaze snaps away. "I did receive a message, Zu. A generic recruiting call from that academy to all mederas and mederos – they've got such a high need. It wasn't about you specifically, though. Except now, after everything that's happened, it's a solution, and *hear me now.*" I wait for her to bang her cane, but she doesn't. "It's only temporary. I will continue to search for a more appropriate placement. All other jobs, however, require you to reach the age of maturity before you can formally accept them."

I am not yet twenty.

I nod numbly. *Temporary* ba'rmship. Perhaps a junior mederaship position will open up at the academy while I'm there. I know very little of what is taught at military academies, but they must start with the basics.

"I confess that I'm not having a lot of luck with other placements," she sighs. "I must implore that you reconsider the undertech position with Maven Ringol. He's very interested in having you, and I think you would thrive there."

I shake my head. Working at GCE without Jal was never an option for me.

She nods. "It wasn't supposed to happen this way, leaving

our burrow before you turn twenty. I am sorry for that. I hear the Woynauld maidship team is a clean group, but beware. At Woynauld, a maid is a maid and no more. Remember your place, and know that you will be sent for upon your birthday. In the meantime, make friends, and stay on Woynauld's favorable side. You will need his final approval for outplacement."

I stand and pace the small platform a few times. I'll be working with children at least, for all that is good.

"There's one more hiccup," Medera admits closing her eyes as if she doesn't want to continue speaking. "Although *I* allow my students to celebrate their Name Day earlier than graduation, Common Good only registers the names of students who have reached majority age. I regret to say they wouldn't permit me to add your name to your record."

"What are you saying?" I haven't been nameless since I left the nursery. She can't –

"You will always be my Zuzan Cayan, no matter what name you're given at Woynauld." She takes off her necklace, and removes the bead I'd given her years ago. She kisses it and threads it into the very front strand of her hair at the bottom with all the other beads her former graduates have given her and fixes it in place. My nurserymate was right – it really does look like I painted droplets of water frozen in the air onto the bead. "You are my last graduate, Zuzan of the Cayan Burrow, and I am very honored."

My face tingles, and I rush to sit next to her. "Where will you go?"

"Pah. My place is here, Zu. There is no better place for an old medera like me."

No.

"You are a wonderful, wonderful teacher. They can't leave you in this contaminated burrow." Not alone, not with the ghosts. "It will collapse."

She pats my hand. "They aren't leaving me here. I *choose* to stay. After all the children who have come through these tunnels, they allowed me to make my own decision. It is funny, really. I cannot take a bit of credit for any of our members' accomplishments. I just stood around and guided these beautiful children through the next phase of their lives, the next phase of our history, really."

"But what about food? Medicine?"

"They will send me adequate supplies twice monthly," she says. "And I can easily live in the higher section of the burrow. *Pah*, now. Do not vex yourself into ill health."

I nestle into her shoulder as she folds her fingers into mine. None of this seems real. I don't want *any* of it to be real. I breathe in the smell of Medera – the smell of my home.

"This was all my doing, Zuzan," she says.

I shake my head. "No. I'm sorry for accusing you about the ba'rm message – it was wrong of me. But you didn't flood the burrow."

"No, that was the rebels." She sighs.

Rebels? I tense up.

"But once Maddelyn fell ill and prone to paranoia, I suspected she had begun hacking into my private messages. She discovered my plan to protect my students from the harsh realities happening in the world."

"What realities?" I recall terrible things from Maddelyn's outbursts.

Medera puts her hand on my leg, calling for silence. "She had always been good with technology. There were other messages, though."

"I don't understand."

"The powder," she stammers. "I–" Her head collapses into her hands. "Oh, Zuzan. I ordered it from the black market." She pulls her hand from mine, and rocks back and forth. "I swear I am the last of my peers to have done so, and I changed my mind by the time the procurer arrived."

"You ordered the peanut powder?" My mouth goes dry. "Why?"

She presses her eyelids together until they release tears. It's only the third time I've seen her cry.

"The last of your peers? You don't mean *mederas*?" My stomach tumbles over itself. How can this be? It's... sickening. When Maddelyn had been under the influence of her mold poisoning, she babbled about euthanizing me. Medera wouldn't–

"It would have been a last resort!" she chokes out. "There have been many brutal attacks on other burrows, Zuzan. Raids on our children. I have kept this from you – we have kept this from all of our children – to protect you. But I cannot protect you now."

Her words are rushed, and I do my best to keep up. My magnetran will arrive soon.

"Hear me, Zuzan. These rebels think *we* are trying to kill *them* off. They believe even Subter *children* are a threat."

I start to tremble. Would my medera really have euthanized us all if we were attacked?

"If you only knew what has befallen these innocent children in other burrows. They've been exploited, tortured. But I told myself – the decision to possess the powder isn't the same as resolving to use it."

"Stop. Don't tell me anymore." My hands shake as I rise from the bench. Medera's peanut powder killed Jal. Even if she changed her mind, it was Medera who smuggled it in – not Maddelyn. I glance at her face, the one I've loved for years, but now everything I knew about her has changed. She is not the same stand-in mother I'd always believed she was. "You don't need to wait with me, Gelia Cayan."

"Please, don't. We need these last few moments together. I've more to explain, about you, about everything."

I back away, my mind spinning. "I wanted to be like you, to teach in your honor. But that dream is gone, Jal is dead, and everything is ruined. I don't know who you even are anymore." I can't look at her, can't sort through everything she's just admitted. What else has she done?

"Zuzan, please sit with me. This isn't how it was supposed to happen." Her voice cuts off as she begins to sob. Gelia will likely die here with nothing more than a canarymouse to keep her company. She is no longer my medera, and I am as nameless as if she'd never had been. "You are my heart," she whispers.

I cry and ache to go to her, but my breath is heavy in my chest. What has she done to us?

When she doesn't leave, I move to the side of the platform where Maddelyn had waited. I slump down by the opposite wall, arms clutched around my knees. I might have four-plus years of LE, but today I feel like I have already died.

CHAPTER 8

Heartily Sorry

Thirteen hours later, I arrive at the burrow that houses the Woynauld Military Academy. As I step onto the platform, the pungent wave of soon-to-be incinerated garbage penetrates my airmask.

The magnetran station's walls are coated in a shiny, tin-like metal, reflecting every flicker of light and radiating heat, and yet I shiver. The architect who designed these tunnels used mirrored skylights to maximize the use of light, tunneling it down tubular shafts from far above.

Judging from the lack of large, rounded columns that typically reach downward into the burrows near the tran platforms, the burrow's energy must be generated from solar panels rather than wind turbines – the new preference of Common Good, according to the chatter I overheard from magnetran riders. As turbine towers go hundreds of feet above ground, and the propellers can be seen for miles, Omnit rebels are attracted all too easily.

I try to reconcile this new information with what Medera Gelia wanted us to believe – that we Subters and Omnits are forever linked by blood – but all the while, she had prepared for the worst: an Omnit attack on her burrow.

A thin woman in dark clothing, perhaps in her mid-twenties, waits for me and flashes a tight smile. "I am Miss Yelda, Head Burrowmaid. Are you the pre-grad burrowmaid sent from Cayan?"

I narrow my eyes, though she can't see them. This is the first time I've been addressed as a maid. *Make friends*, Gelia said. I'm good at *having* friends, but I don't know if I'm any good at *making* them. I straighten my shoulders and extend my hand. "Good health to you. My name is Zu –" I stammer because there's no record of my name, so I rattle off my identification number instead.

Her expression sours when she realizes she can't make eye contact with me because of my goggles. "Like I said, you're the pre-grad burrowmaid, yes?"

"Yes," I say with a sliver of impatience. "Though I'm only here until I reach full employable age. My former medera is working on a more permanent calling for me. I'm supposed to be a medera." Like Gelia, though I'm not so certain I know her anymore.

Miss Yelda flashes a look, as if I were the source of all that rotten, smelly garbage. "You think you're too good to be a ba'rm?"

"No, Miss –" I forget what I'm saying, distracted by the design imprinted into her skin at the crook of her collarbone: a circle with intersecting lightning bolts inside, forming the letter in the center. I assume it stands for *Woynauld*.

A tattoo? In this day and age? The risk of infection for a Subter makes it a ridiculous, hazardous practice.

"Girl?" she snaps.

"Yes! Sorry, Miss Yelda." I swallow. "As long as we're breathing and doing our best for all good, then nobody is above or below any career."

She eyes me with a skeptical pursing of her lips. "I read that you were trouble back in your nursery. You'd better not be planning on any imprudent behavior here. I can warn you that I have seen others heavily penalized for such recklessness."

"Surely, you have the wrong idea of me," I say. "We've started out on an off-note, and I'm hoping I can try again. Good health, Miss Yelda." I hold out my hand, hoping she will shake it.

"Good health. You may leave your travelmask on for twenty-four hours. Do not try to claim medical necessity for longer as it is not tolerated at Woynauld Academy." She gives my hand a brief shake, motions to the left, and I follow her up the steel-gridded staircase. I've never heard of a magnetran station situated below the burrow, but the only staircase available leads upward, higher than the station. This burrow must sit closer to the surface than Cayan.

"You didn't graduate, but a moment ago you hinted that you have a name, for all that is right."

I blink fast, wondering if some regional difference is the reason for her to use "for all that is *right*." Medera taught us that the saying originated from Common Good's philosophy – *doing what's good for all people*. It's just one substituted word, but it throws me. It feels argumentative, as if she were assuming someone is right, and someone else isn't.

"Members at my home burrow choose names when they pick an occupation, not at graduation. It was one of the ways our medera taught us that we were people who mattered."

"Minors chose their own names?" She glances at me sideways without turning her face, and I don't think it's due to my shaved head or overbearing goggles. She must disapprove.

"My medera believes that each of her students decide who he or she becomes, not her. Who better to pick our own name?" A pit settles into my stomach remembering how angry I was when I left Medera Gelia, and now I find myself bragging about her methods. "Even when we first arrive without knowing what we want to do, she assigns each of us a letter, so we have something other than our identification numbers. Most students keep that letter as their first initial, out of respect for her."

Miss Yelda harumphs.

My cheeks warm, mostly because I want to defend Medera Gelia's process but I can't risk alienating Yelda any further. "How do you address your students?"

"We try not to address them individually." Her eyes grow wide as if I'm crazy. "Unless we need to for disciplinary reasons, and then it's by their age and gender. Allund Woynauld plans to name his members on their Graduating Name Day. As a newer burrow, our oldest members are but twelve."

We approach a steel door, and Yelda swipes her finger across a lighted oval. It flashes on and off. A buzzing sound makes me jump, but she turns the knob to swing the door open, holding it for me. "This way to the staff dormitory."

As a newer burrow, it was constructed with more of a contemporary design, using sleek materials. I don't care for it, though. The cold metal resembles the inside of our decontamination chambers at Cayan.

We move through three passageways and across a central tunnel running the other direction. Again, Yelda swipes her finger across a lighted plate and the door buzzes. The ceiling of the room we enter hangs lower than all the others. The beds, bunked four levels high, remind me of the old bookshelves in Medera's library, except these are stacked with sleeping maids and servants. There must be twenty bunks.

"We all share the same oxygen while we sleep?" I whisper, careful not to wake them. Back home, our servants shared a room, but slept in individual drawers. Without the benefits of the hyperbaric oxygen, there was no way that our immune systems could adequately refresh. Someone blasts a hacking cough near the far wall and I jump, glad to be wearing my travel mask for another day. "Numerous studies have shown higher risks of cross-infection for communicable diseases in open dormitories."

She gives me the same glare like when I told her I was supposed to be a medera. "Yours is there." Yelda points to the top level of the center bunk – directly below the tubular skylight, which must stretch all the way to the earth's surface. "Here are your bedclothes."

"Will the sun reflect all the way to this bunk in the morning?"

I point to my goggles. "If so, I require an accommodation."

Her brows come down on her forehead. "You'd need to request that through Fundamental Force Recruits. But I warn you, medical necessity requests will be seen as a weakness by Allund Woynauld, if he approves the request at all."

I rub my stubbled hair. I suppose I can sleep with my goggles on until then. He can't legally stop the request from going through to FFR. Can he? "I'd like to make the request just the same. My light sensitivity is considered severe."

She shrugs. "It's your fate in jeopardy then, isn't it? The staff tablet is in the lunchroom."

"I'm afraid I would need assistance with that as well." My neck tenses as she blinks slowly at me. "But it can wait until tomorrow."

"If you'll excuse me, I must chase some rest," she turns away but continues to talk. "We rise at five o'clock for breakfast, and we raise our youngest members at six."

She walks off, leaving me alone to climb to the top level of the bunkbed, past three other sleeping staff members who don't stir, even when the metal frame shakes.

The reflected sunlight from the tubular skylight burns down on me two hours later. I turn onto my stomach to avoid it as much as possible. A mechanical beeping rings precisely at five o'clock, and the room stirs to life.

When I climb down to the floor, Yelda is already waiting for me and hands me a folded, dark dress along with a vest without speaking a word and then walks off. Medera told me to stay on Medero Allund's good side, but I'm clearly terrible at getting on someone's "good side" in the first place.

My co-workers rush through a silent breakfast of unidentified, mushy fruit and stale bread. No one even looks up, and they all have that awful crest imprinted in the crook of their collarbones. I'm barely done with my last scoop of pureed mush when Yelda hurries me to the first-year burrowlings' chamberroom.

"Miss Yelda," I say as a few maids turn as if they've just noticed me. I keep my gaze directed at Yelda, pretending not to notice. "About that accommodation request – the light proved too much for me."

"Later!" She snaps. "The school schedule won't wait for your special needs."

I follow her and the other maids through a long corridor. The children sleep inside hyperbaric tubes, thank all good, which aids in cerebral development. The bedchambers at the Cayan Burrow were nothing more than metal drawers. Woynauld's horizontal cylinders are separate from the wall, made of tinted glass. As soon as Yelda flips on the lights, the young members stir. Maids rush to release and dress their assigned children. Not one child in the mixed-gender group appears embarrassed to be stripped, groomed, and dressed in front of his or her peers.

The children, like the servants, have the same circular symbol of a lightning-bolted *W* tattooed at the base of their necks. *Incredible.* I will *not* allow them to carve such a primitive marking on me. Besides, this placement is only temporary – Medera promised.

My poor medera.

"You," Yelda commands, "take that last one to your left." A maid snickers behind her. I turn to the tube, and the nameless girl inside waves through the glass. Her eager smile reminds me of myself.

"Only one?" It doesn't seem fair. Everyone else cares for at least two children.

But my question earns sharp laughter from the other ba'rms. "One is plenty for your first day," the round-faced maid says.

As soon as I open her chamber, the girl barely waits for it to split apart like a chiseled geode before she hops out. "Please," she says. "Are you a fair mathematician?" She hands me a workboard with twenty double-digit multiplication problems.

"Math is one of my favorites," I smile at her sweet face, though she cannot see through my mask.

She frowns, sliding off her sleeping gown. "This is my homework. I must ensure all the problems are correct *before* Medero Allund checks them this morning. We have to hurry."

I'm impressed by her enthusiasm to excel. "We?"

"You'll help me." She reaches for her clothes and takes the brush from my hand, using it to taper her white hair back like an expert. "Or I will earn negative reinforcement."

But I hardly hear her. A rash on her forearm looks like it might be spreading. I rub my fingers over the tiny bumps and then touch her forehead. "Are you well?"

She pulls away, and covers the rash with her hand. "That's not funny." She glances around. When she's satisfied no one's watching, she quickly walks through the low-UV washbeam and then dresses herself. Yelda was mistaken. This child doesn't need help getting dressed at all.

"My numbers," she says. "Are they correct?"

I check the workboard and frown. Of the twenty problems, only one is correct.

"I knew it," she says, flopping onto the floor. "Medero is right. I am nothing but a dullard, and I will soon become the dullest maid." She gasps while widening her eyes at me, and places her hand over her mouth. "I'm sorry."

I barely register the insult, not accustomed to seeing myself as a maid yet. It's her use of the word 'dullard' that catches my attention.

She drops her head between her knees like she's about to hyperventilate, and then she covers her neck with her hands. "Cremate me now. Better yet, let me rot right here in this spot, and then I shall become a moldy, brown blob on the floor for everyone to step on."

I raise her chin. "Maybe you learn differently. Has anyone taught you how to compute using your fingers?"

She drops her voice to a whisper. "Like counting on my fingers? Medero Allund says that's for dullards."

I wince at such a word coming out of her innocent mouth. "Not counting. Digital computing. That's how my friend Maddelyn learned her math." My voice falters, wondering how Maddelyn is right now. "She progressed to elite trigonometry. I can show you."

"Quickly?"

I take her hands and place them palms down, an inch from the floor. "Listen up, then." I wish I had a cane to bang. I explain that her index fingers are in control of all the others, and show her how to tap and compute while keeping track of the running total. I'm not sure if it is her determination or her fear of punishment, but my girl works through the first fifteen problems with no errors before Yelda returns. For a fleeting moment, the pride of a medera shoots through my veins.

"What are you doing?" The head ba'rm asks. "Stop at once."

"But I understand it," the girl says. "Look, I multiplied all of it myself. I can even see where I went wrong before. I *see* it in my head, Miss Yelda. It's so *viral*." She stresses the word *viral* like it's a good thing.

"She requires different instruction for this type of math," I say, "so that she can excel."

"No one is allowed differences here," Yelda warns. "Mind me, now, Miss. You may regret challenging the medero on your first day." She storms away.

I pat the girl on her shoulder. "He will be happy with your success. Now, finish your work so you can eat."

"Breakfast?" She glances at the table in the adjoining room filled with her classmates already eating and chatting. A smile breaks out on her face. "I haven't eaten a morning meal in months. I've always been so behind with my mathwork."

Medero Allund enters the Lessons Gallery as the maids wipe

the resin tables clean for class. His mouth clamps closed so hard that his cheeks jut out, his small chin disappearing into his fleshy neck. His skin lets off an odd sheen like I have never seen before, so I cannot guess his age. Perhaps it's a cosmetic alteration of some sort. He could be twenty-five or he could be forty for all I know.

"Good health to you all," he says. Something in his eyes causes me to shiver. He doesn't look at any of his pupils like a person who believes he plays an important part in growing minds and character, like Medera did or like I would if I had the chance. Instead, he looks upon these children with an expression of burden and repugnance. My heart sinks immediately for them all.

Everyone, including the maids and fourteen burrowlings, jumps to attention. Their feet part a perfect ten inches, their hands fold neatly behind their backs, and their chins rise. I follow suit. Maybe I have a problem with disliking people too quickly? Medera intimated that I had no reason to dislike Ringol.

"To pure and righteous lives, Medero Allund," they all say in unison.

His eyes bulge as he scrutinizes each child, nodding his approval as he passes. But then his eyes settle upon my girl. "Do we have a dullard to ferret out?"

My mouth drops open, hidden under my temporary travelmask. I am only allowed to wear it for today to adjust to the air filtration differences. Medera Gelia required visitors to wear travelmasks longer to account for any potential viruses or bacterial transmissions. It was as much for our sake as it was for the visitor. It saddens me to think Mederal Allund cares so little for his burrowlings.

"Well?" He says impatiently.

The girl steps forward. "I am the dullest of all, Medero." She produces the workboard with her addition. A confident glimmer shines in her eyes despite how he belittled her, and how she agreed to it.

He sweeps the board from her hand, and that glimmer vanishes. The entire room remains still as he checks over her work. She stands at attention, stoic as stone. How peculiar.

His face tightens. "Who did this for you, girl?"

Her eyes flicker over to me, and Medero's face snaps my way. He flies to my side in three large steps.

"Did you do the work for this girl, maid?" His hot breath hits my forehead, and I step backwards.

"No, Medero Allund."

His hand flies across my cheek so hard and so fast, I have to play it again in my mind to be sure it happened. A burning sting sets into my cheek, and painful slivers of light flash through my crooked goggles' seal. I straighten them so I can see again.

"You liar!" he screams. He readjusts his shirt, and lowers his tone. "You are *not* one of my students, and I am *not* your medero. In the future, you will call me Lord."

I stiffen. *Lord?* Maybe it *is* okay to despise someone at first sight.

"Look at her goggles," he sneers. "This must be the weak one who wants an accommodation?"

I glance at Yelda, whose eyes remain downcast. "Yes, Lord," she says.

"Your request is denied." He sniffs as if he is the final decision-maker.

"But my rights," I say. "With my visual disability, FFR can review my request and grant the accommodation at no cost to the academy."

His face jerks about, like he's trying to swallow something awful. "Kneel."

What is this?

The round-faced maid nods at me, eyes wide with terror.

So I kneel.

"You are to repeat these words over and over until I believe they have penetrated your thick maid's mind. '*I am but a dullard.'"* He says them slowly, exaggerated, as if I could not possibly understand him if he spoke normally.

I shoot him a daggered glare, though it's hidden by my goggles and travelmask. "What?"

"I am but a dullard." He repeats it slowly again, as if his earlier inclination was right. "I am but a dullard." This time, he's louder. The maid standing nearest to him begins to tremble.

This can't be good.

The phrase slips quietly from my mouth. "I am but a dullard."

"Again, louder."

"I am but a dullard." The words move like tar over my tongue.

He turns his back to me. "And again, and again. You will continue to utter this phrase until you understand."

The nervous maid takes a deep breath, like she's relieved.

I close my eyes, and while I recite the ugly words over and over, I see Medera's kind eyes, stringing my bead onto her hair. If only I had another chance to fix that day, to tell her how much she means to me.

The medero addresses the children. I keep repeating the words. "Do you see that girl kneeling on the filthy ground?"

They all look over to me. *"I am but a dullard."*

"She is your burrowmaid. In her own confession, a dullard. Never heed her advice, and never allow her to do your work."

"I am but a dullard."

He stops in front of my girl. "Do you swear that you did this work on your own?"

Her eyes fix on me.

"I am but a dullard."

She nods defiantly. He grabs her wrist and pulls her to a large workboard attached to the wall. "Then we must demonstrate your new skills." He writes a math problem. Only this time, it is a three-digit calculation that stares my girl down. He hands her the stylus. "If you get it wrong, we will all know you as a liar as well as a dullard. You have ten seconds, girl."

"I am but a dullard."

I begin to shake for her. I didn't show her how to compute hundreds, but she's smarter than he realizes. I hold my breath, waiting for her to figure it out.

She places the marker down and moves her fingers over her belly. In five seconds, she writes her answer. The correct one, thank all that is good.

"I am but a dullard."

She looks to me and I nod to let her know she has done well. He should apologize for decency's sake.

But he doesn't smile at her victory. Instead, Allund grabs her wrist and pulls out a small contraption that buzzes as it touches her skin where her rash broke out.

She pulls her wrist away, whimpering only for a second, and then snaps to attention.

"Stop!" I shriek, breaking my chant. Those bumps on her skin – those are scars, not a rash. How dare he? "Her answer is correct."

He laughs. "Correct?" And then he paces in front of the children. "Can you imagine this girl when she is called to subdue a mob of a half-thou' Omnit rebels, and she has to calculate the precise coordinates for the satellite counterattack?"

How can Common Good allow this curriculum for our youngest burrowlings?

He makes a face, squinting his eyes as people do to make fun of the thinner-eyed Omnits. Then he twitches his fingers across his belly to mock her. *"No.* Not my first choice in a weapontech."

A boy near him giggles, and then his gaze slides over to me. He mouths the word *dullard*.

For all that has ever been good! It can't be that we're training these children as if it's their *calling* to kill Omnits? Don't they all realize their mothers and fathers are Omniterranean?

My girl stands at attention. Yelda waves her hand and

catches my eyes, shaking her head. I want to obey Yelda and I don't want to further anger Allund, but my chest might split open if I don't speak up.

"She won't need to finger-compute for long," I blurt out. "Some people begin to understand calculations through alternative ways, and eventually end up in the right place with everyone else."

Medero Allund twists around, and in no time, he's pulling me from my knees to my feet. "Not in my burrow!"

His hand tightens around my bicep. I push my arm towards him and then quickly snap all my weight back against his thumb – the weakest point – to break free. *Page eleven of the self-defense journal.* He looks surprised and even more rageful.

"Your methods are draconian!" I spit. There's no way he passed his teaching boards.

His cheeks puff out as he exhales like a dragon. "What is her status, Yelda?" His voice booms, echoing in the space. "Are we bound to her?"

"She's the pre-grad from that liquidated burrow. She claims to be a temporary placement, and says her medera allowed her to name herself. She came with an excellent reference, Lord." She shoots me a stern look, as if I were one of the young burrowlings disobeying her.

I don't blame her really. She did warn me, and I've put her at risk of punishment too.

"A name? At her age? She's a *crypt* who graduated from nowhere!"

I flinch at the term. There are many reasons burrowlings become detached from their former burrows – some choose the last name "Crypt" if they believe the reputation of their burrow is beneath them. Usually, though, *crypt* is synonymous with *flunky*, for students who cannot successfully graduate.

"No. She has no name until I assign her one. For now, let it be Miss Dullard."

The children laugh nervously.

"I see she does not yet bear our crest." His shiny cheeks puff again. If I am Miss Dullard, he will be Lord Dragon, unworthy of the medero title.

"No, sir," Yelda replies. "Should I prepare the painter?"

My head snaps to her. "No. There's been a mistake. If you could contact my medera—"

Medero Allund grabs me by the collar of my uniform. "I will deliver her to the painter's myself, Miss Yelda."

She bows.

"I am *temporary*—"

"Begin lessons!" He yells to the class. Then he turns to point at my girl, "And make certain no one assists her. Break her fingers if they dare so much as spasm!"

Yelda's expression falls, as if she might cry. "Yes, Lord."

As he yanks me away, my girl remains at attention. She doesn't cry or even blink.

He pulls me out of the room and down the hallway faster than I can walk. "I won't sit for a tattoo. I have rights!" I fall to my knees as we round a corner, and he wrenches me back to my feet. He's not as tall as Ringol, but still large enough to throw me around like a doll. He leads me into a room that reminds me of a state-of-the-art infirmary, and shoves me to the floor.

A man, chubby for a Subter, looks up from his desk. "New inductee, sir?"

"I have fatal allergies." I hold out the emergency shot on my necklace. "I'm exercising my right to refuse the tattoo for medical reasons."

The medero ignores me and takes an injection needle out of a jar on the counter, and approaches. I flail across the floor, all arms and knees, trying to get out the door.

"Stop her! Hold her down!" He says to the painter, who quickly lifts me up and into an empty plastic chair.

"Your rights died when you became a ba'rm." Allund jabs the needle into my arm.

"Ow!" I flinch, eyeing the infirmary bed under a light where the painter must do his tattooing.

"That will help you remain still while this man works on you."

"What?" I say, my tongue growing thick.

"It won't knock you out, and it's by no means a numbing agent." Lord Dragon grinds his teeth and what can only be a smile – the first I've seen on his face – flashes spitefully and then is gone. "I guarantee that you will feel *every* needle prick."

I try to get up again. I want to run, to fly from here, but my legs wobble. The drug has paralyzed me. When I try to speak, I make odd, sheep-like sounds instead of words, and a few seconds later, I can't move at all.

"The crest, then, sir?" The painter asks.

Medero Allund huffs, and then turns to the man. "No, actually. She hasn't yet earned the crest, I think. She will likely never earn it, in fact." He squats before me, grabs hold of my uniform blouse, and yanks me up and onto the stainless-steel infirmary table, with straps attached to the sides of it.

My limbs flail around. None of my muscles will work. I am at this man's mercy, and my heart lunges into overload.

He rips open my blouse, buttons flying everywhere, and exposes my thin underslip. He pulls the straps down my shoulders, stopping just above my breasts. To Ringol, at least I was a "human form." To Allund, I am a piece of meat.

"Right here," he says to the painter, tracing a line just under my collarbone with his finger and just close enough to my breasts that hot shame runs through my core. My body wants to lurch off the table at his touch, vomit at the filthy sensation, but I am held down by the serum and my own weight.

"Looks like she's recovering from some bruising," the painter says when he notices the spot where Maddy hit me. "Perhaps it's better to wait –"

Allund stares the painter down until he stops talking, and

then ignores the recommendation. "I want it to read, 'I am but a dullard.'" He sings the words slowly again, a gluey sound of hate filling the room.

No! I scream inside my head, *No, no, no!* But my lips don't move.

The painter hesitates. "I'm sorry, Lord?"

Medero Allund spins around. "Do you need help spelling it, man?"

"What I meant to say," the man stammers, "is yes, Lord. I mean, no. I don't need help spelling."

"See to it," Medero says. Without looking my way, he leaves.

Instead of a scream, I manage a gurgling sound, but the man doesn't stop. He covers my chest with a sterile towel and takes a heavy breath. Sweat forms above his brow as he slides a wheeled light over my body to work.

I have no way to shield my eyes, and the crack in my goggle is more like a canyon with the direct light.

"You must have clipped his last nerve." He speaks in a hushed tone. "And for that, whatever it's worth, I respect you infinitely more than I pity you."

He taps the side of my goggles, and then rubs his hand over his face. "Here, here. You are about to drown in your own tears. You don't need glasses now – for all that is right, *I* don't even want to witness this process. I can help this much, at least."

Jet, no. Jet! He slides my protective goggles off and the released tears run down my temples. I try to form words, to speak, but nothing comes out. The drugs have won.

"I would not choose this for my worst enemy." He dabs at the wetness from my tears with a soft cloth. "I am heartily sorry, my poor girl."

He closes my eyes for me, but the light penetrates my thin eyelids. Burning white. Then, nothing but white pain.

CHAPTER 9

Deranged Madcap

I awaken in my top bunk. My shallow breaths come and go. I am marked forever by a vicious medero. *Lord Allund*, the dragon tyrant insists to be called, for all good. His crude manner makes me wonder how I could have been so angry with Medera? How could I have questioned her intentions? Compare her – my extraordinary, wonderful Medera Gelia Cayan – to Medero Allund Woynauld and my heart is sick.

No comparison can be made.

The flesh on my chest burns, but that is the least of my worries. The roaring pain of a migraine crashes over me in waves. I cannot see anything but blurry static. I remove my travel mask – I'm sure the prescribed time has passed. Besides, I'm no safer with it than without it in this forsaken ditch.

When the morning alarm rings, Yelda climbs all the way to my top bunk and brushes her fingertips across my forehead. "Rest today, girl." She has not yet addressed me by my new name – Miss Dullard – for which I'm grateful. "Everyone rests the day after painting. I will have someone change your dressings after breakfast. Why are your bandages so large?" She moves the gauze a bit, and then gasps.

She doesn't move.

I shift, trying to contain my humiliation. It's no use. My pulse quickens and heated blood rushes to my face – I'm sure I'm flushed. "Please leave."

She presses her wrist to my forehead. "You're feverish."

"Subters shouldn't get tattoos," I say hoarsely. Why wouldn't they put me in an infirmary? But I can see now that I'm not a person as much as I am property here. They won't spend an extra dime on me for anything medical. "It's as hazardous as it is irresponsible."

She shushes me. "I have some antibiotics," she stammers, applying a patch to my arm. "And this second patch will help you sleep."

"For sleep?" I'm confused because the gesture seems too humane after I've been made to feel less-than human.

"It's black market. We, the maidstaff, have been working on building up whatever supplies can be traded or bartered. We have a small stock of the essentials. I'll be severely punished for giving this sedative to you if Woynauld finds out." She pauses, perhaps reconsidering the potential consequences of her actions. "Please don't tell anyone."

"You don't have to—"

She places it under my sock just above my ankle. "Yes, I do. You were unwise in your actions, but you weren't wrong in your words. You meant well for the child. We all saw that plain as death."

"We should report him for cruelty," I mumble. "These children deserve more."

"The only staff member who tried to report Allund Woynauld was intercepted somehow, and then she disappeared in the night," Yelda says. "She was my predecessor."

I close my eyes. I can't stay here, not for another few weeks, not even for another day. Gelia said the medero would need to cooperate with the transfer she was working on. There's no way he would approve it now. Even if I have to dig my way out of these tunnels myself, I must leave.

"I made a mistake, Miss Yelda." My breathing deepens, and the tension throughout my body eases as the sedative takes effect. "Please, I beg you, contact my medera."

"Chase some rest now, child." The bunk shifts as Yelda begins her descent, and I hope my words were clear enough for her to understand. I want to lay my head in Gelia's lap, to feel safe in the arms of the only mother I've ever known.

White pain hits me once again, and I scramble for my goggles only to realize I'm already wearing them. I'm still in my top bunk, and the sedative Yelda had given must have worn off. All of the events from the tattooing wash through my mind, churning over and over.

I struggle to sit up from weakness, and try to read the clock on the far wall. No one else is in the dormitory so it must be midday – the children should still be in class. A chill rages through me, and I fear I've contracted an infection from the needle. I work my way slowly to the edge of my bunk, and nearly vomit when I peer at the distance to the floor.

But if I'm ever going to get the chance to alert Common Good of the atrocities taking place at this academy, now is my chance, while Allund Woynauld is distracted at work. Yelda mentioned a tablet in the cafe. If I could just find it and flip it to text-to speech mode, that might do the trick. I don't know how to make calls, but how hard could it be?

I swing my legs over the side of the bed and I take some slow steps down the ladder until the room seems like it's swaying a bit and I have to hug the ladder for fear of crashing down to the ceramic tiles below. My feet, though, slip underneath me and I slide down a few rungs, banging my chin on a rung before I'm able to grab fast onto one of the bars.

"Whoa little miss," calls a woman from below. My eyes are having trouble focusing. The bright light I endured in the tattoo room has scalded them. It will be days before my sight is back to normal.

"You'll crack your skull open," she warns. "I'm just here to fetch my sweater while the students are occupied." I recognize her voice. She's the round-faced ba'rm who looked terrified earlier.

"Hello there," I call to her, grateful that someone is nearby. "I'm sorry but I don't know your name."

"I am a second-year staff member here at Woynauld. My name is Qarmovi." Her voice is deep, but musical like she's always in poetic rhythm, without actually rhyming.

"Hello, Miss Qarmovi. It's very nice to meet you." My arms start to shake from the strain of climbing down, and I can't figure out what's safer to do – return back to the bed or finish the decent. "Would you be able to assist me?"

The rapid scuffle of her feet makes me think she's rushing over. "Surely, little miss, though I think it's best you stay put and heal some more. Miss Yelda said you were nearly a ghost's shell, and fretted that you mightn't pull through." She grabs hold of my legs to lend me some support while I ease down the rungs slowly. I have to stop for a moment just to regain some strength.

"I cannot rest. I must get a message to my medera." I begin to shiver from fever, and it's all I can do to get the words through my chattering teeth. If the infection doesn't clear up soon, Yelda might be right about my near-ghost state.

"You were a tower of brave the other morning, miss, and I'm not the only one saying such. All the ba'rms were alit with your praise." Qarmovi chuckles melodiously.

"Please," I say before having to catch my breath again. "Call me Zuzan."

"Well Miss Zuzan, you'll be the talk of the burrow for a quarter year or more, I'd wager."

"Something had to be said, that's all," I reply as I make it safely to the floor.

"Jetfire, miss! Your skin is hot to the touch. Can you walk?"

I nod and try to keep my words steady. "Can you help me to the tablet where I might make a call? I believe Miss Yelda said it would be in the dining area."

"I ought to be heading back to the classroom," she stammers. "And yes, there's a tablet in there, alright. It's a bit quaky."

"Quaky?" I ask. "I want it in speech recognition mode, if you can just get me to it."

"Well, it works when it wants to, which is not very often," she says. My vision clears up a bit and I'm finally able to make out the silhouette of her face. "Except I don't know anyone who has made a call from it. But if Yelda said it's possible, then I trust her."

I sway a bit and hold out my arms to balance. Qarmovi catches one of my arms, which helps to steady me. "Thank you." I frown, though. Yelda never actually said the device had the ability to make calls. "Can I message someone directly from the tablet?"

Qarmovi shakes her head. "As far as I ever knew, any calls or messages out of the academy had to go through Lord Allund Woynauld's office, just behind the classroom area."

"Please then, can you take me there?" I ask. "I have to get a message out to my medera that they made a mistake. I cannot stay here."

"You would need the medero's permission, miss, and I don't think he's about to grant you any privileges. I'm half surprised you haven't been sent to the undercellars already." She guides me to the dining area and shows me the tablet. "You see? It won't even turn on."

I take a seat at one of the long tables and put my head down. "I wouldn't be able to see it anyway, Qarmovi. My eyes don't tolerate the light. It's useless. I should have listened to my medera. She told me to take the undertech position Maven Ringol offered at the GCE, but—" I swallow back the nausea. "I had just lost a good friend. Two, actually. And I was unsettled."

"Oh, Miss Zuzan, no," she says. "I'm sorry to hear of your pain. Let me get you into my bunk for now. It's bottom level, and you get your rest. Yelda and I will figure out something better for you if we can."

"Allund is the cruelest person I know," I mumble. "I don't want anyone else to get into trouble. I would like to stop him altogether if I could."

"It's not likely that you can stop him. Especially not without winding up in the undercellars."

That's the second time she's mentioned undercellars. She helps me up, and guides me back into the dormitory. "Is that a prison of some sort?"

"I don't entirely know, to be frank. There's speculation and rumors." She drops her voice. "It's under this very structure. I hear it's run by former military officers bent on straightening out whatever they deem wrong with the world. They hate Omnits, for one thing, and they hate Subters who try to help Omnits. So, rumors spin wild about torture and whatnot. I don't know it's true, mind you, but it's not a place for decent Subters like you and me. Even so, I can't help but think our last head ba'rm was sent down there. She was never seen again."

Qarmovi puts me into a bunk that must be hers, and covers me with blankets. "You look peaked and ever so frail, Miss Zuzan. Catch rest and I'll do what I can for you. That Maven Ringer is your best bet.

"Maven Ringol," I say stupidly, "from the Genomic Center."

"Yes," she says. "I can see how you're better suited at a place like that, though you helped that girl plenty, I think. I knew you were too good to be stationed here. I suppose we all knew, really. I would think Allund himself knows it, too."

My ears ring, and weakness and fatigue take over my body. Maybe I'm hallucinating, but I could swear Qarmovi is humming a lullaby a little too slowly. I feel like I'm a brand new burrowling with long hair that she wants to brush for me.

I'm jolted awake by two medtechs who lift me up and onto a gurney. Before I know it, they strap my arms into restraints.

"Hey," I mumble.

"Hush now," Miss Yelda says with heightened tension. "You mustn't speak another word, child. Your fever is run away, and you need medical attention."

"Qarmovi?" I say.

"Never you mind about Qarmovi," she snaps. "I'll not have you straining yourself. Qarmovi acted of her own accord, that's for certain. What she did shouldn't impact you. If anyone asks you, tell them she acted on her own."

I blink, trying to understand what Yelda is trying to tell me without actually saying it. Is she afraid for me, and can't say so in front of these medtechs?

"Your fever is excessively high right now," she continues as if to excuse my behavior, "and you need to concentrate on getting better. No more, no less."

I try to sit up, but severe nausea hits me from the movement of the gurney, and my arms are stuck in place. "Where is she, Miss Yelda?" Qarmovi said she was going to try to help me. What have I done? "Where are they taking me?"

Yelda frowns, and right when she's about to answer me, one of the medtechs holds out an arm and stops her from walking any further.

"This is as far as you're cleared to go," he says to her. *Oh jet.*

"Yelda?" I say hoarsely. "Am I a prisoner?"

"No more talking!" she shouts. "Wait until your fever breaks."

"That's right," the medtech says in a mock-caring tone as soon as Yelda is out of earshot. "Listen to your superior. We're going to fix you right up so you're fit to move down under."

"To the undercellar?" I ask.

He and the other medtech make eye contact. "You'll find out soon enough."

The other medtech murmurs under his breath, "It doesn't make sense to cure them just to euthanize them later."

"Euthanize?" I ask. "Is that what they've done to Qarmovi?"

We stop inside a dark room, and they start me on an IV

without another word. The fluid runs like ice into my body and I shiver anew. After the techs are done, they leave me strapped in place.

That's when I hear the moaning from across the small room, and my stomach falls because I'm sure I recognize her.

"Miss Qarmovi!" I whisper. "Is that you?"

"I tried," she whimpers. Her voice is thicker like she's been crying. "I'm not sorry though. For once in my life, I was brave because of you. You're too good for this place. Now, no more squawking over there, eh? Keep yourself alive, little miss."

Like Yelda, Quarmovi seems to be telling me not to talk, as if I could incriminate myself. Moments later, a man in a military uniform enters the room. Qarmovi stands up slowly, and I can see she is cuffed in full shackles. She doesn't even look at me, yet I can tell she's disheveled. He motions to her, takes her arm firmly as she winces, and she leaves with him without resisting. I could swear her face was bruised.

"What's going on?" I say loudly.

That's when Allund appears in the doorway. Although my sight remains fuzzy, I can tell it's him by the strange profile of his head.

"Do you see this dullard, girl?" he says. That's when I finally notice her – my girl with the math problems. "This is what failure looks like. Would you like to wind up in her shoes?"

He pauses for a moment, during which my girl's quiet crying echoes through the room.

"I can't hear you," Allund says loudly, and I hear the buzzing sound of the contraption he used to shock her.

"She's just a child!" I shout at him. "You jetting monster!"

"I see her," my girl says finally. "I see her and she's a dullard. Okay? Can I go now?"

"Not until you appreciate what happens to people like her, girl. This dullard isn't worth anything to our world. She is to be mended and then taken to the same place they've taken the dullard Qarmovi. Do you understand?

"Yes," she says in a tiny, frail voice. "Yes, Medero Allund. I understand everything."

"Very well," he says. "Run along and tell your classmates what failure looks like, or there's no evening meal for you."

She scurries off, but Allund stays put. He calls for a medtech, who hands him a vial with a needle. Allund then shoots it into my IV, and it instantly hits my nerves. It's the same thing he injected into me earlier – the paralytic.

"You are worth nothing," Allund says. "Qarmovi thought you were, but she will be dead soon. You see, Miss Dullard, when someone undermines *me*, they undermine the entire Subterranean population. That is a treasonous offense, and it is punished in that vein."

"She's put to *death*?" I cry, though my tongue is too paralyzed to make the words form clearly.

"And as soon as you're well enough, you will be next in line. The thing I regret most is wasting so much tattoo ink on you. I should have sent you to the undercellar immediately." He sighs deeply. "Well, I've learned my lesson, and you will have learned yours too late. I've given the medtechs permission to give you trial injections of different substances which might prove helpful to the Subterranean people. Of course, they are all in the experimental stages, so even if the infection doesn't kill you, the injections just might."

I close my eyes and decide to ignore him. He's not there, he's not there, he's not there, I say to myself. At some point, I fall asleep again.

Maybe I'm dreaming.

About a man whose voice I do not recognize.

Yelling.

Shouting. "In here, Sir! Is this her?"

I could swear the person shouting is right next to me, loosening my restraints.

I open my eyes, but my goggles aren't straight. Once my hands are free, I adjust them. Some blurriness lingers, but my vision has mostly returned. The terrible shivers have subsided, and the nausea too.

"Are you here to take me to the undercellar?" I ask him, but he doesn't appear to hear me. He seems to be listening to a radio transmission inside his ear Maybe there's still time for me to thank Qarmovi for trying to help me. If I could go back in time, I wouldn't have asked her for help in the first place.

I pull back the bandages that stick to my tattoo wound ever so gently and wince. It begins to bleed again. The painter clearly doesn't subscribe to the *smaller is classier* idea – his large letters are obnoxious and ugly. The words stretch all the way across my chest, armpit to armpit. I button my uniform blouse all the way to my neck, then sit up, shaky and weak.

A more familiar voice rings out nearby, in the adjoining hallway. "Where the blazes is she?"

"Ringol?" This can't be a dream. I blink at the dark-suited guard who must have been the one to free me from the arm straps. "Please," I mumble.

"I think I heard Maven Ringol. Is he here?"

Again the guard seems to be listening to voices over some device instead of me, and he hastens toward the doorway.

"In here, Maven," the guard calls. He said *maven*. It must be him.

Ringol slides to a stop outside the doorway, holding onto the frame as if he'll fall – or carry on flying past – without it. When his eyes find me in the center of the dormitory, his shoulders relax.

Another guard follows him into the room, squinting in my direction. Ringol smiles, and holds out a hand. "There you are, Undertech Allele. I've come to fetch you for the work you promised me."

Undertech Allele? I glance around to make sure he couldn't be talking to someone else.

Medero Allund hurries in behind them huffing, his shirt untucked from his pants. He stops, composes himself, fixing his clothes in a harried way that makes him look more absurd than ever.

I glance from Ringol to Allund. The resolute gleam in Allund's eyes tells me I'm not in the clear.

Ringol holds up his hand to me, as if I was about to say something. I wasn't – I don't know what I'm supposed to do.

"And here *you* are, Allund," Ringol says. "I've come for my undertech. It took a hefty effort, but I was able to track down a remarkable string of mistakes and bumbles, only to find her here. Thank all good I got here in time, for it seems she's ended up in your infirmary almost immediately."

"*You're* the only one making a remarkable mistake here," Allund replies. "*That* is my new ba'rm." I know he's calling me *Miss Dullard* right now in his head. "I've already paid for her transfer and uniform."

Ringol grins, but the expression doesn't make it to his eyes, intense as ever, although a tiny bead of sweat glimmers on his brow. "I called her for work weeks ago, and the allotted timeframe to challenge the offer requested through Fundamental Force Recruits has expired. I'm afraid you'll have to make do without her. FFR sincerely apologizes for the inconvenience. Once Undertech Allele's former medera corrected the error on her records, they adjusted her placement straightaway."

"Are we talking about the same girl?" Medero Allund looks at me and pulls out a minitab from his pocket. "Surely not. Not with her temperament. GCE would never take–"

"Let me see," Ringol says casually.

Allund flashes a confident smile as if he's helping, and turns his screen toward Ringol. My birthday is still weeks away, and my LE is too low for GCE work. I'm singed.

Ringol squints at the screen, then pulls out his own minitab. Tapping the surface, he nods. "Ah, I see where the mistake is.

There." He points, turning *his* minitab to show Woynauld. "You had two characters in her identification number transposed. It's no wonder she was sent off to the wrong position. Had she ever mentioned that she was sent here by mistake?"

Allund Woynauld's cheeks puff out and he blows out a breath as his eyes scan Ringol's minitab screen. "Be careful, brother. This one is tricky for all that is right."

Ringol tilts his head when Allund uses the word "right" instead of "good," but Allund doesn't respond or appear to notice.

"She cannot be trusted in such a coveted position." Allund waves a hand like it's settled. "She's better off right where she is, and you're better off without her."

The Central Force guards who came with Ringol step forward as if to intervene, but Ringol closes in on the medero first, standing inches away.

"Trusted? Tell me, brother." He spits out the word *brother* as if it leaves a filthy taste in his mouth. "How long have you known her?" Ringol's jaw clenches and a vein bulges across his temple.

Allund stands nearly two inches shorter than Ringol and has to look up to the maven's face. The pair stand unusually tall for our kind. Although Allund appears older, it's honestly hard to tell because of the oddness of his skin. It's shinier than any I've seen, and he looks almost bloated in the hollow of his cheeks. His eyes, though, have a more youthful shimmer to them like Ringol's. I try to shake off how disconcerting I feel comparing the two of them.

"I know her snaky nature," Allund says.

"*Snaky*?" Ringol sounds interested, with a hint of mockery in his voice.

"She caused a large disturbance in the first-year lessons gallery on her first day." Allund leans away from the maven. "Nay, her first hour."

"Maven—" I start, but Ringol hushes me with a pointed look.

"I can only guess," Ringol says, "that something you did begged for this disturbance."

Medero Allund, huffing at Ringol's remark, pushes past one of the guards and glares at me with his bugged eyes. "She is no one. She should be wiping my students' snot, not strolling into a lavish position in scientific research. In fact, I'll do you the favor of contacting FFR with my evaluation of her performance. I won't be signing off on this transfer, or *mishap* as you call it. Trust me, it's for the better."

I know I should keep quiet, but again, my chest might split open if I do. "You couldn't keep me here if you chained me, you a rotten excuse for a human!" I explode. My words come out a bit slurry, but I'm happy that the drug seems to have mostly worn off.

Ringol steps nearer to the medero before he can say anything back. Even I squirm at how close he stands. "I don't need you to sign off unless you require reimbursement," Ringol says quietly. I thought Medera Gelia said Allund *did* need to sign off on a transfer? Is Ringol trying to trick Allund?

"Your review won't matter. *I* know her better than you do, Allund." Ringol smooths the medero's shirt, and then straightens his collar. "I've been recruiting her for some time now, and I've witnessed her true nature." Ringol keeps his hands on each of Allund's shoulders. He looks to sag under the weight of them. "*My* testimony to FFR has been this: I have witnessed her save a life based solely on her wits and self-taught academics. I have seen her lose everything and still have enough humanity to spare the life of the very person who took it all away from her. And I have seen her nearly die and come back into health when others might have given up." Ringol glances over to me with his confident smile.

I realize that this is a man I can work for. How stupid I was to walk away from him. I stay frozen in my spot trying not to feel too hopeful. An hour ago, I believed I would be experimented on and then euthanized. But now!

Can I actually leave this place with Ringol?

Allund shrugs his shoulders out from Ringol's grip, and rolls out the discomfort. His eyes then cut to the door and he sniffs. "What do I care for one lousy maid?" he remarks, quietly. He moves backwards, but trips before catching his footing. Allund looks to be as nervous as his trembling maids. "I'm the winner in this transaction," he blusters, "so thank you for taking her off my hands. I expect reimbursement for her magnetran fare and for the boarding costs while she's been here."

Ringol nods. "The transaction will be completed by tomorrow through FFR."

Allund smooths his shirt as if he can gain some dignity back, and barks for Miss Yelda.

She scurries into the room. "You called, Lord?"

Ringol flashes a bemused look. "Lord?"

"Gather her old clothes, Miss Yelda." Medero Allund ignores Ringol. "For all that is right, we are now rid of this burrowmaid."

Out of nervousness, I reach for my emergency shot but my hand bumps the tattooed area, and I wince. Ringol doesn't notice, and I'm not about to bring it up until I'm long gone from here.

Yelda leads me to the dressing room, and I begin to change into my old Cayan uniform. I take a deep breath – I feel like I've forgotten how until now. "Is Qarmovi?"

Yelda glances at me for a second before shrugging. "Gone, and I suspect forever."

"I've made a mess of things," I say. Allund was probably telling me the truth about the death penalty for Qarmovi. If I ever thought my heart couldn't sink any lower, I was wrong. "I just wanted to help."

"No," Yelda exclaims. "Don't think that. It's good for us, the maidstaff, to know that other types of people exist in this world."

"Other types?" I slide my old blouse over my shoulders,

trying to hurry before either Ringol or Allund changes his mind. The lighter, thinner material does not cover the bandages as well as the dark maid's uniform had.

"Kind souls." She looks away.

"There isn't a particular type of person that can claim kindness." I kick off the hard ba'rm boots and slide into my old moleskins. "Anyone can be kind if they set their heart to it."

"I don't know. If anyone can be kind or evil, then what of Allund Woynauld? Do you think he is capable of both? Are you capable of the depths of his evil?" She finds a long cloth to tie around my shoulders like a shawl to conceal the bandages better. "It's easy to forget, living in a tunnel, that there's a world out there with different ways to exist. I refused to help Qarmovi on your behalf. What say you to that? You must think my heart has shriveled away."

I touch her arm the way Medera does to comfort me. "I'm confident you will resist Allund's influence."

She sighs heavily. "You give me too much credit."

"Thank you for the sedative," I say, and she smiles shyly. "Only a kind-hearted person would have done that. I'm grateful that Qarmovi got in touch with Maven Ringol."

Yelda's eyebrows shoot up. "She couldn't have. She tried, but I told her we have no way to make any calls without the medero's password-protected code. Please, don't say another word about her if you hope to get out of here safely. Medero Allund has an army of ex-military people on call for him. Get out of here without delay. If I can be happy for anything today, it would be for you to make it out of here alive."

I take Yelda's hand and make her swear to take care of my girl who craves kindness, who may very well be brainwashed into thinking I'm a villain.

When we return to Ringol, he's pacing back and forth, but he lights up when he notices me.

My cheeks warm. For the first time ever, I am utterly thrilled to see him.

Only, the maven's smile melts away. His bottom jaw pulls downward. "What is that?" He asks, pointing to my phony shawl.

Yelda gasps, and my eyes follow her gaze. A bloody stain has soiled through the bandage, and through the scarf, as if my tattoo refuses to be ignored.

"I earned negative reinforcement for my disturbance," I say as my gaze slides to Allund who still stands nearby. "I will heal."

"Come now," Ringol says in a soothing voice. His eyes flash to Yelda's tattoo, and then he blinks slowly as if he has to work hard to control himself. "I'm sure it's fine, but a medtech should look you over before we leave." He turns toward Allund. "For travel clearance."

Medero Allund scoffs at him. "A medscreen for a maid's travel? She's already been on an IV drip. For all that is right, you've gone soft. I've humored you to this point. Do not push me."

Ringol's jaw juts out, but he quiets himself. "Very well, then. I will tend to it."

"*Please don't,*" I beg when he moves toward me. The bandages are stuck to my wounds already, and it's ugly, and I don't know how Ringol will react. "It's not infected, and I'm anxious to leave."

Yelda's hands go up too, as if to stop him from coming any closer.

Ringol glances at each of us, and something in his eyes changes. "How, exactly, does negative reinforcement work with *employees*?" he asks, his voice louder than before.

"If you're so concerned, Yelda can change the wrap." Medero Allund says quickly and motions to Yelda.

Yelda hurries to my side. "Please, Maven. Her privacy."

But Ringol hushes Yelda, towering over her and never taking his eyes off me. He gently moves my scarf to the side, revealing my soiled bandages.

I shake my head ready to protest, but he quiets me with that look of his. He peels the bandage away with care, and I wince at the bloodiest part – the two *Ls* in *dullard*. Tears line the inside of my goggles. I don't want him to see this.

His eyes narrow. "What is this? It's no wonder she's infirmed from the looks of this barbarous inking. Are these words permanent?" He takes something out from his inner jacket. It is a medpatch, which he opens and applies to my arm. My body warms almost instantly.

Allund raises his chin. "It is customary in my burrow for all to wear our crest. But after the disturbance…"

Ringol ignores him. He squints at the words below my collarbone. "I am – but a –" He will not say the last word. His warm coffee-scented breath hits my forehead in increasingly faster puffs.

My hand goes to his chest to still him. "We can report him later." I speak in hushed tones so only he can hear me. "Please, get us out of here."

Ringol's hands roll into fists and he quakes. "This is criminal," he whispers, lips moving in jerking motions

"I need out," I say, only slightly louder. He doesn't know the half of it. Qarmovi is gone, they'll be coming for me next. "Please."

Ringol nods and grips my hand before releasing it. For a moment, I am surprised at his ability to gain control over his anger. On the other hand, I am surprised that he would be so protective over me in the first place.

Not a second after the calm, though, Ringol twirls away and his fist soars through the air, landing squarely on Allund's jaw. Yelda shrieks when Allund falls on his backside with a thud.

I grab Ringol's wrist. He is breathing so hard and it's only then I realize – unlike his guards – he's not wearing a filtering travelmask. What the jet?

"You deranged madcap!" shouts Medero Allund from the ground. "You've loosened two of my teeth." He cups his hand around his mouth, and a dark liquid spills over his fingers. Blood. "Get out of my burrow now before I call in an arrest warrant for battery! These CF guards are my witnesses."

Ringol steps forward as if he'd like to strike the medero again. I try to pull him back with all my weight, for all the good that will do. When he finally notices me, the tightness in his muscles eases.

"Send your dental bill through FFR, and I'll gladly pay it. Don't ever address me as brother again. You bring shame to your profession and to the Woynauld name." Ringol glares at Allund, and I swear the vein in his temple is about to burst. "I would bid you good health," Ringol says, towering over the dragonman, "but I'm a lousy liar. Instead, I'll leave you with a truth: If we *ever* meet again, I will make sure *your health* is no longer an issue."

Medero Allund tries to stand up, but topples over and falls into an empty bunk.

Ringol ushers me to the door. I try to wave at Yelda, but she's too busy tending to Allund. One of Ringol's guards leads us in front, rushing through the corridors. The other follows behind.

With every step I take away from Allund, the promise of hope grows and the fear tying me in knots loosens. My body strengthens by leaps and bounds.

When we're almost to the end of the hallway, Ringol stops. "I need you to know that I circled back to Cayan, but I missed you by half a day. I was so angry that I hadn't forced you to come with me when I left. I should have done it –" he shakes his head "– even if I had to carry you off myself. Your talents are too valuable to walk away from. And when I found out you came here–" He looks away like he's at a loss for words, and he's never at a loss for words. I watch his Adam's apple while he swallows. "I believe in you."

The mirrored reflection of my face in his dark eyes makes me feel significant again. Seen. In such a short time, I'd forgotten what that was like. I will never take it for granted again.

"Thank you for not giving up on me."

"I took your advice," he shrugs, looking at the ground, "about having faith."

Ringol leads us up two sets of steel-grated stairs, down a warm hallway and into a tubular, steel elevator. He hands me a ventilating hood made of a thick canvas-like material that slides over my head with a transparent plastic material windowing my face so I can see. We all stand in silence as we ride it to the top.

As the elevator moves, my ears begin to pop with the pressure change. The ride to the top seems like it takes forever, although now I know that there are lower sections in this area. Undercellars, and I wonder if Qarmovi was taken there.

"Brace yourself," he says, as the doors slide open and a wave of heat swooshes over me. He slides his arm behind my back and sweeps me out, the others following. "The medpatch I gave you briefly protects you from any known bacteria or viruses you might encounter, long enough to make it to our transportation."

The doors close and the cylindrical protrusion that houses the top floor of the elevator collapses into the earth, a mechanical hatch rotating shut in its wake. My body can't adjust, and I still feel the rumble of the hydraulic motor in my bones.

The four of us stand on a cement platform above ground in the middle of a desert, met by the night's horizon. I inhale so deeply that it feels like it's my first time breathing. The smell – I can't place it. Wisps of moving air, warm and completely dry. I can even *taste* it, like salt.

Every sensation is foreign. Even with all the novels I've read, I've never imagined anything like this. I turn to find Ringol watching me.

Insect chirps start a few feet away. Bugs...? *No!* Fear shoots through my muscles and everything tightens. Ringol said the patch will protect me from known germs, but what about the unknown? *Jet. Oh, jet.*

There are no walls, just openness, and it's as exciting as it is overwhelming. How does one know which direction to go without a tunnel as a guide?

I squat and my hands graze the concrete, warm to the touch, perhaps still heated from the daytime sun that I've read so much about. I can't help but look up. Hazy specks of light stretch across the dark sky – tiny sparkling stars so dramatic and gorgeous that I never thought I'd see, yet *here they are*.

A single star glares a little too brightly, irritating my vision, but I'm mesmerized by the faint rings it produces against the darkness. "It's gorgeous." I'm trying to figure out this strange sensation building inside my chest.

My heart beats low and hard. I'm afraid to stand up, like I can't possibly allow so much of myself to tower above the earth. Staying down, I inch off the platform and my boots sink into the grittiness of the ground.

"Sand," I say stupidly. It cascades through my fingers when I try to examine it. A breeze zips around me, stinging my ankles with the granules. No ceiling blocks my view of the vast sky and I can only think of one word – perpetuity. A stubborn part of me wants to scream in fear but a bigger part of me wants to give in to the joy of it all.

A low laugh bubbles forth from the depths of my soul.

I feel alive.

"You *can* stand above ground without falling, you know," Ringol says as he helps me to my feet. But as he does so, I catch another view. A winged vessel at least twenty-five yards in length hums in the distance. It sits on top of a paved runway. On its side, a painted double-helix of DNA wraps around the barrel of the plane. It's a good thing his arm still supports me.

"A *jet?*" I say, dropping to the ground again. "There's a reason the word *jet* is a profanity."

When Sterling's Plague traversed the world, it was largely spread from continent to continent via passenger planes.

Air travel has long since been taboo, until recently when it resumed with improved antimicrobial-filtering technology.

"You'll be fine," Ringol says soothingly. He directs his guards to notify the engineer that we will be ready to depart momentarily.

The sand seeps into the crevices of my boots, as if to contaminate them. If Ringol has flown in the jet, and he's still alive, then logic says I have nothing to fear. The problem is, the part of my brain responsible for being terrified is never on speaking terms with my logic center. I want to, but every muscle in my body tightens, and I find I cannot move.

"I can't."

"Let's go." He brushes sand from my shoulder. "We have a full pantry of edibles on board."

My stomach growls. I haven't eaten all day. Still, my feet won't go.

"It's only twelve stair-steps into the plane. And it's a newer iteration of technology: a hoverjet. You won't even feel it once we've hit our altitude."

When I don't move, he huffs. "What would Gelia want you to do?" Ringol walks around me, baiting me, watching for my reaction. It irritates my last nerve.

"Medera would say *'manipulation of sentiment is a heartless man's sin.'* *But she would also order me onto that plane*, I think grudgingly. I glance at it again and my heart races.

"Maybe I don't use beautiful analogies like your medera," Ringol says, "but I am here to help. Did your medera have a pithy saying about stubbornness? Or recklessness?"

Medera would bang her cane.

"Just give me a moment."

"One never knows where rebels can show up, and we have clearance to take off *now.*"

And then he does something that surprises me, even with the telling smirk he flashes right before. Ringol reaches for me, grabbing me around my waist and throwing me over his shoulder like a sack of laundry. One of his arms keeps my legs still, the other is placed directly across my rear end.

"Ringol!" I didn't think he was serious about carrying me away. "Set me down!"

"I'm not taking any more chances, so be still. I will have a medtech waiting to check you when we arrive at GCE." He takes gigantic steps in the sand, carrying me without effort, and without hurting my wounded skin. He carts me up the twelve steps and into the plane and straps me into a cushioned seat in the center of the cabin before I can say any more. Then, he taps the flight engineer on his shoulder. They exchange hushed words. The man nods and then fiddles with his control panel.

Everyone looks at me like I'm as crazy as Maddelyn had been. Maybe I am.

"You may remove your mask in here," Ringol announces, collapsing into his seat. His guards have already removed theirs. One flashes a friendly smile, but the other doesn't even look my way, squinting and blinking. They both unbutton their shirts, peel them off, and throw them into a side-chute in the aircraft's wall. Their pale skin pulls tightly against their ribs and abdominal muscles, like most Subters who can't quite reach optimal body weight. They remove their combat boots, and they unbuckle their belts. They wouldn't dare strip down with me sitting right here. Would they? Maybe the Woynauld Academy's method of mixed-gender changing is more the rule than the exception outside of my home burrow. But I find I don't much care for it.

"This was the best excursion yet, Maven," says the guard who won't look at me. Excursion? He reaches into an arched cubby and pulls out a pair of glasses.

When they begin to drop their pants, I turn away.

"Your mask," Ringol points to my face. I barely hear him over the humming engine. "This cabin contains the purest form of usable oxygen. There's no safer breathing on Earth."

I rip the mask off my face and throw it on the floor with a dead thud. I then hold my hand up to block my view of the guards. "What are they doing?"

"They're changing from their costumes. Did you *really* believe I hired Central Force guards?" Ringol snorts.

"Then who–?" The aircraft jerks forward a bit, and I grab hold of my seat. "Who are they?"

"Undertechs," he says simply. "I had to convince Allund Woynauld that I had the backing of Common Good, that my documentation proved the law was on my side, and that nothing was questionable. He believed it." Ringol shrugs. "They are decent now. Meet your co-workers."

Co-workers? The first young man, the one with kind eyes and a gracious smile, approaches me. He's now wearing light-colored pants while buttoning a matching tunic shirt.

"Good health. I am Undertech Griffith Diggs, and this is my second year at GCE."

"You may call her Undertech Allele," Ringol says. It takes me a minute to respond to my new name. Alleles are the differing forms of a mutated gene, so I have to admit that the name is clever. But it's also a lie. I am Zuzan Cayan, of Cayan Burrow. Except, maybe that girl no longer exists.

I return Griffith's easy smile. "Good health." He plops into a seat next to me and straps himself in just before the jet staggers forward again.

I grip his arm. I can't help myself.

"Takeoff is the worst," he whispers. "You won't even know we're flying once we reach altitude."

Ringol pretends not to watch me from his one-seated bench, but a wry smile twists across his lips. I wonder why he'd waste so many resources on an inexperienced first-year with such a low LE as mine. Nevertheless, of course, I am grateful.

The pilot speaks over an intercom. "In four, three, two–"

"Hold on," Griffith says, wrapping his fingers over mine.

A high-pitched whine crescendos from under the plane

until I can barely stand the noise. *This is just like a magnetran,* I tell myself. The terrible sound settles into a solid grumbling, like an earthquake. When the vessel sounds like it's about to implode upon itself, I can feel it slowly hover into the air higher and higher, and then it blasts away. My skull is thrown into the headrest, and I try not to swallow my tongue.

After a while, I realize how tense my muscles have been because they start to relax, and ache. I open my eyes. Ringol, Griffith, and the other fake guard watch my every move. "You were right," I say. "Takeoff is the worst." I unwind my fingers that are clamped over Griffith's arm. Half-moon marks from my fingernails speckle his skin. "Sorry."

"You're a pro at flying now." He rubs his forearm. But Ringol lets out a loud puff of air as if he's held back his laughter for too long.

"I don't think I caught your name," I say, turning to the other man opposite me.

He shoves his glasses up the bridge of his nose with his forefinger before unfastening his safety strap and walking over to me. "Chen Zamption, intelligence tech," he says with a formal tone. "Good health."

"You'll find the stash of edibles in the front cupboard," Ringol cuts in. He rubs his temples like he's suffering and takes out a medpatch. Rolling up a sleeve, he slaps the patch inside his upper arm. He winces, leans his head back, and covers his eyes with his hands. "Help yourself."

My stomach growls again. Never in a hundred eons would I consider walking around while flying through the sky, except when starvation is involved. I unbuckle and stand slowly, when something eerie outside of the line of windows stops me cold. Clouds. We are flying through them. They appear like thick smoke.

A bump sends me scrambling for something to hold onto, and I reach for the empty seat. Hands out for balance, this time, I make my way up the aisle to look for the food. I choose a protein chunk from the supply Ringol pointed me to as we move out of the cloudy vapors. A blazing glow upon the earth below pierces through the windows.

"What's that?" I hold my hand out to shade my face. Dangers thrive on the surface of the planet, like volcanic eruptions and lightning strikes, and it makes me glad I don't normally have to deal with these things.

Ringol stands, glancing out of the small window alongside me. He shakes his head, and then guides me back into my seat.

"Is it a rebel demonstration?" asks Chen.

Ringol nods, and it takes a minute for things to sink in with me: the rebels are Omnits, and they are burning something.

"Rotting dullards." Chen crosses his arms. He stressed the word *rotting* on purpose, since Omnits tend to bury their dead instead of using cremation. We Subters don't like imagining countless Omnit corpses buried at ground level, above us. "They should be blasted from the planet."

But Ringol snaps around. "Undertech!"

"I'm sorry sir," Chen complains. "I just don't understand them. Why burn their own hospitals, or murder the Subterranean medstaff who risk their lives each day to treat them? In my view, they've turned holocaustic."

"The phrase *'they should be blasted from this planet'* is holocaustic." Maven Ringol counters, his tone serving as a warning. "I employ no one who harbors prejudicial thoughts. These people are our brothers, sisters, and parents. Omnits gave birth to us, only to lose their children to the burrows. They are motivated by *fear*, whether we understand them or not."

"My deepest apologies, Maven. I'm trying to re-think everything, but I was brought up on different beliefs. My medera often complained how even the non-rebel Omnits refuse to identify the offenders." He sniffs. "But as you say, we aren't hearing the whole perspective."

"The Omnits who are afraid to talk have been terrorized by

these same faction groups, so they are afraid for their lives," Ringol says. "The rebels are vicious, but they don't speak for all Omnits. Make the effort to open your mind, Chen. Subters are already separated from our Omnit families. Don't allow the misguided actions of angry rebels to separate us even further."

Chen may have been fed all the negative things about Omnits from Medera Zamption, while I was fed all the positive things from Medera Gelia. Neither of us heard the whole truth.

Goosebumps pop up across my flesh. This is what Maddelyn ranted on about – she wasn't *completely* crazy after all. I wipe my hands across my skirt and try to glance out the window too, at the bright haze one more time. But of course, it's too intense so I turn away.

"We land in five hours," Ringol mumbles. "Rest."

CHAPTER 10

French Braids

The morning after arriving at GCE, a soft alarm inside my bedchamber wakes me. I pull my goggles over my eyes, and then press my thumb into the oval-shaped button to open my bedchamber. As the curved lid splits open from the top, the door slides sideways and downward into the wall. I step into a room that I share with only five others, which wouldn't even fill two bunks at Woynauld's maid dormitory. The other women busy themselves getting dressed.

A small locker next to my bedchamber is marked with my newly acquired name: *Allele Crypt, Undertech.* I frown. Cayan was my proud home, but no one can tell. Inside the locker, I find ample toiletries and a white uniform, pressed and hanged. My fingers slide over the smooth material, soft to the touch yet sturdy. It must be silk or some modern imitation.

The hope for a fresh start washes over me; the same feeling I had when I first arrived at Cayan. During my early years while I endured Na'rm Anetta's hatred, I learned to see myself as *she* did, but then Maddy and Jal showed me I was likeable and Gelia taught me I was even loveable, so my self-hatred faded in time. Mostly.

I smile shyly at a woman whose locker is next to mine. *Make friends*, Gelia said before I left Cayan. Here, away from the toxicity of Allund, I might.

"I wonder when those goggles were last sanitized," a woman

whispers at the other side of the room. They don't know me yet, so I can't blame their curiosities. I turn to respond.

"Or her bandage," another one says, not even trying to whisper. I glance at her, and she stares at me with a look of disgust. "Crypt is the perfect name for her. She looks like she crawled out of a grave."

My heart sinks as I turn back to my locker.

I work diligently to keep the humiliating words on my chest hidden as I dress. How would I explain it? My bandages stick to my skin, so I wait until I can slip on my blouse, and then I peel them off slowly. The words are now bumpy, swollen over the black lines of each scorching letter, as if someone sewed a rope underneath my skin.

The louder woman snorts. "For all decency, it's almost painful to look at her shaven head." She may as well call me *Ratgirl*.

Without thinking, I stroke my now-stubbly hair at the nape of my neck, shaved like a person who had been infested with some sort of parasite. My face warms. There's a small part of me that wants to set the record straight – and a larger part that wants to tell them off.

The thick-haired woman stares at me while she works a French braid around her head sideways from ear to ear. Even when I grow my hair, it never grows long and healthy enough to braid it like she does. Her eyebrows, high at the corners, decline sharply down to the top of her long nose, giving her an ever-angry appearance. "I'd like to know why our maven placed you in this room. We've all earned it with our high ranking."

Another woman nods.

Make friends, Ratgirl. I bite my cheek, trying to keep quiet, at least until I know them better. I can barely look at them. "I can't say," I mumble.

"Well, I intend to ask him about it first thing," French braid says.

My white uniform boots fasten too loosely around my

ankles, so I watch how the silent woman tightens her buckles. French Braid has different boots – platformed several inches to make her taller than everyone. She doesn't wear a skirt like the rest of us. Instead, she wears tight-fitting cropped pants.

My overcoat fastens along the left side over my ribcage. I roll my sleeves like my roommates have. Jalaz would have loved to see me here, like this. Maddelyn, too. Even my medera would smile.

As much as I try to avoid it, I glance down at my chest. My overcoat's neckline plunges too far down toward the left with the way it snaps off center. Through the thin white blouse underneath, I can make out the tops of the letters.

I rifle through the items in my locker, but there's nothing to help hide it.

"This way, Undertech Allele," calls a voice.

I spin towards the door to find a maid in a dark uniform. "Sorry?" I straighten my goggles over my eyes. The worsening crack in my lens breaks her image into two people, allowing in a flash of light that makes me flinch. French Braid snorts at me again. Could I possibly appear more freakish?

"Maven Ringol has requested a meeting with you before breakfast." She stands at attention. Her voice sounds similar to Maddelyn's, though from the lines around her mouth, she must be close to forty. She has a similar accent to Ringol's, pronouncing the vowels much rounder than I do. There's something about the droopy shape of her eyes that gives her an ever-sorrowful, worried look.

Medera never specified who I should attempt to "friend." I was a maid just yesterday. Until I became a maid, I'd never do what I'm about to, and I'm ashamed for that. A job is merely what a person does, not who a person is. I extend my hand. "And you are?"

Her lips purse and she eyes me down to my boots.

I take the maid's hand from her side and shake it. "Good health."

She flashes an amused smile. "My name is Miss Kriz. Good health upon you."

I glance at French Braid, who has now forgotten me and drop my voice to a whisper. "Could you help me find a thicker blouse? You see, I have this noticeable – um – mark." I open my overcoat's neckline wider, revealing only to her the bloody letters on my chest.

She gasps, but quiets herself as her eyes dash around the room. "Hurry. We cannot keep Maven Ringol waiting too long." She grabs me by the elbow and begins to pull me away, but then drops her hands. "Apologies, Undertech. I didn't mean to be so casual."

"Pah." I tuck my hand under the crook of her elbow. "I'm a new fan of 'casual.'"

After a quick stop at the medtech station for clean bandages, Kriz secures a dark maid's blouse in exchange for the white silk one I'm wearing and escorts me to Maven Ringol's office.

As soon as we walk in, I shade my eyes from the glare of lit squares on the wall.

Ringol flicks a switch from behind his desk which turns off the screens, and he stands. "I should have shut these down before you came. They are faux windows, so I can sit in my office and pretend I can go outside whenever I want."

Now that I've been to the surface, I sort of understand what he means. But I'm his employee at this point, not a random student at a burrow, not someone partnering to save C's life, and not a co-quarantine-mate. I don't know how to act with him anymore.

I stand awkwardly at attention. "Good health, Maven."

"Right." He eyes me sideways. "Good health." Our words fall flat, but he's my supervisor, and Medera would have it no other way.

Maven Ringol straightens his shoulders, but his brow twitches and he smiles. His eyes then settle on the dark blouse Kriz found for me and his expression softens for a moment.

"Kriz, fetch the optotech."

"Optotech?" My voice cracks.

Kriz turns to leave, flashing a buoyant smile, as if she approves.

"I don't need a new pair of goggles." I struggle to tighten my old pair, as if they're arguing with me in front of my maven. "I'm ready to get straight to research."

He smirks like he did when he offered me this job. "The examination isn't for a new pair of goggles."

I bite the inside of my cheek. "My eyes just took a beating from the tattoo painter's bright lights, and my migraines have finally stopped. If we could just delay–"

"You will be examined," he barks.

I flinch at his raised voice. "My roommates already think I've been shown special treatment. What am I leading them to think if I don't start working?"

"You're not leading your colleagues to think anything." He rubs his temples. "Directing their thinking is *my* job."

"But, Maven–"

"I'm not looking for your opinion on this subject or on any subject unless I ask for it," he says with tensed shoulders as he stands and paces around his desk. "This is how things work: I inform you of your assignments, and you are to reply, *Yes, Maven,* and then you are to smash every one of my expectations." He stops directly in front of me. I smell a trace of coffee on his breath. Java catalyzes a whole host of biological issues for Subters. Clearly, temper is one of them.

He stares at me for a moment, and then I realize he expects a response. "Yes, Maven."

"Medera Gelia did you no favors by raising such a contrary, categorical snob."

My eyes turn instantly wet at the mention of my medera, at his harsh judgement of her.

"For such a praised medera, she bumbled this one."

My stomach twists. "Maybe *you* bumbled in your pursuit to hire me." I face him directly. "You knew my personality, and you came for me anyway. Why?"

His face freezes and his arms stiffen. He opens his mouth but no words come out. I can't figure out how to read him.

"Medera Gelia Cayan's methods have been revered and duplicated by her peers," I continue. "Her character, her poise, and her intelligence are surpassed by none." My voice breaks. All I did was give her trouble when I left. "Insult *me* if you think it's necessary, but don't ever insult my medera. I can't work here if you do."

Kriz clears her throat, and both Ringol and I spin toward her. "Pardon." Her gaze darts between the two of us.

A man flanks her side, open mouthed, pulling a wheeled cart of equipment. My fists tighten at my sides.

"Thank you," Ringol says. "Good health, Optotech Hahn."

"Good health, Maven Ringol. Is this our patient?"

"No," I say as I start to walk toward the door, but Ringol catches my arm.

"Yes," he says. "But don't expect her to display any patience. This is Allele Crypt, our newest undertech. She must be able to read from tablets and chip projectors to perform the duties for which she was hired. Will you explain how you plan to examine her without the use of light?"

"I use black light," the optotech says, "and as I told Maven Ringol yesterday, the rays should not bother you any more than light irritates you through your goggles."

"If you've reviewed my records then you already know that nothing can be done." I blurt, even though I'm relieved about the black light. "Please explain this to my maven."

"I understand your records have been misplaced." The optotech's eyebrows go up, and he looks to Ringol.

Of course. I have a new identification number. What saved me from Woynauld causes problems for me here. New number, no records attached.

"Regardless," the optotech says, "this examination is more thorough than those provided at the burrows."

"Excuse her, Optotech. She's suffering from her first case

of jetlag. Call if you need assistance." He retreats to the door, leaving the optotech standing by his desk. Ringol winks back at me like the hatless man I remember him to be. "Although, I'll pay you a ten-percent bonus if you complete her examination without calling me."

My mouth drops. "What–?"

"I could stay with Undertech Allele." Kriz turns to Ringol. "She's clearly shaken."

"The only thing shaking Allele is her inability to follow orders. She'll learn." Ringol holds the door for Kriz and motions for her to leave. He nods to the optotech. "Best of luck, sir. And Undertech?"

I tilt my head, biting my cheek because the words that want to fly from my mouth are what Na'rm Anetta would call *wicked*.

"Behave." He stands there, almost daring me to respond.

First he insults my medera, and then he ridicules me in front of Kriz and this optotech, and now he wants to put me in my place after I've escaped a tyrant like Allund Woynauld. Is that who he's trying to be like? Allund?

I snap my body into a military salute. "Yes, Lord Ringol."

The maven's eyes widen like saucers, but I remain at attention until he leaves. Once he slams the door behind him, I twirl around and flop into a chair.

The onyx desk, the granite floor, the screens made to look like ground-level windows, these are all things that speak to the wealth here at GCE while the Cayan Burrow floundered for watered-down cleaning supplies. I shake my head.

"Shall we begin?" asks the optotech.

He rolls his cart with two shelves full of apparatus toward me. I lean away as he approaches. I have yet to meet an optotech who doesn't harbor sadistic tendencies.

The optotech blinks and presses his lips together. He holds up his hand, perhaps needing an extra moment to figure out what he's going to say while I squirm. Then he pats my knee like he's comforting a child. I feel like one.

"I'll describe each step in detail and will answer all your questions. None of the testing involves a process that should cause you alarm." He folds his hands across his waistline, nails bitten to the quick. If anyone knows about anxiety-causing things, it might be him.

"I have nothing against you." Except for the fact he's an optotech. "But I'm up to date with my examinations."

"This isn't a standard examination, Undertech. This goes deeper. The first step is a simple bloodlab using microscopic needles."

After my tattoo, I cringe. I will never think of needles in the same way again.

The optotech hands me a flat strip. "You simply roll this band around your finger and then press your forefinger into your thumb."

"There are needles in this?" I hold it up sideways to examine its silhouette, too blurry through my goggles.

He smiles. "Tiny, tiny needles. One for each test." He sits back and waits with an amiable, calm expression.

I wrap my thumb and press it into my forefinger. It's a little abrasive to the touch, but not painful.

He takes the wrap and slides the strip into a reader. "Maven Ringol sets you on edge." His tone is quiet and friendly, and it puts me at ease.

"I don't have a good track record with supervisors." Yet despite his temper just now, Ringol came back for me at Woynauld. He didn't have to, but he did. He said he believed in me.

Hahn's eyes scan the almost instantaneous bloodlab results. "Intriguing."

Intriguing could mean a lot of things, but if the results were good, Hahn probably would have said so right away. My heart quickens. Clearly this is something Ringol overlooked. The maven can't possibly convert everything I need into paper format for my undertech work. So what job can I do here at GCE instead?

"It's okay," I say tightly, steeling myself for the disappointment of his diagnosis. "Believe it or not, a labmaid position beats my last job."

"No, Undertech Allele. The results are certain, and fascinating. Your immune system has made antigens against your own pigmentation. Even if we attempt pigment remediation – surgically inserting color into your eyes – it would fail. Your body would reject and attack the foreign pigment as if it were an infection. At some point, with the right researchers, we can figure out what can be done, if anything, for a permanent solution."

"In the meantime, I'll be scrubbing Petri dishes."

He chuckles. "In the meantime, you'll wear full-coverage contact lenses – sort of like a prosthetic pigmentation, protecting your eyes like your goggles do, only better. They will be worn directly on the surface of your eye over your iris and the exposed white. You see, the pink in your irises is actually the visible–"

"Blood vessels inside," I finish for him.

"Quite right. The polymer used in the prosthetics is smart enough to automatically adjust depending on the degree of light present, which makes it possible for you to read from tablets or do anything an undertech would need to do."

"So… no goggles?" A tiny smile creeps over my lips. Even so, I might cry. "Really? How long until–?"

"About ninety minutes."

For the first time since I've met him, I gaze into Optotech Hahn's eyes. They're brilliant and soft, and I want to hug this man I hardly know. "What about my color-blindness?"

He blinks slowly. "There's a special tint that helps with people who are challenged with colors. I worked on the visual development team for this technology. We're going to add it to your lenses which will help. It's not a perfect correction for color-blindness, but it's a wonderful improvement."

Wonderful? *Miraculous,* really. Maddelyn described the

different colors to me over and over, and I have tried to imagine them in my mind and guess what color different objects might be. She once caught me staring at Jalaz during gallery studies, and whispered how his green eyes could mesmerize a demon, before she remembered I didn't know his eyes were green.

I touch the Optotech's hand. "I'm sorry for how I behaved when you first came in."

"I'm sorry you've waited this long to see properly." He turns and takes out a stainless-steel container. "We start by having you choose an eye color. Blue is most common for the albino coloring we Subters suffer through. Though, something tells me that you're galaxies away from common."

CHAPTER 11

Magnificent

An hour and a half later, I open my eyes, goggle-less and blinking. Images swirl before me: the desk, Optotech Hahn, his cart. Light bleaches everything into flashing splotches, so I close my eyes again. What if this ruins what little sight I have? My heart races as I brush away the tears dripping down my cheeks. They are normally caught inside my goggles, but now they are free.

"A little burning or an itching sensation is normal," the optotech says. "But that should ease in time."

When I open my eyes again, a soft glow radiates from each of Ringol's fake windows. The blurriness clears, and one of the screens shows an animated bird perched on a tree limb, jumping and cocking its head. Different shades define everything more vibrantly – *colors*, for all that is good! – and sharper lines. Tears keep falling, but I wish they'd stop. They blur everything before me. Colors. Light. Dimension like I've never experienced it.

"This is what everyone else sees all the time?" My voice breaks, but I spin around and glance at everything I possibly can, my eyes greedy for the sight. Another picture window shows a stream of water surrounded by a muddy embankment. The leaves on the animated trees are green, *I think*, not gray. They're beautiful. "What color is the bird?" It's brilliant.

"Look here." Optotech Hahn hands me a tablet – a *tablet* for all good – with a color chart, where each hue is labeled, and I don't have to turn away from it. I scan the different squares, and a lump forms in my chest. I've always wondered, and here they are.

"The bird is a light blue." I smile, glancing around the room. "Your cart is red, and that wall is a shade of yellow. How does anyone pick a favorite color?" A laugh tumbles out of my throat and my tears blur everything, despite trying to keep them in. When I turn back to the optotech, he's got tears in his eyes too – his kind, pale-blue eyes.

"These are the rewarding days one lives for. That emerald green suits you beautifully." He holds up a small mirror.

My full face appears before me, my mouth gaping. The goggles have left some fading indentations in my skin. I blink, hardly believing I can see my own eyes staring back at me, the color that Jal's would have been. In a small way, he still made it here, through me. "Thank you."

"I've merely done my job. Perhaps you might thank someone else." He begins to pack his equipment, smiling because he's right. I should thank the maven. "I will ship an extra pair for you just in case. Should you need additional replacements, camcall me straightaway. I will deliver new lenses to you the next day."

"I'll be able to see video camcalls?"

"Camcalls with your maven's permission, of course." And educational projections and videos. My heart drops into my stomach; Ringol had pointed out how I wouldn't be able to keep up with the newer technology used by mederas. Now that I can, I'm not even close to becoming one. A burrow could have hired me and paid for these lenses, even if I had to pay them back over time. But that's not how things work in burrows. Mederas scrape to make ends meet. How unfair that they don't have the kind of resources GCE does.

The door on the other side of the room opens, and Ringol enters. I stand for him to see that I am not wearing my goggles.

His gaze bobs from Optotech Hahn to the images on his fake windows, and finally to me.

"Maven," I say, amazed at how clear everything is. So bright. I want to thank him, but I'm trying to figure out what color his eyes are – brown? That's not quite right. His skin is a shade darker than the optotech's, and his uniform is a dark gray with dark red pinstripes.

He walks toward me and then freezes like he's unable to take another step. Kriz follows him into the room. She, too, freezes when she turns to see me, and she smiles.

"Magnificent," Ringol says.

My body stiffens. *Magnificent*? Maddy once said that my face without goggles was elegant. But he seems truly awestruck. Ringol continues to stare in my direction, motionless.

"I can't possibly thank you enough," I say, trying to smooth the hair at the base of my neck, before remembering it's been shaved off. My cheeks turn fiery under his intense stare, and I wish he'd say something. "For this, for the time you helped me in quarantine, and for finding me at Woynauld's. Thank you."

Ringol finally clears his throat, dismissing Kriz with a small wave of his hand. She curtsies and leaves, the optotech joining her. He begins to walk to the table in the back of the room, but then spins around like he's thought of something else, looking lost in his own office.

"Maven?" I start.

"I–" he stammers, "have research to supervise in the laboratory over the next week." Instead of looking at me while he speaks, he fixes his gaze on the floor beside me. "You – can – I mean, *you will* stay here and review this material until you are ready for the ranking exams." His expression is muted, but I know him well enough now to realize he's faking his calm demeanor.

He holds up one of his brow-chip-projector-button things and then places it into my hand. "This adheres just above your eyebrow. It's called a ChiPro, and it's registered to you."

When he looks into my face, I almost jump away. It's different now, how his eyes lock onto mine. His gaze doesn't just meet the approximation of where my eyes would be behind my goggles – he's staring directly into them. It's like he can see the insanely deep pieces of my soul. I feel almost bare before him, but strangely not uncomfortable.

As his gaze shifts from my left eye to my right and back again, I find details in his features that I couldn't see with my goggles. They fascinate me: the way his lashes curve, the many shades in his dark irises dancing together, the way his pupils dilate. Magnificent.

But it's not him who's changed. It's me. I've become less blurry to the world – more seen than ever before. My insides tingle, though the way he's staring at me makes me want to look away. He knows exactly who I am. With all my faults, he's helped me anyway. A hot flush burns from my neck to my cheeks as I fumble with the ChiPro, trying to place it on my temple.

"I always put it in the most comfortable spot." He points to his ChiPro above his eyebrow and backs away. "It will take you some time to get up to speed, but your colleagues will tutor you on the genomic material until you are ready to be ranked. It's a grueling initiation process. You'll be quizzed in front of everyone."

"A public test?" I smirk, because it almost sounds fun.

"Most undertechs study genomology for years prior to placement here. You're at a severe disadvantage, which is why I've placed you in the chamberroom with the highest ranking labtechs. Nukleo has been directed to tutor you. She's the one with braids."

My insides cringe. I'd like to stay as far away from French Braids as possible. "You think I need tutoring?"

The maven's mouth forms a straight line, and then he presses the button at his temple. "Send the v-clip compilation of GCE initiation failures to Undertech Allele Crypt," he instructs the ChiPro.

My button projector automatically beeps and lights up just above my center of vision. I flinch before I remember it won't hurt my eyes anymore. Ten-second clips of labtechs play one after another. The first man trembles and stutters, and it cuts to his rank at the end – the absolute bottom of his peers. The next is a woman who freezes, as if she knows the answer but is too terrified. She fails initiation altogether, and her final scene shows her leaving GCE.

"Current GCE staff members watch these videos before each initiation," he says. "Mostly for amusement."

I frown. That seems unnecessarily cruel. I press the button and the projection disappears. "I study better solo."

His expression hardens. "Fine." He reactivates my projection and quickly shows me how to access the genomology table of contents on the ChiPro. "Study all of these two texts, all of the research, and the corresponding notes. Memorize dates, tables, and any data that seems even remotely relevant. You'll need it all."

With that, he marches out of his office, leaving me alone.

The texts he told me to read are the same that Jal studied, so I'm more than familiar with them. I devour the reading material much faster than usual because the pages are programmed to automatically scroll with my iris movements. The accompanying videos are also spectacular – everything is blown up into animated holographic projections: viruses infecting healthy cells, cells multiplying, DNA duplication, coding errors forming mutations, gene-editing videos, and so much more.

When I am finished with all that Ringol told me to study, I want to know more. I have questions about the intersection of genomics and immunology, which seems to be at the heart of the Subter-Omnit divide. I've never been able to accomplish this much so quickly, so I dig into the other genomic textbooks lingering out there, the ones he hadn't yet assigned me to study.

Hours later when I'm finished with those, Ringol still has not returned, so I decide to explore my ChiPro's other functions. I press the button at my eyebrow and it chimes. A few seconds later, it speaks. "What is your command?" The animated female's voice sounds sincere, like she wants to help.

"Find a person."

"Whom may I help you find?"

"Camcall to Medera Gelia Cayan of the Cayan Burrow," I annunciate while trying to keep my voice low, and I look for a volume control on the holographic ChiPro display. I have so many questions for Gelia. And a huge apology.

"Checking for the Cayan Burrow." One second later: "No camport found at Cayan Burrow. Medera Gelia Cayan was not found. Would you like to camcall someone else?"

I slouch over. Medera inactivated the camport on her tablet? But I have another idea. "Yes. Camcall Maddelyn Cayan at the Central Psychiatric Institute." I miss her so much, as hard as that is for me to reconcile on some level, but I haven't seen the real her since before her bizarre breakdown. Is she better now? Is she close to her normal self, or did the incident take its toll?

A chirping sound beeps intermittently in my ear, as if it's found her and its waiting for her to answer. My heart picks up pace. At least she reached majority age before leaving Cayan, so she was able to keep her name, even though we didn't get to spend her birthday together.

"Maddelyn Cayan is unavailable at the moment," explains the digital voice. "If you would like to leave a message, you may do so now." It beeps.

"Maddelyn?" I say, hesitating. "I miss you." I want to say I forgive her, and none of it was her fault, but maybe bringing up the horrible memories would be harmful to her recovery. I take a breath. "May good health be with you."

A chirp sounds in my ear once more. "Do you have any further commands?" my ChiPro asks.

I'm about to say no, to study all the practice material again, but according to Medera, I have perfect memory recall – a long-term eidetic memory – so I haven't forgotten a single word. There's nothing else left to study, so I decide I want to find out more about the Omnit rebellion that has been kept secret from me. "Find current news events related to Omniterranean uprisings against Subterraneans."

My chip beeps three times and a projected screen illuminates. "I found five-hundred and thirty-three v-clips on recent Rebel uprisings." A list of each clip appears, all credited to the Central News Agency for Common Good.

I flick my forefinger across the light so the projection radiates into the air just as I did for the RNA manipulation video. The screen is now fully dimensional in front of me, and I begin to watch clip number twenty-nine, *Omnit Rebel Attack an Academic Burrow*, though I'm not sure I want to.

The hologram of a man appears before me, the news anchor, who explains the scene as it unfolds. Security cameras show footage of Omnit men and women dressed in unfamiliar uniforms – dingy brown clothes with boots and dirty knit caps – rushing into an unprotected burrow full of children. The medero, identifiable by his long, checkered robe, holds his arms out as if trying to peacefully stop the group. The first rebel to reach the medero – towering over him by at least a foot in height, bulkier by at least eighty pounds – uses a rod to electrify the poor man. The medero falls lifeless while the burrowlings scatter, screaming. Militants grab them before they get too far.

One of them hollers at a crying child. There is no sound, but I could swear he's mouthing, "Where are the babies?" How would a burrowling know where babies are? Subter babies are sent to nurseries, not burrows.

I skip to another v-clip segment titled *Reported Rebel Targets*.

"*This week alone,*" the news anchor explains as images appear, "*the Common Intelligence Agency warns that Rebels plan to attack major hospitals, burrows, and centers of research. Reports about Omnit rebels obtaining military-grade anti-bunker bombs have not been confirmed or denied by the agency."*

"Undertech Allele?"

I jump to my feet at Ringol's voice, and then stand at attention. I press at my ChiPro, but miss as the projection swings around the room as I turn, stopping at Ringol's chest. I slap my temple to get it to stop.

He's brought a tray of food for me.

"Maven, I was –" Not following his instructions.

"We are not news reporters or historians, Undertech," he says. "I gave you specific files to study. This is not a good start."

My face warms. "I read them. Maven Camu's work is fascinating." Camu was Ringol's brilliant predecessor, another one of Jalaz's favorite genetic heroes.

He drops the tray onto his desk from just a high enough point that the clanging sound is maximized while the food stays mostly in place. His jaw tenses. "Eat."

He has placed the tray in front of his chair at the desk, so I hesitate, but when he looks expectantly at me, I move to the other side and sit down. In his chair. Folding my hands. "Thank you, Maven Ringol."

After tapping his finger above his brow, it beeps. "Show me Allele Crypt's data."

My muscles tense.

"Do you know how competitive an environment this is, Zuzan?" His voice softens on my real name.

"I'm beginning to understand." I take a bite of the bread. The airy-soft texture is only surpassed by its freshness; yet I find it difficult to swallow.

"Send life-size v-clip CD88 to Allele Crypt," he says. "This one's my favorite."

A giant image of an Aslan-like lion tucked behind some tall grass appears before me in a hologram. But then, another projection flashes over by the door as if in the distance, one of a deer eating some leaves. A fawn, judging from its size and spots.

"I understand, Maven." My voice tightens. "The competitive-ness here is serious."

"I'm not sure you do. This fawn over here? Let's name her Zuzan. The lion, for lack of a better label, shall be called Cut-Throat-GCE-Staff. This lion is the cleverest beast, since we recruit only the brightest, most promising scientists this world has to offer. Most of them study hours every night after finishing their shifts just to stay ahead of the flurry of scientists clamoring to get into GCE. They voluntarily re-test to increase their rankings when they are brave enough."

I scrunch my face, swallowing the bread that goes down like dry pebbles in my throat. "I've completed the assignments, Maven."

Too late. The lion darts into the field, chasing the fawn across the grasses. The lion's tendons stretch and contract with every move. Anytime the fawn changes direction, it stumbles just a bit and the lion gains on it. Shortens the distance. The two separate projections merge into one as the lion closes in. The situation is hopeless. Finally, Zuzan-the-fawn trips for the last time, and she gives up, panting. How can she just give up? *Get up!* The lion pounces, grabbing her hind with its claws and snapping its teeth into her neck.

I shut my eyes, pressing my chip to remove the images, winded as if I'd been running with the fawn. I push the tray of food away.

"The stronger, faster deer are free. Safe. They outlive their unfortunate cousin. In a few short hours, they'll forget she ever existed."

I swallow again, pushing down the lingering crumbs in my throat, and think about Jalaz. GCE may have forgotten him, but I never will.

"Name the theory." His voice booms over the sterile surfaces in his office causing me to jump slightly. Maybe coming here was a mistake. The alternative, though, is Allund.

"Survival of the fittest," I reply in a barely audible voice.

"And the maven?"

"Charles Darwin, sir. 1809-1882." My voice cracks. "This, along with his natural selection theory, has been proven again and again over the course of evolution." He must not realize that I'd studied everything Jalaz did so I could quiz him properly. It was excellent practice for a future medera.

The maven's brows remain low on his eyes. "You read both text books?"

"I'd read the two you'd assigned me before coming here. And then I read two other textbooks that happened to be in the portal, along with the notes from Maven Camu's research experiments."

He calls up data from his own chip and taps the air in front of him to navigate. "I only assigned two textbooks." His eyes scan the projected "Undertech Allele Crypt" statistics in front of him.

"I read fast," I say stupidly. "I figured it wouldn't hurt to just keep going to the other files."

"Impossible words-read-per-minute stats." He murmurs, then clicks his tongue. "Skimming the information won't get you through the ranking."

"I always read from paged books, but it's easier with the auto-scrolling. I don't skim, and I don't forget. I have perfect memory. Medera Gelia even developed a specialized test to confirm this."

He doesn't respond, but crosses his arms. I stare at him, directly into his pupils, and I wonder if my eyes are as readable as his: he doesn't believe me.

"Ask me anything."

"You really think you're ready?" He narrows his eyes at me and taps his finger on his projected display. "Because I've just arranged it. You'd better have the contents of our two major textbooks and all of Maven Camu's notes committed to that perfect memory of yours."

"I have the textbooks, but the notes–"

Maven Ringol's face turns stony. "This is no game, Under-tech."

"I understand that, sir. But Maven Camu's notes are not complete." Maybe he's testing me. "I studied everything you gave me. Her way of detailing every procedure is systematic. Consistent. I would estimate a good thirty-percent of her data is slightly off. I assumed it was too classified to publish the real stats."

He taps in the air, reviewing some of the former maven's charts. "On what do you base that claim?" he says in clipped words.

I tap my own projector button and start to search for examples. "It's in her pattern of summarizing, Maven. There are certain sections where the patterns falter – equations that disappear altogether. Without that material, the notes appear to be evidence of completed research with inconclusive results. Although, I think if the studies were repeated, they would reach definitive conclusions. Am I your first recruit since she left?"

He frowns.

"The numbers were likely altered after the fact." I press my chip. "Find Maven Camu's notes, figure fifty-two." Once it projects the data, I sweep my finger over the screen to display the chart above us. "There. It's just odd."

"There, what?"

I motion to the chart. "The standard deviations aren't calculated correctly. You can't see it here unless you refer to the raw data." I double-tap the chart to open the underlying figures in a side-by-side projection. "There's no way these numbers," I point to the table, "produced that standard deviation."

Maven Ringol stares at the numbers, squinting as he goes through a mental calculation. "I think you're right," he says slowly. "It must be off by a point."

In some weird way, I like that he can calculate so quickly.

"Here, look," I say. "It changes the results from what should be significant findings, to insignificant. When I compare Maven Camu's earlier notes, you can see that she's the model of meticulousness. She would have had these calculations quadruple-checked. Either she lost her obsessively perfect personality in these later studies, or something else impacted the figures. And this isn't the only example."

Ringol pages through a few of the later studies over his projection. I watch his eyes shift as they travel across tables and numbers. His eyes are a denser, darker color than most Subterraneans, his pupils almost blending with his irises.

"They're just slightly off here and there," he says. "Undetectable unless you're paying painfully close attention." He turns to me, and his pupils enlarge.

"Were you assigned to this particular study when you worked under Maven Camu?"

He shakes his head slowly.

I wait for more of an explanation, but he doesn't offer one. According to the information provided in my reading from earlier, he's only been in charge of GCE for two months. "But you knew her, right? You'd know that these later figures don't match her –"

"Don't breathe a word of this to anyone until I have a chance to review it." He rubs his temples as if his head aches. His face grows somber, from the evenness in his brow to the frown that spreads across his lips. "I look forward to working with you."

He puts out his hand to me and I open my palm in reply. In it, he drops the rock I thought was lost forever – swept into decontamination clean-up and disposed of with the wreckage. Jal's rock, the gift he gave me just before he died. It's red, not gray. How did Ringol get it?

"I can't believe it," I breathe. My skin prickles with goosebumps, and I meet his gaze. "Thank you. For everything." Tears sting my eyes, because Jalaz should be here. Not me. I blink hard – I'm not used to crying while other people can see. Being seen comes with drawbacks.

He reaches out and wipes a tear from my cheek, and then pulls away like he's done something he didn't mean to do.

"You will need to be ready in two hours," he says, retreating to the door. "That should be plenty of time to eat and change. I'll send Miss Kriz to help you prepare."

"Prepare?"

He flashes me a look like I'm joking. "Have you forgotten? Even with your photographic memory?"

"*Perfect* memory," I clarify. "There's a difference. And no, I have not forgotten about the initiation videos." Or what should be called the formal hazing with questions. My shoulders tighten, but not because I'm afraid of what they might ask. I'm simply not looking forward to pretending I'm *Allele Crypt,* who always wanted to land an undertech position.

He looks into my eyes, and again, his entire body freezes. The odd way he's gawking at me is the way people normally do the first time we meet. At least, it was when I wore the goggles. But now he stares at me as if he never met me at Cayan, or came to fetch me at Woynauld's. Maybe I've become a different person to him – perhaps a *magnificent* one.

I hate to admit there's a growing part of me that wants more of his attention, something I didn't have until now – it's not a sense of belonging, because I don't think I belong here. It's more of a sense of purpose, or importance. Am I important to him beyond scientific labwork, as his look suggests? Would he ever be able to see me as more than a "human form"?

He shifts, coming out of his daze. "You've nothing to worry about. There's a formal reception before the peer examination. Your co-workers look forward to blowing off some steam under the circumstances. It is good for morale. It reminds us there's more to life than work – and that is of course *why* we work."

"Reception?" My stomach churns. Jalaz had been excited about initiation, and ongoing testing was the biggest reason he had me help him study. He never mentioned a reception.

"You give a short speech as a general introduction."

Ah, the speech. The one Jalaz wrote emphasized his lifelong ambition to come to GCE.

"Then," Ringol continues, "you spend some time in the room meeting our undertechs one-to-one." He smirks as I stiffen. "They size you up, and vice versa."

I never wanted this. What do I say when people ask me personal questions, like "at what point in your life did you know genetics was your calling?" Admitting "I only considered it last Tuesday" won't go over well. Ringol mentioned there's a waiting list of applicants for GCE. Besides, all the women in my room already hate me. "Mingling isn't my strong suit. Could we skip right to the peer examination?"

He looks down at his feet, puts his hands in his pockets, and then raises his eyes to me. "I am determined for you to succeed at GCE, which means you will need to gain the respect and confidence of your peers. Therefore, you will not only have to attend your own reception, you will also have to mingle and charm your coworkers. Like you have me."

Heat rises to my cheeks again, and Ringol smiles. But this can't possibly work. I'll stumble on every conversation, and I hate fibbing. I wanted to teach children like my determined C, or the poor girl I left at Woynauld's who just needed a small hint to conquer math. I'd give up my position as an undertech in a heartbeat to live that dream.

"Undertech!" His voice is loud, and I jump.

It's as if he knew I was silently arguing with him and he won't stand for it. "I'll do my best, Maven Ringol."

He nods and leaves.

After a few minutes, the tightness in my legs eases. I flop into his chair and stare at my food, and I can't help but think: the last thing *Zuzan-the-Fawn* enjoyed before the *GCE Lion* attacked was her final meal.

CHAPTER 12

Wholly Improper

"You've not eaten?" Kriz's voice echoes as she enters the room some thirty minutes after Ringol left. "Are you well?"

My food has grown cold, and the wonderful bread has hardened. "I'd be better if tonight's reception is canceled."

She blinks. "You're worried about the reception, not the examination?"

"The maven wants me to mingle so my peers can size me up. Sometimes I think he just likes to see me squirm."

Kriz folds her arms. "He prepared for your arrival like no other. He recruited you from Cayan and was detained longer than he intended, fetched you from the military academy, assigned you to the chamberroom with our best staff members to help get you up to speed, and then paid for an optotech so you could hit the ground running. And he's commanded me, his head maid, to ensure your evening runs flawlessly. No, our good maven hasn't the slightest intention to 'see you squirm.'"

I consider her words and nod. "But those women already mocked me," I say meekly, touching the nape of my neck where my fingertips are tickled by stubble. The burning from the tattoo on my chest flares up as I swallow. My goggles might be gone, but in so many other ways, I'm still Ratgirl. "I'm so different from them." It's the truest thing I've said to Kriz, and it may be the most embarrassing moment of the day.

When my eyes return to Kriz, she stands with her arms

crossed. "I beg your permission so that I might voice my observations, Undertech Allele."

Zuzan. My name should be Zuzan. "Of course."

"Whenever we have a new staff member come to GCE, they believe deep down that they are different. In some slight ways, it's true. They study hard to get here, and when they succeed in coming to GCE, they pound their figurative chests, desperately trying to prove themselves."

Jalaz fit that mold, that perfect GCE academic, and he wanted to be here more than anything, which makes it worse because I'm here, and I don't cherish it like he would have.

She points to my tray to get me to keep eating. "The problem is, they aren't different. They've all studied the same texts and research, they've all taken the same preemployment boards and practice exams, and when they get here, they're swept into GCE's divisive, competitive culture."

"Competitiveness?" Ringol kind of said the same thing, but more to advise me of what to expect. But Kriz isn't trying to advise me about it – she says it with disdain.

"Aye. But that's where your differences will serve you well, because you're *not* the same. You can see past what most new hires cannot." She pulls out a palm-sized tablet, taps it, and returns it to her pocket. "Now we must hurry. What theme have you decided upon?"

A small wave of panic shoots through me – the theme of my speech. I shrug.

Her eyes widen, but she recovers. "You can practice your speech with me. We'll figure out your theme."

"I need more time, Miss Kriz. Please talk to Maven Ringol."

"Calm yourself, Undertech." She chuckles. "New hires normally go on and on about their undying passion for genetics, boring the rot out of their co-workers. You won't have that problem."

My chip beeps and begins to flash words in the air: *Maddelyn Cayan, Central Psychiatric Institute*. My heart quickens.

Kriz's eyes harden. "Receiving camcalls is a privilege you have to earn."

"But it's my best friend!" I say in desperation as I swipe at the blinking words. The projection illuminates. A small version of Maddelyn floats just above eye level. I swipe again to make her life-size.

"Zuzan? Is that you?" she asks. Her eyes drift between happiness and nervousness. "Where are you?"

"Why can't you see me?" I glance at the projected words, searching for anything that I might need to switch on. What am I missing?

Kriz taps the word *cam* projected to the side. "Make it quick, then."

"Can you see me, Maddelyn?"

She nods, a tear spilling over her cheek. "I – I've missed you. And your eyes! Oh, Zuzu, you're beautiful. I always knew you were, under those gargantuan goggles."

"I go by *Allele* now." After my new roommates revived my *Ratgirl* insecurities, just seeing Maddelyn again is a reminder: I'm more than what they see. She taught me that. At her nursery, her na'rm used to sing to her and fix her hair in different ways, while miles away, mine made fun of my thin locks that wouldn't grow and called me wicked. I believed my na'rm until Maddelyn told me the only wicked person in my nursery was her. She helped free me from believing that evilness was an inescapable part of my genetics.

"Are you well?" I ask.

"I'm better. Except, I can't forgive myself. And you shouldn't either. I can't stop thinking about those awful days." Her fingers sweep through her spiky hair, shaved at the same time as mine. "Jal–" Her voice catches in her throat.

"Stop." Even just the mention of his name, the image of him struggling for air haunts me. "You were poisoned, you weren't yourself." She's no more evil than Na'rm Anetta claimed I was. "For now, I just want to talk with my oldest friend."

"I don't deserve it, but thank you." Hollowness surrounds her eyes, giving her a washed, worn-out appearance. A thump sounds in the background and Maddelyn jumps. "I can't say it's pleasant here." She leans in. "Some of the residents are jetting insane." Her mouth twists into an unsure smile.

We both giggle as if we're back at Cayan, walking halls we felt like we owned.

"Has your vision been fixed, then? Those specialty surgeons can do wonders." She squints as if to see me better. She wears a baggy jumpsuit with a rolled towel tied around her waist. "Oh, they're green," she says. "Truly elegant, and such a wonderful tribute."

"They've made protective lenses – like goggles but better – so I can read on any device."

"There's no stopping you now, then," she smiles. "But, what is it? You're holding something back."

"It's silly." At least, it seems so now, especially compared to Maddelyn's situation. And anyway, here is the kindest friend I'll ever have. Who cares if I can't befriend the other undertechs at the reception? "Tonight's my initiation and I have to give a speech and go through a public examination with my peers, and – hold onto your rocks – *mingle*."

"Oh, no. No." She covers her mouth. The edges of her stubbled hair have been molded around the face as if it's a purposeful, new hairstyle.

"The maven warned me about my colleagues here at GCE." I tell her about the lion hologram.

She shakes her head in disbelief. "Cruel man. Scientists are as mad a lot as my own."

"At least I was able to see you. When will they release you?"

She shrugs, only half listening. "What, precisely, do you plan to say in your speech?"

I glance at Kriz, who sweeps her hand for me to hurry.

"I'm ironing that out."

Her eyes widen. "Perfect. I have thoughts." Her eyes twinkle and her lips part into a smile. "Anyone at GCE who heretofore regarded you as a fawn will have trouble ever misjudging you as such again. Hear me now."

I smile, not because she wants to help, but because she's back. My Maddelyn.

She tells me her ideas, and we quickly come up with a plan. My spirits are boosted which I sorely needed, but the euphoria fades after the camcall ends, as Kriz walks me to the auditorium.

"Do my bandages show?" I smooth out the neckline to my blouse under my jacket.

"You look fine," Kriz says. "Try to have fun, if you know how."

We stop before the doors and I shiver. "I've had fun before, gobs of times. We played cards every Thursday at my burrow," a game called Crazy Mavens, but that's not important, "and we did theater group on Saturdays."

She nods dismissively. "Remember to look everyone in the eye."

"Thank you." I silently add Maddelyn's advice to the end of hers: *especially into your maven's eyes.*

She pulls out her mini-tablet, taps several times, and then speaks into it. "She is ready."

"It's about time," replies Maven Ringol in an irritable tone over her device. "And her theme?"

"Courage."

Ringol stays silent for a moment. "Very well."

Kriz flashes me a tight smile. "Someone will be out to fetch you." She hastens down the corridor, leaving me at the double doors. I'm tempted to run away. Instead, I squeeze Jal's stone in my fingers.

A million doubts race through my head so fast I'm surprised my skull doesn't spin off my body. I'm *not* Allele, I've never wanted to be an undertech, and science-y babble makes my eyes cross. My chest heaves up and down, and I don't know why I let Maddelyn talk me into such a provocative speech.

"Undertech Allele?" It's a voice I recognize from the plane ride.

I twist around. "Undertech Griffith."

He flashes that sweet, friendly smile. "I didn't recognize you without your – face thing."

"Do you think you can forget you saw me just now?"

His eyes pop. "I don't think that's possible."

I grab his arm, my fingers pressing into his skin. "Or better yet, help me escape?"

He stares at me as if I'd just landed from outer space, speaking some alien language. If only I had a space ship to call and rescue me. "This is a mistake."

"You are a funny one. So skittish." His easy smile twists ever so slightly.

Behind the doors, our maven speaks in muffled words, inaudible except for the tone of his voice. When the crowd begins to clap, I startle.

Griffith juts out his elbow like a gentleman. "May I escort you?"

Although I string my arm into his, my stomach kinks and my hands sweat. I go through Maddelyn's litany of rules: *Don't trip on the way to the stage. No stuttering. Speak clearly.*

The double doors open, and we thrust forward like a hoverjet. Hundreds of eyes set upon us. Upon me. The sea of people parts, spreading a path directly from us to the podium, leaving me dizzy in the middle of all the bright colors of the universe.

My boot snags on the floor, but I baby-step a few strides to recover.

"Kindly welcome our new recruit, Undertech Allele Crypt, to initiation for our elite GCE staff," says Maven Ringol from the podium. His dark, sleek suit shines in the lighting, reminding me of no other person I can remember. "Her theme for this evening is–" He glances in my direction and back at his staff members in the audience. His jaw flexes, and then he opens his mouth like he's about to speak, but only manages a hoarse mumble when his head snaps again to me.

Courage, Maven.

Wink at him, Maddelyn said. *He'll try to wear you down, and you must preempt him.*

Wholly improper, Kriz countered. *He is her maven.*

He'll never expect it, Maddelyn replied. *It's edgy, and she needs to gain the edge here.*

Instead, I smile weakly. Everyone here has survived initiation. I squeeze Griffith's arm for support as we climb three steps to the podium, stopping beside our maven.

Make eye contact with five different people in the crowd, Maddelyn had advised.

Maven Ringol stands silently. I wish he would move, change the frozen expression on his face. My cheeks warm under his gaze, though I haven't broken eye contact with him. My insides melt, with his dark eyes and confidence. If men could be described as magnificent or exotic, my maven would be on that list. For so many reasons I can't look away from him, this person who's given me another chance at hope, and I can almost hear Kriz's thoughts from wherever she's hiding.

Wholly improper.

CHAPTER 13

No Artificial Mind Boosts

Griffith waves to catch Ringol's attention. The maven's eyes shift to Griffith and then to the room full of people, all waiting quietly until he speaks again.

I can't glance into the audience without trembling.

The eye contact is important, Kriz had finally agreed with Maddelyn. *It signifies you see yourself as an equal. You will gain instant respect.*

The problem is, I'm not as passionate about genomics as the *least* passionate person in this room. I'm a ghost girl hidden by goggles that are no longer there. I'm Zuzan Cayan, which is a name that never really was. Aspiring medera, a dream that will never come to pass. I'm stripped of everything I ever was, except for numerous lies which piece together a new me.

A person who isn't *me.* Everything that Medera Gelia taught me about becoming the person I want to be has been erased in a matter of days.

The maven shifts and clears his throat. He turns to the audience and smiles. "Our newest undertech will explain her theme in her own eloquence." He holds out his arm as if to invite me to the podium. The maven moves aside, and he and Griffith leave the platform to join the crowd.

I am an imposter, wearing a uniform as counterfeit as my prepared speech, as phony as my practiced smile. The crowd's murmurs die down.

"Good evening." My voice flattens and catches in my throat. I have yet to look anyone in the eye. The words branded across my chest should read *I am but a phony*. I steal glances into the sea of faces before me. Nukleo whispers something behind her hand to a man with deep-set eyes and a long jawbone, and they both giggle.

Wave to Nukleo, the alpha woman, Maddelyn advised. *Everyone will assume she's already approved of you. It's key.*

But I can't. The whirs of mumbling overtake the room.

I am but a phony.

With my thumb, I roll Jal's rock up and down my fingers. He was a fine example of someone who was never fake – he was as pure and tangible as this rock. The sweat from my palm slickens the surface, and the stone slips from my fingers and rolls to the edge of the stage. The painted flower on the rock whirrs around, slows, and steadies. I hold my breath as I rush over to rescue it, as if I had to rescue Jal himself, from falling over a ledge. But I never rescued him. He saved me, and now he's gone. When I try to stand up again, the room spins.

I steady myself by grabbing the edge of the podium. Whispers fly as I return to hide behind it. *Breathe, Zuzan.*

"Good evening," I say again, louder, quieting the noise from the crowd. Maven Ringol rolls his finger as if to hurry me along. "My theme for tonight is –" I catch sight of Kriz in the back of the room. She waves and nods. "– Courage."

I am but a phony.

Several people in the room chuckle.

I clear my throat and look down at my uniform, clearly different from everyone else. My chest rises and falls.

Ringol smiles and takes a deep breath, prompting me to do the same. As I exhale, the speech Maddelyn and I had prepared fades away. How can I talk about courage, for all good? There has to be something else I can stand for, something true to myself – the real me. I glance down at Jal's rock.

May good health find you always. The red he used to paint the rock is beautiful.

"At the heart of courage lies truth." The truth is, I need things to happen on my own terms.

Kriz covers her mouth, and I'm not sure I can do this. She realizes I've veered from what we'd practiced, but I can either come clean or become someone I'm not.

"I knew courage by the name of Jalaz Cayan," I continue, holding up Jal's rock although no one knows its significance, "a young GCE recruit who would have graced this podium if he were still alive." The undertechs shush one another. "Jalaz stood up to protect me, with no thought of his own peril. In a way, it's only right that I dedicate myself to carry out the work he loved – I owe him that and more.

"He dreamed larger than I ever could, and his absence from GCE is a tragedy for all who knew him, and for all of you who will never meet him." My eyes flash to Ringol. Maybe I'm not as worthy of this position as the people in this room who worked their entire lives to get here, but maybe working on Jal's behalf makes me worthy. "I am not like Jalaz, or any of you brilliant scientists who stand before me today. I wanted to pursue another calling, but now I'm committed to work in Jal's honor, and because of that, I refuse to fail."

The entire room falls silent. Ringol's jaw sets tightly forward. Kriz wipes a tear. Even Nukleo stands perfectly still, like a fawn with her ears cocked, trying to detect danger.

My fingers tremble as I close them around Jal's rock.

"I can only hope to be as courageous as he was."

I step back.

The room rings with silence. I am done. Maybe Maddelyn's speech would have been more strategic and intimidating, but at least I told my truth – as much as I could.

And then, slowly, my colleagues begin to clap. Someone from the back whistles. Griffith rushes up to the stage, takes my hand, pulls me down the stairs, and through the middle aisle. He introduces me to some undertechs, and I shake hands. Make eye contact. Smile. I have to keep wiping the sweat from my hands on my skirt, and I can't think of anything to say to all these new acquaintances, except "nice to meet you," or "I look forward to working with you, too."

It's stiff, and forced, and I'm sure they sense I don't belong here. I catch Nukleo's French braids from the corner of my eye (something new for me), and she's having an animated discussion with Ringol. I strain to lip-read anything I can, trying to figure out if it's about me, but I give up after a minute.

I lean into Griffith and he leans closer to me.

"How am I doing?" I ask.

He smiles, but then he's jerked away as someone cuts between us. Nukleo.

Griffith stands at attention. "Good health, J'Mave Nukleo."

J'Mave? As in *junior maven*?

"Undertech Griffith." She puts on what looks to be a forced smile, and Griffith doesn't move a muscle. "Seems you're always tucking our new recruits under your skinny wings. But this one? She's admitted to taking this job not because she's got a passion for genomics, but because her buddy died. The *truth* – if I have the *courage* to say it – is that she's beyond *hope*." She stresses the words in a mocking way, to make sure I realize she's poking fun at my speech. "Wait – do you smell that?"

Griffith shakes his head.

"It's fear." She leans in to me and sniffs. "Examination time nears."

Every muscle in my body tenses, but I meet her steely gray eyes dead-on. "I'm not afraid."

"Undertech Allele!" She barks, and I flinch. "You will address me with respect and stand at attention."

"Yes," I answer simply. "Of course." I straighten my body, thinking about Allund. He demanded to be treated this way too – which is partly why I held so little respect for him. "I am not afraid, J'Mave Nukleo."

She sneers at my response. "You may have duped this entire organization with your weepy words, but you've not fooled me. Practice tests are child's play compared to the peer initiation exam." She pulls out her tablet and taps it a few times. "Kissing up to more of our undertechs won't help you now. If you're as ready as you say you are, then I'm dying to test you."

She spins away.

"*She's* testing me?" I ask.

Griffith lets out a sigh. "The highest-ranked person tests new staff members on behalf of all undertechs, probably because the highest ranked person has the most to lose in ranking."

We watch her stomp away. "I'm not afraid of her."

"You should be," Griffith warns. "I'm not testing today, and I'm afraid."

As Griffith scrambles off to find his seat, I search for Ringol. What did Griffith mean by she has the most to lose? Jal never mentioned anything like this, and neither did Ringol. I hate that there's so much I don't know. The lights flash three times and everyone in the room returns to their chair while tapping the projector chip at their temples.

In the airspace just over the stage, words and figures project from a lightbeam originating at the center of the ceiling. My personal data, one item at a time, flashes. Each piece of information blinks several times before the next one appears.

NAME: UNDERTECH ALLELE CRYPT, it flashes. Silently, I argue: *my name is Zuzan Cayan, and I'm a medera deep in my heart.*

AGE: 20.002 YEARS, it flashes. I turn to Ringol and he shakes his head – I'm only 19.833 years, but that's not an employable age for the GCE. He must have altered it to cut through red tape when my identification number was changed. Of course, if he hadn't, I'd still be a ba'rm buried in Allund's burrow.

HEIGHT: 54.5 INCHES, the lightbeam flashes more and more information, supposedly about me. These scientists have really bizarre practices. It goes on to my BMI, my pre-test scores –

ninety-nine percent? *Never.* I have to blink a few times before my LE statistic registers.

LE: 18.7 YEARS

Pah. That's utter nonsense. I have less than five years on my life expectancy. I'd give anything to have that much time, nearly two decades. Inserting incorrect data onto my record can't be legal. Although giving me a new ID isn't legal, either.

"Undertech Allele," Ringol calls. I twirl around as his jaw flexes.

"Did you see–?" I point.

"That's the least of your worries. Nukleo already has you on her radar, and that's not a good thing."

"I swear I've done nothing." The statistics continue to pop up. How much is there to know about me?

Eye Color: Green

They're pink.

"She sees you as a threat." He takes my elbow and guides me to the stage.

"I never intended to work at GCE, so I'm probably the least threatening person here."

He chuckles. "The ranking system doesn't care if you never intended to come here. You're here now."

I roll my eyes, only a split second after I realize he can now see my eye-rolling.

"Undertech," he says through his teeth. "Hear me this one time. Maybe you think I'm too uncredentialed for this job, or I'm too abrasive. You don't have to like me, but you should trust that I have your welfare in mind. Heed my advice: do not appear cocky. Don't answer immediately, as if you find the questions too simple – you will gain more enemies than you'd like. And never answer the question before it's fully asked."

I only half-hear him. Does he really think I don't like him? Maybe not at first, but now? After all he did to come back for me.

His staff members all begin to quiet down, and they

start to gawk at us. I've been disrespectful, and of all the people I need to respect, my supervisor should be at the top. "Maven–"

"And –" His gaze slides around the room as if he's worried he'll be overheard. " – you must give some incorrect responses."

"I – what?"

"One or two. I know it goes against your nature, but this is critical. You'll rank high enough in due time." His gaze slides around the room again. This is a huge leap from where he was earlier today, when he didn't believe I had studied the texts sufficiently enough. "It's best not to skip to the front of the line right away."

"Ranking ahead of everyone in this room?" Now it's my turn to peek out at the crowded auditorium, and my gaze slides over to Nukleo. I couldn't possibly–

"No new inductee has ever gotten all the questions right. The jealousy here is as dense as granite, and we don't have weeks to waste on backlash. A simple 'I don't know' will suffice."

We start moving towards the stage. "I would hope to gain more credibility among my peers by doing my best." His plan feels too manipulative. Calculated. Which is just another way of lying.

He grabs my elbow a bit too roughly as we make it to the stairs. "What you possess in superintelligence you lack in common wisdom. We can't afford extra attention – trust me."

What does he mean by *that*? I bite the side of my cheek and glance at the podium where Nukleo flips through something on a tablet, probably picking out the hardest questions for me.

"Mind me, Undertech." Ringol growls.

As he pushes me up the stairs, he remains on the lower floor. Somehow, my feet continue onward and I make it to the chair that's situated directly under my faulty stats. As the audience taps on projected images in the air in front of each of them, I sit and wait.

Nukleo stands a few feet to my right. Her beaming smile

controls the scientists in the room, hushing them into a long silence before she speaks.

"I'd like to extend a warm welcome to Undertech Allele Crypt." She drawls out the name "Crypt," like there's something wrong with it. Her neck cranes so she can glance at me with her toothy grin. Her eyes, however, are set in a cold glare, as if *I'm* the one who's insulted *her*.

I force my mouth into a smile and bow my head graciously. Kriz explained that the test consists of thirty questions, that they start basic and then progress from there. The more a person answers correctly, the deeper they skip into genomics subject matter. Everyone here has already gone through this, and each one of them probably worried about getting the right answer. That's what I should be worried about – instead, I'm stressing over when to say, "I don't know."

"First examination question," Nukleo says, reading from her tablet. "Compared to Subterranean newborns, Omniterranean newborns' physical characteristics include better pigmentation, thick hair, smaller head circumference, and larger size. Other than physical traits, name two indications of the Omniterranean phenotype for newborns."

The question flashes above my head in a holographic projection for the audience, although I can't read it well from underneath. With the silence in the room, I could almost believe she and I were alone. Kriz stands behind the back row, and nods at me.

I pause for a moment, but not because I'm struggling to answer. I'm trying to do what my maven instructed – not appear to be too eager. The earliest questions are the easiest, so it'll just get more technical from here on out. "Omnit infants have the original grasp reflex when an object touches their palm." I push my index finger into my opposite palm and then grab it. "While Subter infants typically don't. They tend to open their fingers or flinch away." I demonstrate again. "The other way is to pull bloodlabs. Of course, labs that indicate genetic trait differences would be an accurate test, but even routine bloodlabs show basic biological efficiency where Omnit infants fare much better. Omniterraneans have healthier reference ranges."

The room shuffles about. As far as I can tell, everyone in the audience except for Kriz taps an entry on their projections.

"Correct," Nukleo says. "Question two." Before she asks it, a number appears above my head, rotating in a three-meter diameter so that each person, no matter his or her angle, gets a straight-on view: *71% endorsement.*

What in all good does that mean? I search the room for Ringol, and he grins like I'm doing fine – like it's okay that twenty-nine percent of my peers already don't endorse me. The examination continues on like this with the questions becoming increasingly challenging – where I have to calculate things or go above and beyond memorization of facts to answer, and I'm careful not to respond too quickly. The endorsement figure that circles around my head changes wildly after each question when my colleagues tap on their chip projections.

As I progress, an odd correlation emerges proving Ringol's point. The faster I respond, the lower the rating. I would have hoped for the opposite: that the more competently I answer, the more respect I would gain because I'd bring that knowledge to active genomic projects. As I near the end of my examination, I've dropped to fifty-nine percent endorsement even though I haven't missed any questions. My heart beats like a tight drumroll, and I can barely look out into the crowd.

"Question twenty-eight," Nukleo chimes in her high-pitched voice. "What is the overall Life Expectancy for the average Subterranean over the past ten years? Give your answer for each year."

She stops talking, and I wait. That can't be the end of the question. Does she want it split between males and females? Does she want the December figure for each year or the average LE for all months put together? My newly improved eyes find Maven Ringol, who's now moved to my left, standing at the bottom of the stairs.

He *knew* this question was ambiguous. If I answer it one way, then she could say the correct answer should have been given the other way. To what decimal point should I report the life expectancy? Should I give the figure in total expectancy months? Years? A combination?

I try to check the question projected above me to see if she skipped this information, but I can't view it from my angle.

"Undertech Allele, do you have a response?" asks Nukleo, a wry smile twisting over her lips.

Sweat tickles my skin above my lip. "Would you please repeat the question?" My eyes shoot to Kriz – her hands are clasped together under her chin – and then over to Ringol. He rolls his hand to hurry me. A simple "I don't know" was what he wanted.

"I will not repeat the question," Nukleo says.

The men and women before me tap on their minitabs, and my approval ratings get messy.

65%

51%

70%

It seems my colleagues can't make up their minds about me.

Nukleo smiles before me, and this time, her eyes curve with genuine pleasure. She's made up her mind about me, if no one else has. She hopes I miss this question as much as Ringol, but for completely different reasons. "Undertech Allele, do you have an answer, or don't you?"

What score did she receive on the induction exam? Ringol mentioned that no one, ever, answered everything correctly. Did she get one wrong? Two? He must not want me to do better than *her*. I've never answered a question incorrectly, and the thought of pretending I don't know something goes against every instinct imbedded in my spine. But the possibility of not knowing an answer – *that* petrifies me.

Maybe that's part of the test – how well I perform under this type of ambiguity and pressure.

Fine, then. I will not fail.

Average life expectancies – the question must have come from the same textbooks I'd reviewed earlier. My mind races through the information, recreating the words verbatim. An image of one chart from the second text assembles and I no longer see the room, just the bolded row at the top of the table with the breakdown of data, the double-underlines, the sans-serif font, the months listed down the left side. The only problem – the year-to-date averages had not been calculated. So, I need to do the math in my head. I *have* to try to get this one right. What if the next two questions are worse?

My fingers wriggle just a bit with each year's figures as I triple-check my computations.

"Ten years ago, the cumulative average life expectancy was 45.439 years for Subterraneans, both genders combined." Someone in the audience chuckles, and then coughs to cover it up. Griffith. As I respond for each year one by one aloud, I silently note the sharp drop in life expectancy – about a half year of life for each progressive year of time. My eyes remain on my fingers, my mind on the calculations, and I finish the final string of math. "And this past year's Subterranean life expectancy was 39.981 years."

I lean into the back of my white resin chair, clearly not made for comfort. I'm sure Nukleo picked it just for me.

She raises her brows. Her head nods with exaggerated hesitation, as if she'd prefer not to confirm. But it's official: twenty-eight done, two to go. I peek at the rating above me.

Seventy-seven percent. My eyes flash to Ringol, who bows his head. There's a twinkle in his expression, like he's entertained.

"Question twenty-nine," Nukleo says. "What would happen if we attempted to solve the biological weaknesses of our race using cloning technology with the DNA from pre-plague humans?"

Nukleo turns to me, her lips pulling into a tight line. *Cloning?* Something Jalaz said to me about my non-Omnit traits, that he'd found on my genome, presses to the front of my mind. Manipulations. Edited codes. Questions.

"Undertech?" Nukleo looks out into the crowd like she expects someone to laugh at me with her. "Any thoughts?"

"The virus that initially caused Sterling's Plague has mutated," I begin to say. But then I wonder if this response it too simple. "Although scientists have developed inoculations, they were developed on post-plague humans – on Subters and Omnits, after our DNA structures were altered. If we clone humans using the former DNA structure, but then intend to protect this cloned group from the virus using a post-plague vaccine tested on Omnits and Subters with different DNA structures, the inoculation might not be effective. We'd have a cloned group of people suffering the same eighty-nine-point-six-percent death rate as the group of people alive when the everything initially hit."

People begin to make entries, and my eyes flash over to Nukleo.

"Does that complete your answer?" she asks, almost too calmly.

I wipe my hands on my thighs. Why would she ask that?

"No, ma'am," I reply pointedly, trying to maintain the same blanket of calmness in my tone as Nukleo had. "There's – more." Only, I'm not sure what. Chapter titles and the opening thesis of each text I read today shoot through my thoughts. My knee begins to bob up and down again, and the inside of my cheek is raw from biting. There's got to be something.

My endorsement rating edges upward – now at 79%.

I mentally page through all the sections again. Maybe it's something simpler. I close my eyes and picture the indexes with all the charts. But then Jal's assertion about my genome breaks through all my thoughts. Whatever manipulation happened on my genome – if it happened – was probably illegally done.

That's what I'm missing: the law part, not the science. "Cloning isn't allowed as a viable solution in general because it doesn't help advance a species. Bylaw eighteen-point-sixty-two clearly states that unless the technique used allows for the most natural evolutionary processes to occur, it should be avoided at all cost. Cloning simply duplicates a version of genes that already exist. Common Law has ruled it unsustainable."

Nukleo's eyes turn to fire. She jerks her chin in a terse nod.

The room taps at their minitabs. In a matter of seconds, my approval rating has dropped by ten percent. *Jet*. Ringol predicted this.

"Your final question," Nukleo says, "is as follows."

My shoulders squeeze toward my spine. This is it – the last chance to obey my maven and respond wrong, after I declared in front of everyone that I wouldn't fail.

For the first time in my life, I hope I don't know the answer.

"Question thirty: What was Salas Sterling's position on the use of his genetic manipulations during the first successful use of bioengineered viruses for mass devastation?" Her fiery eyes slide over to Ringol. She's fuming.

What an absurd way of ending the test. Of course Salas had been against it. Jal idolized Salas Sterling for his breadth of skill, his edgy innovation, and his idealism. Jal wanted to impact the world as greatly as Salas did. Jal never would have been so passionate about a man who'd caused the very dilemma we're trying to solve.

I open my mouth to answer and then clamp it shut again. *No*. I twist around in my chair and review the stats blinking above my head. My eye color *is* green now. No one will see them as any different, not in the light, so they are technically green. My name *is* Allele for all official purposes, since my Cayan name was never made permanent – Medera said so herself.

Why was my pretest score reported at ninety-nine percent? When I answered this same question with the text-to-audio mode on the tablet at Cayan, the response I gave would have been correct according to all publicly available documentation.

But is the publicly available story correct about Salas? Was Salas actually at fault? *Jetty rotting jet!* Jalaz even named himself after Salas. I stare at the rock in my hand, wondering if Jal's faith had been misplaced.

Ringol shifts. He's more tense now, standing straighter. He'd told me I answered all of the questions correctly that day. In theory, if that was what everyone is taught, then I suppose I was right in a way – as much as I could have been wrong. Maven Salas isn't what Jal thought he was.

"Undertech Allele, your response?" My j'mave's face wrinkles into angry lines, as if I've disobeyed her by hesitating.

I shake my head and it feels as if the floor rumbles underneath us. Maybe I'm dizzy.

This cover-up for Sterling makes little sense. And yet, even these scientists don't seem to know. Ringol does – that's for certain. If I reveal the truth, no one will know I'm right. They'll think I'm crazy. *Crazygirl* might be a step up from *Ratgirl* but it's not a term I prefer. But if I go along with the historical lie, I'll be perpetuating the ruse. I'll be lying too. I hate lies.

Facts don't change, though, just because everyone believes a different story. This room of scientists might think I'm wrong, but I can't go along with common belief when I there's evidence to the contrary. "My answer–"

My words are muffled by another rumbling, this time, more intense. The stage shakes and Nukleo grabs both sides of her podium. An alarm sounds, howling like a thousand banshees.

Ringol takes several long strides and leaps onto the platform. He takes hold of the podium. "Everyone to your oxygen chambers, immediately! We're on emergency lockdown."

A burning panic spins my stomach into knots. I glance at the walls, hoping I won't see the spectral faces of dead children. I don't. I can see colors and shadows but nothing morphs into a ghost like it had before. My sight is too sharp for my eyes to play those games.

Kriz hurries to the stairs, but I'm having trouble letting go of my chair.

"Make haste," Ringol says in my ear, his hand hooked over my elbow. My chills settle against his warm touch. He shoos Kriz away, and she backs off. "Follow me. I've reviewed the discrepancies you uncovered on Camu's project notes, and I need you to see something now, in case we end up evacuating."

He takes me through a hidden door behind a panel at the rear of the stage. It leads to a series of dingy corridors, rough compared to the smooth-walled hallways I'd taken to get to the reception, and I feel like these halls are rarely used. Hidden, perhaps. We eventually come out into a regular corridor closer to the transportation platform area. He heads straight for an unlabeled door, bioscans inside, and we're suddenly in a darkened hallway, lit only by an occasional reflective light.

"Where are we going?" I ask.

"I can explain better once we're there. Once you see what's there," he says, looking back at me every once in a while.

By the slant of the floor, I assume we're headed lower into the earth, like the undertunnels at Woynauld. At each corridor turn, flashing yellow lights blink in the center of the floor as a warning. Ringol's hand remains hooked under my elbow, his fingers gripping as if he risks losing me at any moment.

"Stop," I say after we make another sharp turn into the darkest corridor yet. For a second, I'm taken aback. My eyes normally adjust to dimmer lighting with relish – focusing more sharply on the lines and curves around me. Now, however, everything has faded. My eyes seek any hint of light to make out my surroundings. Maybe this is "normal" vision, but right now, I don't like it.

Questions fly through my head – the violent quakes, the altered data, my maybe-true-maybe-false stats, the ranking process, Salas Sterling's history, my approval ratings, the danger behind the alarm that still rings throughout the structure, Nukleo thinking I'm a threat, and Ringol's expressions when he looks at me. As these issues whir about like blood pulsing through veins, as the earth continues to tremble beneath us, only one question makes it to my lips.

"My life expectancy – the eighteen years listed on my stats – it's false, isn't it?"

My elbow brushes against the granite wall, and the wet condensation sends chills through me. The meandering corridor's damp smell reminds me of my small library at Cayan. I hug myself to stay warm, waiting for an answer.

Ringol rubs his head with both hands, checks something on his ChiPro, and then groans. "Someone leaked our location to the rebels. This area is not habitable at ground level, and no one knew we were here, but now they do. Unbelievable." He pulls me by my arm deeper into the cave-like halls. "We're being attacked by bunker bombs. *Why now?*"

Targeted bunker bombing at GCE can do a lot of damage, and if I were him, I'd want to get to the bottom of it too. But I can't seem to focus on that right now, because I've been directly hit by something else. "Please. What is my LE?" If I do have an additional eighteen years to live, and I can see with my new lenses, *that* would be life-changing.

He stops, one vein in his forehead bulging. "Let's focus on the emergency at hand: we're in grave danger. Or maybe you could tell me why you deliberately disobeyed my direction."

"To throw a couple of exam questions?" I yank out of his grasp.

He remains still, his eyes boring into me so deeply that I shiver.

Another rumbling in the earth causes dust particles to fall, crackling as they hit the hard floor. I struggle to remain standing.

Ringol catches me, and by the confused expression on his face, I can tell he's not thinking about my question. "Rebel use of anti-bunker bombs were supposed to be under control. What a load of lead."

A sizable particle of stone hits my shoulder and the sharp pain makes me cry out in surprise.

"Let's go." This time he grabs my wrist. "You've no idea what you've done, Undertech." He speaks over his shoulder. "You've usurped your colleagues by doing so well on the exam – Nukleo most notably. The plan was to get you here with as little notice as possible."

"I've done nothing wrong." I've simply answered each initiation question as the rules of this GCE process dictate. "Besides, I was never meant to end up here. You're not rational right now."

He whirls around until he's directly in front of me, both of us panting from our quick pace. "Never meant to be here? Hear me. It's my belief you are the one person who *is* meant to be here." He stops, like he wants to explain but can't. Instead, he takes off again with me in tow.

"Where are you taking me?" My muscles tighten until my hands clench, fingernails biting into my palms. When he doesn't respond, I ask him again. "Maven Ringol, what is my LE?"

He grunts, and stills before he finds his voice. "I need to ask you something."

"With all due respect, Maven Ringol, you haven't answered any of my questions yet."

"Zuzan, please." He rubs his temple.

He's used my real name, but instead of relaxing me this time it puts me on alert.

"From the first time I met you, you've been willing to give your life for other people. For your young burrowling – running to her aid even after an attack from Maddelyn. For Jal – offering to give up your only antidote injection. And to top off the list, you spared Maddelyn, whose shot you might have saved for yourself. Some might call you heroic."

I smile, because it's the nicest thing he's said to me.

"Others would say you're institutionally insane," he counters as my mouth drops. "So, my question is this: did you do these things because you valued your life so little? Did you think the people you saved deserved to live because of their more favorable LE?"

"No. I had to save them," I say trying to recall my thought process at the time. "My co-burrowlings and my medera – they are my heart," I echo Medera's words which have become a part of me. "The only thing I could think of was saving them. I wasn't sacrificing my limited time. I did it because–" Moisture tickles the inside corner of my eye, threatening to fall. His question is too personal, and he still hasn't answered mine. I could do so much with eighteen years: nearly two generations of burrowlings.

"Because why?"

Logically, with my minimal LE, of course they deserved the exchanged risk. But if I had a longer LE, would it have mattered to me? I breathe deeply and remember their faces – Jal, Maddelyn, Little C. No, my LE wouldn't have mattered, and it wouldn't have changed my actions. I would do it all again. "Because I love them."

He lets out a long-held sigh, and does the unthinkable. He wraps his arms around me in an embrace. "I have people I care deeply about, too. And everyone we love, Zuzan, they all need us." His words tumble in slow motion over my ears, but my brain slows as the warmth of his body seeps into my chilled bones.

"They need *us*? Do you mean your group of undertechs at GCE?"

He releases me and I instantly chill. "By 'us,' I mean *you*. With my help. At least, that's my hope. The important thing is that you're here, *finally*. I trust you–"

A thunderous clap sounds and the walls shake, cutting off his words.

"They're going to jetting crush us!" I say.

"Hurry!" He raises his voice and begins to drag me down the hall again. "These insurgents believe some very twisted facts, and they're afraid we're planning to kill all of them. I don't blame them for their uninformed fears, but this bombing doesn't help their cause."

After the mysterious questions about Salas Sterling, I'm not sure what to believe myself. But the bombing begins to quiet, and the only rumbling comes from my pounding heartbeat. This deep into the cave, the sirens are far enough away that my ears can adjust to the normal sounds around us. "Are we harming them?"

"Of course not, but it doesn't matter," he says without hesitation. "Lies and misperceptions prevail over truth in dark times. We need to solve all genetic deficiencies in future generations – physical and intellectual – and reunite our people. Subterraneans and Omniterranean are the same species, just with a few trait differences."

"*You* might believe we are the same," I say as my fingers glide over the ropey scar from my tattoo. Even through the material of my blouse, I can make out the raw bumps of each word. *I am but a dullard.* "But Medero Allund Woynauld strongly disagrees. As do others."

"*Allund.*" He slows down. "Of course. Blasted fool. *He* did this: he arranged for the targeted anti-bunkers. It's revenge."

It takes me a moment to catch up with what he's said. Allund Woynauld runs a military academy. "Allund would give away our coordinates?" The unrelenting alarm still screaming in the distance, reminds me of that dragon medero's temperament.

"I'd bet his teeth on it. He must have also misled Central Forces because they didn't even warn us." Ringol cocks his head and puts his forefinger over his lips to shush me.

The faint echo of footsteps taps in the distance.

Ringol starts taking off his boots and motions to mine, whispering, "Remove them."

I comply, shivering once the soles of my feet touch the frigid rock floor. But it's more than the cold. Ringol's secrecy unnerves me. "Why are you afraid of whomever is following us?"

He checks his ChiPro and shakes his head. "It's Nukleo. We're coming up on the classified area I want to show you. No one can know about it, not even her. Can you keep up?"

Before I can answer, we're off, running like deer chased by a lion. I clutch my boots to my chest as he cuts around corners. The floor turns to a rougher, unfinished rock. Fewer lights pepper the corridors as we progress.

"Here." He stops in the middle of nowhere and reaches for the wall. When he rubs his hand along the side, his entire arm disappears, like it's been sucked inside. "Here's the entryway. It's made to look like continuous limestone, but it's low-projection imaging." He takes my hand, and we both disappear into the side of the wall the way I used to believe my child-ghosts could at the burrow.

Once inside, we jog another ten meters as motion-sensor lights awaken on both sides of the floor. We stop at a light-colored steel door stenciled with smeared letters.

BIOAUTHORIZATION REQUIRED

The Q and I in *required* have messy streaks tailing underneath them, like the stenciling was hastily removed before the paint dried. Ringol places his thumb flat on a marble-like surface above the knob, much like those at the Woynauld burrow, which causes the door to buzz and click. A tiny light shines in the center of the oval.

The door slides upward, rolling into itself with a slight rattle, and lights flicker lazily until they illuminate the room at full strength. He presses a button closing the door, and he turns to me. "Welcome to Maven Camu's private study." The thick, metallic walls of the space mute the sound of the alarm still shrilling through the tunnels.

The room holds four desks, a steel bookshelf that stretches up to the ceiling complete with real, page-bound textbooks, a large silver cart filled with glass equipment of all shapes, and a couch – the same style as the one in Ringol's office. Which, I gather, had been Maven Camu's office before him and her choice in furniture. What work did she do here in this hidden office, then, that would be considered so top secret? Scores of handwritten notepads and unlabeled tabdrives litter the surface of the couch and each of the desks.

Above the main desk on the very back wall, an inscription had been painted in freehand on the steel.

"Destruction
is an easier, speedier process
than reconstruction."
-Albert Camus

Interesting that Camu had clearly named herself after a writer, rather than an admired maven. I stare at the lettering – a perfect cursive with even script. It's exactly what I would imagine her writing to be like. By destruction, perhaps she meant Sterling's plague and the split of human beings into segregated subgroups. And reconstruction – maybe this refers to her life's work?

"When did Maven Camu pass away?" My shoulders tighten as the last word escapes my mouth. Ringol spoke of unnamed people he loves. What if he adored Camu as much as I do Medera Gelia?

But he shrugs with no sign of inward pain. "She disappeared several months before I was stationed here, so I didn't get the chance to work with her directly. Nukleo held the interim maven title until I arrived."

"She's not dead, then?"

"Nobody seems to know," he says as he takes a seat behind the desk. The word *reconstruction* hovers just above his head. News clippings and other snippets have been tacked up onto the wall beneath the quote in what appears to be the chronological order of Sterling's Plague outbreak, with colored string showing connections to related notes.

"So many undertechs worked at GCE for years under Maven Camu, but Common Good placed you in the top maven position instead." I turn to him. "Isn't that odd?"

"Maybe a little." A bemused expression dances across his face, one that hints of secrets. "But you'd have to know the entire story, and I don't have the time or the permission to tell it. Would you like to get to work, or retire to your oxygen chamber like the others?"

"My chamber?" He's switching subjects so fast, and I wish he'd slow down.

"You are allowed – and in all honesty, advised by Common Good – to take shelter in your room during an attack such as this. You would remain relatively safe in your bedchamber, equipped with enough oxygen, water, and pelleted nutrients to last you for two weeks. Or you can help me figure out why Maven Camu's experiments fell apart. The answer has got to be here somewhere, and I need to know this before I decide upon the corrective course of action."

"No." I narrow my eyes. "I won't help you, not until you explain my LE discrepancy. And don't try to tell me it's classified information. Everyone knows his or her own LE."

He switches on a monitor built into the wall using his ChiPro. The screen shows the corridors we'd just traversed. "The LE on your published stats during your exam is as accurate as it gets for anyone, provided we live through this attack." He then picks up a notepad and starts to flip through it.

I scurry around the desk until I'm face to face with him. "Why wouldn't you tell me this? Why did I have to find out in a roomful of strangers? How could it change so drastically?"

"It was the shot, Undertech. I injected you after you were exposed to the peanut flour. It contained a largely unproven stem-cell therapy to correct immune system functioning."

"What?"

"For some people, it stabilizes the immune system through unprecedented stem cell activation, enhancing cell productivity, in turn increasing their LE. For others, it causes minor side effects with relatively no positive outcome. A small number of subjects have nearly died from it. You were a responder. Actually, one of the few."

"I see." I've never heard of this treatment. "So you gambled with my life?"

"Common Good hasn't released the injection for the general population yet. It's one of Nukleo's experimental tinkerings, and it's got to go through clinical trials first. Her team continues to tweak the bugs. It's an expensive concoction, wrought with minor legal roadblocks."

"Nukleo?" I let it sink in, trying to decide whether this eases my loathing for her.

Nope. But it might explain why she instantly hated me.

"And if you'd never shown up at Cayan, I'd still be at my lower LE?"

"Yes. But you'd likely have dropped more in your LE after the peanut powder exposure."

"Does Nukleo know you injected me with it?"

He nods slowly, and my mind instantly jumps to how poorly she treated me from the start. "She's not as bad as she's led you to believe."

She didn't agree to treat me, though. But why should she?

"Hear me. After that toxic exposure, the risk to your life in not giving you the treatment was higher than giving it to you. Your life, whether you believe it or not, is worth a lot to GCE. Having you here has paid off already. Look how you've cracked part of the issue – Camu's misrepresented data – and it only took you hours to discover. Just hours," he laughs as if he can't believe it. "And if you discover the pattern of issues in Camu's research, or at least determine where her figures were breached, we might correct them, which may lead to a better solution. Can't you see how big this is? Or how many people may be impacted?"

"Stop." He's full of ifs, mights, and mays. "To work together, you can't hold anything back. No lies, or stretched truths, or misperceptions. Not anymore. The truth is important to me, more than I can say."

After a moment, he nods. "All right. I will tell you anything that's *unclassified* information if you agree to help me." He waits for a moment. "Or I can escort you to your chamberroom."

"No." I owe Jal, and I'm willing to dedicate myself and work towards *his* goal, which happens to be similar to Camu's. And Ringol's, I think. "I want to help." He might have risked his career by giving me this shot, and I gained more years of life because of it. It seems I owe him, too.

The relief spreading across his face hits me like the brilliant stars he showed me in the sky. A strange sensation shoots through me, a burst of something, like taking a bite of Medera's frosted pastries on someone's Name Day.

Oh, I miss Medera.

"I have a few conditions," I hedge.

Ringol's smile melts. But maybe he expects complications from me by now.

"I need to speak with Medera Gelia. And C at Zamption, too."

"Zuzan–" he says, but I don't give him time to object.

"Maddelyn Cayan should transfer to GCE's infirmary for the remainder of her recovery. She's improving, and I won't have her mental health impeded by subpar institutional care."

"We don't know what Maddelyn's current state might be, Allele." I sense his impatience from his switching to my new name. But I am undeterred.

"I spoke with her today while I prepped for the initiation. Please hear me, Maven. She's been punished for events outside her control, and I can't allow anything else to happen to her." My skin warms, causing the scar across my chest to burn, and my voice cracks thinking of how awful it must be for my Maddy. "Lastly, my girl that I left at Woynauld's burrow – we need to transfer her out. Here, if necessary. She has suffered great abuse at the hands of that monster. You should have seen the scars on her arms."

"Impossible." His voice stiffens. "Do you think I can cater to your every demand? I am a chief maven, not a wizard. You didn't have my permission to make camcalls, and you're forbidden to contact anyone else without my authority."

"And," I say without hesitation. "That qualification you noted about sharing information with me – only telling me the things you can, based on confidenti–"

"No clearance, no knowledge-sharing. That's how the system works. If I divulge top-secret material, I face incarceration."

"Listen to me!" My voice echoes in a shrill mess. How could he not tell me about my years? After I help him, if I am in fact able to help, I will want to spend some of them as a medera. "I need to know anything that pertains to Camu's research, to me, and to my former burrow. Find a way to grant me access legally, based on my assigned work. I'm not asking to know anything more than that. But if there is something that I should know – anything important to me or my work – you have to tell me."

He huffs and stands up, moving to the other side of the desk to pace like a caged animal. "Important to you," he says when he reaches the wall, as if it could answer him, and then he twirls around to pace the other way. "We're under attack, for all that is decent and good."

I take the seat he's just abandoned behind Maven Camu's desk. I struggle to play calm, folding my hands across the messy desk and wait for him to stop pacing. I will not break. Heat begins to radiate from the floor, which must have a motion-sensor start, thawing my icy toes.

After a few minutes, the maven sighs.

"Here's what I can do, and I will promise you no more. I am trustworthy, whatever you might think of me, and I intend to keep to my word." His eyes grow soft. "When I ensure it's safe, you may contact your former Cayan members. I will inquire about Maddelyn's conditions, and if I find they are inadequate, I will see what can be done to alleviate them, but a transfer to GCE would be the last resort. I will freely share information with you if it is needed for the sake of deciphering Camu's research or, in my sole judgment, for your state of mind, *only* if I have not already been sworn to complete confidentiality. I intend to keep the integrity of my post intact."

I raise my eyebrows. He's snipped and trimmed my demands, but he's also conceded a few. I should be happy.

"Here is what I can't do: I will not be pressed into anything that will jeopardize our mission. You must have your former burrow members address you by your new name, understanding that it is for everyone's protection. If I deem even the most mundane conversation with a former Cayan member to have put you at risk, you are to cease contact. That brings me to the Woynauld girl. We cannot cause any more rifts with Allund. After tonight, you must see this as clearly as I do: there can be no contact with her or anyone else at Woynauld."

No. That poor girl. My insides melt. I know what it is to be picked on and bullied by everyone, from my na'rm to other burrowlings. This girl has suffered enough under Allund's tyranny, and someone has to step in, the way that no one did for me. No one, until Maddy.

But if Allund Woynauld is behind this current attack on GCE because of me, then I have to trust Yelda to care for her like she promised.

"And finally, you're to take my directions and my rules without questioning every single one of them." He gives me a side-long glance. "I don't tolerate that from my staff members, and no matter how much I need you, I won't tolerate it from you either."

Somehow, this moment makes me think of when Ringol brought up how I questioned Gelia, who was too much of a saint to be bothered by my antics. And, if I'm honest about my relationship with Na'rm Anetta, I'd have to admit I questioned her each time we spoke. But people have blind spots. Things they don't know.

I look at the exhaustion knitted into his face and I melt inside. I wish he weren't so tired, or worried, or annoyed with me. I wish there was something I could do right now to get him to smile like he had before when I made him happy, except I don't think I'd asked for too much.

"Hear me, Ringol," I say in a softer tone. "I care about my work and about my people." I want to tell him that I care about him too, because I do. But I can't bring myself to say it aloud so instead I place my hand over his. The warmth in his hand spreads to mine. "I couldn't stop if I wanted to."

A monitor on the wall beeps. Nukleo walks into view on the screen, glancing over her shoulder as if she's lost or scared. She passes the hidden corridor, and the monitor switches to another camera that follows her movements.

"I need to take care of this." Ringol says, as he reaches for the door with his thumb. He hesitates before leaving. "Do we have a deal?"

He looks defeated. Have I done this to him? I've pressured him into things he's not comfortable doing. But isn't that what he's done to me?

"Yes."

CHAPTER 14

I Heard Them

The heated floor works its warmth up my toes, into my feet and legs, and eventually my entire body. Once my shivering quiets, I begin to warm up to my surroundings. The room – the size of a small lab – may be in disarray, but it's a perfect space for quiet research. It reminds me of my library, where I always lost track of time.

I ignore the chaotic pile of tabdisks and focus on several notepads, decorated with full pages of writing. Some of the scribblings are written in standard shorthand – an easy module I'd taken at the age of eight, though Maddelyn didn't understand my interest in such an archaic mode of writing. The rest of Camu's notes are written in a blend of English, French, German, and Latin. The writing doesn't follow the horizontal lines of the paper, but rather takes on any direction her hand might have approached the paper at the time, sometimes curling around corners if her thought had kept going.

I smile at the script, remembering how word phrases meld into single short-hand words, and start looking for some clues. My biggest question, though, is who messed with Camu's research data in the first place? It's too hard to tamper with written notes, I would notice the change in handwriting. So this information at least has been preserved as Camu intended. Any number of the tabdisks, however, where the data will be typed, could have easily been altered.

As I read through her theorems, genetic code hypotheses, and the explanations for her reasoning, I gain a better sense of Camu's personality. She was an extremely intelligent woman driven by curiosity, one who needed to solve the mystery before her just for the sake of solving it – almost like she needed to win. So passionate. Her well-documented hypotheses come complete with scientific evidence to back up every minute detail.

I like her.

The alarm ringing in the outside tunnels finally stops its horrific blare. By the time I catch sight of the monitor in the wall, Ringol has already confronted Nukleo. He tilts his head and crosses his arms. I slowly rise from the desk and move in for a closer view, bending over yet another clutter-filled desk. A light flashes at the bottom of the screen.

MUTED.

I press the blinking light. The *MUTED* symbol disappears and Ringol huffs over the digital speaker.

"You didn't notify anyone that you were in the lower tunnels, Maven. I stopped to check on my test subjects on the way back to my chamber, when security alerted me that someone had been seen down here." Nukleo is wearing labgear, with the pin-striped blouse that I assume denotes that she is a j'maven, rather than the plain, white blouses undertechs wear.

"Did security call me per protocol?" Ringol booms. "We could have avoided this whole misunderstanding."

"They did," she retorts.

He taps at his ChiPro, and his shoulders slump as if he's guilty.

"You didn't even hear it, did you?" she asks in an accusatory tone. "You couldn't possibly hear it over the alarms down here. The upper burrow could have collapsed, crushed the entire GCE staff to death, and you wouldn't have known. We lost power in the uppermost labs, which will be fixed shortly. We're also assessing the extent of the damage to the parcel of land directly above us. Maven, what are you doing down here?"

He hesitates a nanosecond too long before he speaks. Even I narrow my eyes.

"I wanted to check the viability of the tunnels in case we all need to evacuate the upper stories."

He's lying to her, and he's lousy at it.

"Ah," she says, obviously unconvinced. "And what is your conclusion, Maven? Can we all live in the under tunnels? Without the oxygen machines at the surface pumping in breathable air? Because they would be destroyed if the upper floors implode."

This time, he drills into her. "Kinks in the design need to be worked out by the facilities manager. Clearly, though, we need some sort of escape plan."

She nods, but doesn't look a bit convinced.

"You should go check on your test subjects and retire to your chamber."

"I would–" Nukleo stammers. "But I'm not sure how to find my way back. I've never traveled this far into the tunnels. My maven – I mean Maven Camu – insisted it wasn't safe. The wisest of leaders, she was." Nukleo shivers while pulling off a sneer. She doesn't realize that Camu kept them away because she had a hidden office, and she didn't want anyone to find it.

Ringol nods. "Then, why did you risk coming down here?"

Nukleo places her hand on his forearm. "Let's not argue, Maven. Just help me back."

They turn to leave.

"If this kind of attack happens again, we'll need to remove our subjects from GCE," Nukleo adds.

"Subjects?" I say aloud, although they can't hear me. Maybe this has to do with the shot he administered on me, the reason my LE is extended. He promised to tell me about anything that has an impact on me, but he said nothing about these "subjects."

"Maybe, but I am not sure when it would be safe to do so." Ringol motions for Nukleo to start walking.

"You know," Nukleo says as she stops him. "I don't care how your newbie scored today. This is my project, and I will not share it with her or anyone else. Don't brief her on it, don't let her near it, and don't ask me to assist her with anything."

"We're all on the same team," Ringol starts, but his voice fades away as they meander away from the camera.

My shoulders tense. What type of test animal is she using where she'd be concerned enough for their safety to want to move them? If her study has anything to do with lengthening LE based on a genetic weakness found in me, then Ringol should agree to let me in on it. One thing is for sure, I need to find out. If I leave now, maybe I could catch up with them?

I spin around to grab my boots, knocking some miscellaneous papers every which way. And then I see the words *Sterling's Plague – Human Virus Conspiracy* across the top of hand-written notes tacked to the wall. I scan the page, which outlines how Salas became obsessed not only with HVC (where humans are considered a virus, destroying the earth), but also with a more recent theory of his, that plagues are nature's way of cleansing itself. Camu asserts that he went mad in his later years; if all this is true then I'd have to agree, because he eventually believed that the world had been way overdue for a cleanse. He worried that a plague-like cleanse wouldn't happen naturally because too many advances in medical science prevented a large-scale outbreak. I shiver.

This is jetting insane. Camu has this report attached with a piece of yarn to a news release where they discovered the plague had been bioengineered. The news release also noted that Salas was abducted – just like the history texts say.

Another yarn connects Camu's notes to a black-and-white photo of a letter from Salas Sterling. In it, he says he's dying of his own plague, and that he has no regrets. He claims ultimate success, and he further notes that even if people survive, he made sure their offspring would not.

I follow another string of yarn to a note penned by Camu,

clarifying that Sterling's genetically altered plague-virus mutated and did not create a failure-to-thrive condition in all human offspring. Jal would be crushed to know Sterling's dark side. I'm crushed for him.

But with each passing second, Ringol and Nukleo move farther away. I don't have time to review everything. I scramble toward the door.

Locked.

On the outside chance, I press my thumb onto the black oval bioreader. The door buzzes and clicks. It worked. *No rotten way.* Ringol must have pre-programmed it for me since this is where he meant for me to work.

Before I leave, I scan the room once more. Nukleo might ship out the animal subjects before I get a chance to review her work. I imagine a labroom full of genetically altered chimps or rhesus monkeys who, like me, have low LEs. It takes years to get the genetic alterations just right. What an unprecedented opportunity. Subters' LE issue is top priority. We have lost too much in our average life expectancies in the past ten years, and with it, too many brilliant minds leave this world prematurely. Where will we be in another ten years?

The door slides up and I rush out, hoping to catch up.

I'd forgotten my boots in Camu's room, and by the time I realize that my feet have chilled to ice again, it's too late to turn back. Every twist and turn Ringol took through the tunnels replays in my mind, and my feet pound on the rock floor until they go entirely numb.

Within a few minutes, I catch up with them. I stop at each corner and watch until the two reach a further turn and disappear. I run, breathless. They continue their conversation, but their words are too hushed for me to make out. Has Nukleo talked Ringol into excluding me from her project? I stare at the back of his hatless head, hating even the milliseconds he might have been swayed. Maybe he won't listen to her.

When we near the exit out of the lower tunnels and back

into the regular corridors, I tuck away into the shadows on the far wall and wait. Nukleo continues out of the tunnels, and Ringol makes the excuse that he's lost his tablet before turning back towards me. I hold my breath as he passes. If he walks, he'll reach Camu's room in less than ten minutes. If he jogs, only five: hopefully enough time for me to find out more about Nukleo's project.

All other GCE staff members must have already retreated to the safety of their chamberbeds – the hallways are perfectly empty.

Nukleo quickly makes her way to the lab. I follow her though several rooms and then down a few hallways until she stops at a shiny door. She presses her thumb into a scanner, the door slides open, and she enters.

I hurry over, but the door closes behind her, and clicks when it locks. *Jet.* There's no way she would allow me to enter – no possible way my thumbscan would unlock the door. The clicking of Kleo's boots fade down a hallway. The sound of yet another door clicks and opens further down as I scan the words on the closed door in front of me.

BIOAUTHORIZATION REQUIRED, stenciled just like Maven Camu's door, except the lettering on this sign is pristine.

A guttural cry from inside the labroom reaches my ears, all too close to the haunting cries I used to imagine coming from the ghostly walls of Cayan. The second door clicks closed, and the halls are silent once again.

Those were *not* monkeys.

No. *That* wailing was human.

I shove my thumb onto the bioreader. I'm shocked when it buzzes and clicks, and when the door opens, I stand motionless for a second. Ringol arranged for my access here, too?

I pad down a narrow hallway as the cries grow louder. Not just one cry, but many. My throat closes. I want to turn around and run as much as I want to reach the next shiny door. All studies approved by Common Good are limited to animal subjects. *What has Ringol done?*

When I press my thumb to the reader this time, the haziest words blink at me. *BIOAUTHORIZATION FAILURE.*

Come on! I dry my sweaty palm on my sleeve and try again.

"Stop!" Ringol's voice pours through the hallway.

I whoosh around as the door I'm trying to open buzzes and clicks. Ringol's eyes grow large.

The door takes forever to slide open, but I keep my hand on it and take a step inside. "I can hear them!"

The wails are from living humans, more piercing than my imagined ghosts. More horrific than my heart can bear.

He grabs my wrist and pulls me out of the labroom. When the door slides closed, I'm in the connecting hallway again, but not before I witnessed what I already knew: an illegal experiment. Wailing Omnit subjects with dark hair, lined in glass-domed chambercribs.

Babies.

CHAPTER 15

In This Together

I catch a glimpse at an open-mouthed Nukleo before Ringol pulls me back into the connecting hall. He can't take away the nightmare I've just seen. My stomach wrenches as I twist my wrist out of his hand the same way I had with Medero Allund.

The newsclip I saw back in Ringol's study flashes before my eyes again. It clicks immediately. The Omnit man wasn't asking burrowlings about where Subter babies were. He was asking about *Omnit* infants. Stolen Omnit infants. *What the jet?*

Ringol straightens his striped maven's jacket. "New rule. You mustn't wander."

My arms shake as the bawling of innocent Omnit babies trickles into the corridor. "How dare you use babies like this!"

I pant while I stare at his eyes where before I've seen many things – kindness, anger, amusement, and even innocence – until now. *This* explains why Omnits are attacking Subters. It probably explains why GCE was under attack; it wasn't just some petty revenge from Allund. "How dare you!" I repeat. "If we're using Omnit babies as test subjects, we deserve to be attacked."

"Well." Nukleo steps into the hall. "You've recruited a feral one, Maven. After her testing, I admit I was a little worried about my ranking. I'm not worried anymore." She turns on her heel and disappears behind the sliding door.

"Monster!" I shout. Everything about her now rings wicked

in my mind – her shrill voice, her spiteful nature, her disgusting, immoral research.

"Enough!" Ringol shouts.

"Yes, I've had enough!" My voice shakes. I trusted him. Believed him when he told me he cared about people. I admired how he defended Omnits to Chen, but how can he still claim to defend them now? He can't. "And you will, too, as soon as I contact Common Good and have you all arrested! How could you, Ringol?" I want his name to sound like a curse, but instead it sounds like the deep betrayal that it is.

He grabs my wrists and holds them still, trying to quiet me with that intense look of his. I won't be quieted. These babies must be returned to their parents and nurtured. They deserve a better life than this, living in glass chambers in a labroom. Of all the long, lonely days I'd spent as a young child, feeling forgotten and insignificant, none of it can compare to this.

"Come now, Undertech. J'Maven Nukleo is no more a monster than you are." He's trying to console me, but his words are also tainted with a degree of shock, like he can't believe I'm angry.

"Pah!" I retort, tears stinging my eyes. "I would never use children in an experiment. It's unthinkable. I resign! Do you hear me Maven? I can't work here knowing–"

"What do you know?" he asks. He still holds my wrists.

His question catches me – it's obvious, isn't it? I've just seen the most wicked experiment I could ever begin to imagine.

When I don't reply, he continues, finally letting me go. "So, you would prefer to go back to the Woynauld Academy and pledge loyalty to Medero Allund's leadership rather than mine?"

My hands go to the tattoo on my chest. Both situations are inhumane. Allund is abusive to his burrowlings, but using babies as lab rats is unspeakable.

"Yes, Maven. I prefer to work under Medero Allund. Compared to this, he's a saint!" My voice cracks.

He shakes his head. "How can you think this poorly of me without gathering facts?"

"What facts do I need after what I've just seen!"

"This is highly classified work." His face turns stony.

"You mean illegal?"

"It is one-hundred percent sanctioned by Common Good. Assigned by them, in fact."

"I don't believe you."

"Zuzan, it's—" his words cut off, his mouth opening and closing like he can't decide what to say. "Someone engineered a new virus called Drake's Plague, after the scientist who allegedly created it. Its latest mutation has surged across the entire planet, now attacking Omnit infants as soon as they are born. When they're infected, they don't live longer than four months." His eyes remain downcast. "We're dedicating our best resources to reverse it."

The air feels too thick to breathe. "*All* babies? None of them survive?"

"None." He drops his head to his chest. "Common Good has managed to keep this quiet from the Subterranean population, but they can't for much longer. The Omnits are afraid, and they have reason to be – not because *we* want them dead, but because Drake, and others like him do. For some reason, Subterranean infants are unaffected. Drake must have discovered some genetic loophole in Omniterraneans that he capitalized on. Come." He turns to the research room – a makeshift infirmary. Or hospice. A roomful of dying babies.

The numbness in my feet travels to the rest of my body. The population shrinkage has already reached emergency levels. Even if Subter babies don't get sick with this particular plague, it is only Omnits that can reproduce. If none of the Omnits survive infancy from now on, it will eventually lead to humanity's extinction.

Tears tumble down my cheeks.

Ringol bioscans his thumb and leads me into the room full

of screaming babies. After a few minutes, it's not the crying infants that capture my attention. It's the quiet ones who lie motionless, barely breathing. The babies farther on their journey to ghosthood.

"For all good, Maven!" Nukleo yells above the din. "Maybe I wasn't clear before. We've enough to handle without her histrionics!"

I wander down an aisle. She and several other medmaids wear masks over their mouths. The medmaids change diapers and administer injections into tiny IV tubes. I count fifty babes in all. Not only do Omnits have to turn over their Subterranean babies, but now they have to turn over their Omnit newborns too. It's that, or watch them die. Their parents must be going out of their minds.

"Rebels attack the hospitals because they think all medtechs are evil baby-snatchers." My thoughts spin this way and that. Ideas form into theories at lightning speed and then dissipate into nothing for lack of information. "Show me the research to date."

Nukleo rushes down the aisle and stands nearly nose-to-nose with me. "You cannot have my data."

I step back for a moment, but then refuse to be intimidated. This is much bigger than she or I. "I need to help."

She jabs her finger into my chest. "Go fly."

Ringol rushes over and stands between us. "You will share the data with Allele, Nukleo. What have we got to lose?"

"We've got our whole *species* to lose!" Nukleo spits. "You're not cut out for GCE mavenship, Ringol."

"One week of docked privileges." Ringol speaks through his teeth.

She stares at him, her lips forming a tight line.

Ringol doesn't look like he'll back down anytime soon. "It's done now, anyway, Kleo," he bites back at her. "We need to involve her as soon as possible. Grant the access, or I will."

Her eyes struggle between anger and calculation. She takes

a deep breath and rearranges her posture. "Of course, Maven," she says, faux contritely. "It's all filed on the classified central drive, accessible to all who have been cleared. It seems she has bioscan clearance to this area – have you already granted her access?"

Maven Ringol's eyebrows press down for a split second. "I haven't granted any access rights to her. I'm assuming you didn't either."

Nukleo rolls her eyes. "Nope, it didn't make the top of my to-do list. Yet another mystery lying at the feet of our newest staff member." She turns to me. "Use your ChiPro. I'm sure you'll find the information you need." She closes the space between us. "You should have finished that last question, Newness. So now we're tied. Because of the bombing, your incomplete endorsement ratings don't count as the tie-breaker. You would have had to answer the final question, and then everyone needed to submit their final approval vote. I checked the rules."

She trudges off, and I shoot Ringol a *what-the-jet-is-she-talking-about* look.

"You could have won the junior maven ranking by correctly answering the last item, or, in the case of a tie if you had been wrong, with a higher endorsement rating. It rarely works out where endorsement ratings have to be used for the top ranking, but you came very close to that."

"You wanted her to outrank me?" Not that I want the j'maveship, but that's not the point.

"No." He replies curtly. "I wanted you to stay under the radar, but clearly you're not able to do that."

A baby shrieks, an ear-splitting sound, and I can swear it's stabbing right through my chest.

"I'd like to get to work immediately." I glance around the room and anxiety pinches every square centimeter of my flesh. The handful of medmaids here can't possibly care for all these wailing babies. Whichever baby screams the loudest gets their attention. "Where are all the medtechs, or nurserymaids?"

He shakes his head. "If I order more hands, they'll send more babies – Common Good uses a ten-to-one ratio, and their central infirmaries are overcrowded. We can't possibly take more. With all the hospital attacks, space is a luxury. Someone decided that all five scientific centers of excellence should run concurrent research studies to combat Drake's Plague, and we all have the same ratio of medstaff to infants."

It's a crazy, zero-sum plan: five separate research centers all trying their best to correct the plague while babies die. "Then we should use our own staff. Our undertechs."

"No," Ringol replies without pause. "They are overworked as it is."

"Participating in drawn-out ranking ceremonies?"

His eyebrows flatten across the top of his eyes. I don't mean to insult him, but these babies need help desperately. They aren't at all comfortable the way they're set up. And he's the only one who can do something about it.

"These poor souls will cry themselves to death without proper care," I plead. "The ratio should be two-to-one, depending on how sick they are. Think this through, Maven. Even if we come up with the correct solution for their sickness, we haven't eliminated the outside variable of a high-stress environment."

"I don't see how–"

"For the sake of these innocent children, we've got to have some undertechs whose work can be spared temporarily. We need twenty-five workers around the clock for a two-to-one ratio. That would mean the five medmaids you already have, plus twenty undertechs."

His eyes dart around the room as he ponders my suggestion. "I'll work out what I can in the morning. You should get some rest, J'Mave. You'll have a full plate tomorrow."

I grimace at the title. I didn't know I could possibly rank up to junior mavenship during initiation, not that I would have changed my answers. It's just another reminder that I'm stuck in a place where I don't know how things work, and it's getting to me. I've gone from Zuzan Cayan to Miss Dullard to Undertech Allele to J'Mave in a *very* short matter of time. But honestly, I don't care what I'm called as long as I'm allowed to help with this project.

"Thank you, but I'm going to stay for now." I grab a pair of medical booties, and cover my bare feet. When I stand, I find him staring at me as if he's ready for orders.

His expression changes to that of concern. "You need to rest so that your mind is fresh when you review the data."

"I won't be able to rest until I check the IV fluids, the feeding formulae mix, and temperatures for each of the chambercribs." I meet his eye, and it hits me that I'm doing exactly the opposite of our "deal" – the part where I'm not supposed to question him. But some things are more important than blindly following directives. Who else will speak up for these children?

Instead of getting angry though, he huffs a chuckle and hands me a face mask. "I'll help you check vitals to cut the work in half." He turns and I look up at his broad shoulders as he holds up a finger and says back to me: "But don't think I'm letting you off the hook for dismissing my order. We'll discuss your consequences in the morning." I don't find much threat in his tone and try to quash the smile rising to my lips.

I open the glass hatch to the first chambercrib, liberating a screaming babe from his mattress. "Shhhh," I coo instinctively. He's much larger and more plump than the Subter infants from the nursery. "Good health, baby." His face has turned bright red. His body warms against mine, and I think about the writing on Jal's rock: *May good health find you always.* The chart lists his birth date as just over a month ago, which means this baby's "always" will expire in about three months.

His arms flail and his head flops back, so I support it with my hand. I sway gently from side to side as if I'm slow dancing, and then I pat his back like I used to do to help the nurserymaids at the sublery. The baby quietens, though his chest jerks a few more times as if it's too difficult to relax.

In an instant, I'm pulled back to the memory of how Medera Gelia hugged me when I arrived at Cayan. Before then, I'd felt like a lone soul in this world. No one should ever feel that way. Not this child, and not any of these babies.

I kiss his soft cheek. "We're in this together now."

CHAPTER 16

You Get Sterling's Plague

The next morning, I open my chamberbed drawer before anyone else is scheduled to wake up. The haze of darkness catches me off guard. Before having my lenses, I would have basked in this lack of light, but now the edges of the walls disappear into shadows. Still, I catch another shadow moving silently in the room. "Who's there?"

"I have your clothes," Kriz says. She took my measurements yesterday since my uniform fit too loosely. "These should work." The sound of her voice is so like Maddelyn's, except her slight accent is more a match to Ringol's. She also hands me my boots, which I had left in Camu's hidden office yesterday. Ringol must have gone back for them.

"Thank you," I say.

But she doesn't respond. Instead, she turns and leaves the chamberroom. I dress in the dark, but not quickly enough. Nukleo descends from her bedchamber before I can leave, and flips on the lights. Her mouth drops open at me as I head out the door. At least I'll have five minutes of peace at the lab before she shows up.

Kriz waits for me outside. "I trust you found the new underblouse to your liking."

I glance down. Burgundy with black pinstripes, like Nukleo's, and similar to Ringol's suit except in opposite colors. "What in all —"

207

"J'Mave Allele, surely you've been informed of your ranking by now?" She frowns.

I pinch the material between my fingers – it's a thick polyblend that hides my scar. I doubt Nukleo's was made from the same material. Kriz has thought of everything.

"I'm not ready to wear this."

She scoffs, walking away.

I narrow my eyes and chase after her. "Are you angry with me, Kriz?"

She spins to face me, several feet ahead. "It's Miss Kriz, J'Mave. I'm just a maid. I've been reprimanded for your unauthorized camcall yesterday, landing me a week without privileges."

"But that's not fair at all! You warned me–" Tension builds under my ribs. Ringol knows this was my fault. Why would he dock Kriz's privileges?

"I neglected to inform my maven of your transgression. So, you see, we are not permitted to be friends. Whatever you do from now on, I am to report back to our maven."

He's punishing me through Kriz, turning her against me. "I'll talk to him."

"Don't." She huffs. "He's not happy with you. You are to report to the undertunnels immediately."

"The undertunnels?" I start. "But I was going to make a stop first." I'm not sure how much Kriz knows about Nukleo's project, and I don't want to get her in trouble again.

"Regardless of your talents," Kriz says as she leaves to return to her work, "you'll not find success unless you curb your impulsivity. I highly recommend that you start now."

My early-morning energy sinks as the baby boy's face flashes in my mind, creeping into my heart with his genuine attempt to calm down when I held him. He craves human connection, and if I am honest, so do I. Now is the only time I'll have without Nukleo in the labroom. It's on the way to the lower tunnels, and I woke up earlier than required. No one should care if I check in on him. I won't have time to check the vitals of all the babies, but I can check his.

Instead of walking, I decide to run to make up the time. When I reach the bioauthorization door, I slam my thumb onto it and glance over my shoulder. The halls are empty. After a few seconds, those blinking letters appear across the onyx panel. They're orange.

BIOAUTHORIZATION FLAGGED.

I just now decide to hate orange. What has he done to my authorization? My projector chip begins to beep, so I press it and Maven Ringol appears. "Miss Kriz reports that she informed you of your assignment this morning." His mouth closes into a straight line.

"Yes, Maven."

"You chose to ignore it," he says.

"Please." My throat tightens. "I just need a minute with–"

"One minute? What can you possibly do in a minute, J'Mave? Even *you* won't be able to find a cure for the virus that quickly."

"I just want to check one child."

"Report to your *station* at once." His face disappears.

This must be the punishment he mentioned last night. This, and Kriz's anger. I suppose he was more serious than I thought. I sigh and turn to leave, almost colliding with the person behind me: Nukleo, with her hair in a messy bun rather than her usually ultra-neat braid.

She snickers and starts in with her grating voice. "Our maven is a strict one, no? Maybe especially so with you. I hate to play favorites, but he's never spoken to *me* with that tone."

For a split second, I consider begging her to allow me to come inside the labroom once she opens it. Or I could trip her. But there's that blasted second door. As I walk away, her projector chip sounds with the same beep mine did a minute ago.

"Maven?" she answers.

I walk a bit more slowly to stay within earshot.

"See to it that we reassign some undertechs to care for your subjects. Twenty of them."

I smile.

"I believe a two-to-one ratio, around the clock, would be optimal considering how sickly the infants are."

Her voice drops to a whisper. "Has someone deleted your brain cells? We don't have any undertechs to spare, let alone *that* many around the clock."

"J'Mave Nukleo, heed my orders," Ringol says in very much the same tone he'd used with me.

Nukleo continues to argue with Ringol until I'm out of hearing range, close to the undertunnel entrance. If nothing else, Ringol is open to reason, at least when it comes to the better treatment of those infants. He's also stubborn as slate.

I slide the door open to the undertunnels – it's manual, without bioauthorization, although I'd bet there's a camera watching me. Without the alarm sounding, the tunnels don't scream with that terrifying sense of emergency. My arms prickle with goosebumps, which fade quickly with the brisk pace of my hike.

When I reach the hidden door covered by the lowlight projection, I hesitate. This fake wall of rock would trick the most astute paleontologist. A faint hum rings across the silence, maybe a side-effect of the projection. I press my hand into the wall, and as it disappears, I pull it back.

And then I leap in.

I spend four straight hours in Camu's hideaway, alone. Going through each of the notepads on her main desk, I scour through her unpublished theories and hand-written notes outlining the stats as proof. Her notations are meticulous. Absolute. Unwavering. Jal would have loved working with her, and she with him.

But then something else in the stack of papers I'd knocked over yesterday catches my eye. Across the top of the page, the French words *De Réserve: Susanne Poivre* are written in

Camu's writing. My breath catches as I make the translation. *Contingency: Susan Pepper.* As in cayenne pepper? I shiver. It's too close an approximation to my name, my chosen name. And this page was dated a year ago. It even has my old identification number on it. Ringol's statement from yesterday echoes in my head: *You are the one person who is meant to be here.*

The French words spattered on the page slow my normal reading speed down as I translate.

Career aspiration: Medera >> It's normal to give away a little of one's life in order not to lose it all. Another Albert Camus quote, like the one painted on her wall. But this time, she's applying it to *my* life instead of hers. This is as close to unbelievable as it gets. I've been on Camu's radar for a long time. A nervous anxiety begins to build deep within my bones like a whirring of a magnetran preparing to leave the station, and I have to pace around the office to tame it.

I am code-named Susan Pepper. Clearly, she didn't think I'd become a medera, even a year ago. Her meticulousness in notating everything extends to the information she had on me. She knew all my academic test scores, and the time it took to get through each module. She knew my favorite authors and even my favorite educational theorists.

There's only one person who could have fed this information to her: *Medera Gelia.*

My heartbeat rings in my ears. Why? She never mentioned anything to me. But no. There was the day I left the burrow. She said she wanted to talk more, but I shut her down.

The door to the hidden room suddenly buzzes and clicks. Maven Ringol enters carrying a tray of food.

"Time to eat," he says. "Your new meal plan is prescribed by Medtech K based on deficiencies he found in your recent bloodlabs." Ringol shoves the clutter on the desk over to the side, the Susan Pepper document included, and sets down the lunch tray.

He catches my expression, and must be able to see that I'm fuming. "Come on, Zuzan. I warned you to prepare for the consequences of your disobedience yesterday. I also asked for help on Sterling's Plague and Maven Camu's corresponding research. Just because you happened upon another plague in the meantime, that doesn't make this work less important. If anything, it's more important. Now more than ever. You get the lead on Sterling's Plague, and Nukleo gets Drake's Plague."

I jump to my feet, grasping the Susan Pepper notes in my fist. "I agreed to work on the Subter-Omnit division for you, but only on the condition that you tell me everything." I wave the notes in front of him. "Explain this!"

He takes the piece of paper, and his eyes narrow, soon glossing over the page without focusing on the words.

"You can't read it, can you?" He never learned French. Come to think of it, I was the only one at Cayan who did, and my heart floods with even more suspicion. *It is high time you learn Latin*, Medera said during my second year. *You never know when you might need it. French will be next, and any other languages we can get to after that.* She said I needed to know these languages because I wanted to be a medera, but now I'm not sure. She didn't teach Maddelyn anything past Latin.

"You can read this?" He rubs the side of his forehead. I must be the cause of all his headaches. "I'd have to put it through a translator."

"Maven Camu knew all about me, and she must have gotten most of this information from Gelia Cayan. It says I'm a contingency plan."

Maven Ringol raises his eyebrows, evidentially surprised. "Then, these notes are classified." He reaches for the paper but I pull it away too quickly.

"The terms of our deal were that I work in this hole to unearth questions on Camu's research, putting aside my true desire to teach. In exchange, you will share all pertinent information about me, including *how* I came to be part of this assignment."

"I've never read that document; I can't tell you things that I don't know." His forehead creases with deep lines.

"Then find out!" I slam the paper in front of him again.

"Hear me." His cheeks quake with anger. "We are not friends. You will maintain respect."

I've been fooled like a child by my own medera. Another possibility that's almost too horrible crosses my mind. Jal's GCE interview was the happiest day of his life. "Jal's placement at GCE – was that staged?"

Ringol crosses his arms. "I would have gladly welcomed him as an undertech. Jalaz Cayan earned his placement just like everyone else here."

"Except me."

"You've earned every second you're here and more. Your initiation score will likely set a long-standing record." He lowers his chin to his chest and he takes out a medpatch from his pocket. Removing an older one from underneath his sleeve, he replaces it with the new. I bite the inside of my already-raw cheek. He must be in pain. Maybe I should back down until he's better, but I can't.

"You don't have to tell me we're not friends. We can't be, because you've lied to me." My hands shake. "You have, *and* my medera has."

He blinks, as if hurt by my words. "I'm not lying. I can't tell you about information I've never seen, or about whatever communications Gelia Cayan had with Izodora Camu. My impression, though, was that Gelia didn't know much."

"Let me talk to Gelia." I curse the tears forming at the corners of my eyes. She let me believe I could be a medera, encouraged me. All along, she knew otherwise.

"I can't," he stammers.

I throw the paper at him. "Don't tell me I've lost my jetting privileges–"

"Gelia's been unreachable since your transfer."

"Stop lying." I narrow my eyes at him.

His gaze doesn't break from mine. "I scrambled to have your identification updated in FFR's database. We – Gelia and I – had planned to convince you to come to GCE, but the burrow was empty when I came back. I searched every tunnel, and finally found a note from Gelia left in the blasted decontamination chamber. She said she had little choice but to send you to Woynauld's, of all places."

"She's... gone?" Medera Gelia had no placement, nowhere to go. A woman of her age, in her condition, can't just roam the earth. I sit down in my chair and take a sip of tea from the tray of food he brought me. "Did she say where?"

He shakes his head. "When she and I last spoke, she expressed remorse in keeping things from you, saying you deserved better."

"Why did she keep me in the dark then? If anyone had explained all the things that were at stake, I might have decided to help review Camu's research on my own."

"You can't hold something like this against her. She knew some things about this, but not a lot." He holds up the paper. "You said it yourself: you were a contingency plan. Plan B, if plan A failed. I don't know everything plan A entailed, but I'm assuming that if it hadn't failed and if your burrow didn't flood, you'd be well on your way to mederaship in some technologically-devoid burrow with oversized saucers on your face."

Maybe that's it, then. Gelia had hoped for the best, that plan A would work out and I'd be left alone. Still, though, if there was a chance that my entire life would be turned upside-down, I wish she had told me. "I'm Susan-the-Contingency Pepper."

"You're not the only one in this contingency plan, piecing things together." Ringol sighs, and I realize he means *he's* part of it, too. What happened to him? Did he have to leave his people behind, the ones he loves, to come here? "When I first heard about you, I doubted that you even existed – a burrowling who is a perfect genetic match for this type of research. That is until Jalaz sent your genome structure my way, and then I saw for myself. You have super-patterning skills, which you must know, among other things – excellent memory, quick reading, the list goes on. Anyway, Camu realized there were risks in her work so she needed a backup plan if and when she wasn't around to see her work completed, but your LE stats left your undertech candidacy in question."

"Until the shot," I say. "The day Jal died."

"After I met you and saw for myself what you might accomplish, I would have done anything to get you to come and review Camu's research. Gelia fought the idea for a few days, in her defense, but she knew you were needed. Even so, she left it up to you – something about your right to decide who you were for yourself without undue influence. She really didn't care what your genome indicated, or what Camu had been insisting upon. She only cared about the person you were determined to become. Whatever you decided, she was ready to support you."

She is my heart. As she always was. I brush a tear away, wishing for just one more hour with her.

"Subters are a dying race, Zuzan. The year you were born, Subter births accounted for only ten percent of all newborns. Now it's dwindled to two-and-a-half percent. The laws of nature have taken over, and nature, in all her glory, has banked on Omnit survival and Subter extinction. All the advances we've made, the scientific discoveries – they will be wasted in the hands of Omnits. Without us, they will be useless at best, or at worst, dangerous."

I close my eyes. "Instead of *fighting* nature then, we must help her."

"What do you mean?" he asks. "You can't mean we allow people to die."

"Of course not. We first need to focus on Omnit survival. Drake's Plague – it's a newer outbreak, and may help us uncover clues. It's an odd triangulation of events: Camu went missing, someone tampered with her data, and Drake's Plague was released at approximately the same time. Allow me to work on Nukleo's research during the rest of my day's hours. Whatever time I spend with the Omnit infants over there, I promise to work an equal amount on Sterling's Plague here."

He stiffens. "It's too much. You're still recovering from toxic exposure, and I have to guard your health above anyone else's."

"Then guard it. But the longer it takes to curb the Omnit newborn plague, the angrier the Omnit rebels become. They already know our location. If they attack again, then we're less likely to finish Camu's research, or anything else."

"You can't negotiate everything, Zuzan," he huffs. "Your demands are impossible."

"Only because we're in an impossible situation."

He reaches over the desk and places his hand over mine until I look directly into his face, and the expression of concern in his eyes stops me cold.

"At least take care of yourself. I want you to eat, rest, and stay healthy," he says. "It's important to me." He turns my hand over and runs his index finger from my wrist into my palm, sending a spiral of electricity through me that I was unprepared for. And then he laces his fingers into mine. "You're important to me."

I watch as he moves his thumb in tiny circles over mine, and for a moment I want to stay like this forever. And then sense floods back into my brain. He is my maven, and nothing else. I pull my hand away.

"It's not fair for you to call all the shots," I say. "To announce when we're friends and when we're not, and when to hide the truth or divulge more information."

"I'm sorry." His eyes drop like a scolded schoolboy's, but then they rise again to meet mine. "You're right."

Maybe his apology should have tempered my mood, but instead, it hits me like he's confessing something he wouldn't have acknowledged unless I'd called him out.

"I will eat and rest," I say, "so that I can continue to work. Now please–" The word lingers in the air while he searches my eyes as if to ask for mercy. Instead, I stand and hold up my hand to head off any objections. "You must excuse me."

But Ringol walks around the desk and stands directly before me. He takes a step closer and my heart quickens. I hold my breath because the sensation of his touch lingers. A deep warmth washes over me.

There's a magnificence between us. He named it when I first arrived, and I feel it now.

His gaze bounces across my face, reading me. Can he tell I feel it? That I want him to take another step, that I want him to kiss me?

As quickly as he stood before me, he turns on his heels and leaves.

CHAPTER 17

Try Not to Maim One Another

I try to concentrate after Ringol leaves, but Camu's notes and disks and charts all mix together. What was it that Camu thought I could do with all this? Her work to solve the Omnit-Subter divide appears to have progressed to where she could have started clinical trials – that is, if her data proved her theorems. From everything I've examined in her notes and raw numbers, it should have. The published numbers just don't agree with the raw data. The big question is: Why? Did Camu change the results to protect herself? Did someone else change the published results to conceal her success?

I work for a few hours making little headway. Finally, I press my ChiPro button and give it a search command.

"Find connections between Izodora Camu and Gelia Cayan."

The chip beeps a few times, and then responds in its overly kind, automated voice. "Allele Crypt does not have clearance to access information pertaining to Izodora Camu. Do you have any further commands?"

I hit my palm into the desk, and the corner of the "Susan Pepper" paper flutters from the small breeze. "Yes. Find information on Susan Pepper."

The chip beeps, and then responds. "The Susan Pepper file is retina-scan protected. Shall I scan your retina?"

"Yes," I say. The ChiPro beeps, and something lights up

above my brow. The automated voice says there's a verification failure, so I press the button to make it stop.

Rotting jets. I'm getting nowhere. Camu has set me up to figure out parts of what she's left here, but why would she restrict my access to these files? Ringol couldn't have done it. He can't even read French. Unless he's lying through his perfect teeth and playing me once again. *Jetfire!*

After my scheduled work hours, Ringol camcalls to release me from my Sterling's Plague duties. I side-eye him because he could have easily just messaged me instead. But now I can go to Nukleo's labroom – and I couldn't be happier to flee my lack of progress in Camu's musty office.

I bolt for the door. The hurried walk through the lower tunnels takes only a few minutes, although I'm so distracted by the notion that I'll be holding the Omnit baby again soon that I almost make a wrong turn.

When I arrive outside the labroom, I press my thumb into the bioscanner, and this time I'm admitted inside the connecting hallway and make it through the next door. Ringol kept his word: at least twenty-some people crowd into the aisles. I can't help but smile and search for my baby boy. Dodging through the undertechs, though, I realize that none of them try to comfort the babies. They're all staring into the glass chambercribs as if they're afraid of the infants inside. When I make it to my baby's chambercrib, his face is purple from the stress of screaming.

I shove the mousy undertech out of my way. "What in all good is wrong with you?"

"Sorry," she squeaks. "What am I doing wrong?"

Opening the hatch, I gently lift the child and lean his head over my shoulder and begin to sway. His frantic screams quiet to half-hearted cries. "You're okay, little one."

"You," I say to the mousy undertech. "What is your name?"

"Rozalind, Rozalind Porter."

"Undertech Rozalind, I need you to hold this child exactly as I am until he stops crying. Do you understand?"

She exchanges glances with another undertech, and then her gaze falls upon my pin-striped blouse. "We're not supposed to expose the subjects to agents outside of their chambercribs unless absolutely necessary."

"This *is* absolutely necessary!" I say as I hand him over. "Hear me: you are not to refer to him as a 'subject.' It's too clinical. Almost cruel. Call him by his name."

"Name?" she scoffs. "Children don't have names until they come of age."

"His name is Jal," I say flatly. I scan the room for Ringol or even Nukleo, but there's no sign of them. "Talk to Jal like he matters to you. Tell him everything will be okay. Sing. Tell him how DNA transcribes into RNA. Anything! Just don't stop talking until he stops listening."

"How will I know he's stopped listening?"

"Because he'll be sleeping." I ball my hands into frustrated fists. I should cut her some slack really, since I studied childhood development as part of the mederaship coursework. None of these maven-hopefuls have. But it feels like a lack of compassion in them.

"Attention!" I yell. But no one hears me. The screams from the babies drown out every decibel of my voice.

Griffith approaches with a giant smile. "Congratulations, J'Mave Allele. Well earned."

Every molecule of my body cringes with his recognition. "Where are your assigned babies?"

"Over there." He points to a section of infants in their chambercribs, and I'm not sure which ones are his, but it doesn't matter because all of them are crying. "I don't quite understand why the maids aren't able to change the diapers as they always have, but—"

"Change diapers?" The words explode from my lips. "Is that what you've been told?"

He shrugs. "I'm to alert the medtechs if any of the vitals go awry."

I turn to the room, yelling one more time. "Attention!"
Three or so turn to face me.

Griffith sticks his fingers in his mouth and blows. His whistle echoes throughout the lab, and they all turn to face us. Griffith straightens his labhat. "J'Mave Allele has asked for our attention!"

"Thank you, Undertech." But the sudden whistle makes the babies cry louder than I can yell, so I'm forced to take then undertechs into the hallway between the two bioauthorization doors. I take a handful of them at a time. Group by group, I explain the health benefits of keeping the babies calm, which was easy enough. Rozalind demonstrates how to rock the infants, using baby Jal as her example. When I insist that they name their babies – to call them anything other than their subject-identification code – most of the undertechs sneer or roll their eyes.

"What do we name them?" asked one curious worker.

"Name them after your favorite dessert, your favorite element on the Periodic Table, or your old medera or medero. Just name them something more meaningful than a number and write the name on each chambercrib."

"Omnits prefer earthy names, like Rock or Leaf or Autumn," Griffith suggests.

"I heard that Omnits name their children at birth," another tech says. "And that each of us has an Omnit name from our parents, our real names." I turn away from him to fetch another group, doubting whether that's true for me.

In an hour, the labroom quietens so that only a few babies cry at a time. Almost half of the babies sleep in the arms of GCE undertechs, and when one of the younger undertechs looks my way, she smiles proudly. Griffith speaks softly to his charge, whom he named *Cat*.

Fighting the urge to take Jal from Rozalind, I return to the desk to review Nukleo's data and open file after file. Scans performed at the first week of age indicate microscopic lesions all over the surface of each child's brain. At four weeks, the lesions grow by a hundredfold, and at four months, the babies suffer from sixty to eighty rice-sized spots across their brains. Each of them is bound to die from seizures.

In the midst of the semi-quiet, an undertech shouts from his station. "Medtech, please! Medtech!"

I rush over to the chambercrib. The baby convulses in seizures, jerking slightly at her neck, her limbs flailing and then slowing, then flailing again. Her stats blink at the bottom of her chamber, dropping as we wait for medical assistance.

"Where is the anti-seizure patch?" I scream.

Griffith, with Cat still draped over his shoulder, pulls me away. "This is difficult to watch for all of us, J'Mave." He speaks into my ear in a somber tone. "Your undertechs will look to you as an example."

I glance over my shoulder and nod, trying to blink back tears.

Medtech K jogs down the aisle with a limp. His face is pocked with scars from some former illness. He checks the infant's vitals and begins to work on her. "She's a few days past the four-month mark," he says.

"What is her name?" I ask.

"Twilight," her undertech responds. "But I don't think she knows it. She's been asleep this whole time."

Or unconscious, more likely. The example brain scans that I just looked at for babies her age were speckled with terrible sections of dead tissue. An anti-seizure patch – that was my solution? What about the holes dug out of her brain?

Nukleo barrels down the aisle. "Get out of my way!"

Twilight's seizures cease almost as abruptly as they came on, and her vitals drop.

My co-j'mave's eyes pop as she shoves Medtech K out of her path. "No, no, no." She rolls the child onto its side and scans her with a handheld device that sounds off a series of beeps. But then the beep changes to one long, humming tone.

Twilight's limbs fall limply as Kleo gently puts the child back into its chambercrib. She stands back slowly, clicking off her device. "Medtech, please note her time of death."

Just when I think Nukleo will shed tears, she lifts her chin. Rozalind, however, didn't make it through Twilight's last moments dry-eyed. As if she could smell tears a mile away, Nukleo marches up to her while she, of course, has my baby sleeping on her shoulder.

"How, exactly, are you going to work with these subjects if you can't keep your cool?" Nukleo screeches.

At the word *subjects*, Rozalind's eyes dart my way. Baby Jal, startled by Kleo's voice, wakes up and begins to fuss. Around the room, more than a few undertechs rush to wipe their eyes before Kleo notices them.

"Sorry," she stammers. "It's – it's my first time." She immediately begins to sway back and forth.

I knew she had it in her.

Nukleo's eyes dart from undertech to undertech. "What are you all doing?" she asks no one in particular, and then her eyes settle on me. "Of course. My cryptic twin, Newness." She smiles at me with that cold expression of hers, eyes full of fire. "Conference. Hallway. Now."

She doesn't wait for me to agree and storms past. She presses her ChiPro and hisses, "Ringol! I told you this would fall before it had a chance to stand. Kindly come down and see for yourself."

After she exits, I wait for baby Jal to calm down once again.

Griffith eyes me with concern. I wink to let him know I'm okay before following Nukleo into the hallway. She has a lot of bark, but I have yet to see her bite.

Nukleo holds her forehead with one hand, her eyes concealed in a way that could hide tears. Did I have her wrong?

I put my hand on her shoulder, but she shoves me off and jerks away. "It's bad enough you go behind my back and rearrange the staffing through Ringol. But you couldn't stop there, could you?"

"For all good, a baby just died!" Any sane person would appreciate more help on a project like this.

"What makes you think you can take over? Of all the soft-minded moves, this must be the softest, Newness!"

"Ringol clearly agrees with the increased staffing."

"I won't allow it," she continues. "Do you realize this is illegal? Our manpower levels are approved through Common Good based on pre-approved research and the estimated hours required to complete each project. Any changes need to go up the approval chain. I'll report this." She gets too close to me, right in my face.

Okay, so maybe she does bite. But I bite back. "Step back, Nukleo."

"There you go feigning innocence one minute, throwing demands around the next. There's something strange about you, and I'm going to figure out what it is. Here's a bit of data you won't find in any research summaries: I am going to re-claim sole j'mavenship tomorrow. I've scheduled our face-off. Afterwards, I'll delete your bioauthorization to *my* labroom."

"What?" My gaze bounces to the bioaccess panel by the door, and I think of the baby Jal on the other side, the warmth of his little body against mine. She can't separate us. I hate to admit I might need him as much as he needs me. "How did you feel when they didn't offer you Ringol's spot after you served as temporary maven?"

She hesitates a moment too long. "Opportunities come and go. He still might fail as maven."

I stare coolly into her eyes. "I bet it would sting more if you lost the j'mave title too?"

"You think you can beat me?" She snorts. "I've written or co-edited most of the text published by GCE over the last five years. I've defeated every challenger who's ever stepped forward, hands down."

"I know about your papers. I read them all." I step closer to her like she did to me a minute ago. "Yesterday."

"Speed readers tend to be sloppy." Her tone slows down a bit, like she's worried.

I smile as evilly as she does, hoping my eyes are just as fiery. "My memory is perfect. You might want to brush up on things. Five years is a long time."

"You don't scare me, Newness." She laughs. "Feinhold and Hooling's research proved there's no such thing as photographic memory. Their subjects couldn't recreate the minutiae – they left out smaller details."

"I didn't say *photographic* memory." It took me a couple of months to realize once I began our lessons at Cayan that other students – smart as they were – couldn't see the material in their minds like I did after reading it. Some came close to photographic memory in their areas of interest. In Jal's case, science and genetics. But for me, it's everything, which is why Medera Gelia named it something different. "I said *perfect* memory."

Nukleo scoffs but her expression turns to one of confusion, probably worried that she doesn't know what I'm talking about. She couldn't know.

"I can recreate memories from the time I was a year old onward." Almost painfully so. "I can sing every syllable of every lullaby my nurserymaid ever sang. I can see every lesson I studied in my head, every letter, and I can read each one to you from memory and tell you where the typos were."

"If you're so sure you can win–" She cocks her head.

"I'm not one-hundred percent certain I can win, but you shouldn't be so sure that you can, either."

Her mouth twitches with nothing to say. She's concerned, or perhaps she's softening.

"There's middle ground here, though," I say. "We can each risk losing tomorrow, or we can delay the face-off."

She narrows her eyes. "Delay it?" She stops, as if she's calculating her possibilities of losing.

"We'll both keep j'mave status until we solve the Omnit newborn issue. Afterwards–"

"I've been working this project for months. No solution has even been hinted at, and you think we'll succeed just because *you're* here now?"

There's some commotion in the labroom past the door, and we both jump. "I hope so."

She scoffs. "I doubt it." She waits until the commotion dies down. "You're more likely to distract us from our goals. What's in it for me?"

"Saving babies." I glare at her, for all good. What else might matter to her more? "You can have all patent rights to whatever treatment we discover."

"*If* we succeed in treating them. That's a ginormous *if*. What if we don't?"

Then baby Jal will die and it will be like losing Jalaz Cayan all over again. Then I will have failed at one of the most important things I've ever tried. "Then I will ask for reassignment."

"Maven Ringol already won't allow that." She scoffs. "That's an empty offer."

I need her cooperation. I know in my bones I can help, and Nukleo will know it too, once we work together.

"I can put a request to FFR to leave GCE altogether." I shiver, wanting to take it back as soon as I say it. I want these babies to live, but I want to honor Jal by working on Sterling's Plague, and pick up where Camu left off. I never thought I'd want something more than I wanted to become a medera, but somehow, I feel like I belong exactly where I am. Yet, here I am offering to leave.

Voluntarily.

Her arms drop to her sides, and she slowly smiles. And then her face hardens again. "I have a counterproposal." She lifts an eyebrow. "Step down from your j'mave position now and stay on this project for a few weeks. If we don't find a solution in that time, then you'll make good on your promise to transfer through FFR."

I shake my head. "You'd have full authority to override my input if I step down as j'mave immediately."

"I won't."

I stare into her eyes, and through her stony glare, there's fear. "I don't trust you. It's either my offer as proposed, or risk losing tomorrow."

She lets out a sigh that turns into a hiss. "You're impossible."

So I've been told. "It's an impossible situation."

"We need to agree upon how long this deal will last. I don't want you bothering me any longer than necessary, and I'd like to know when you'll request the transfer."

Jal's soft brain tissue won't last more than a month and a half before it's damaged beyond repair. "Six weeks."

"Two."

"I'm giving you full patent rights and all the glory, Kleo."

"Three."

"Five," I say, doubting any fully developed treatment could be tested by then, but I'll take as much as I can.

Her ChiPro beeps, and she answers.

"What is it, Kleo?" Ringol's voice comes off tinny and small over the microspeaker. "I've stepped away from the premises, believing you and J'Mave Allele could get along for a few hours without coming to blows." I hate that he's treating this like a joke. At the very least, he should have warned us that he'd be gone. "Try not to maim one another. This errand took longer than planned, but I'll be back in four hours."

"Sorry to bother you, Maven." Nukleo flashes me a dead stare. "We're fine here. J'Mave Allele and I have come to an agreement."

CHAPTER 18

In Short, It's Negligent Genocide

Before starting anything else inside the labroom, I take a medmarker and walk over to the longest wall lined with chambercribs. Standing on a chair under a blank section of the wall, I write in capital letters.

TWILIGHT

She was a person, and I don't want to forget her. My childhood nightmares of infant ghosts reaching out of the walls cannot haunt me anymore. Not when babies are dying right in front of me. Nothing can ever haunt me more than this.

For the rest of the afternoon, Nukleo and I work together with no arguments and no further cause for alarm. All in all, we enjoy our first close-to-normal interaction. She sneers at our undertechs every so often who coo or sing lullabies. Still, her transformation has been nothing short of metamorphic. I don't trust it for a second.

However, she's sharing pieces of information I didn't have before our arrangement. For example, the babies arrive within three days of birth. They are fed enriched formulae, usually growing at the expected rate. Head size – the circumference pops out as the only measurement out of range for Omnit infants – starts normal but grows to the 120th percentile after eight weeks. The lesions found on the brain scans can't explain this discrepancy. There must be a significant amount of inflammation in their brains as well as the lesions. In medical terminology, the lesions and inflammation paired together predict a diminishing prognosis.

"What anti-inflammatories are we using?" I ask Medtech K. If we increase the dosage, the inflammation may ease, and we could head off some of the early seizures.

"Anti-inflammatories are *ICE* territory," he responds. The maven for ICE, the Immunological Center of Excellence, may not see things the way I do. "We rely on narcotics for pain management," he continues, "and all bloodlabs marking inflammation indicate a normal range."

The bloodlabs must be missing something – I'm sure there's swelling that can be fixed with the right medicine. When I find Nukleo and suggest this change in drugs and tell her my reasoning, she doesn't shoot me down.

"We should gradually wean our subjects from the narcotics," she offers. "I'll write up the explanation for Common Good's review. Jet." She rubs her eyes. "We have to watch what we report to CG. They'll grow suspicious if we veer too far from our discipline. I'll have to relate everything we do back to genetics somehow. I can assign my best minions to come up with a genetic link to the treatment change." When she turns and calls for Griffith, I can't tell if she's being sarcastic or serious. Did she just indicate he's one of her best workers?

I sink into brain scan images again, studying one after the other looking for patterns or clues of any type. After several hours, I shut down the files and take a break. Baby Jal sleeps soundly in his chambercrib. In fact, GCE staff members have been successful in keeping most of the babies calm. Using the message system on my projection chip, I send a note to all the undertechs present.

Be proud of your work today. You've shown your babies they can depend on you.

I attach an article to the message that summarizes various studies showing the positive effects that comfort and a serene environment have on recovering patients.

When the shifts change, a new group of undertechs report for duty. The first shift explain the responsibilities to their replacements, how important it is to react to the child right away, and most importantly, they relay the babies' new names, now written on all the chambercribs.

Most of the first-shift undertechs remain at their posts an extra hour to help transition their comrades to the tasks at hand. If I had to guess, though, they probably don't want to leave their babies, just like I don't want to leave baby Jal.

Kriz interrupts me through chipchat. "J'Mave Allele," she says. "Maven Ringol has requested you meet him at the upper reception hall by the travel platform." She no longer seems angry like she was this morning. Maybe she's forgiven me.

"Did he explain why?" I ask.

"He didn't. I'll meet you at the annex and we can walk together."

When we reach the reception platform, the light above the surface elevator lights up. Kriz taps her minitab until Ringol's face appears on her screen. "Access code?"

"Eta, seven, gamma, forty-one, pi," replies Ringol.

I suppose one can never be too careful, especially after a recent attack. Kriz taps again to open the hatch.

Five people exit the elevator with Ringol in the lead. The next person wears medmaid garb, two are dressed in undertech labjackets, and the last one wears a light-orange jumpsuit. She's got spiky hair yet there's something about her height and manner of walking that makes me wonder.

My heart stops when she looks up at me. Maddelyn screeches and runs to me. I kiss her masked cheeks repeatedly.

"You look fantastic," she smiles, hugging me. "I'm so sorry," she says and continues with *I'm sorry* over and over.

I shush her and hold her tight. I never thought I'd see her again, but here she is. Tears pour from my eyes. I can't believe the joy and ache I feel altogether at the same time. In the middle of our reunion, Ringol walks away.

"Thank you," I call to him.

Without turning, he raises his hand as if to say, *It's nothing.*

But this is far from nothing – it's everything.

I can't stop smiling as I escort her all the way to the staff infirmary, which is now devoid of medtechs, all having been dispatched to help with the Omnit infants.

Once Maddelyn settles into a small room, the nursemaid who accompanied her insists that she eats before taking her medicine.

"But it makes me so sleepy," Maddelyn complains. "And we have so much to talk about."

"What is it?" I ask, taking the capsules from the nursemaid's hand. I'm shocked that it is in the same family of psychotropics used on the infants. "I'll need to see all her medical records immediately."

"Yes, J'Mave," replies the nursemaid.

"Take note of our inventory supplies at the central cabinet," I say. "Make a list of the items you'll need for Maddelyn's care."

The nursemaid hesitates before nodding.

Maddelyn hugs me again. "I so miss everything from home, and having you close again is like a dream. C went to Zamption, didn't she?"

When I nod, her face falls.

"What is it?"

"They are one of the strictest burrows out there, save Woynauld's. I heard a lot about the different burrows at the crazyhouse."

"Don't call it that."

"It's true, though. Full of all kinds of crazies. The only escape I had was outplacement occupational therapy, where they allowed me to study technological systems. I had to teach myself most of it, but if you know the basics, you can pretty much pick up anything. I thought you were going to Zamption, too?"

"They wouldn't take me. I was stationed at Woynauld's for

a few days as a ba'rm until Maven Ringol was able to bring me here." The gory details aren't important, not at this minute.

"Medera Gelia really did send you there?" She blinks, maybe remembering some of the things she told me when she was under the influence of mold. Maddelyn doesn't know anything about medera's disappearance. Now isn't the time to break that to her, either, so I shrug the question away.

"At the looney bin, I heard how Medero Woynauld uses corporal punishment," she whispers. "And he tattoos his crest on all students like he owns them."

"I don't know how he got such a job in the first place."

"I'll tell you how," she says. "If rumors from the crazies are true, he's in line to take charge of the Central Forces. He's to be kept away from combat for his own safety until he's needed."

The only thing that makes sense about this information is the fact that he's not a trained medero. But Allund would stage an attack on Omnits like no one has ever seen in his first few minutes of command. I hope the day never comes. "What have you heard about Zamption?"

"Like Woynauld, Medera Zamption is anti-Omnit. She believes she needs to prepare her burrow members for an impending clash. She's swift to send members into isolation when they veer from her strict rules."

"Poor C." I can still feel her fingers squeezing my arms when she begged me to go with her.

"I know Medera didn't have a choice," Maddelyn says with a blank look. "With our burrows under attack, I'm sure many children were displaced and transferred wherever there was room. It's sad though, isn't it? Our children represent all we can be in the future, and we're preparing them to expect nothing but doom."

I'm late for supper, even more late in reporting to Ringol. Since my bloodlabs indicated deficiencies in certain minerals, I'm not allowed to skip meals. I head over to the cafeteria, and message him, asking if he can meet me.

As I walk the hallways, every staff member goes out of his or her way to greet me, bowing their heads or flashing tense smiles. Luckily, Ringol had provided me with some "leisurely reading material" about GCE, including the files of every staff member as a reference. Still, each person seems genuinely surprised when I respond with his or her name.

"Welcome to GCE, J'Maven Allele," one man says with a pat on the shoulder.

"Thank you, Undertech Pascal."

"Good evening, J'Mave," a younger man says shyly.

"Good evening to you, Medtech O."

"Nice to have you on board," says Juanita, one of my sharp-tongued, whispering roommates.

She's almost walked by before I get over my surprise. "Nice to be here."

While waiting in the mess line, Cheftech Bol smiles as I approach and holds up a finger.

"Oh, J'Mave. I set your tray aside." He runs to a backroom, and returns carrying a tray full of high-protein, high-calorie foods. There's enough for two of me.

"Thank you." I take a seat at an empty corner table. Permanently-affixed stools surround brushed-steel tables, four seats on each side. As soon as diners finish at a table, cafémaids come and clean behind them. According to the operations manual for GCE, the café shuts down following each meal so the room can be sealed and sprayed with sanitizers.

I lift an orange-ish protein chunk several inches from my plate, and then drop it so it hits with a thud and crumbs fly. "Yum."

"Good evening, J'Mave. May I sit with you?" Griffith asks.

"Only if you stop calling me j'mave or j'maven or junior maven."

He laughs and takes a seat at the stool across from me.

"You're ultra-unique." He smiles, as if he meant it as a compliment.

"You have no idea." I take a bite of my orange chunk, and nothing about it tastes orange. It's dry with a vague vanilla flavoring to it.

"Some of the undertechs think you're cutting edge."

I laugh. "Some?"

"Others think you'll eventually crash and burn. But still, they're all fiercely interested in everything you do. *Everything.*"

My eyebrows raise, and I try to keep my head still as my eyes scan the people around me. Many of them peek over their shoulders to see what I'm doing. Heat rises to my cheeks. This isn't exactly "staying under the radar," as Ringol put it.

I turn to Griffith. "What do you think?"

"All I can say is: I like GCE a lot better now that you're here." He smiles, and all of a sudden, he reminds me a little of Jal. "Don't worry about everyone else. Your *yeas* greatly outnumber your *nays.*"

Before I finish chewing my bite of protein chunk, someone approaches with a scowl. He slams his fist into the table. My food jumps on its tray, another protein chunk sheds orange crumbs every direction.

"I demand to be reassigned to a different project." Angry lines crease this man's forehead. "I need to return to my original project, curing infertility in Subters. I will not work on J'Mave Nukleo's research."

"Speaking of nays," Griffith stands, "allow me to introduce you to—"

"Good health, Undertech Crick," I finish for Griffith. Like Undertech Chen, Crick

came from the anti-Omnit burrow of Zamption, according to his files. "Please join me."

"Good health." He mumbles, taking a seat. "I'd no idea what J'Mave Nukleo's study was about until today. I'm scheduled for the next shift, but I won't do this – this – *nanny* work. I came here to work on solutions for Subterraneans, to find a way to strengthen our constitution so we can live longer, have our own children, be free to roam the surface of the earth and soak in the sun, for all that is right!"

Griffith winces at me when Crick uses the altered saying. I'm immediately reminded of Allund. "Common Good ensures that our research is unbiased and helps both segments of the population, not just Subters," I say. "That's why we call it Common Good – the good for all people. If we don't help the Omnit infants, then who will?"

"Do you think they actually give a jet about us? They're killing us every chance they get." He scoffs. "What a waste of precious Subter resources. Common Good has yet to punish the Omnit population. Our new, Omnit-loving maven prefers to help those filthy pups than to help our own kind. It's a rotten disgrace."

My face warms from anger and my hands begin to shake. I think about the dying babies, and it's hard to believe anyone could see them as anything but victims. "And what has any Omnit done to you personally, Undertech?"

"They just attacked GCE, J'Mave! They've murdered mederas and burrowlings alike. Let them all perish, Kleo's infant subjects included. How can you expect us to make headway on our issues if we spend our time raising the brainless animals who'll someday grow up to kill us?"

My eyes widen. He truly believes the haze he's spewing with his twisted logic. "Undertech –"

"You're new here, and I can respect that you'll have fresh ideas. But I refuse to help a dullard child whose people keep turning on us."

"Undertech!" I stand. It isn't true – not a bit of it. The more I read about the rebels, the more I understand why they're afraid. I don't agree with their attacks, but they're misinformed and they represent a small minority of the

Omnits. "Omniterraneans are different by phenotype only. We've all been born from Omnit parents. You can't mean—"

"I mean what I say, J'Mave," he stands to meet my gaze. "They throw us away at birth, like discarded scraps. Our worlds have separated, our features so different we may as well be a disparate species. With some targeted splicing of genetic code, I believe Subters can succeed. I've prepared all my research findings for Common Good's review. It's not perfect and it technically breaks some of their scientific precepts, but they should consider alternative solutions. We must save our own kind, first and foremost!"

My hands shake. In all honesty, I understand living separately from the Omnits for our health, but that's not what he means. He's proposing something close to negligent genocide. "Unthinkable."

"Isn't it a proven fact of nature that the most intelligent species best adapt to the environment and survives all others? It's also a proven fact that Omnits don't have the intellectual capacity we have. Certain leaders at Common Good have held us back long enough. We don't need Omnits, we just need free reign to complete the necessary research."

My stomach wrenches at Crick's view of the world. "You are relieved from your duties from the Omnit newborn study," I say. "Not because I agree with anything you've said, but because I don't want you to set foot near those children. I will work your shift until we find a replacement." I've worked all day except for the hour I had with Maddy, but I don't care at this point. "Maven Ringol will find you another project. Report to him at once." I just now realize that Ringol hasn't responded to my last message.

"Gladly," he says as he dashes away.

I plan to message Ringol over chipchat to warn him about Crick and update him on all my findings thus far, but before I can give the command to connect with him, my chip beeps.

"Maven Ringol," I say. "I was just about to—"

"Never mind that." His voice explodes like I've never heard him before. "Kindly make your way to the labroom. Stat."

"Yes, sir," I reply in a small voice.

Now what have I done?

CHAPTER 19

Not a Rotten Thing

On the way to the labroom, my chip beeps. It's a message from Maddelyn's medmaid with all pertinent medfiles attached for my review. I slow down to read the file.

One note refers to her need for meds to be able to sleep. The medtech who wrote the report refers to it as *rehabilitation*. All her bloodlab numbers however appear normal. Completely fine.

Except for the most important one. Her LE. It's now listed as only eight months. *What the jet?*

I open the portal to her overall prognosis. She's developed many, many fatal allergies after her peanut powder exposure, and all the allergens that were formerly low levels are now a level eight or nine toxin for her. It's like her system has decided everything is extremely dangerous. Apples, insect feces, rodent fur, rodent saliva, straw, leaves, chalk dust. *Jet.* That must be it, then. Her shortened LE takes into consideration how many agents she reacts to, the prevalence of those items, and the probability that she will risk a deadly exposure in the foreseeable future.

My chip beeps again from Ringol. "Where are you?"

Instead of answering, I break into a run.

My muscles tighten entering the labroom, until I check the wall.

TWILIGHT

No other names have been added, so I relax. The lights have been dimmed for nighttime. Rows of undertechs rock the infants, hushing the babies who cry, singing softly to sleeping babes.

My heart swells at this beautiful sight. I send a quick chipchat message to everyone working: *You've shown these babies that you care. You are phenomenal.*

As some of the undertechs receive the message, they turn to me and smile.

Maven Ringol sneaks up behind me. "Is this your doing, J'Mave?"

He hadn't been around since I instructed our undertechs to interact with the infants. Regardless, I'll stand by my ideas – they are based in research and well, general humanity. "Actually, it's yours. You redirected staffing to this project."

"Don't play with me, J'Mave. Look around at our highly trained scientists. Is this your suggestion or not?"

"I can explain–"

"No, *I* will talk. *You* will listen." He activates his projection chip at the same time mine automatically alights. I inch my bottom into the seat he points to. "I've pulled our labstats for today."

"Ah." Research cost per hour? Of course that's up based on staffing alone. Heating costs, too, since Nukleo and I decided to raise the baseline temperature of the room. The infants are out of their chambercribs more now.

He activates some charts over his ChiPro, and then flicks them over to me until they're displayed on mine. "See for yourself. Pre-seizure and full-seizure activity is down by seventeen percent compared to the same time of day from the preceding week. Our subjects–"

"I prefer to call them infants, sir." I smile. "Or babies."

"Yes, well these *little people* are sleeping twelve percent longer, eating twenty-two percent more, and overall, crying less." He leans in so he can see the projection from my chip, and he points to all the positive stats. His breath hits my cheek.

I try to keep my head still so the chart doesn't shake. "Our highly trained scientists deserve all the credit." Maybe it's because I didn't expect his praise, but goosebumps prickle my skin.

"At any rate," he says as he claps his hand on my back, and deactivates the charts, "I approve of all your changes, except for the names. To be specific, it's not that we've named the subj – *little people*, but you never should have added a name field to our research database."

"A name field, Maven?"

"Their identification codes are now followed by a name. Only a maven or j'maven could have–" He looks into my face and stops short.

I straighten my back. "Nukleo?"

"Impossible." He chuckles. "Kleo?" he says, as if he's trying to figure out how to pronounce her name. "Your influence knows no limits."

"I'm pretty sure she still hates me."

He smiles at me for a while, and then he's back to business. "What's your progress on Camu's work?"

"From everything I've seen, she had been on the right track. It's possible to recreate some of her experiments and check the data."

He shakes his head. "Common Good would never fund it. Not after they've funded the original research."

My shoulders slump. "There's always a way. We just don't see it yet." Maddelyn would tell me to hard-as-diamonds hope at this point. "I wanted to talk to you about Maddelyn, sir, to thank you for rescuing her from the clinic. I can't tell you what it means to me to have her here, safe."

"I realized that the amount of stress you've been under can impact your work, so one less thing to worry about was worth the hassle." He frowns. "Though I can only keep her until she reaches maximum medical improvement."

MMI, of course. The healthiest condition the individual is expected to achieve, even if it isn't back to her original state of health. If she's as good as she'll ever be from that point on, they will deploy her elsewhere.

"But her LE –"

"FFR will find her suitable maidwork for the rest of her employable time."

I flip on my minitab and check Maddy's records. Prognosis. Recovery time. Estimated MMI date. "Twenty days?"

He nods. "Twenty days with her is better than none."

I slump into the chair, stunned. "Someday, I will repay you." I could swear his cheeks flush. He never offers any information about himself, but I should know something more about him when he's done so much for me. "Maven, at which burrow did you study?"

He glances away. "Burrow?"

"Don't tell me it's classified." I tilt my head playfully.

The side of his mouth twitches into a lopsided grin. "Our agreement only covers information that pertains to you."

"You directly relate to me."

He breaks into a full smile and heat rises in my neck and cheeks.

"I mean – you are my supervisor. My mentor. You're–" He's what? He's broken into my circle, inside the small group of people that I care about. My maven.

He raises his eyebrows, and then glances around the room as if he's wondering who can hear. "Not this time, Zuzan. You'll have to survive the disappointment of not knowing."

"Jacoby?"

"No."

"Handelle?"

He shakes his head. "Get some rest."

I huff and turn to leave. And then I realize I can't. "Actually–" Would he approve of me working a third shift in one day? "I thought it best to relieve Crick Zamption of his shift."

"Pardon?"

"He has *beliefs*," I say, choosing my words carefully. I'm not able to look at Ringol, who has strong issues with anti-Omnit sentiment. "Sentiments that make him unfit for this project."

"Ah." Ringol cracks his knuckles. "And he's expressed these beliefs to you?"

"I wanted to observe the third shift, anyway." As I speak, I fight a yawn from surfacing. I don't want him to think I can't handle the work.

"You will get some rest, and I will find a replacement for Crick's assigned hours."

I want to object, but the suppressed yawn surfaces again, and this time I can't hold it in. Ringol turns me around by my shoulders and leads me to the door.

But then someone runs from the last row of chambercribs. "Medtech! It's Aurora. She's not breathing."

"I need a medtech over here, too!" cries another undertech.

My heart races. It's too much. More babies will die before we can do anything about it. I turn to help, but Maven Ringol finds the crook of my arm and stops me before I run to the babies' chambercribs.

"Don't," he whispers. "Once the subject gets to this point–" He pulls up the baby's stats on his chip and points. "The lesions in their brains have left nothing of who they were meant to be. It's the same tragedy each time. This one is already gone."

"We have to try something!"

"The *something* we are trying is to find a cure before it gets to this point with the other little people in our care."

I stop and glance at him. I hate that he's right. I backtrack down the aisle and out of everyone's way. Running for the door, I block out the noise – the beeps, the tense yelling – and I wish I could block out the what's happening too. I make it into the hallway, between the two bioauthorization doors.

For so long, I wanted to honor Jal's memory by being here. Now, though, it's different. These babies are taken from their families after birth and are brought here to die. They don't even have nurserymaids tending to them, just medstaff and scientists. It's heartless. Now I want to honor *them*, care for them before they're gone.

The door to the lab slides open, but I don't turn. Only one person would follow me with all the commotion inside.

"Zuzan," he says.

"I didn't know how lucky I was," I say. "When I had insufficient LE and then everything turned upside-down, and I had to say good-bye to my friends and my dreams, winding up in a burrow with a horrible man who hated me. I thought nothing could be worse."

He puts his hand on my shoulder.

"But this? This is worse. These children will never learn lessons, won't know anything as simple as love. They die like rats in cages."

"No." He wraps his arms around me, and I remember how he held C's hand while we were in quarantine. I rest my head on his shoulder like C did back then. The tightness in my muscles eases a little in the warmth of Ringol's arms. My problems have been nothing compared to what these Omnit babies have been going through. I have to do more for them.

"The infants here will not suffer like they did before," Ringol says, "because of you. Because of the changes you've already implemented."

I shake my head. "They're people, Maven, and they deserve better."

He sighs. "Our main focus must be to find a cure."

I shrug out of his hold. "That's not good enough." My voice shakes. "More babies will arrive in their place, and everyone will go on as if they didn't matter, like the fawn."

"Of course they matter," Ringol says. "But what more can we do?"

"You told me you have people you love. They're out there, somewhere in the world, aren't they?" I think of my girl at

Woynauld, hoping she's okay, and about C, hoping someone is showing her compassion. "If someone else were in charge of your loved ones' care and believed they were doing good enough because trying just a smidge harder causes problems – what would you say to them?"

Maven Ringol looks off, like he's thinking about his people.

I can't back down now. "Can we do better?"

His jaw clenches, and he turns back to the labroom door. "Go get some rest, J'Mave. Report to Camu's undertunnels first thing tomorrow. Get your mind onto the genetic divide. If you can't, then you'll have to keep away from the Omnit infants."

"But Maven!"

"Not another syllable, J'Mave. Or I will delete your bioauthorization myself." He stares me down for a moment and turns. The door buzzes and clicks, and he's gone.

When I return to my bedchamber, I fall asleep instantly. I dream of a roomful of a hundred girls who all look like my C. One by one, they cry out. *Zuzu, help me!* But before I can get to the one who calls me, baby ghosts reach her from the floor and consume her body with their fiery arms. The next one calls out and as I run to her in horror, the life burns out of her with a swarm of screaming, fiery infants.

And there's not a rotten thing I can do to stop it.

CHAPTER 20

Asleep My Entire Life

Maddelyn's eyes flutter spastically when I attempt to wake her the next morning. The medmaid presses Maddy's finger onto a bloodlab strip and then checks the results on her minitab.

"What's wrong with her?" I ask.

"Not a thing. I don't know why I'm here to monitor such a healthy person."

But Maddy's complexion is especially pale this morning. "She's completely out of it."

"It's her psychotropic meds. They allow her a full night's rest and they keep her calm when she's awake."

I pick up her wrist from the infirmary bed and then let go. Her limp arm falls to her side. "Calm, or comatose?" Activating my chip, I check the drugs listed in Maddelyn's medcharts. "I want her dosage lowered steadily each day. She'll be off them in just over a week."

"All due respect, J'Mave. Dosing changes require approval from a central psychtech."

I stand. "What is the proper dosing for this drug?"

She blinks at me, her face flushing.

"A hundred micrograms per kilogram, maximum dose," I say. I've recently studied this drug because of its use on the Omnit infants. "Your patient is at twice the maximum. You'll reduce it, or I'll report you and the entire central psychiatric staff to Common Good."

The medmaid's eyes widen as if she's trying to figure out if my threat is serious, and then she nods.

Griffith joins me once again at breakfast. My specially prepared meal is twice as big as his. I'm supposed to gain three-percent of my body weight before my meals will go back to normal. I can't worry about my own health, though; not with so many others worse off than I am.

"Why so glum?" Griffith asks.

I hardly noticed how silent we've been. "What do you know about immunology?"

He grins, but glances around to make sure no one hears. And then he leans in. "We have one undertech who worked a year for the Immunological Center of Excellence prior to coming to GCE."

I raise my eyebrows.

His cheeks flush. "Maven Camu recruited him because he was a talented up-and-comer."

Perfect. "You?"

"I wish." He chuckles. "It's Crick Zamption."

I wince. It had to be Crick. *Fan-jetting-tastic.* But still – maybe he *could* help Maddy. I glance around the cafeteria until I spot him huddled over his meal, alone in a quiet corner. My lip curls just thinking about our last conversation.

"I was wondering something, J'Mave." Griffith adjusts his hat. And adjusts it again. "I wanted to know if I could just call you *Allele*? Do you understand?"

I want to say I'd prefer Zuzan, but I can't. "It is my name." I stand up to leave.

Griffith flashes a confused look, and then nods as I hurry away with my tray.

"Do you mind if I eat here?" I ask when I reach Crick's table.

Crick eyes me cautiously as he mouths a forkful of his brownish protein chunk.

I'm doing this for Maddelyn, though. I sit without his permission. "I'd like you to complete a consultation on a female subject, twenty years old, who has developed severe multiple allergies."

He stops chewing.

I give him a quick rundown of Maddelyn's history. "This is your new project."

He crosses his arms. Ringol came down hard on him after he asked to be taken off the Omnit infant duties and he probably blames me for it. "I didn't come to work at GCE for the least important projects, J'Mave Allele."

"Conduct your evaluation first thing this morning. Chipchat me with your recommendation."

"May I refuse, J'Mave Allele?"

I'm not sure. Can undertechs direct their own work? It's not like Ringol gave me that option when he ordered me to a project. "Of course. Gentleman's choice: this project or Nukleo's Omnit infants."

He leans back and pushes his tray away. "I see. This is retribution. Very well, J'Mave Allele."

I hate how he keeps using that name with me every chance he gets. It's like he can tell it irritates me. But he's agreed, so I get up.

"On one condition," he continues. "I want to continue my former project. The funding was already approved through Common Good."

I freeze. Do I need Ringol's permission to negotiate like this?

"Don't look so worried, J'Mave Allele. I want to solve infertility in the Subter population, a worthy goal." His eyes grow lively. "If Subterraneans could reproduce, then extinction is less a risk."

"Camu's research from ten years ago concluded even if Subters could have children, we would produce the same ratio of Omnit to Subter offspring that the Omnits produce, probably with more health problems."

"I have new ideas," he scoffs. "At any rate, that's my trade-off. This Subter girl's allergy consult for the infertility project. And, J'Mave Allele, I will need a team of three undertechs. Going once, going twice…"

I glance at the time. "I'll look into it after your initial report on the Subter girl." I'll have check in with Ringol later. "If you give her your best effort."

For the first time that I've known him, Crick Zamption smiles. A big, crooked-toothed grin.

I run off. Baby Jal is sleeping when I get to the labroom, so I quickly check his bloodlabs and wince at his miniscule LE score. What's worse, I catch sight of the wall.

TWILIGHT

AURORA

BREEZE

"I'll figure this out for you," I say with my face pressed up against the glass of Jal's chambercrib. "Good health, Baby Jal. I will not fail."

To keep my promise to Ringol, I head down to the undertunnels, hopping through the fake wall and bio-scanning to unlock the door. Too many issues remain unresolved. Something has to give soon, though, or I'll break.

Tabdisk after tabdisk, I review Camu's information. The images of genetic sequences burst into the air above the old minitab on the desk. Camu's voice fills the void of silence as she explains the importance of each pairing. Her tone sounds both frustrated and confident at the same time. *"Deletion at gene sequence B7HT4 results in a missing allele in Subterranean offspring related to pigmentation and subpar immune system performance. It's why Subters are primarily albino."*

I understand why Camu was frustrated – she was so close. It's like being at the end of a story but, unlike a book, she couldn't skip to the end to find out how everything turned out. She had to struggle her way through and write it herself. But now that's my job. Two hours pass like two minutes while I rummage through information, when my chip beeps with a call from Crick.

"She's a zany mess, J'Mave Allele," Crick says in his mocking tone, in the projected display hovering over my desk.

I close my eyes and sigh. "There's got to be a way to help her. Anything."

"He's as personable as hot lava," Maddy yells from the background.

"You're discussing this in front of her?" I'm happy her meds are wearing off, but I'm worried his gruffness will upset her.

"She's of legal age. I've already explained it to her. In short, she shouldn't be here," Crick says. "Based on the specialized bloodlabs I ran on her, she could have a severe reaction to practically anything at almost any time. And she can develop new allergies as time goes on."

A million solutions flash through my head, each with deal-breaking risks. "Your recommendation?"

"Besides putting her into a sealed hypoallergenic bubble and hope it doesn't pop?"

"You rotten creep!" yells Maddelyn. "I'm going to pop that oversized bubblehead of yours right off your neck."

Crick narrows his eyes. "Who decided decreasing her psychotropics was a good idea?"

"Your recommendation, Undertech!" I repeat.

He grunts. "It's risky, and I wouldn't call it a recommendation. It's the last resort in a desperate situation. It's an old pre-plague therapy – replace her immunoglobulin, which has gone as whacko as she has, with donor immunoglobulin."

I nod. Immunoglobulin is the part of her blood responsible for defensive immune responses.

"The dated technique has been recently refined in conjunction with newer immuno-corrective treatments, used in extreme situations." He continues. "And then we have to convince the new immunoglobulins to play nice with all the things her body thinks it should be allergic to."

"How do you do that?"

"Controlled exposure to her known allergens." He smiles, like it'd be fun.

"No." Expose her to things that we know might kill her?

"So be it, then. We're back to the bubble." He shrugs. "I've already ordered a bodysuit and full-head mask. She'll need them until she's treated, or not treated, regardless."

"I'll speak to Maven Ringol."

"I already have," he says with a smirk.

"What?" I hadn't even told Ringol that I assigned Crick to check Maddy's allergies.

"Relax, J'Mave Allele. He deferred everything to you. Did you think I'd go along with this feeble project without checking with my Maven?"

"Carry on then, and if you have to check anything in the future, see me first." I try to sound intimidating, but my voice sounds more shrill than sharp.

"Yes, J'Mave Allele." He ends the call. I still can't stand talking to him, but if he helps Maddy, it's worth it.

I reach for the next tabdisk, and the pile I'd already gone through shifts. Most of them drop to the floor. When I bend to pick them up, I inadvertently drop the pile I hadn't gone through. They fall on top of the others, mixing together underneath the desk.

Jetting jet! It will take me forever to sort them out again, and time is so short as it is. I breathe deeply to control my building frustration and scoop up a handful from the floor and place them on top. Several tabdisks are farther underneath the desk where the chair rolls. I have to pull out the chair and stabilize myself with one hand on the left panel of the desk. It's the side with a shorter leg, making it wobbly and causing my hand, which is wedged in a corner, to slip until my fingers find purchase as they slide over a thin panel of wood glued to the surface. It looks like it was added by someone who tried to make it look like the wood of the desk. I would never have noticed it unless I was this close.

What the jet are you hiding, Izadora Camu?

I yank it off, and an envelope falls to the floor.

The words *Project Helix-Q: Carillon Au Petit Lait* is written in Camu's script across the front of the envelope. A chiming of whey? The seal to the envelope ripped open when I pulled it off the desk, so I take out the contents. Two pages, also written in French, and one tabdisk.

The pages outline a failed experiment of genetically altered subjects, embryos that were supposed to produce people with the physical benefits of an Omnit and the intelligence of a Subter – the way the human species existed pre-Sterling's Plague. However, my mouth drops open as I read that Camu purposefully averted Common Good's guidelines and used illegal methods. Of the six-hundred embryos implanted into surrogate Omnit mothers, only eight survived to birth. Of those, only four survived past the first year. And the surviving children, living in the Omnit world, didn't fit in. So much so that they were shunned entirely by the Omnit society. They suffered ridicule and physical attacks from Omnits. One was even set on fire by someone within his Omnit family – an older son of the surrogate mother's.

How unimaginable.

A sound outside the room makes me jump. At the buzz and click of the door, I shove everything back into the envelope and inside my desk drawer.

Maven Ringol appears with a meal tray. Our argument from yesterday burns hot through my veins after he threatened to keep me from the Omnit babies. I tense at the sight of him.

"Leave the tray." I say tersely.

"I trust Maddelyn is well," he says, perhaps trying to remind me that he's helped me once again.

"For now. I hope Crick lives up to the hype."

"You think he won't?"

His question surprises me – he knows what Crick is like. "He sets off my inner-alarm."

"Don't let your biases take over, or you're no better than he is. Hunches lead to misguided decisions and needless worry." He sits in the empty stool.

"It's nothing for someone in your position to worry about."

"Zuzan." He says my name in a near whisper.

"Allele," I correct him. "You can't call me that whenever it suits you. 'Zuzan Cayan' doesn't exist any more. She died along with her identification number."

"You've never been more wrong." He places both hands on the wobbly desk. I slide the panel underneath the desk with my foot, out of view. "Zuzan Cayan is one of the most perplexing and frustrating human beings that I am honored to know. She's an outspoken advocate who says *infant* when I say *test subject*; who says *try harder* when I thought I already had, and who waltzes into a room and captivates everyone. Zuzan Cayan absolutely exists, and she is both a brilliant scientist and an outstanding teacher. If I'm honest with myself, I learn something new from Zuzan almost every day."

I can't meet his gaze – all I can do is fiddle with the tabdisks in my fingers. He brought me here to GCE and kept me safe. He brought Maddy here for *me*, and he's allowing me to work on the project that means the most to me. He's the most gruff and the most kind man I know. But these things he's saying about me now… His words can break me into two.

"Stop, please," I say. My heart is pulled in two directions. One where Ringol is my maven and mentor and I should give him the respect that his position demands, and the other where he's been a true friend and his actions and words touch my heart. I don't know how to respond or act with him most of the time, and I'm so tired of trying to figure it out.

"Nukleo and I agree with your assessment from yesterday," he adds. "We can do more for our subjects. She has a team

working on defined enrichment activities mimicking the
methods, equipment and toys we use and have in Subter
nurseries. After you eat, please join her and give your input."

"Of course, Maven." I turn awkwardly to my tray, pinching
crumbs from my protein chunk. I hold my breath waiting for
the sound of the door closing behind him.

Instead, he walks towards me, and moves around my desk
to sit on it beside me. He ignores when his large boot hits some
of the tabdisks I had piled on the floor, and they cascade down
into a heap, hitting the broken panel underfoot.

"That's it? *Of course, Maven,*" he sings in high voice, a
poor impersonation of me. His knee brushes my elbow and
goosebumps sprout across my skin.

My heart thuds with heavy beats and I can hardly look
him in the eye. "I'm trying to take your instructions to heart,
Maven."

"Which instruction?" The corner of his mouth tilts up. When
I don't respond, he continues. "No thank-yous? No guesses on
which burrow I might have crawled from?"

"You told me we can't be friends." My voice cracks as I speak
because it's the last thing I want to say. Now more than ever, I
need his support. "You are my supervisor."

He stands up, and takes my hand gently, pulling until I'm
also standing up, facing him. "You're using my words against
me?" I watch his full lips because I can't look him in the eyes.
His fingertips glide the length of my jaw, and then he tilts my
chin upward so I have to look into his dark pupils, sparkling
at the edge.

"I suppose I deserve that." He lets out a heavy sigh. "I speak
harsh words before my brain has a chance to catch up. What if
I apologize in all sincerity?"

"I remember how you apologize, Maven."

"The hoverjet incident?" He laughs and folds my fingers into
his hand. I move in closer until the warmth of his body melts
the chill in mine.

My breath catches. This isn't something we should be doing, I should pull back. But I don't want to.

He gently cups my face with both his hands. "I am truly sorry for my behavior, Zuzan. In all honesty, you have been my only friend, the one who confronts me with my faults. When I'm proven wrong, I own it." He leans in and kisses my right cheek, and then my left. And then there's a soft, brief touch of our lips.

He gazes into my eyes with the same expression he had when he called me *magnificent*, and now I can't look away. Every inch of me pulses, as if my body's been asleep my entire life. His fingers stroke through my stubbly hair and then gently trail down my neck. He plays with my collar and his thumb slides under the material at my collarbone, and his breath quickens. His forehead touches mine, but it's as if I have to hold him up – like he needs my support to stand. My mind whirs with nothing that makes sense. *Kiss him*, it's saying.

"Ringol," I whisper, accidentally breaking the spell.

He backs away too quickly, like he had forgotten he's my superior, and releases me with an apologetic look. The chill in the room hits me immediately, and I shiver. I want him to come back – to touch my hand, to kiss my cheek, to feel him against me again. But in a moment he's gone.

The door buzzes and clicks.

What just happened?

CHAPTER 21

Reaching for Shadows

Baby swings, rattles, and musical toys greet me when I stop in to see Jal again. Whole sections of the large labroom have been cleared of the cold, metal desks, and arranged into play areas.

I can't help but smile at Ringol's efforts. Thinking about him makes my mind spin and my insides flare and fluster, so I brush it aside and concentrate on the labroom.

"Don't look so smug." Nukleo walks up behind me. "We've got issues."

"You and I always have issues," I counter, but smile as I say it. The room looks more lively, like a nursery instead of a deathbed infirmary, so nothing she says can get to me today.

"True," she says with her wicked smile, and then she begins to walk while talking, forcing me to keep up with her long strides. "However, since we've established playstations for our subjects, Undertech Griffith noticed something unusual. Which is unusual in and of itself, since Undertech Griffith is typically useless." She pulls Griffith, who had been working with a group of undertechs on charting some stats, by his sleeve until he's walking with us. "Your findings, Undertech."

"Yes, J'Mave. Good health, Allele," he says.

Nukleo scowls. "That's J'Mave Allele to you, Undertech."

"There's no harm," I interrupt. "I don't require formal titles."

For some reason, Griffith's cheeks flush.

"Not in my labroom," Nukleo says. "Not unless you two are a couple."

"Excuse me?" I ask, watching Griffith's shoulders pull in as he turns a darker shade of purple.

"You are!" she continues, her evil grin working its way over her face. "How adorable. No, honestly – adorable. Like creamy baby vomit." She points to a spot on her labcoat.

Griffith clears his throat. "We figured out that the infants who were best at motor activities are twelve weeks old. However, the babies who are best with eye contact and babbling are somewhere around ten weeks old, and then the eye contact and babbling drop off rapidly in older infants."

"Thank you Undertech." Nukleo shoos him away while we keep walking. "Oh, sorry." She says after he's gone. "Am I keeping you two apart?"

"Knock it off, J'Mave." I glare at her. "We're platonic."

"You'd better tell him that, *J'Mave*. Rumors spread faster than the nastiest virus around here. Not that I care about your personal life, but I should warn you. There are strict guidelines for relationships which are outlined in the FFR guide. But even if you're not romantically involved or breaking any rules, you can't afford to have friends as a J'Mave. Friends take advantage of your weaknesses. Make friends after you relinquish your post."

There are probably two thousand reasons why Nukleo doesn't have close friends, and it has nothing to do with her j'mavenship.

"What do you make of your undertech's findings?" she asks.

"It's odd that some normal development continues while the social aspects, such as eye contact and language, regress. It gives me something to work with, though. I'd like to review the brain scans again."

She waves me away. "Suit yourself. Your weeks of J'Maveship keep tick-tick-ticking away."

I roll my eyes and walk over to Baby Jal's crib. When Undertech Rozalind sees me coming, she smiles and hands him over to me. "He's so good," she says.

"Of course he is," I reply, cooing at him and holding him in the air. And then something spectacular happens.

He smiles at me.

"Did you see that?" I ask her.

"You're his favorite."

I kiss the child on his cheek. "I love him."

Rozalind's eyes snap to me, and I realize what I've just said. I clear my throat and bounce him a little more, ignoring Rozalind's gaze.

As I hand the baby back to her, I catch a glimpse of Griffith pointing to a chart. He glances up and smiles. I'm going to have to fix our previous misunderstanding. But not here, where we could be overheard.

Instead, I look up FFR's guidance on relationships with supervisors, only to find that romance between a Maven and a scientist is strictly forbidden. Common Good doesn't want to mix scientific decisions with scientists' emotions. They found in the past that these relationships lead to differing flavors of corruption. Nukleo was right.

I review the scans on the Omnit babies again. As I go over them, I notice that the brain scans indicate an increased amount of lesions in the areas of the brain related to language and pragmatics. How did I miss this before? No wonder the older infants lose these skills.

My minitab beeps, so I find a quiet corner before answering Maddy's camcall.

"I'm ready," she says. She's wearing a full helmet and body suit. After she's gone unprotected for so long, the suit seems like overkill, and it's heartbreaking to see her this way.

"Ready for what?"

"For that high-risk treatment bubble-head told you about

earlier. I want to do it. I've been wearing this suit for about two hours, and I'm about to scream. I'd rather die than live this way. Do you realize what I have to do to relieve myself?"

I frown. "You'll get used to it. Give the suit – I don't know – say, three hours before you give up? Seriously, Maddy. I want to research all the options before we decide."

She sits straighter. "It's not your call. I know you're doing all you can for me, but this should be my decision. My life, my prerogative. Right?"

"Let me review Crick's information. Things have been so hectic today–"

"And they're not about to get less so." She knocks on her helmet's glass faceplate. "You can't want this for me."

I don't, but what happened to Jalaz is fresh in my mind. "Death is forever."

"Undertech Crick explained how my immune system is hosed up. My body wants to start wars against things that aren't enemies, which wreaks havoc on my health. He fully outlined the procedure, the possible outcomes with the risks. It'll be difficult. I'll spend days in isolation, but if I make it to the finish line, it'll be worth it."

Maddelyn is one of the few people who's ever out-negotiated me, so I'm sure she drilled Crick, leaving no question unasked until she was convinced. "Okay."

"You know," she sighs. "I'm sorry. I never understood what you were going through with your lower LE, and how it makes you look at things so differently. Not until now."

I swallow hard to fight back the tears. "I didn't want you to *have* to know."

"I'll beat this. Maybe my body is stubbornly amiss, but my will is just as stubborn."

"More so," I say. "I'll let Undertech Crick know."

"He's preparing treatment now, but insisted I speak with you first."

I pull the short hairs at the base of my neck.

"He's still irritating, conceited, and obnoxious. But underneath that he's got some so-so qualities."

"Sure," I say without meaning it. "Everyone must."

I try to get back to studying the Omnit babies' brain scans, but find I'm distracted, stuck on Maddy's words – that her body wants to start wars against things that aren't enemies. Could that be what's happening to these babies? Not an allergy, per se, but a virus containing proteins or DNA strains that look enough like that of brain tissue, to trick their immune systems into attacking their brains? Autoimmune activation that goes too far is known to cause such lesions in other debilitating conditions.

I search for Nukleo to get her input, and find her frowning over the stats on her favorite infant, Horizon. I explain my theory while she stares at the baby.

"It's possible," she says. "But don't you think it's more likely that the virus itself is attacking the brain tissue, rather than the immune system attacking the tissue it's supposed to protect?"

"The bloodlab data shows no sign of viral activity past the second week after birth. The only process that can continue to cause the brain lesions we don't see until the babies are older, is the babies' own immune system. What if it's just very stubborn immune cells that become overstimulated from the initial infection?"

"The Immunology Center of Excellence should have caught this if your theory is valid. Common Good would shut us down if they knew we're exploring anything outside our discipline. Our job is to determine if we can solve anything at a genetic level. ICE is immunological, so our hands are clearly tied. Besides, Omnits' immune systems are stellar – almost perfect compared to ours. When an Omnit gets sick, they're usually down for a few hours or at worst, a few days."

"Maybe the virus uses Omniterraneans' amazing immune

systems against them," I say. Sterling's Plague had some convoluted impact on genetics inside of his virus, according to Maven Camu's theories.

"Not likely," she replies almost too quickly. "If the virus-maker found a weak spot in Omnit DNA then it would impact the entire Omnit population."

"Do you mean the virus would sicken older children and adults? If my hypothesis proves out, we will eventually see issues there as well. The completed brain development in Omnits means that lesions wouldn't cause symptoms for a much longer period of time." I shiver at the thought. What if we have massive plague deaths again? There's no way that Omnits would believe we're on their side if word got out that this is a genetically-altered virus targeted at them.

"Look, we're assigned to look for genetic issues and solutions. Nothing else."

"Maybe," I mumble, "but my idea is a little of both – genetic loopholes with an altered immune system that wreaks havoc. I've got to run."

She raises her eyebrows, but I ignore her. I need somewhere quiet to flush out some ideas. A place like Camu's Cave. I rush over and kiss Jal, and then leave. "Good health, baby."

But I glance somberly at the three names on the wall first.

TWILIGHT
AURORA
BREEZE

They matter. They will always matter.

CHAPTER 22

You Appear Undamaged

As I near the open lobby near the transport platform, with the door leading to the undertunnels, I catch the sound of someone's footsteps up ahead. I slow down and stay hidden in the adjoining hallway to see who, besides Ringol and Kleo, would know about the undertunnel entrance. Someone is hovering near the unmarked entrance. It's not the fact that he bioscans and walks through that sends my internal alarm into panic mode. It's how he acted just beforehand – as if he were going to pass it up, glancing around first, and then doubling back to sneak inside.

The fact that it's Crick Zamption doesn't help. Maybe there's another hidden labroom in the tunnels that I don't know about. But then, why would he act so guilty if he's supposed to be here? I chipchat Ringol to ask. Shouldn't Crick be checking on Maddy anyway?

Ringol doesn't answer.

The last thing I need is another confrontation with Crick, but I doubt Ringol would want anyone to find Camu's stash of personal notes, so I chase after him.

When I enter, the tunnels take on the same eerie persona they had on my initiation night when all the alarms had blared. A shiver runs through me.

"Undertech Crick?" My voice bounces and echoes against the walls, but with the air filtration system humming, I doubt he can hear me if he's further ahead. I pick up my pace.

My ChiPro beeps with a return call from Ringol.

"Don't answer that," Crick warns me from a dark space a few feet away, and I jump.

"You scared me to death," I reply. "Why didn't you answer me when I called you?"

He crosses his arms. "Maybe because we're not supposed to be roaming around back here, eh, J'Mave Allele?" He comes closer, and stands four or so inches taller than me.

"*You* shouldn't be here." I want to take a step back, but I don't want him to think I'm afraid. I'm his supervisor. But still, something feels off. "What are you doing?"

He narrows his eyes. "Maven Camu used to travel through these tunnels all the time. Everyone knew she had some hidden materials down here. I saw a quote about *destruction* and *reconstruction* during my camcall with you – the same quote that I noticed during a camcall with Camu. Jetting dishonest maven if ever there was one, and that goes for Maven Ringol, too. I wonder how long it will be before *he* disappears."

"What do you know about Camu's disappearance?" I ask, not caring how accusatory it sounds.

He holds up his palms as if he's innocent. "It's my best guess. Camu was sympathetic to dullards, much like our new maven." He shrugs. "Sooner or later, all dullard-lovers will have to answer to the coalition."

"The anti-Omnit group?"

"A pro-Subter coalition – the Proliferation of the Subterranean Species for Eternity to be exact. When one side forms an offensive strike, the other side has no other choice but to defend themselves. It's self-preservation."

"What about fixing the genetic break that caused the divide in the first place?"

"Playing dumb doesn't suit such a gifted person as yourself.

PoSSE has a great need for people like you. Speaking of gifted, your sickly Subter girl has a decent mind behind that sass-mouth of hers."

I slide my hand into my pocket and grasp Jal's rock with my fingers. There's no use talking with him. He's got a way to twist everything until it fits his argument.

"In all reality, J'Mave Allele, can you see yourself living above ground, conversing with masses of drooling dullards? You wouldn't have a thing in common. All past integration attempts have failed. They've even bludgeoned hospital medstaff in cold blood. They hate us."

We take all their babies, now, not just Subters. I remind myself of this fact. *They're terrified.*

"Not all of them," I say weakly, because I worry if so many people have closed their minds, how can we live together peacefully? The options aren't binary: integration versus segregation. We've now moved to a much worse reality. Conflict.

"Even if half of them hate us, or only a quarter of them – it doesn't matter. We're still so outnumbered and they won't rest until we're gone."

Camu's failed experiment with the genetically altered children may prove his point. They would have looked more like Omnits than we do, and they still weren't able to escape victimization.

"Omnits are too biased and too stupid to understand."

They'd have to listen if we are able to save the Omnit babies. "We should try harder."

He smiles and takes a step toward me. "Funny, Maddelyn is from the Cayan Burrow, J'Mave Allele. Wasn't the boy who died before making it to GCE – the one you spoke of on your initiation night – he was from Cayan, no? He sent over a genome when he was applying to GCE."

My eyes drop to the ground. What has Maddy told him? Ringol warned me to stay under the radar, and here I am dancing in it.

"It always seemed odd that you took on the Crypt name, since most people who take that surname try to distance themselves from their burrow, sometimes out of shame, sometimes out of differences in philosophy, *J'Mave Allele.*"

What does he think he's got on me? I stare at him coldly.

"I've spoken with Medero Allund Woynauld." His words sound practiced and prickly, like he knows exactly how they'll affect me. My scars burn. "Can you believe he had a run-in with Maven Ringol over a nearly blind maid?" His eyes narrow. "There's another girl – a first year who transferred to Zamption, my old burrow."

"I'm not sure where you're going with this." He's trying to get to me, and it's working.

"This Cayan burrowling keeps asking for her old burrow sisters. There's one sister in particular –"

I cringe, knowing what he'll say.

"– Zuzan."

He laughs when I snap my eyes to him. I glance at his knee. The last page of the self-defense journal in my library promised the next issue would focus on how to sweep across an enemy's knees to disarm them – no breaks involved. Unfortunately, the next issue wasn't donated to my library. How hard could it be, though?

"As a former Zamptionite, I could see this girl is well cared for." He moves in closer. "If," he continues, "her former Cayan sister cooperates with my cause." His *PoSSE* cause. His mouth twists and he continues to come at me. "*Zuzan.*"

"Keep your distance," I say.

He lunges forward, grabs my arms, and shoves me to the floor. Then he peels my ChiPro from my forehead.

"Get off!" I roll on to my stomach, but it's too late. He's on top of me with his arm wrapped around my neck. I claw at his arm and gasp for air. His other hand rips a seam on my labcoat. He digs his hand under my blouse, fingering my ropy scar.

As quickly as he grabbed me, he releases, panting. He

activates his ChiPro to message someone. "Tattoo confirmed."

The air that couldn't make it through my compressed windpipe now whizzes through me. I sit against the wall, trying to recover while watching his every move.

"Apologies, Zuzan," he says. "I had to be certain. Medero Allund is quite apologetic as well. The tattoo mishap occurred *before* he knew your real identity. He's reviewed my findings about your genome, and we're very interested in you. We had already identified the genome as female when it was sent, but we thought it might be Maddelyn's. I confirmed it wasn't hers after running her bloodlabs during her immunological workup, thanks to you. It took a bit of sleuthing, but I eventually realized what was right under my nose."

Crick has been watching me more closely than I care to think about. I shiver. He must have known I'd follow him inside the tunnels. "You sicken me," I hiss. "As much as Allund Woynauld does."

"This isn't a game." Crick brushes off his jacket. "Everyone is in danger because of the Omnits. But maybe the people who put Omnits ahead of Subters are also in danger, or the ones they care about – like the students who transferred from Cayan to Zamption, or an old medera–"

"Get out of here!"

My ChiPro rings again from Crick's pocket.

He smirks. "I will, and you, *my dear Zuzan,* will remain loyal to PoSSE's directives for everyone's safety."

"With Medero Allund? You can go and rot, for all I care. I'll never be on his side, if that's what you mean."

"Allund Woynauld – right. Let me help you with that. He is the only leader capable of ensuring the protection of Subterraneans. Some people consider him to be excessively punitive, but when we need to conquer enemies, that's a sorely needed trait. Regrettably, you found yourself on the wrong side of his temper. Obviously, you'll want to be on his *right* side next time."

"You know how he treats the burrowlings under his care?" I ask.

"I'm not here to debate his instructional methods. Make sure Ringol doesn't transfer me, and I won't have you transferred out of GCE for being underage. I'll leave peacefully when I've fulfilled my mission. Furthermore, I'll need access to the infertility research. And, of course, today's encounter with me is to be kept confidential."

He holds out a hand as if to help me up, but I stand on my own. "If you harm any of my people–"

"All Subters are your people. Keeping them safe is up to you. Beware of our Omnit-loving maven – he's not who you think he is. If you tell him about our partnership, all deals are off."

Including Maddelyn's treatment? He wouldn't.

He makes a fist over his heart, holding out his pinky and thumb. "Eternity."

"Zuzan!" Ringol's voice booms from the darkness, echoing like the roar of a lion. No one is supposed to be in the undertunnels; he probably thinks it's safe to call me by my burrowname.

Crick grins as if he's proven his point, tosses me my ChiPro, and then backs into the same dark corner he must have hidden in before. It would have been so easy to surprise Maven Camu the same way.

Crick has Maddy and C in his hands, and he can send me away for my age discrepancy. Or worse, for faking my identity. All he wants is the infertility project, and my silence. I wanted to prove I could manage these projects on my own terms, but I can't even figure out what those are anymore. Can I agree to Crick's deal? It sickens me but seems like an easy enough trade.

"I'm here, Maven," I call out to Ringol.

"Zuzan!" He's at my side in seconds. He touches my face, worry and anxiety lining his. "You look fine. Why didn't you answer my calls?"

"I fell, but I'm okay." My hands shake as I replace the chip at my forehead. "I'm sorry." Sorry that I couldn't stay under the radar. Sorry that I failed to keep up the Allele façade. Ringol only brought Maddy here because of me, and now I've put her in danger.

Ringol pulls me into an embrace. I stiffen, knowing Crick is out there watching us.

"Are you injured?"

I shake my head, lowering my eyes. My teeth begin to chatter. What would Ringol do if he knew that Crick tackled me down and shoved hands down my blouse? Would he react the same as he did with Allund? Probably.

But I can't tell him without risking everyone I love.

"I missed your camcall. I've been battling migraines." He massages his temple as if to demonstrate. "Fortunately for me, you appear undamaged." Ringol smiles as a chilling emptiness fills me. I watch Crick's shadow as he sneaks out of the undertunnels behind Ringol's back.

CHAPTER 23

Chiming of Whey

What did Crick mean when he said Ringol isn't who I think he is? I'm trying not to allow Crick to throw a shadow between Ringol and me, but I have to admit I follow him a little less closely and with deflated energy. I'm on my guard.

The cold settles into my bones as we make our way to Camu's office, and I have questions pulsing through me that want escape. *What else has Ringol kept from me?* I want him to be the Ringol I've come to know: fiercely passionate, rough around the edges, and one of the few people who challenges me. I want him to be *this* person, for all good, because I need to trust him.

Of course, I used to believe that Medera Gelia wouldn't hide things from me too. And I *never* thought Maddelyn would try to murder me. If I could only predict people as well as facts and numbers, I never would have misunderstood these situations. But human beings are full of emotions and deception, thereby defying all logic. Is Ringol another one of my blind spots? With or without goggles, it's possible that I see people through the filters of who I hope they are. But why wouldn't he warn me about the anti-Omnit coalition?

When we make it to the hatch, Ringol opens the bioauthorization door, smiling patiently for me to continue.

"Ringol," I start once we're inside, but I'm not even sure what to ask. If I tip him off and Crick finds out and harms

Maddelyn, I'd never forgive myself. I don't know who to trust. "Why can't anyone know that I'm from Cayan?" Crick knows it now, and my stomach twists at the thought of his fingers pressing into my scars. And then images of the day I'd been "painted" at Woynauld flood back – Allund slapping me, drugging me, throwing me onto that table.

How he touched my skin while telling the painter what to write.

My eyes sting but I fight the tears.

He raises his eyebrows. "Many reasons."

"Because of my age?"

"You've got to suspect the reason by now, Zuzan. Someone might connect you to the mysterious hand-mapped genome sent from Cayan." He flashes me a confused look. "Why do you ask?"

"Who gives you orders?"

His soft expression fades and his shoulders tense.

"Common Good, of course. What's gotten into you? I thought you had your mind on the infants?"

The dying babies: an experiment condoned by all scientific centers of excellence.

"If Common Good knew about me, or knew what you did to get me here, I wouldn't be standing before you, would I?"

By the lost look on his face, he's either truly confused, or he's a talented liar. "I follow my own moral code on some things, just like you do," he says. "But Common Good is always in charge." He's turned gruff. "Hear me. To save just one of those Omnit subjects – *babies* – would be miraculous. But if you were able to impact the survival of the entire lot of them – all of *us*? How much more can we ask?" His fingers press into his temples again and moves them in small, circular motions. Deep circles have begun to form under his eyes, and to think he lectured me on getting my rest. *Pah!*

"Medera Gelia said in her letter that she regretted not telling me things. Is there anything you regret not telling me?" I ask this gently, and watch him while he shifts and loses himself in thought. But he doesn't answer me. *Manipulation of sentiment is a heartless man's sin.* I don't repeat this aloud – he didn't like hearing it the last time, but it's still true.

His ChiPro beeps, and he touches the button, turning to leave. "I've got to get this."

I take a seat at my desk. When the door buzzes and clicks, I know he's gone. For a few moments, I play back our conversation verbatim in my mind, and each time I run through it I worry more and more about his migraines and his pallor. What is going on with him?

I send him a quick message. *Consider a quick bloodlab check for yourself. Get some rest.*

I try to take a cleansing breath. It's more than his health that bothers me. It's the man himself. Every time Ringol opens up to me, he soon shuts down again. It's this fact that bothers me most. My chest tightens uncomfortably as I replay our interaction on repeat in my head. But there's not a jetting thing I can do about it.

I pull myself together, choosing to ignore it for now, and push my frustration away so I can get to work. At least here, I can make a difference in ways that matter.

Activating my chip, I begin to search archives of recent events hinting at increased medical issues in the general Omnit population, age two or higher. If my theory holds true – that the virus over-activates their immune system, the one thing considered a strength in Omnits, – then the virus will eventually affect all Omniterraneans, no matter their age. And if that's the case, the world is a short-wicked bomb with Drake's name on it.

I wait for the results of my Omnit searches. In the meantime, I open the desk drawer with the hidden envelope, Project Helix-Q.

I devour the French words scribbled on the pages, front and back, though I'm not familiar with all the scientific terms.

The genetic combination was considered a mild success – Omnit strength mixed with the intelligence of Subters. The experiment didn't fail scientifically, even with the low birth survival rate, it was hailed as cutting edge.

But it did fail the social-integration tests. The combined subjects couldn't reintegrate above ground. They'd been abused, even attacked, and finally sent to live with us, the Subter population – almost like what Crick described. *Oh, jet.*

I stare at the French words written on the top of the notes. I take out the page where Camu outlined her information about me to compare the two. Using one of her blank notepads and a pencil, I sketch out my thoughts trying to decode what she meant.

I copy Camu's words first. *Réserve: Susanne Poivre* And then I write out what I believe Camu meant. *Contingency: Susan Pepper (Zuzan Cayan).*

I use a similar conversion on the information I found inside the envelope.

Carillon au Blé could possibly translate to *Chiming of Wheat* and *Chiming* is close to the word *Ring*; which I'm guessing refers to *Ringol*.

And finally, *L'amande Blé* translates to *Almond of Wheat* which could be in reference to *Allund Woynauld*. Although this one doesn't feel quite as on-the-nose, it still works. *N'est pas?*

Could Ringol be a Woynauld? Is this why Allund called him brother?

I flip to my chip's electronic records to find Ringol's personnel file, but it is protected. All I can see is his name: Ringol Crypt, and a few places of residence. One of the locations catches my eye but only because I remember seeing it on another staffmember's history when I reviewed everyone's files after becoming junior maven. Kriz. I flip to her record. She was stationed at the same place as Ringol for a number of years, although her job there is redacted on the file.

The tension inside my chest tightens even more, and I keep

taking notes as I read Camu's hand-written status updates.

If *Carillon au Blé* really means *Ringol Woynauld*, then could it be that Ringol and Allund were Camu's subjects for Project Helix-Q?

According to Camu's notes before me, the surviving subjects of Project Helix-Q included two boys who were twenty-nine months apart in age with different genetic makeup, yet both born of the same surrogate Omnit mother. They lived with their surrogate mother's family after birth. During one of Camu's visits, the younger boy brought up issues with fitting in. The older boy was later tormented by a cousin in his surrogate family, who doused him with gasoline and set him on fire. The younger brother kicked dirt and sand on the flames, and rolled his brother until they were out, which minimized his injuries. The boy survived, treated with stem-cell skin regeneration, and both subjects were pulled from the Omnit population. The older boy became obsessed with revenge.

It must have been Allund. I begin to shiver again and can't get warm.

Soon after, the subjects were taken to an undisclosed burrow and educated by a private medera. They were promised high-level jobs in the Subter world to make up for their pain and suffering. Allund and Ringol fit this entirely – their massive size, their seemingly undeserved jobs. And Ringol's speech about the mysterious people he loves. For all good, he lived with a woman he called "mother."

My ChiPro beeps with the search results I requested on Omnit illnesses. I look up from Camu's notes and start devouring the statistics before me. Early onset Alzheimer's is up by twenty-four percent in the past two months. Psychiatric disorders of every type have risen by thirty percent. I wonder if this might explain the rise in violence, too? Strokes are up by twenty percent. These are all conditions that could be exacerbated if one's immune system is attacking brain tissue. But the disorder that scares me the most tops the stats with a forty-one percent increase.

Migraines.

One medtech noted a sharp increase in deaths with Omnit patients who present with these unusual ailments, theorizing the cause of death to be brain aneurisms. But this medtech's reports stopped suddenly a few weeks ago. I search his name and wait again for the results.

Jet. The medtech was killed in a fire at his assigned hospital a week ago. I press my eyes shut, not wanting to read any more.

How much Omniterranean genetic code does a person need to have to be susceptible to the effects of Drake's Plague? How much Omnit coding did Camu include in her Helix-Q subjects? Ringol, a genetically spliced Omnit-Subter, has been exposed to the plague for as long as the infants have been at GCE.

I need to call the maven, stat, except my chip beeps with a call from Maddelyn.

"Zuzan," she starts. "Get over here, now."

"You know you can't call me that." As soon as I snap at her, I'm sorry. "What is it?"

"Not over chipchat. Hurry. Now!"

CHAPTER 24

An Extraordinary Combination

Rushing to the infirmary, I have to force myself to breathe. It could be anything – her condition could have worsened, or her treatment could have gone wrong, or perhaps a combination of the two. It must be serious, though, if she wouldn't tell me over chipchat.

Rounding the corner to her room, I almost knock Crick over. "If you've done anything–" I start. Somehow, even in the regular light, I can't help but see the darker shadows in his features.

But Crick's demeanor isn't tense. He looks at me like I'm insane. "Your girl is fine."

I slide past him, darting to the doorway of Maddelyn's room, where she's still wearing her full-body protection. Her left arm is stuck inside a rectangular tank, large enough to house her IV. It works like a mini-decontamination chamber.

"Close the door," she says.

"What's happened?" I sit on her bed next to her. "We're alone."

"I've done some snooping." Her voice turns a bit sheepish.

I blink. "From your bed?"

"From my minitab." She holds the device up. Medera Gelia used to praise her for her technology skills, until she went paranoid. "It's not hard if you know shortcuts."

"Why?"

"I looked into the weird thing with your bioscanning, for one thing. Do you know that your thumbscan pulls up a record other than that of 'Allele Crypt?'" She pulls up something on her tab, and then shows it to me. The times I go into the cave, the lab, and a few other bioscan areas, it shows my identity as BLOCKED RECORD.

I sit back. "What might Ringol have done to it?"

"Nope," Maddy says. "He didn't do it. This blocked record was created a year ago."

"What?" I glance at the date. Ringol wasn't here a year ago, but Camu was. That's the simplest explanation, but I can't go into this with Maddy right now. "Did you find anything else?"

When she nods, I frown.

"It's Ringol." She taps the device with a stylus since her hand is gloved in the bodysuit. "I found some of his camcalls on the central network. Your intelligence staff needs to work on updating their database passwords."

"I'll let Chen know."

"Not yet. Right now, it's good that I can get in. This was one of Ringol's last camcalls made to someone overseas. I can't quite decode the entire encryption, so I've only got Ringol's side of the conversation, and only a few seconds worth."

"Maybe we shouldn't listen–"

"It's about you." She taps to play the recording. Ringol's voice enters the space, and I jump as if he's in the room with us.

– Zuzan keeps asking questions, and whether or not you provide answers, she's going to figure it out.

There's a pause, where someone else must be talking, but it's all staticky. I can't even tell if the other person is male or female.

No one is safe now that she's here. I suspect at least three GCE staff members are associated with the PoSSE. If she weren't making so much progress, I'd recommend moving her out of GCE for everyone's security.

Another staticky pause.

Yes, I can manage her until you make a decision.

Manage me? What could he mean by that? Maddelyn plays it again and my stomach twists. He's been lying to me, pure and simple. How could he have kissed me yesterday as if he cared? Maybe it was just part of his plan, although he hasn't warned me to leave for everyone's safety. Theories about his motives race through my mind, but they only lead to more questions.

"When was this camcall?" I ask. Ringol and I had been arguing about everything, and then he turned a corner. Yesterday.

"This is time-stamped two nights ago, just before midnight."

I blow air from my mouth. So many things about Ringol keep piling up – the connection to Allund, for one. But did he ever say they weren't related? No. In fact, they called each other *brother*. And then there's the PoSSE group that Crick belongs to, but Ringol has confronted prejudice head on. But now there's this recording where he's agreeing to keep me in line. Who could he be talking to?

"You don't look so well," she says.

When he held me yesterday, I felt safe in his arms. This doesn't make sense. He was the one person I thought would help me no matter what. Instead, he's biding his time with me. How can I trust him now?

"I'm fine – especially now that I see you're doing better." I pat Maddelyn's hand.

"What does he mean by *posse*? Is there any connection to Allund? Are you in danger?" She touches my hand, her eyes full of concern.

I shrug, glaring at a dark spot on the floor that morphs into Crick's shadowy face from the tunnels, his threats echoing in my head. Crick already informed them of my genome – my true identity. Questions bubble at my core, but I have nowhere to go with them. I can't trust anyone working with Allund Woynauld.

And maybe now, that includes Ringol.

"Thank you for sharing this with me." Ringol fought to retrieve me so I could piece together the holes in Camu's research. I don't understand why he would be talking with someone about me without telling me. "Please don't tell anyone about this, especially Crick."

After checking her medstats, I leave Maddelyn so she can rest. My boots pound against the hard marble tiles as I rush away. After spending time at the Woynauld Academy, I'm certain that this *PoSSE* spins everything into bigotry.

The only person who might know more of the truth is the one who hates me most – the one person who doesn't trust me worth a rot.

"Chipchat J'Mave Nukleo," I say into my device, my voice eerily steady.

My stomach growls as if it knows how angry my entire body is.

"Why, hello, Newness," she says as her face appears before me. She doesn't bother to stop changing out of her uniform as she speaks, now standing in just her underslip. "Another idea for the infants that can't wait until morning?"

"Stay where you are," I respond. I can't talk to her over the device, not after seeing how Maddelyn was able to hack camcalls – who else can tamper with this technology?

"You've got about five minutes before I lock myself into my drawer for the night. I'm ashed."

As I fly off to our chamberroom, I begin to replay the recording of Ringol in my mind. *No one is safe... three staff members are part of the PoSSE.* I already met one of them. Who else does he suspect?

I round a corner passing someone, when they reach out and grab my arm just a little too tightly. My body tenses, and I spin out of their grasp. Squatting, I kick out my leg, *page-sixty-one-style*, twisting a hundred and eighty degrees until my assailant falls squarely on his back.

He grunts, and then chuckles. "Allele?"

"Sorry." I hurry to Griffith's side. "Did I hurt you?" I take his arm and pull him onto his feet.

"Everything seems to be working still," he says. "You've got some surprising power for your size."

"Self-defense is all physics theory," I blurt out. "I'm – I'm a little skittish at the moment. Please excuse me." He's still calling me Allele instead of J'Mave and I cringe at the thought of having that conversation.

"Hey." His face flushes again. "I'm at your beck-and-call. Tackle me at your whim."

I laugh nervously, and it sounds more like I'm faking someone else's laugh. Then I scurry to my chamberroom.

As soon as I enter, Kleo crosses her arms and opens her chamberdrawer. "You're too late." She yawns. A long, dramatic, drawn-out yawn. It's an hour before regular chambertime, so no one else is in the room yet. "I told you, I'm ashed."

I reach around and slam her drawer closed. "Can it, Kleo." My words come out hot as fire. Her face draws in as if she's about to yell at me, but I stop her. "Tell me. Was it a GCE staff member who created the Omnit-infant plague?"

Her mouth clamps shut and her eyes widen. "What is your clearance? I'm reporting Ringol for breaching confidentiality." She reaches for her chip. "He'll be stripped of his title!"

For a second, I'm too stunned to move. It was only a hunch, a million-to-one shot. It can't be true. I grab her hand. "Ringol hasn't told me anything. You're the one who confirmed my suspicion just now, so if there's anyone to report, it's you."

"You tricked me." Her voice slows like I've injured her pride. "What do you want?"

"Information. You knew Camu."

"It wasn't her fault." When tears form in her eyes, I'm shocked she's capable of such a deep emotion. "I let my guard down. I trusted the wrong person and he took advantage of our relationship. Drake acted independently. When I found out, I reported it to Camu but it was too late. The virus had been deployed using common birds. At first, we hoped it had been ineffective but a few months later, babies began to die." She clenches her jaw tightly and wipes her eyes. "It's my fault for trusting him."

If Nukleo had a relationship with Drake, the individual responsible for the newest plague, she'll never be promoted to maven. He's the reason her career's been stunted. She's the most qualified, but Common Good installed Ringol here instead. It must absolutely rot to be her.

"Camu didn't know?"

"Of course not, you mite! Her work ethic is beyond reproach. But it didn't matter. It happened under her watch, and she ultimately decided she had to step down." Nukleo's expression turns grim. "If it weren't for Drake, Camu would still be in charge of GCE."

"Did she step down officially then?" I ask. "She didn't just disappear?"

"She was here that morning, gone by midday. There was a chip message sent to GCE staff members, but it didn't seem like her wording. It was too simple and trite. Most of us here at the time suspected some sort of foul play." Nukleo presses her lips together and hesitates like she's not sure how much to tell me. "Drake was part of this crazy alt-Subter group, as we all found out later, known for 'disappearing' people." Her words strike me hard, because Gelia disappeared too.

"If you're right about all this," I say, "then Camu was framed for Drake's work." Which may be why Camu needed a Plan B. *Me.* Not because her experiments failed – all her notes line up with anticipated success – but because she must have feared *someone* would stop her from doing it. Plan B was for me to discover her altered data, figure out she was on the right track to solve the Subter-Omnit divide, and finish it for her. I shiver.

Can I?

"Most GCE staff members, like me, would give anything

to have her back. Not many people here trust your precious Maven Ringol."

She shouldn't call him *my* maven. I'm not sure he's ever been mine, and I don't even know how trustworthy he is. But I'm trying to figure something else out. "What do you know about Project Helix-Q?"

"You don't have the clearance to know." She glares.

"You and I together are the best chance to fix past mistakes. This is important for Drake's plague. Camu left notes on the project, but not enough to go on." I stare into her hardened eyes, hoping she'll see I have nothing to hide. "Can't we team up on this?"

But she doesn't budge. Her bottom lip pulls in like she's about to speak, but then she sighs, like I've put her over the edge.

"Please." I touch her arm.

Her expression softens. "Helix-Q was some sort of half-breed splicing experiment that Camu worked on as one of her first projects here at GCE – before my time, when Common Good still allowed Omnit surrogates. She manipulated genetic code in human embryos to create offspring with normal intelligence and healthy bodies. It was groundbreaking because of the implications for fertility. She succeeded where her predecessors had failed." Kleo lets out a long exhale. "The pre-birth death rate was high, though, ninety-something-percent, and the surviving offspring didn't successfully integrate into the Omnit world.

"Still, every project goes through modifications and fine-tuning. But Camu never got the chance, because Common Good shut it all down: no more Omnit surrogates for spliced embryos, and unless the genetic manipulation would pass through to future generations, then our government argued it wasn't sustainable. According to Camu, it was a political hot button." She gives a half-hearted shrug. "That's all I know."

I sigh and then smooth my centimeter-long hair down. "Who am I?"

Her eyes comb me from head to toe. "I really don't know. And it's not for lack of trying. I have connections, but your records are tightly sealed. All I gathered is that you're special somehow, to Maven Camu."

"But she vanished."

Kleo nods.

"Why can't we fix the Omnit plague, if we created it?" I ask.

"*We* didn't create it. Drake did, and he was as brilliant as Camu. Drake didn't exactly leave any clues nor did he ever intend to reverse it. PoSSE believes that if Subters could reproduce, then killing off the Omnits would be a proactive defense, a purging of our biggest threat."

"We're not going to let that happen." I throw her labcoat into her hands. "Come with me."

She narrows her eyes. When I turn and leave her behind like she's done to me so many times, I know she'll get the hint. On the way to her research lab she catches up with me, so I show her the statistics for all the current ailments reported for Omnit children and adults.

"Great research." By the look on her face, I know she's not being sarcastic. "You were right about the immune-system-on-overdrive theory. Drake came from Zampion. He and Crick had always been close."

"Maybe they combined their expertise – Drake's genetics plus Crick's immunology."

"We've got to get Crick out of here. He should be with Drake in the Central Penitentiary." She reaches for her chip.

"Wait." Crick said that I needed to make sure he could stay here and work on his research. "I need to clear up treatment for Maddelyn before we report him." I can't tell her everything – if she finds out I'm not twenty, she might be the first to send me away, no matter what it does to Maddelyn or C, or even her own project.

She pulls away from me. "That's not how we do things here, J'Mave. Why should Drake alone be punished?" She pulls her lips in tight. "No. We're taking care of this now."

Ringol and Chen once talked about how Omnits don't turn in the rebels, and Ringol said it's because the rebel-Omnits threaten the peaceful Omnits. Is that what I'm doing by protecting Crick right now? I hate him even more.

"People are dying," I remind her. "I have so much to go over with you. Our first order of business is saving the lives of the infants who depend on us." She has to agree that some things are more urgent. "Agreed?"

"Let's get to work." She nods and sighs wearily. "One talented geneticist plus an exceptional immunologist equals a catastrophic Omnit-only plague. Where do we start?"

"They'd need an extraordinarily complex combination," I say.

She nods. "Something that would seem impossible: a virus that infects Omnits but not Subters. We've been exposed to the same virus hundreds of times. We should be dead already."

My eyes snap over to her, but she doesn't notice. I won't let that happen to baby Jal.

I will not fail.

CHAPTER 25

Like a Barnacle

We brainstorm, Kleo and I, working into the late hours of the evening until long moments of silence pass between us. My head droops a few times, and then I jerk awake again.

"Look at this," Kleo says, pointing to the master chart of all infants. "We have no significant change in body temperature noted from fourteen days on."

I squint at the figures. "Why wouldn't the babies' immune systems try to fight the virus once they become infected?"

She pulls up archives of other Omnit baby populations who are now as sick as ours. All the data shows the same thing. "The virus must somehow bypass the normal immune response, and trick their systems into attacking the healthy tissue in their brains. We'll never figure this out. We don't have enough immunology expertise."

Something Camu mentioned on one of her tabdisk files might shed some clues. *Deletion at the u-level of gene B7HT4 results in a missing allele in Subterranean offspring related to pigmentation and subpar immune system response.* "Or maybe we already know."

Kleo blinks at me as if I started speaking in French.

"It's *because* we're Subters that we're protected. Our protection relates to that genetic deletion – a missing allele. Have you heard of B7HT4?" I laugh numbly. How could they have constructed something so menacing and so exact? "The Omnit's immune system, in this case, has been tricked into seeing a problem where none exists, and that kicks it into overdrive."

Kleo clicks her tongue and searches on her ChiPro for research. "Here it is. The Immunological Center of Excellence conducted a study two years ago concluding that Subterraneans are completely devoid of this particular immune capability – the only thing we have that comes close is our freakishly hazardous allergies. It's related to the B7HT4 allele, and the findings were written up by both Drake and Crick Zamption."

"Our faulty immune systems – in this case – keep us from reacting to the virus."

"Crick made sure of it," she says. "It's brilliant how the virus works, like an enemy combatant walking into camp unnoticed, then convincing the resident soldiers to attack one another. But even if we're right, it could take years to come up with a remedy."

Sterling wanted to cleanse the world of humankind so the other living organisms could reboot our ecosystem naturally, but he failed because ten percent of the infected humans survived. Viruses morph, or become ineffective in differing climates. Did Drake consider all possibilities? "We need to find a region or population of Omnits where this virus has been less effective." I activate my chip. "Look for Omnit populations with a lower infection rate."

She crosses her arms. "I don't need to research that topic – I've been on this project for months, and we already explored this."

My shoulders droop. If they looked and found nothing, then my idea is "ashed," as Kleo would say. "You're right then, we'll never–"

"There's a subpopulation of Omnits in the Southwestern hemisphere reported to have a lower infection rate. However, this population is also fighting through their third straight month of the feline flu, which is a virus that produces meningitis-like symptoms originating from the overrun cat population in that region. Therefore, statisticians believe that the Omnit-infant plague has simply been overlooked or underreported. So, we're singed – back to square one."

I let out a squeal and activate my chip to search for this information. When it pops up on my screen, I jump up and hug her. "This is perfect! I don't believe the information has been underreported at all."

Kleo smiles, and then curls her lip as if to catch herself. "How do you figure?"

I close my eyes and think through what I'm about to say without making it sound insane. "This feline flu launches a major 'kill all invaders' immune response. Nothing would get by the omni's 'stellar' immune system at that point – not the feline flu and not the Drake-Crick virus. The feline flu works as a pro-virus against Drake's Plague. I'm guessing whatever mechanism it uses to sneak past a normal infection response is nullified by the feline flu."

"Because the population is already sick, and the immune response is already attacking in a way that kills Drake's Plague," she says.

I nod. "We need something just as effective – an infection that can cross the blood-brain barrier, like that meningitis-like feline virus."

She smiles, but then frowns. "It's not like we can just order a bulk shipment of a stupid-dangerous virus. Those Omnit-survivable viruses don't just make us sick; they *kill* us. This is something the Immunological Center of Excellence should test. They have the resources to prove or disprove your theory."

I gawk at her. "Your plan is to camcall Maven Tunna and explain our theory, beg her to seek Common Good approval, and allow *her staff* to be exposed to a pro-virus that *might* save the Omnit babies, but it would unquestionably endanger the lives of her employees? If we say *please*, maybe she'll do it in time to save our labroom full of babies."

She spins away, walks down an aisle and places her hand

on the glass chambercrib with the only baby she'd named. Horizon. She strokes the glass as if she could feel the baby's soft skin under her fingertips.

I follow her. "It has to induce a solid fever, producing enough of an immune response to attack not only the new infection, but the hidden virus as well."

"It's crazy to further sicken a sick population in order to cure them," she says.

"Without getting sick ourselves." I sigh. "We'd need to be inoculated like the Subter medtechs who serve at Omnit clinics and hospitals."

She crosses her arms. "Without Common Good approval?"

"That's not even our biggest problem," I say. "Unless we have viruses stored here at GCE."

She narrows her eyes. "We do. From past and present research projects, in partnership with ICE."

"Then some of our undertechs have already been vaccinated!" I begin to review personnel files on my ChiPro. "If we're lucky, bloodlabs will help us figure out which others can be vaccinated too."

She turns to me with fear in her eyes as if the reality of my proposal has pulled her underwater. "How do we explain to the staff what we're doing? Something that surely puts them at mortal risk?" She rakes her fingers through her hair, loosening a strand from her braid that falls to the side of her face "How do we get Ringol to agree?"

An undertech caring for babies turns our way.

"I suppose," I lower my voice, "we tell them the truth."

"The truth? Like they might die to save an Omnit baby, but we don't even know if the baby will survive. We'd tell them that?"

She stares at me, breathing too quickly as if she might hyperventilate. Her eyes are wide like she's hoping I'll fold and tell her I've changed my mind. No chance.

"I've been lied to my entire life. With everything that's

happened to me, I should be dead. But I'm alive and I have the chance to keep these babies alive too. All I know is that I've got to try harder. At some level, I'm sure most undertechs will feel the same if we just tell them the truth."

Her expression freezes. "Even if this hypothesis of yours works, Common Good will lock us up for scientific crimes before they allow such a protocol to succeed. We'll be in a cell next to Drake."

"I know."

"So why should I risk my entire career for a long shot?"

I rub my face, wishing I could sleep for just a few minutes, clear my mind, and come at this with new energy. But I can't. "Sometimes a situation is bigger than a single person."

She starts to walk away like she's given up, or won't go along with the plan, as feeble as it is. But then she turns around and closes in, her face inches from mine. "How did you get to be this way? I've met no one who cares as much as you."

"Everyone has the same capacity as I do when you remind the person what they care about." I think about my people: Medera Gelia, C, Maddelyn, *Ringol*, and if I'm pushed to be brutally honest, Kleo too. "Aside from Horizon, who do you care about?"

"No one." But the tears in her eyes make me wonder.

"Come on, Kleo," I say. "There's a heart beating inside you, and it works the same as everyone else's."

"You're right," she starts with a shaky voice. "I had a twin. Do you know the odds of having Subter twins that both survive to birth?"

I shake my head.

"Nobody does. We were the only ones on record. She and I thought we were the luckiest ones, because we were true sisters – which is more than anyone else had in the burrows. My sister was so much sweeter than me, but she was always sick, and so other kids picked on her. I had to fight her battles. She died of pneumonia during our third burrowling year, when we were ten. There I was, no friends and all fight, destined to be alone. The next time I tried to care about someone, it was Drake. Look where that landed me."

"You care about these babies." I touch her arm, and this time she lets me. "The Omnit infants need the *'all fight'* Kleo. Fight in your sister's honor."

She closes her eyes as if I've fired up her pain. "That is different. This is my project. Every dead subject is an indication of my failures. Don't assume things about me without facts."

"I saw you that day right after the baby died in your arms. That's a fact."

She snorts, but her face contorts until tears line her eyes, and then she returns to pretend stoicism. "What are the odds that Ringol will approve any of this?"

"I'll speak to him."

She nods. "I don't want my name associated with this trial."

"What?"

"Our deal – where we come up with a fix and I get full credit – I don't want the patent rights. My name can't be attached to something controversial ever again. I almost went down with Drake, and I'm sure some of the GCE staff still doubt me. It's someone else's turn to take the hit."

"J'Mave–" I start.

"We're done for tonight." She cleans her desk in haste, clicks her tongue, and stands up. "You've already cut into my mandatory rest hours." She walks away, but I'm relieved she's agreed to move forward.

I've got more things to do, so I tap my chip and search for GCE's inventory of viruses and full-body suits. Seven hundred and thirty-some available viruses. Staggering. But the availability of fully developed vaccinations safe for Subterraneans will be key.

Kleo huffs at the doorway. "Are you coming?"

I jump, thinking she had already left.

"You can't keep going on hunches alone. You do sleep,

don't you? You know, refresh your brilliant little evil-scientist mind?" Her eyebrows rise.

I nod, not that she's ever shown an iota of concern for my health.

"What?" She tilts her head as if reading my thoughts. "You're growing on me, Newness."

I scramble to deactivate my chip and follow her, because maybe Kleo and I have made headway on our partnership. We could both use a friend. I lower my head so she can't see my budding smile.

"Growing on me," she adds as I catch up with her, "like a barnacle grows on the underbelly of a ship."

CHAPTER 26

Begging the Common Good to Come Knocking

After I bathe and dress the next morning, and before I stop in to see baby Jal, or discuss my pro-virus proposal with Ringol, or begin my day's work in Camu's cave, I rush over to the infirmary to check in on Maddelyn. I haven't spoken to her since she played the recording of Ringol. My ears burn with humiliation all over again at the thought of it.

As I skip-walk down the corridor to the infirmary, my chip vibrates. The entire device lights up like never before. The word *urgent* flashes in the center of my sight.

Ringol couldn't know my plans already... could he? Kleo wouldn't have told him. Would she?

"Ringol?" I ask just milliseconds after pressing the screen, but it's not his face that appears. It's Kleo's. I hadn't even noticed she'd left the chamberroom before me.

"Get down to the infirmary stat," she says. Her voice shakes.

"Jet!" I break into a run, because it's got to be Maddelyn. I knew Crick's treatment was a mistake. "Almost there."

Maddelyn isn't in bed when I reach her room. Sweat prickles my forehead. My throat, my lungs, and my stomach tighten. "Maddy?" I call, my voice echoing.

I'm about to scream until I notice the shouting at the other end of the infirmary.

"This way!" Maddy appears, her body suit clinging to her

legs and arms, loose around her middle. "Hurry! The medtechs wheeled him in about ten minutes ago."

A rush of relief washes over me with her by my side, until we reach the emergency treatment pod.

Kleo glances at me as we enter. Her eyebrows furrow like Medera's did the day I left the burrow. Beyond her is a bedchamber glass pulled from whatever wall held it. The tube-like vessel holds a quaking person inside. It reminds me of the freestanding chambertubes from Woynauld's Academy, but this one is adult-sized.

"We have to get the maven out!" Kriz screams.

A crowd of medtechs surround him, Kleo behind them, biting her lip.

No.

My hands find the surface of the glass. Ringol's cheeks pull down, his eyes tightly closed. His body tenses and then releases and then tenses again.

"Here!" Kleo yells. "Press here!" She points to a plate on the side, a bioreader similar to the one on the labroom door. "We have to press at the same time. We share second-in-command."

Kleo shoves a medtech to the side so I can move closer to the biopanel. "It's a security measure. It protects our maven from unforeseen hostile attacks. He is the only one who can open it, from the inside. If he fails to do so, his J'Mave must open it from the outside. In this case, both of his junior mavens." I barely hear her explanation, barely see anything except Ringol's tremors.

Kleo presses her hand onto the metallic scanner and I do the same. The panel illuminates at the top and the light slowly passes over our hands. "It first identifies our bone structure," Kleo explains. One of three small lights blinks and then stays on. "And then it confirms that we are alive." A second light blinks, and stays lit like the first. "And then–"

When the third light blinks, the entire vessel buzzes and clicks, releasing the outer hatch. Kleo thrusts it open, but Ringol doesn't notice.

He's still seizing, spittle dripping from the corner of his mouth.

"Get him out!" I scream.

Four masked medics lift him from the tube and place him on an extra-wide, steel gurney.

"I found him this way." Kriz's teary eyes are red and puffy. "I called the medtechs to bring him here, and I asked J'Mave to meet us straightaway. I didn't realize we needed both of you."

"Pah!" I push her out of the way. She fetched Kleo before me? "Get him on his side."

Medtechs surround me as I struggle to stay close. "If you please," Medtech K hisses at me. "Step away."

"They'll take care of him." Kriz's eyes do not rest upon me, but on the havoc surrounding Ringol. She says it as if she's convincing herself rather than me. "He'll be okay now."

He won't be, though. The medtechs roll Ringol's gurney into a private room and close the door. Kleo blocks my way as I try to follow. "They don't need interference. They know what they're doing – they're Common Good's finest medstaff." Perspiration beads on her forehead.

My chest heaves up and down as the medtechs yell orders to one another.

Ringol has contracted the Drake-Crick virus. It's only a matter of time for him.

For some reason, Jal's tortured last breaths flash before me – the way he told me he kept his promise and then gave me the rock – and I freeze. There was no way to help Jal that day, but I'll burn in the cremation chambers before I stand by and watch Ringol die.

"I need to *treat* him!" I meet Kleo's glare. "I believe he suffers from the B7HT4 anomaly we discussed last night." In other words, he's non-Subter. "He's related to one of Camu's cancelled projects."

Kleo flinches, indicating that she understands what I mean. Her pupils enlarge, but then she recovers as her hand flutters to straighten her labcoat. "Impossible. Give the medtechs a chance."

I shake my head, pulling her to the side. "It's the same as the infants, Kleo."

She now grabs my arm, pulling me farther away from the crowd. "How can you make such a claim?" She hisses, as if I've told her the earth is flat. "He's as Subterranean as the rest of us."

"Trust me: I have strong evidence, which I can show you in confidence later. But consider his height, bodymass, and his features." We're all different sizes and shapes, on a general continuum, so it's easy to miss. "Not exactly Omnit, but not entirely Subter either."

She backs away, her hand covering her mouth, staring at Ringol's empty chamber tube.

"He may pull through *this* episode," I continue, "but what about the next and the next? If anyone is fit for a test trial, it would be him. I've already selected the pro-virus."

"Pro-virus?" Kriz asks.

We both snap our heads to her. She and Maddy walk closer to us in the hallway, gawking wide-eyed. "What do you mean you've selected a *virus*?"

"Miss Kriz," Kleo speaks in a sharp tone. "Kindly tend to our resident beekeeper." She motions to Maddelyn, who shoots her a daggered glare. "Take her back to her honeycomb."

Kriz hesitates, glancing at the closed door to the emergency treatment room.

"Don't ever," Kleo hisees, "mention our theories, studies, or ideas around common staff unless we're cleared to do so." She directs me to a private infirmary room and slides the door closed with a clang. A cold blast of recycled air shoots from the vent just before the heated air kicks in.

Kleo sits on the infirmary bed and crosses her arms. "Now. Which one?"

I stare at her, not knowing what she means.

"Which pro-virus?" Kleo asks.

My body stiffens, and I hope she's ready. "Indigo flu. It's a level three sickness for Omnits, rarely deadly for them. It's the mildest virus we have in GCE inventory that crosses the blood-brain barrier like meningitis, for at least forty-eight hours on up to a week. Patients develop bluish bruising under their eyes and sometimes over the upper torso."

"Charming," she says sarcastically. "And the drawbacks?"

"It causes fatality in an unvaccinated Subter within six hours."

"Of course." Her eyes clamp shut. "We can't do this."

"Can't and won't are two different things." I pull up our inventory on my chip and flick it over to hers. We have twenty-six body suits, five quarantine rooms with decontamination enclaves, an entire separate labroom big enough to hold a subset research study, and five dozen vials of the indigo flu virus. The vials have been sitting for almost five years, though. Still, we should be able to culture more if this works."

She glances through our supplies with hesitation. "We could all perish."

"Without protection, yes. The good news is that Camu had formed a partnership between GCE and ICE to develop an *IndiFlu* vaccine for Subters. It was a joint effort to create a small population of medtechs who were able to treat Omnits above ground. It was cutting edge and controversial." I smirk because, like us, Camu didn't seem to shy away from controversy.

"I'd never heard of the joint effort, and I worked under Camu's mavenship."

"You can't possibly know everything." I message her the supply lists. "We have exactly thirty-two doses of the *IndiFlu* vaccine still in storage."

"That's not enough," she retorts. "And I wouldn't put any of my staff under the risk of a vaccination if it hasn't been approved by Common Good for the general Subter population."

When will she fight for me, not against me? "They're my staff, too."

Her brows lower. "Not for long, though. Right?"

I put my face close to hers, like she does with me. "I will take the first dose. We'll put Ringol into a quarantine room close to the infirmary, and I will inject him with the virus. If neither of us perish, we can consider it a successful alpha trial."

"Guard your heart when it comes to him, Newness," she says, a disgusted look spreading across her eyes. "Scientists make rotten lovers."

My cheeks heat up. "That has nothing to do with this. He's our maven. We need to save him."

"Once we move the GCE staff members who can't tolerate the vaccination out of the premises, we're calling attention to ourselves. Common Good will break down our door and audit our collective asses."

"I'd like to see them try to audit a contaminated facility."

She laughs. And then she covers her eyes with the heart of her palms, pressing hard into the sockets, and I worry she might change her mind.

"We have forty-seven babies we can't fail." As soon as the words leave my mouth, I want to pull them back. *Manipulation of sentiment is a heartless man's sin.* Is that what I'm doing with Kleo right now, manipulating her?

Before I can apologize, Kleo turns to walk away. "We need to draw your basic bloodlabs first," she says. "If your readings are favorable, then I will allow you to be vaccinated."

"Thank you," I sigh in relief. "It's going to work."

"Or you'll die," she sings back but her voice cracks. "One or the other."

She can't fool me, though. She cares.

CHAPTER 27

I'm Not Dead Yet

My bloodlabs come back within marginally acceptable levels. While I'm relieved, I'm also terrified. I could be throwing away the precious gift of extended LE that Ringol gave to me. And if I had to guess what Ringol would say about me volunteering to be the initial tester for this pro-virus plan, I'm sure he'd order me to stop. But I can't watch him die. He hasn't regained consciousness and time is running out.

Jal would have done this for me, and even though I've had my doubts about the maven, I'm sure Ringol would do for me what I'm about to for him.

After an inventory tech digs out the box of vaccinations from storage, we set up camp in a quarantine room across the hallway from the infirmary. I take one glass vial and stare at it. The inoculation could either protect me against the virus – a virus that is lethal enough to kill me without the vaccination – or it could throw my whole system into chaos. Maven Camu had been involved in the research to develop this vaccine, though, and her notes were thorough. I trust her. I have to.

I inject myself while Kleo tries to hide the terror on her face, standing next to me in a full hazmat suit.

"I'll stay here in quarantine, until we know," I say. "You should cleanse in the decontamination chamber."

She stares at me a moment longer, and then leaves without saying a word.

* * *

Ten hours after my vaccination, my newest bloodlabs indicate that I have successfully produced antibodies to the indigo flu, and Ringol has been moved to a quarantined area. A glass wall separates him from the rest of the facility.

But we can't infect him until more staff members are tested and inoculated.

Kleo orders the resident medtechs to perform bloodlabs on the remaining GCE staff members. Anyone unfit for the *IndiFlu* shot will leave the facility within twenty-four hours. In the meantime, the facility has gone dark: Chen has assured us that no unauthorized incoming or outgoing camcalls can be made. We can't risk any rogue staff members alerting the authorities about our plans. Maddelyn has also encrypted my chip. She offered to do the same for Kleo, but Kleo didn't want anyone messing with the Common-Good-approved setup on her ChiPro.

Kleo sent out an internal-GCE video message, explaining that evacuation for non-innocuable staff members is mandatory. The only people who have a choice to stay are those whose labs indicate that it is safe to vaccinate them. Surprisingly, when the staff members learn that the CG-unapproved flu shot was developed by Camu, most of them are willing to move forward. My ChiPro beeps with each staff members' new bloodlab result. The same results are also sent to Kleo's chip. Kriz's results come over, and she's safe to vaccinate, thank all that is good. What would we do without Kriz?

When I go to quarantine to check on Ringol, I press my forehead against the see-through glass wall. I'm so close that my breath fogs into a blotchy circle, distorting Ringol's head. I laugh, because he's growing hair on his face and head like an Omnit male. Everyone must notice. His horrific seizures have stopped, but he still hasn't regained consciousness. Surprisingly, his dark whiskers growing in make him appear jolly instead of out of place.

I blow out a long breath to cloud up the glass, and then wait for the fog to dissipate. For a second, Ringol disappears behind the haze and I have some ridiculous hope that he'll be okay by the time it dissipates. But once it clears he's there again, still as death.

I wonder how much the maven studied his own genome. However much he knew about his Omnit-Subter mix, it was more than I knew about myself. It doesn't matter though, because how much does it help him now? Besides, he did something that no other Subters got to – live above ground with a family. He was caressed by his surrogate mother as a baby, and he has memories of his parents' love.

When he was forced to give them up, he had to start living a lie, just like I have. He had to stop being someone's son, and became a Crypt. That's why he didn't tell me what burrow he came from. He didn't live in a burrow. He used to be free and loved. He probably never thought he'd wind up down here.

Who are you? My silent question floats in the space between us, and coats the molecules of air like my breath, fogging the glass and retreating. Will I ever truly know Ringol, or will there always be some part he hides from me? Regardless, I want him to pull through so I have a chance to find out.

"You love him."

I spin to face Maddelyn. She doesn't sneer at me accusingly like Kleo would. A small smile forms on her lips behind the clear faceplate of her bodysuit.

"What do any of us know about love, buried here in the dirt?" I run my fingers through my pixie hair.

"Hear now," she says with the authority of Medera Gelia. I almost look for a cane for her to pound on the floor. "There's no greater human experiment than love."

I laugh. "That's not something I thought you'd ever say."

I have no right to love Ringol. He's my supervisor. He confuses me daily and he's beyond stubborn when he refuses to tell me the things he knows are important to me. From the day I met him, my life has been thrown completely off track. But really, how "on track" was I at that point? Maddy was getting sicker by the minute, and I had no job prospects. It's Ringol who pulled me out of a dire future, who found a way to extend my life expectancy, who cared for me while I was in quarantine, who even came searching for me after I refused to work for him. He found a way to get me out of Allund's employment, and he literally helped me see color.

My pulse races at the thought. Who else could have given me a rainbow underground? For all good, I'm just as stubborn as he is. Sometimes he pushes me too hard, but then he turns around and treats me as kindly as Medera or Maddy would. So if I'm honest with my feelings, if I consider the way my entire body warms whenever he's near and how my heart races without my permission, and how we change each other for the better, I'd have to agree with Maddelyn. I love him as much as I'm angry with him. I love Ringol.

"Well," she says. "There might be someone I'm ready to consider in the human experiment."

"Someone you love?" I ask, wondering when she had the time, while sporting her body suit, to fall in love with someone. A medtech?

"I wouldn't call it love, not yet. But he's growing on me," she says.

I shake my head, trying to figure out who she could mean.

"You wouldn't approve. You hate him."

"Hate him?" She can't mean –

"It's Crick."

"Zamption?" I ask with a sharp tone. He's crass and jaded. Brilliant beyond his own good. But she doesn't know he might be a co-conspirator in creating Drake's Omnit-plague. He's been with her for days now, working to prolong her life. She may see him as some kind of sardonic savior – the only person who can free her from her bodysuit. "Maddelyn–"

"Don't." She turns away. "I don't need a lecture. I may die if my treatment doesn't work. I am as trapped as a canarymouse in its cage, but I know what I feel."

"But how well do you know him?" She doesn't know him at all. Crick Zamption is a bigot willing to do almost anything to further his cause, like shirking off dying babies, attacking me in the undertunnels, or threatening C. He even threatened Maddelyn's health at one point.

"It doesn't matter, anyway. I can't be vaccinated no matter what my bloodlabs show, so I have to leave."

My eyes drop. "But you're in a full body suit?" Even as I say it, my voice tapers off. Why would I knowingly risk her life for any reason? I clench my jaw. I hadn't thought about losing her again. And I'm the one who made it so she has to leave: my crazy plan.

"I'll be sent to the closest recovery center with the capacity to continue my treatment protocol. On the upside, my LE has improved exponentially. I'll never be placed in a political position after what I've done. But once I'm finished with my treatment, I was hoping that a certain J'Mave might call me for my technical services?" She bows.

"You know she will." Of course Maddelyn's health will improve. It's got to. "And Crick?"

"He's put a request through FFR to move back to Immunology." She shrugs.

Good. She'll be away from him, at least.

"Crick told me what happened to you." She takes my hand.

I open my mouth wide. He admitted he attacked me? Does she know he's a coalition operative?

"Tell me," her voice turns accusatory. "Why didn't you tell me?"

"I – I couldn't."

"I would have killed Medero Allund had I been there, as Ringol should have. He may be the next Central Forces commander, but I hate him with every allergy-ridden speck of my body."

My tattoo: *that's* what Crick told Maddelyn. Clearly he left out the method he used to verify that it exists, of course, and everything else he's done. Coward. Someday soon, I'll tell her everything he hasn't – when it's safe.

Maddelyn hugs me. "I'm sorry for all that has happened to you. You are the one soul who least deserves it."

"I'm fine now. I'm just worried about your association with Crick."

Her eyes move beyond me, staring through the glass at Ringol. "I know the feeling."

It's not the same. The intercepted message sounded pretty bad, but Ringol wouldn't intentionally kill people. "In all my dealings with the maven, his concern has been for the welfare of all."

"Of all?" She snorts. "Or just the Omnits?"

I was hoping she would see more clearly, now that she knows about Allund and seen the hatred toward those innocent babies. "Crick has influenced you, I see."

Her jaw tightens. "These are my opinions, Zu. I've been reading PoSSE literature ever since I've been able to hack into their articles."

"But," I say, "their writings focus on the actions of the Omnit rebels – rebels who are misinformed and angry. They don't speak for all Omnits."

"They are murderers."

"The rebels are, yes."

"Rebels?" Her voice rises an octave. "How can we see any of them as friendly when innocent Subters die and hospitals burn?"

I shake my head. "They don't understand what's happening to them. Their babies are dying."

"No, Zu. Those babies won't die because *you* will save them." She puts her gloved hand on my shoulder. "I'd never support the intentional murder of innocent children on either side. I'm proud of you for helping them."

"It's not one-sided, though. Omnits staff our armed forces, and–"

"I know, I know. Medera Gelia went on and on about our symbiotic arrangement." She smiles. "What's happening to these babies is tragic. What Allund did to you was pure masochism. But that doesn't mean you need to be a hundred-percent pro-Omnit from here on out."

"Omnits and Subters, we are the same. You can't separate two sides of a coin – once divided, what's left is worthless."

"Zu," she hisses. "It's already happened. We are separated into our own figurative currency. Crick is working to ensure our future. PoSSE could use your help once you are able to devote the time."

I snort. "I don't think they'd want me."

"They appreciate the intensity of your genius, unlike Common Good or GCE."

How much has she told PoSSE people about me? "Please be careful whenever you talk to Crick, especially about me." Maybe Kleo was right – we should have incarcerated him right away.

Maddelyn curls a lip and motions to Ringol. "Well, I think *he's* using you, so you be careful, too."

My chip beeps with more bloodlab results: Griffith is able to stay, one of my roommates is not. Maddelyn is partly right. Ringol told some unknown person that he would manage me. The next day, he kissed me. That audio clip she'd played for me keeps repeating itself in my head. "Manage" is just another word for manipulation. I'm no longer blind to it, but I still believe Ringol has a good heart and that he's working towards something he thinks is right.

But then, isn't that what Crick said he was doing too?

I stand a little farther away from the glass, and my breath no longer fogs my view. "Yes," I say more to myself than Maddelyn. "I promise to be careful."

* * *

Maddelyn and I walk to GCE's magnetran station just a few hours later, heading to the farthest terminal arm-in-arm as if we're walking through the halls at Cayan. She'll go to a regular medical facility and will gain her health back based on Crick's treatment plan.

We stand forehead to forehead – or forehead to mask – squeezing our hands together, waiting for the magnetran to arrive. I try to believe that this isn't the last time I'll see her. I want to go with her, except I want to stay behind, too.

The magnetran blasts its way into our space, air whipping around us until it's hard to breathe, just before it slows to a stop. It hums in the background and the hatch pops open.

Maddelyn breaks away and climbs down the hatch. Just before her head disappears, she calls out. "I always knew you'd save the world someday!" We laugh – she'd decided it the day we met.

Her face crumples, and it's like I'm looking in a mirror as my facial muscles contort. Maddelyn is my sister, my family. The hatch closes before I can find my voice.

"*We* were supposed to save the world *together*."

CHAPTER 28

Every Decision Falls

I hurry back to the infirmary to supervise the vaccinations for Kriz, Griffith, and the handful of undertechs whose bloodlabs came back okay, before heading to my bedchamber for the evening. We sent all nonessential maidstaff away on furlough, including the laundrymaids. I dress in the only nightgown left for me, one that doesn't cover my scar, and I don't even care. As I slip into the drawer that houses my bed and press the button, I try to stop thinking about all the things that could go wrong. *I will not fail* has been my mantra, but now it's changed to: *This can't fail.* My mind races until my head aches, playing through a million possibilities for failure.

My chamberdrawer closes and slides into the wall, but I don't think I'll be able to rest.

Five minutes later, my ChiPro beeps with Kleo's bloodlabs. *Oh, jet.*

I slam my fist into the button above my head so my chamberdrawer opens. Across from me, Kleo's drawer opens almost at the same time. We stare at one another for a moment. She can't leave me. I need someone, and even Kleo is better than no one.

"We'll rerun the bloodlabs," I whisper.

She nods, but stops and her expression turns fiery. "You planned this!"

"What?"

"You knew," she snarls. "You must have checked my medrecords. You did some voo-doo logarithms and your evil-savant perfect-memory brain figured out that my bloodlabs would come back like–" She breathes heavily and her eyes dart around the room, fixing on nothing in particular, chasing her thoughts.

"Kleo–" I start, but she's not paying attention to me anymore. She activates her chip, looking through data files.

When she gets to whatever piece of information she'd searched for, she sighs. Her eyes slide to me – this time, with a flash of contrition. "My bloodlabs were within normal levels last time. That was before I'd injected myself with a trial of my immuno-cocktail. Flying, blazing, jet steam!"

The stress of everything must be getting to her. "We have the bodysuits," I begin. But if I didn't think that option was safe for Maddelyn, how could it be for Kleo?

She swallows hard. "You will continue as planned. No further delays. I will depart in the morning with the final group. Our furlough placement is only twenty miles away, and I will continue to run other GCE projects there." Her mouth opens as if she's going to say more, but then her eyes travel down my neck and fix upon my scar, visible because of my nightgown.

She gasps.

I cover it with my hands. "It's–" Kleo, of all people, had to see it. I'll never live this down. That *Newness* nickname she'd given me will be replaced by *Dullard*.

She climbs out of her bedchamber in one graceful leap, making it across the room just as swiftly. She moves my hands away and her eyebrows tilt. Then she pulls the material of my nightgown away so she can read the entire message.

But I can't let her stare at it. I cover it with my hands.

"*I am but a dullard.*" Her voice drops, and there's a lilt of sadness to it.

I close my eyes, reliving the day when I had to repeat that

phrase over and over. The image of Allund's angry face flashes in my mind.

"This is what you've been hiding. How did this happen?" Her expression falls like she's about to cry – for me! As if she's more upset over *my* tattoo than she is about *her* bloodlab results.

"It feels like a lifetime ago." And it doesn't matter now, but Kleo's eyes turn pitying. I fight the tears forming in my eyes, because I try not to think about the tattoo or how unfair it was, or how I wish I could scrape my own skin off to get rid of it. Most of all, though, it reminds me that Allund is still the person in charge of a burrow of children who can't defend themselves.

"I briefly worked as a burrowmaid before coming here – it's a long story. When the medero was unnecessarily brutal towards the girl I had helped that morning, I stepped in to defend her. He didn't like my interference."

"Of course you did. You cared." She moves my nightgown back in place. "Medero Allund Woynauld tattoos all of his members."

I flinch at his name. "My LE had been lower when I was about to graduate, and with very few career options, I took that position for all the wrong reasons. But I'm here because of you and Ringol. The maven injected me with your immuno-cocktail, and my LE improved enough for me to take this position. I wish it worked for you like it did for me."

Her chin quivers for a second as if I've overwhelmed her, and then she bites her top lip.

"Thank you, by the way, for creating that treatment. It changed my life." In more ways than I can ever tell her. But the whole subject of Allund makes my skin crawl. "I want your opinion at every step of this pro-virus trial. I will camcall you hourly with updates."

She flashes a faint smile. "You will not, not if you're doing your job. You'll be too busy."

"Co-J'Maving with you is my job," I say. "I will update you on the hour."

"Go to sleep." She's commanding me, not requesting.

"Yes, J'Mave Nukleo." I watch her climb into her beddrawer, hoping this isn't the last night we'll be chambermates. Though my mind won't stop pummeling me with the worst possibilities, because what if it is?

When my wake-up alarm chimes, I open my chamberbed drawer. It's as if Kleo and I just said goodnight, like I haven't slept at all. Kleo has inched her way into my heart and has become my friend, and she believes in this crazy theory of mine, enough to leave GCE. Maybe once she leaves, at least she can claim that she was ignorant of our unapproved trial. In a way, it might help save her career, or at least keep her from being incarcerated.

This gives me some relief. She deserves a blank slate after all this. Why should she continue to suffer for the mistakes of other people?

The babies in the lab, though, suffer more than Kleo or I ever could. Even if all else fails – if I fail – I can prove that I care about them. They matter because they are the same as we are – our people, no matter what Crick believes. He is more *dullard* than he'd like to admit.

Walking through the quiet hallways unnerves me. I'd normally see at least five or so undertechs on the way to the lab, but this morning, I don't see any. They're all packing or have left already.

When I enter the labroom, babies cry from all corners. Our staffing levels have depleted almost to where they had been before the undertechs were sent to help. The corner play area with the toys and swings is vacant, like it's forgotten history.

What have I done?

Kleo sits with a three-and-a-half-month-old female a few aisles down. Before I realize what I'm doing, and maybe out of the disorientation from lack of sleep, I'm by Kleo's side and my hand is on her shoulder.

The baby's stillness marks her fate. She's not dead yet, but it won't be long. Just because Subters can't have children of our own doesn't mean we can't love one as our own. It's clear she loves Horizon.

Kleo doesn't look up at my touch, but glances at my reflection in the glass chambercrib.

"She's first." Kleo speaks in a strained voice. "Inject the maven with the counter-virus. If he's alive after twelve hours, then inject her. No, eight hours – do it in eight hours after his injection. I've messaged you my dosing calculations based on infant weight."

"I'll do the injection myself." I touch Horizon's soft head. "Are you packed?"

She nods, keeping her eyes fixed on the infant. "I can't believe I'm saying this, but I agree with everything you've planned. I'm sorry to leave this all on your shoulders."

I hate that she has to leave, and that I'll be alone, but I think it would be harder if *I* had to leave. I can't imagine what it's like for her to have to say goodbye to Horizon, or how I'd feel if I had to leave baby Jal to someone else.

"Luckily," she says turning my way only slightly "I trust those wonky shoulders of yours."

I turn to leave, lowering my head to smile.

"And when I say trust–" Kleo's stool squeaks as she turns around. I hesitate for a second, waiting to be stung by one of her reverse-compliments. "I mean that I trust your evil-genius judgment more than I trust my own. Don't let me down."

Eight hours later, all the GCE staff who were at too great of a risk have left, and those who have received their vaccinations are debriefed. I've run analysis on Ringol's genome, and the results are conclusive. His markings are entirely consistent with a Helix-Q subject.

Only one trained medtech remains, Medtech K. He will need

to know about Helix-Q, since Ringol's treatment will require modifications based on his genetic status. I'm not worried, though, since K has been a reliable worker from the beginning.

Kleo has prepared a v-clip for our staff to watch, outlining the issues, the stakes, and the research that supports my theory. Surprisingly, she refers to that theory in the video as *ours* – hers and mine, even with the controversy it will no doubt cause. She chose to back me up, and I'm grateful. Through all of this, I have gained a sister, spiky and sharp though she is.

Her controlled expression on the v-clip is calming. She describes the Indigo symptoms and goes over the treatment protocol should the trial be successful, and we can proceed to administer it to all the infants. Her smile continues as the end of the clip catches each member by surprise, myself included.

"You, brave GCE staff members who are capable and agree to run the trial, you are my heroes. Thank you for your sacrifices. Thank you on behalf of our infants and their parents who will never know what you're up against. Finally, thank you to J'Mave Allele, my brilliant partner and caring friend to all."

A warm sensation wraps me like a hug. I knew we became friends, Kleo and I, but it's good to know she's finally figured it out.

Standing over Ringol's infirmary bed, I triple-check his proviral injection, second-guessing everything I'm doing, and then second-guessing my second-guesses. So much of this trial is based on hunches and hopes. Ringol likes facts and certainties, so he might not agree to any of this if he were conscious. The Indigo Flu isn't deadly for Omnits by itself, but Ringol is only part Omniterranean, and already weakened by Drake's Plague. It could kill him outright.

Baby Horizon's chambercrib has been moved into the adjoining quarantine room. Kleo is counting on me to inject her, but I must inject Ringol first. It's jetting crazy. My hands shake. Maybe I should message Kleo and tell her that we need to call this off. This whole, stupid idea is–

Griffith clears his throat behind me. "Is there a problem?"

"Of course there's a problem!" I spin and glare at him. "I'm about to inject our helpless maven with a communicable disease, while at the same time releasing a killer virus in our Subter-staffed GCE headquarters."

He stares at me for a second. "You're skittish again, Allele. Your mind spins so rapidly, and once your thoughts go south, you just can't stop." He takes the injection from my hand. "This is a potentially beneficial, pro-viral treatment plan. J'Maven Nukleo is a hard person to work for, but I respect her. She explained we must inject him because his prognosis is grim regardless." He removes the cap from the needle and hands the injection to me. "You and Kleo have made dual leadership look flawless, something that has shown the GCE staff members that you can both be trusted. Now, J'Maven, is the time for that courage you spoke about."

I take it from him and stare at it for a moment. A thousand what-ifs pulse through my veins, but then I glance at Griffith, who blinks like there's nothing to worry about. So, I insert the needle into the port at Ringol's IV site, and I blow air from my mouth as I release the concoction into his bloodstream.

"Now, we wait for a nice fever to set in." Griffith looks at me and flashes a warm smile. "And we *hope*."

Griffith helped me escape from Allund Woynauld, offered me comfort on my first jetengine ride, and encouraged me just before my initiation speech. And he's smiling at me, all dimply and gracious. I owe him thanks, but I also owe him honesty.

"Thank you, Undertech Griffith."

He cocks his head when I use his title, maybe understanding what I mean by it. Had I known that dropping titles meant something romantic rather than simply abandoning a formality, I never would have agreed to it. I can't let him think I'm pursuing something with him when I'm not. He is a good friend and I adore him, but he is also my employee and I don't have deeper feelings for him. I have feelings for someone else.

He stares at me for a few seconds before bowing his head and leaving.

"I'm sorry," I say after he's already out of earshot.

Within a few hours, Ringol's eye sockets develop large, puffy circles. I expected some discoloration, but there are many shades of blue that circle his eyes – indigo, light blue, purplish-blue. His body temperature rises by three full degrees and his skin burns to the touch.

What have I done?

Kriz tends to him, her face tight and worried. "I hope you know what you are doing," she says through tight lips every so often. "For all good, I will turn you in myself if he dies."

"I'll turn myself in, Medera Kriz," I say in all sincerity. Her eyes widen, but she does nothing to deny her title. In the past few days, though, I'd become more and more sure of it. "Those thoughts are better expressed outside of this room, though. We can't know if he can hear us, but if so, he needs to know we have faith he can get through this."

My ChiPro beeps with a camcall from Kleo.

"How is the maven?" She speaks without exchanging any greetings.

"Showing strong Indigo symptoms but stable," I say, walking out of the room.

Kriz lets out a bitter *pah*.

"Proceed with Horizon at the dosage I'd left for you."

"Already?" I suppose it has been eight hours, but Ringol isn't showing any signs of improvement yet. Injecting an infant to contract this horrible sickness feels impossibly wrong, and Horizon has seized three times already today.

"J'Mave Allele," she says with the same calm demeanor she

exhibited in her v-clip. "Proceed with her as we had discussed. There's no time for needless delays."

An hour later, I have an undertech I've barely worked with – Pascal – help me prepare Horizon's injection. I catch a glimpse of his face while he's not looking, wrinkled beyond his years. The proud way he carries himself reminds me of Gelia. His life partner was shipped out earlier today with Kleo. Why would he have volunteered to stay?

"I'm wondering," he says. "Why we need to prepare separate pro-viral injections for each subject. It's a lot of work to go through the decontamination processes with each infection."

"Do you have a suggestion?" I ask, because if there's something to consider that we haven't already, I need to hear it. I need to be a hundred-percent sure of every decision made from here on out.

"Instead of administering a best-guess dosage for each infant, we could simply expose them, one by one, to an infected person."

"You're not off-base with that idea," Undertech Griffith says as he enters the room holding Horizon, her small body falling limp even though her eyes are open, staring at nothing. "Except we don't have time to ensure that the virus takes. What if the subject's initial immune response puts the Indigo virus to sleep for a few weeks? The proviral effect will be delayed, and that's taking a huge risk when these infants only live three or four months."

Griffith is much brighter than Kleo let on.

Undertech Pascal nods. "Still, there's a risk that natural contagion may occur."

Griffith places Horizon onto the small worktable and nods to me with the utmost professionalism. No more smirky smiles or sideways glances. But there's more behind his eyes. I've hurt him. It's the last thing I wanted to do.

"Thank you, Undertech."

He turns to leave without another word.

After a moment of hesitation, I fill the child-sized syringe with the pro-viral concoction, in accordance with Kleo's calculations. We turn the infant onto her stomach to inject the dose into her buttocks. Horizon jerks her head upward and then settles again.

Biting the inside of my cheek, I proceed to inject her. Her eyes stay open, and she doesn't move as the virus invades her bloodstream.

Now we wait and hope, like we're doing with Ringol.

And then, as if the universe decides to weigh in, the earth rumbles. What must be more anti-bunker bombs pound our area, and the lights flash off and on.

Kriz shows up at the infirmary door, sharp worry spreading across her face. "They're back!" she shouts.

The ear-splitting alarms begin to sound like they had the night of my initiation. I want to curl up in a corner and cover my head. Somebody on staff must've leaked information to Allund.

With Ringol unconscious and Kleo miles away, every decision falls to me. I haven't been trained for this. What is my role, now that I'm in charge? What did Ringol do last time?

"J'Mave!" Kriz shakes my arm. "You must give us orders."

The alarm is so loud that my entire body vibrates with it, and the floor shakes with the bombing. The quarantine room we're in sits closer to the earth's surface than the laboratory a few floors below, so we're more at risk.

Allund Woynauld can still get to me. Maybe that's the point. Maybe that's the message he's sending.

I cover my ears.

CHAPTER 29

I Volunteer

Griffith calls from a few feet away.

Kriz screams from the side of Ringol's bed.

Their mouths move, but the blaring alarm drowns out their words. Griffith's eyes are a mix of panic and determination. How could I have let them both down like this? Every muscle I have trembles. I need time to come up with a plan, but I can't focus. Nothing makes sense. The earth rumbles again and dusty particles fall from the ceiling.

Griffith coughs, and grabs my shoulders. "Don't think!" he shouts directly into my face.

I nod, wiping the tears I hadn't noticed before. "The jetting alarm!" I scream as if anyone could hear me over it, and then I take a breath. I message Chen, asking him to cut the alarm off. We can't leave our posts, and we need to be able to talk. Messages pop up on my chip projector from the two dozen GCE members who'd agreed to stay:

–*Are we under attack?*

–*Should we head to our bedchambers?*

–*J'Mave, please respond.*

–*How can the Omnits do this to us when we are risking our lives for their babies?*

I send a quick warning message to Kleo, telling her about Ringol's suspicion that Woynauld is behind these attacks. And then I blubber on in a way she despises, saying that I wish I

314

were more like her – that I could calm the staff with the same poise that she does. I tell her that I will take all the blame if controversy arises from the trial. I let her know that I'm glad she made it out of here safely, and at the same time, I tell her that I wish she were still here because she is a better leader than I could ever be.

But she isn't here.

When I finish, I catch a glimpse of Horizon, and my heart jumps. "Medtech!" I yell it over and over, but Chen hasn't cut the sirens yet, so he can't hear me. I chipchat *S.O.S.* to him.

Horizon's small body convulses, contorting in ways it shouldn't, a bubbly foam beginning to leak from her mouth. Her eyes roll side-to-side as if she's watching a long magnetran passing. She's seizing.

The moaning sirens continue to blare while Medtech K rushes into the room and takes over. He turns her over and injects something, a drug to stop the seizures. But I've seen this before. By the time he turns her over again, she's not breathing.

Griffith pushes him away and begins chest compressions, blowing into Horizon's mouth. The medtech backs away and shakes his head.

She can't die.

The fear my howling child-ghosts gave me is nothing compared to the terror I feel for this child and the smothering guilt I have for causing her pain. I'm as helpless as I was when Jalaz died in front of me. I caused this insanity, including Allund Woynauld's revenge-bombing.

The sirens stop, and it takes a moment to adjust to the deafening silence.

"Help me!" Kriz's hoarse voice calls out from Ringol's room.

I wipe my face as Griffith continues to work on Horizon, and I dash over to Ringol's room.

My boots slap against the cold rock and my ears ring. I make it to the door to find Kriz, who has pushed Ringol onto his side. He's heaving vomit over the edge of his bed.

When he finishes, Kriz is on one side of him and I'm on the other, hauling him onto his back and then propping his head on the pillows.

She locks the bedrail and brushes her arm across her face. "Promise me he'll make it."

Ringol's eyes have swollen so much I barely recognize him. I can't answer her. Instead, I whisper to him. "Come back to us."

Griffith appears at the threshold of the room without entering. "She–" But he can't say anything; instead, he looks down. The earth trembles again, as if to announce Horizon's death in a way that Griffith can't.

"I've failed her." I scratch my nails across my scalp.

Kriz glares at me, and then storms out of the room.

Why did I think that I could do what no other scientist has? The collective genius of GCE and ICE staff members is staggering. Did I think I could succeed just because Ringol believed in me? Because Kleo did?

Stupid, stupid pride!

Medtech K enters the room and examines Ringol, pulling bloodlabs and checking vitals. He frowns and takes some notes. "We should prepare the staff for the worst. Miss Kriz, especially."

By the time I understand what he means, the medtech has left the room like he's already given up. Horizon's name needs to be written on the labroom wall. She matters.

But the trial has failed. I've failed.

Ringol will die.

The clearest, truest revelation hits me in the middle of everything, and it's something Ringol said to me long ago. *What you possess in superintelligence you lack in common wisdom.* I've been so blind to my stupid pride, so afraid to fail that I couldn't see I've already failed in so many ways.

Unless I want to cause more failure, I have to see myself for what I am.

I grab hold of Ringol's ice-cold hand. Dark splotches mar

his perfect face. Bruises discolor his arms and his joints are swollen beyond what I'd ever imagine. "I'm so sorry."

Walking into the hallway, I call out. "Undertech Griffith?"

The lights flicker, and he doesn't respond. He must have gone back to the labroom.

A thunderous boom echoes throughout the tunnels. It is time to call off this absurd medical trial, so I need to alert my staff. I cue up my chip to record and begin speaking.

"Dedicated HCE staff, kindly cease all preparations for further doses in this trial. Our beta subject, a beautiful baby girl named Horizon, did not make it. I am tending to our maven who has fallen gravely ill. Based on the poor results of these two cases, the viability of this trial is in question. Any failures resulting from this pro-viral study are on my shoulders, alone. Furthermore, the bombing attacks leave me no choice but to remind you of Common Good's safety protocol that recommends you return to your reinforced bedchambers." I swallow hard thinking about the babies being left alone. A million thoughts rifle through my mind, and none of them work. Most of them don't even make sense. "However, our infants would greatly appreciate volunteers to stay with them and keep them calm. Remember, when you're all they have, you're everything to them. Thank you."

A chipchat message comes through from Griffith. *Take care of our maven. I've got the labroom under control.* I'm so grateful for him.

Retreating into Ringol's room, I lock the door behind me, because I'm all *he* has right now. The alarms start up again, and I flinch. There must be more bombs on the way.

Ringol jerks about as if he's in pain. If only there was an emergency injection for everything I caused, some sort of hope at the end of a necklace we used to wear, but there's no such shot. Folding Ringol's large, cold hand into my fingers, I climb into the bed next to him.

"You are a brave man." I touch his burning forehead. "Thank

you for saving me, and for pointing out my faults when no one else would. I should have listened sooner."

It doesn't matter that someone ordered him to manage me, whatever that means. They were right, I obviously needed it. When I kiss his temple, his feverish sweat leaves a taste of salt on my lips. I would do anything to take his place.

I want to lay my head in Gelia Cayan's lap, and feel her knotted fingers rubbing my back, but even Gelia has gone missing because of me.

The heat from Ringol's fever radiates from his body. I rest my head on his shoulder. My feelings for him have grown into something I can't ignore. "Fight this, Maven. Please. Don't leave me here alone. I need to hear your voice again, even if it is to tell me about my mistakes, or to tell me you faked your feelings for me. For all that is good, Ringol, I love you. You're one of my people now, my heart. Can you hear me? I'm so sorry for all of this."

He doesn't respond, and I fear he never will. If he's gone already, then once his body realizes it, he will stop breathing. I lay my head on his pillow and trace his lips with my finger. I will stay here with him no matter what.

A sudden movement wakes me. Ringol sits up to cough, and he moans like it sent shocks of pain through him.

I check the time, realizing that I'd fallen asleep for several hours after the bombing stopped. I immediately reach out to him and feel his pulse, the temperature of his skin, note the reduced swelling in his joints. The bruising around his eyes has eased up a bit too.

"Maven Ringol?" He's better – I feel it. "Ringol!"

He coughs again. "What the blazes are you doing in my bed?"

My breath catches and I laugh. He's breathing and talking. Tears roll down my cheeks.

Someone pounds at the door, and I rush to unlock it.

Kriz sweeps inside. "Ringol?"

He holds his hand up to her. "Exhausted. Can it wait?"

Her face crumples as she fights away tears, and nods. "Yes, it can." She turns to me and reaches for my hands. Her eyes water as she whispers, "Thank you. With all my being, I thank you."

She urges Ringol to sip water before covering him with a warming sheet. Gelia would have done the same for me, a thought that makes me smile.

My chip buzzes with a camcall from Kleo, and my heart sinks again. I'll have to give her the news about Horizon. I wipe my face as I walk into the hallway to answer. "Kleo, I–"

"Save it." She hesitates, looking away for a minute before she continues. Her French braids are gone, and she's cut her hair super short. "It was too late for my baby girl."

"I can't say how sorry I am."

"Thank you." She blinks a few times, as if she didn't expect to care. Of course she does. "You need to monitor the maven until he recovers. Move forward with an infant whose disease has not progressed to the point of–"

"I've already halted the study," I say shaking my head. My heart drops in my chest, and I'm not sure if I'm even thinking straight from my lack of rest. A tiny part of my brain starts to argue with the words I'm saying. "We should begin decontamination procedures here at GCE headquarters so it's safe for all of you to return."

"You're not authorized to abort our co-project by yourself," Kleo says.

My throat thickens, and I can't speak. I don't want to abort the study, and I'm relieved Kleo thinks we should move ahead.

"Listen, Newness," Kleo says with a smirk. "While you were sleeping for six hours straight and not answering your calls, I've been busy sleuthing around and traveling to all ends of the earth. Ask me what I've found out. Go on, ask me."

"Sleuthing?" I ask stupidly. I just now notice she's sitting in a room with what looks like shiny metallic walls. "And traveling?"

"I read your French-to-English translation of Camu's Helix-Q notes. Notice the bombing has stopped? You're welcome."

"Where are you?"

"Well, I'm glad you finally asked. After you messaged me about Ringol's suspicion that Allund might be behind the raids, I went to the most obvious place I could to find out: Woynauld's Military Academy." She crosses her arms, grinning. "Medero Allund has recently experienced some horrible symptoms. Migraines and such. I'm running Helix-Q analysis on him now."

He'd never been exposed to Omnit infants, so if he's infected, he must have contracted it from Ringol. "Rots to be him."

"Right. Those migraines look like they're doozies. But our oversized medero now understands that the only treatment program that has a flying-jet-of-a-chance to save his worthless life, just happens to be in its trial run at our very own Genomic Center of Excellence. It was only minutes after he learned of my news that the rebel bombers were apprehended."

"He admits that he and PoSSE are behind the attacks?"

"This freak would never admit to that, but he takes full credit for capturing the bombers – by calling in a 'favor'. Funny how that works."

"You are truly brave, Kleo." PoSSE has some nefarious connection to Central Forces. Stepping into the middle of everything, Kleo has put herself at great risk. "I'll name my first patent after you."

She flashes a genuine, heartwarming smile that reaches her eyes. She's finally showing her real self, and the real Nukleo is gorgeous.

"Oh, my Woynauld girl!" I exclaim. "The head burrowmaid, Yelda, will know which one I mean. Please – can you find out how she is?"

"Sure." She turns her head askance. "You haven't even said a word about my new *A*-do."

"*A*-do?" I laugh. "You mean that sassy, too short haircut?"

"Yes, the *A*-do. *A* is for Allele. *Allele-do* didn't have the same ring to it."

"Now you're poking fun at me." My hand automatically smooths my hair at the base of my neck.

"Am not," she says. "I'm honoring you. You know, the purest form of flattery and all? I promised little Miss Beekeeper that I'd keep our project rolling forward. She mentioned doing something big for morale. This was practically Maddelyn's idea. I'm pretty sure I pull off the look way better than you, anyway."

There it is, the Kleo reverse-compliment slap, which I love. "Way better."

She rolls her eyes. "Check your messages. People've been trying to reach you, for all good." She waves dramatically and presses the button to disconnect.

My messages? When I check, there must be a chipchat message from every undertech left at GCE.

I volunteer to stay at my post, the first undertech reports.

Your approval rating couldn't be higher, says another.

I trust the joint leadership of my co-J'Maves, one of my ex-roommate says.

I watch each video message one by one, in tears because every female undertech has the new *A*-do, as Kleo called it. I don't know what to say.

Unbelievable. And then I receive a message from Undertech Pascal.

The infant known as Horizon was too far gone in my expert opinion. He clears his throat before continuing. *This female child would have perished within hours regardless. I have developed bloodlab indicators for Drake's plague progression and favorability markers for our trial. With all due respect which I give freely, we cannot allow Horizon's death to halt our efforts. The best way to honor her life is to continue with the trial. I will send an infant with the most compatible markers shortly.*

This message stops me for a moment. Pascal points out something I'm ashamed to think. I've let my emotions for Horizon and Ringol cloud my judgement about the trial. We clearly need to beta test on healthier infants.

When I'm through my messages, Griffith saunters in holding baby Jal. "It's time."

I stand. "Put him back into his chambercrib." My face heats up – there's no way I can allow this. Any other infant but him.

"J'Mave Allele," he starts. "This baby is still very strong, and he's only suffered a few minor seizures. He's the perfect test subject according to Pascal, and the sooner he recovers, the better for his brain."

I can feel my heart drop into my feet, but still, I can't argue. My undertechs are right. Griffith and Kleo and Pascal are right. My choice is to treat baby Jal now, or watch him seize to death later.

My eyes burn with brewing tears. "Bring me my boy."

CHAPTER 30

Encroaches the Space

Baby Jal's fever shoots up an hour after the pro-viral injection. His eye sockets begin to swell and bruise, and I can hardly stand to see him so sick. He begins to vomit after three hours, so I stay with him in quarantine all night. Rubbing Jal's back as he sleeps, I worry he's suffering too much, or that I've put his little body through more than it can handle. Nobody deserves this, much less this beautiful boy.

Like Ringol, the baby's forehead burns and his hands remain ice cold. I watch for any small sign that he's turning for the better, but every time I check, he seems worse.

Ringol coughs in the quarantine room opposite ours, a barking that sounds more animal than human. I rush to his room. He's been sleeping since yesterday when Kriz thanked me. I'm beginning to worry that his conscious episode was a fluke.

"His fever has broken," Kriz reports without looking up. "He's less than two degrees off."

I sigh, relieved. His Indigo Flu should clear up within the next few days and we can reassess.

"When will we know for sure that he's made it through this Drake-Omnit plague thing?" she asks.

"I don't know." It's hard for me to admit that I don't know something so important. I pull out a bloodlab test strip. "We need to stay positive."

"And hope." She adjusts his pillow and dabs the drops of perspiration on his forehead with a cloth. She's quoting my speech.

"Medera?" Ringol mumbles. His eyes are so swollen he can't possibly open them yet.

Both of our faces snap to his. "I couldn't do this without you, Medera Kriz."

I glance at Kriz, who doesn't look my way. "Why is he calling you that?" I ask.

"Zuzan?" he says. His eyes flutter as if the room is too bright. "I can smell you."

Kriz's eyes narrow in on me.

"It's Miss Kriz and J'Mave Allele," I whisper.

His mouth breaks into a weak smile. "Zuzan." My name rolls slowly off his tongue. "So magnificent."

My face warms, but I squeeze his hand which is now warm, thank all good. He squeezes back with healthy strength.

"You will be fine, Maven." I say, hoping he uses my new name.

Kriz shoots me her "wholly improper" glare. "He isn't himself."

But then he pulls my hand, drawing my face closer to his. "My maddening new recruit, what was life like before *you*? Less complicated, less painful, and endless tunnels of monotony."

Griffith walks in and I pull my hand to free myself, but I can't break away from Ringol's grip.

"Jal's bloodlabs show he's fully developed the Indigo symptomatology." Griffith's eyes lock in on us. "What's going on with the maven?"

The more I tug to get loose, the more Ringol tightens his grip. "Come lie with me again, my Zuzan."

"What's going on?" Griffith's eyes fill with rage mixed with confusion.

Kriz tries to pry Ringol's fingers to release my hand, but he pushes her away. She huffs. "We should sedate him until he is more lucid."

"Let go, Maven," I say. "There is no one named Zuzan here."
He growls.

"We can't sedate him," Griffith replies. "Not unless it's medically necessary. It may impact his treatment results."

"Well," Kriz speaks through her teeth. "He can't hold onto his j'mave like a teddy bear. Anchor his arm for us!"

My fingers throb from lack of circulation and Griffith does as Kriz orders. I push his hand towards his chest, and then yank back with all my weight. *Page eleven* comes in handy again. I fall backwards onto the floor, landing on my bottom. Standing quickly while the maven groans, I straighten my labcoat and leave the room.

"Come back, magnificent Zuzan!" Ringol shouts over and over, but I can't visit him again, no matter how it torments me. Even when he calls out *Zuzan* from time to time over the next few hours, I stay away.

I get back to caring for baby Jal in the next quarantine room over, hugging the child tighter every time Ringol calls out. Whatever happened between us in Camu's cave doesn't matter. How I feel about him can't matter. Besides, a relationship between maven and a subordinate is strictly forbidden. No exceptions. Whatever happened between Drake and Nukleo nearly ended her career. I don't care that I could lose my j'maven position anymore, but I do care that he would be stripped of his mavenship.

Medtech K messages Ringol's updated bloodlabs to me, which show only a minor improvement in the markers for Drake's plague. Even with encouraging improvement in his markers for Indigo, the results deflate me. If the pro-virus doesn't resolve his case of Drake's Plague, this trial was a waste and baby Jal will suffer through Indigo Flu for nothing.

For the rest of the day, I stay close to Jal. His fever steadily increases over the course of the evening and peaks in the middle of the night. Small bruises appear on his chest and back, and his respiratory rate increases sharply. I desperately want to take his bruises and put them on myself to spare him the pain. His body remains limp in my arms – no cries, no struggles. Every so often, I feel for warm air exiting his nostrils to ensure he's still breathing.

In the early morning hours, he lifts his head and whimpers. It's a half hour too early to run his bloodlabs according to Pascal's schedule, so I wait and watch his every move. At the end of thirty minutes, I pull out a bloodlab test strip and press it into Jal's heel, and then insert it into my medtab. His Indigo markers are improving. If he survives this recovery, we will finally know if we've cured him of Drake's Plague. For all good, this is his last hope.

"Zuzan?" A man's voice calls from the door.

I spin around.

Griffith stands in the threshold, and his eyes narrow.

Sweat prickles at my brow. "You startled me."

He stares at me without saying a word. He knows.

"Griffith, *oh*." I feel sick. "It's – it's classified."

His face sours, and he turns to leave.

"Wait."

He turns and cocks his head.

"You can't tell anyone, please. For a lot of reasons." He's got to understand – I didn't want any of this. The least I can do, though, is lay out the entire truth for him. "I am Zuzan from Cayan, burrow sister to Maddelyn Cayan. Maven Ringol recruited my wonderful classmate, Jalaz, who died before he came here, and Ringol encouraged me to apply at that time. Due to my own stupid mistakes, I transferred to Woynauld's Military Academy and took a ba'rm position. My Cayan name was never registered since the Cayan burrow was condemned and shut down before I hit legal age. Other issues play into this story, but in short, that's why Ringol called me Zuzan. But my official name is now Allele Crypt."

"I was saddened to learn of Jalaz Cayan's death." His eyes drop to the floor as he turns to leave. "He sent that hand-mapped genome, amazing work for someone without equipment. Someday, maybe you could tell me more about him. I respect that you named the baby boy after him, an honorable tribute to your burrowkin."

"Thank you." I hope this means he'd like to remain friends.

His expression softens. "Like you said in your initiation speech – you're here for him. Good health, J'Mave."

Later, when I'm barely awake, Medtech K stops in. He insists that I decontaminate for the day and retire to my bedchamber. The medtech lifts baby Jal from my arms, and Undertech Griffith escorts me away.

Griffith walks behind me rather than next to me into the decontamination chamber. Afterwards, we walk in silence to my chamberroom, and I turn to him. He knows too much about me, and the truth behind Ringol's feelings for me, and he's been brooding ever since he found out. All it takes is a camcall to Common Good, and he could bring us both down.

"Whatever you might think, the maven and I have never–" I stop. What haven't we done? We're not technically a couple, but that hasn't stopped me from falling for him.

"J'Mave," he interrupts. "Did you really not know I was interested in you when I asked to drop your title and call you 'Allele'?"

He catches me off guard, so I shake my head slowly. "I'd been living in a dark hole."

"I see." He clears his throat. "If you love him, you should go to him. You wouldn't want to have his recovery take longer because he's stressed from your absence. We all witnessed the babies faring better when we increased our staffing levels." Griffith's concern hits me in a strange way. He's acting like it's a foregone conclusion that Ringol has feelings for me, that he loves me. I guess it's something hard to fake when you're delirious with fever. But Griffith seems to be questioning whether I return Ringol's feelings.

I shake my head. I do love him, but I can't. Maven Ringol's work at GCE is too important, and I'd never put him in jeopardy. Not again. "Maven Ringol doesn't know what he's saying."

"I've noticed the expression on your face when you're tending to him."

My face heats up. "We are not in a relationship. And it's clearly not permitted anyway."

His mouth opens, and he takes a step away from me. "I have no doubt that you're shut off to a genuine relationship. But tell me, J'Mave. Before our maven fell ill, did you have any clues about his feelings for you?"

"Yes." My voice turns panicky. "If by feelings you mean irritation, anger, and contempt. Hear me. My whole life has been nothing but a tragic play written by other people, that I'm forced to act out day after day. I'll tell you something, Undertech Griffith. I'm not Allele – I'm still Zuzan, the same girl who is prone to vanity and stupid mistakes, someone who longs for her best friend and her medera's advice. I'm broken in so many ways. I have nothing to offer in a relationship – not for you, the maven, or anyone!" I stop abruptly, breathing heavily, knowing I've never been more honest with myself. Truth is a force that can burn all the lies from the surface of my skin and leave me raw.

Griffith raises his eyebrows and nods. "Well." He grins, and his dimple unarms me. "I had no idea. But now all your skittish episodes make a lot more sense."

I relax at his better humor. "It's late, Undertech. See you in a few hours."

As I walk to the quarantine beta-test area the next day, I camcall Kleo to update her on our progress. She's stuck at the

Woynauld Academy with the GCE jet because of storms. While I'm giving her the status update, she starts twirling her finger in the air as if I'm not speaking fast enough.

"What is it, Kleo?"

"Undertech Griffith already filled me in on all that jabber. And if you're going to camcall while you're walking, please engage your ChiPro's stabilizer mode. I'm getting motion sickness."

"Sorry." I fumble for the right setting. "Better?"

She holds up a hand as if she's afraid I'm going to start talking again. "As soon as Ringol's or Jal's labs hit the threshold marker determined by Undertech Pascal, you will begin to inject the pro-virus into ten more infants." She's not reminding me as much as she's confirming that I have the stamina to continue. "And when those infants recover, ten more until we make it through GCE's entire population of infants. No more delays. There's too much buzz in the scientific community about the mass GCE exodus and 'odd events' going on, so we're running out of time."

"Have you spoken with Yelda?"

She shakes her head. "The new headmaid's name is not 'Yelda.'"

Jet. Allund must have dismissed her.

"But the woman I spoke to knows this girl you'd mentioned. The child has turned around after a "disciplinary incident" according to this maid. Medero Woynauld has made her an example of *setting one's mind right*. He refers to her as his dullard-to-prodigy success story." Kleo's lip curls from having to repeat the slur.

Although I'm happy my girl is no longer under attack, I worry about Woynauld's influence on her. She craved his approval even as he abused her. "Please tell her – my girl – that she should be proud."

Someday this girl might forget all about me.

My first stop at quarantine is my baby's room. I find him in

Kriz's arms, and he's drinking formula from a bottle. When he sees me, he stops drinking for a minute to smile.

He's gorgeous.

When I take him from Kriz's arms, I squeeze his little body with all the emotions stuck inside my soul. The purest sense of peace washes through me. I laugh, because I wanted to make sure to improve the quality of life for the infants in our care, but instead, baby Jal has improved mine in ways I can't measure.

"His bloodlabs?" I ask.

"They've restored faster than Ringol's – for both illnesses."

Both?

My eyes flash to hers questioningly, but she's focused on the baby. Does she mean the markers for active Drake's plague symptomatology? "It's working?" My voice cracks.

She finally meets my gaze, and smiles. "Griffith has alerted Kleo."

Baby Jal will be okay, thank all that is decent and good. Maybe the rest of the babies will be, too. But. "Why isn't it working for the maven?"

"He's different, as you well know, so it maybe that he's just slower to respond. Still – he's eating, so he's improving. I still have hope. A lot of it."

"Of course." Kleo's cocktail worked for me but not for her because everyone is different. But it's a perfect example that there's a chance it won't work on Ringol at all.

The day in the cave when he *managed* me, the curve of his eye shifted as he gazed into my face, and he seemed happy to be there with me. I wanted to feel like I belonged, and I did. With him.

"Have we chosen the first subset of infants for trial?" I ask.

Kriz nods. "Undertechs Griffith and Pascal are preparing them at the lab."

"I'll go help, then." Before I hand over Jal, I kiss the dark tufts of hair covering his scalp, breathing in his perpetually fresh smell. "Good health, baby."

Rushing over to the lab, I worry about unknown details that we might not have considered. Have my undertechs conducted full bloodlabs on the infants they've chosen? Studied the intricacies in their charts? Their brainscans? The first subset of infants must be similar enough in almost every way possible – age, region, progression of disease, gender if possible. Our current trial tested on three people has yielded vastly different results. Horizon had perhaps been too weak to recover. We need a cleaner sample to learn anything.

Baby Jal has been the best responder by far. Our initial subset must include infants with similar bloodlabs and traits to him.

I jam my thumb into the bioreader once, twice, and a third time before it yields. Flying through the door as soon as it opens, I scurry along until I'm all the way down the long corridor. Before I make it to the second security door, the first door opens again. I spin around, startled. Light from the outside hall spills into the darker passageway. The silhouette of a large figure encroaches the space.

He makes it through the door, allows it to close, and then holds himself up on the curved, steel wall as if to rest before continuing.

"Maven Ringol?"

CHAPTER 31

Return Home

Ringol slides the back of his arm over his brow before he lifts himself from the brace of the wall. His chin rises, and he stops the minute his gaze reaches my face. His swollen eyes are slits, glazed over from his illness.

My heart races, and all my thoughts jumble into mush. My first instinct is to run up to him and throw my arms around his neck. I asked him to fight his illness, and he did. But doubt creeps in and fogs my mind. He's lied to me. Besides, we both know that we can't be together. I will not jeopardize his mavenship. *I can't.*

"Hello, Maven. You're not allowed to enter the lab. We can't decontaminate you until your bloodlabs show you're medically cleared."

"I have to explain. Please," His eyes close slowly. "I want to tell you everything."

His voice is strained and weak, and I've already figured out a lot on my own. "Not now."

He winces as if he's still in pain, and his hands clench into fists. "I was wrong. I should have broken procedure. I should have told you as much as you'd be willing to hear."

Heat rises from my neck to my cheeks. "Tell me one thing then, Maven. Is my confidential project – Sterling's Plague – truly solvable?"

He shrugs. "I don't know. If anyone can–"

"Maybe you can explain how you promised your boss that

you'd *manage* me?" My body stiffens. I thought I'd gotten over the disappointment in hearing him say those words, but my hands shake from the confrontation.

"Whether you admit to it or not, I am your manager." His voice grows louder. "I am a human being who makes mistakes, and I will admit to every last one of them if you'll let me."

"There's a difference between a lie and a mistake. It's too purposeful. Calculating."

"I'm confused at times," he continues, "but one thing has never confused me." He paces forward, sliding his hand along the wall the entire way over. By the time he makes it to me, he's winded and his breath hits my face. My gaze drops and I bite the inside of my cheek. With him so close to me, I already want to give him every chance to explain, and I want to forgive him even before I hear his reasons.

His fingers tilt my chin upward again, and I see his eyes are slightly out of focus. Perspiration speckles his scalp. "Won't you ask me why I've decided to be so open now?"

"I can't." Tears line my lashes. "I can't figure out when to believe you."

He kisses the one tear that streams down my cheek. "It's you, Zuzan. You're the one who has changed me. My dear, wonderful Zuzan. How can you be so mean, staying away from me for so long? None of this is fake. I'd set fire to any orders that would keep me away from you. A man who nearly dies and comes back to life doesn't have the inclination to lie. He loves whomever he loves."

He holds my hand, waiting for me to respond. His eyes glimmer with a thousand promises, and I want to be the one to see every one come true. But I don't believe people have the luxury of love – a truly devoted love – here in this hole where babies die underground like they've already been buried.

Still, there's a bigger reason that stops me from giving in to Ringol right now. I didn't know it until the words flew out of my mouth when I argued with Griffith.

"I love you, Ringol." I kiss his cheek and back away slowly. "I won't deny it. But since the day we met in the hallway at Cayan, I've been scarred and broken so often, I don't even know where to look for the pieces. I have to try, though, and I – I need time."

He hugs me tightly, and then kisses the top of my forehead for as long as it takes him to inhale and exhale three times, and backs away.

"I'm sorry for any of the cracks that I caused." He tilts his head and smiles softly. "And I promise to demonstrate 'patience and a tiny bit of faith' for you now."

I laugh at his quoting me from when we were treating C back at Cayan. It feels like a lifetime ago.

The door to the lab slides open. Undertech Pascal rushes out, startles when he notices us, and then hesitates like he's not sure whether he should continue or retreat.

"Respectfully, sir," I say to Ringol. "Go back to the infirmary until Medtech K clears your bloodlab results and you regain your strength."

I nod to Pascal before entering the labroom. "Please see to it that he returns to his recovery bed."

In one swift motion, I thumb the bioscanner and slip into the labroom. When the door closes, I stand inside motionless. I know I've messed up with Ringol so terribly, and I can't even think of how I should have done anything differently. The tears come again, and before I know it, Griffith pulls me into a decontamination chamber, closing the door and activating the decontamination mode.

"You're okay, J'Mave," he says when the chamber begins to hum. "Everything will be okay."

"Undertech Griffith." I dry my face, determined to fix one thing today. "Your work has been nothing but stellar but I rely on you for more, and I need to know I can count on your friendship."

He smiles, and that dimple I've missed shows itself again.

"I apologize, J'Mave Allele. You will never need to question my professionalism or my friendship again. Never doubt that I believe in you. Maven Ringol warned me that PoSSE was bad news, but it was you who proved to me that we should fight for Omnits, not against them. If you hadn't come here, I'm ashamed to say I'd still be struggling like Chen. He'll come around, though, too."

I smile because Ringol must have known, and still, he took Chen and Griffith to Woynauld's. Maybe he thought they needed to meet the dragon for themselves.

Griffith then jumps into the list of infants for the study, explaining that he's checked and rechecked every item on my list, and he's added a few more after speaking with the maven. By the time he's done, I've calmed down and I'm ready to continue our work.

In short, he's fully capable of handling this part of the research without me. He's even identified an additional lab near the tunnels to hold the infants who are infected, complete with its own bioscan entry and decontamination chamber. He's assigned shifts to our remaining personnel to care for the infants once they become infected.

There's little left for me to do, other than give my approval to proceed. "Thank you, Undertech. What time do you anticipate we'll be ready to initiate the first group?"

"We are *T* minus five minutes, J'Mave. All the vials are filled based on J'Mave Kleo's calculations. We've transferred all but two infants into the test facility, and those two are on their way as we speak. The instructions you've left to care for the subjects once they are ill have been disseminated to the crew. Our medtech is on standby."

"Good work." A jittery sensation flurries under my breastbone. It's time to proceed, which can turn out well for the babies like Jal, or it can turn out like Horizon.

The decontamination door opens, and commotion from the back of the labroom makes us both jump.

"J'Mave!" shouts Medtech K. He's holding a male infant named Storm. "He's developed a fever."

Rushing over to him, I feel Storm's brow. The child is burning up. This infant has not yet been injected with the pro-virus. What the *jet*?

Griffith pulls out a bloodlab strip and presses it into the baby's heel.

When he inserts the test strip into his medtab, his eyes go blank until the results clear. And then he frowns, slowly raising his eyes to me. "Put the child back into his chambercrib and begin the treatment protocol for Indigo Flu. And then do a quick medcheck on the rest of the infants."

I shake my hands at my sides and spin around, pacing. This can't happen. We can't handle a labroom full of feverish infants with a skeleton staff. "We've been so careful, Griffith! How did this happen? And now what? I should have seen this coming."

He nods. "You haven't been the one traveling back and forth from quarantine to the infant lab. I have. Medtech K and Undertech Pascal have. We've used all necessary precautions, and endured hours of decontamination at both ends. It's nobody's fault."

"If all the infants contract the disease at the same time, we're singed. We have forty-six infants, fifteen undertechs to care for them, and one lonely medtech."

He begins to blink rapidly, and a smile breaks across his face. There's nothing funny here. "What?"

"None of that has happened yet, J'Mave. We have one confirmed Indigo case and if more break out, we will find a way. Although none of the GCE scientists would ever have imagined working as nurserymaids-slash-medtechs, they are more than willing to do so now. If you want to take blame for something, take blame for this: you and Kleo made them understand this work is necessary and honorable. For all good, our undertechs have shaved their heads in solidarity, at least the ones who have hair." He takes off his labhat for a moment to show his bald head, and I giggle. "They care because of you."

Even without my dear Jal, without Maddelyn and Kleo, with Ringol in recovery unable to help, he's right. I'm not alone. "Thank you."

He and I face the hard reality together, camcalling Kleo for her input. Four babies have bloodlab results showing early signs of Indigo. Of course, these four children are of different ages, different stages of Drake's Plague. Two are female – Grasslands and Cherry – and the other two are male – Pine and Storm.

"We couldn't have chosen a more eclectic group if we tried," I say.

"By default, it's become a study in the natural spreading of Indigo Flu," Griffith shrugs. "This string proves to be more contagious than we thought. It will eventually yield the same result for our purposes, just not as neatly as we had hoped."

"We will need to contain the disease as best as possible, and fortify the decontamination process." Kleo shifts nervously, as if she's aching to help. This is, after all, her project. "So use the smaller labroom in the west wing for these children. The slower we can keep the disease from spreading, the better chance our undertechs will be able to keep up with the workload."

She's called them our undertechs, not *hers*. It's such a small difference, but it's coming from her as if it's natural now.

In no time, the ten infants originally chosen for the study are moved back in their original chambercribs, and the four currently infected have been transferred to the west lab. In a matter of hours, three more babies fall sick and need to be transferred as well.

I take charge of the "Indigo" lab with Medtech K and two undertechs. We plan for baby Jal to be returned to the main lab with thirty-nine other infants and nine undertechs. We're all taking shifts – I've ordered each staff member to take six hours rest each day until the crisis is over. Each hour is an exercise in stamina, but each day is a step closer to recovery.

* * *

Two days later, Storm is over the toughest Indigo symptoms, but his lunch comes back up all over my labjacket and blouse, right when Maven Ringol chipchats me. He still looks fatigued even though the swelling around his eyes has gone down. There's something else weird in his expression, though. Something I can't quite make out. He lowers his head.

"What is it?" My voice is clipped. I peel off my soiled top – down to my underslip – and pick up the infant who now begins to wail. I tug on a medsmock from our cart of supplies, but it falls to the floor before I can drape it over me. "You're scaring me. What is it?"

Ringol nods hesitantly. "I just received a call from Central Dispatch. Along with our regular shipment of supplies, they've included five Omnit-infant replacements. It's routine, ever since the onset of this fiasco. We're always supposed to have fifty."

No rotting way. I rock Storm until he quiets. He rests his fiery cheek on the word *dullard* written on my chest. I shift him to my other shoulder as Medtech K helps me into a new medsmock. "We can't possibly handle more. They're here already in our terminal?"

"They will arrive in twenty minutes," he says. "The shipment requires my signature."

Five more infants. Jet.

"Maven, why *five* replacements?" We've lost Twilight, Aurora, Breeze, and Horizon. "That's only *four*."

He presses his lips together. The muscles in his jaws tighten, and a shiver runs down my spine.

Kriz speaks from the background, evidently standing next to him. "You must tell her."

He scowls in her direction, and shivers run down my neck.

"Please, Ringol," I plead. "What's happened?"

"I've already spoken with Chen to correct the issue," he hesitates like he can't figure out how to tell me. "Our database system has a direct feed to Common Good's, so they already know that Jal has now recovered. At this point, the only legal thing to do is to return him to his parents. He will be sent to a central infirmary to be examined and processed, and then he will be sent home, to his family."

I play Ringol's words back in my mind over and over several times, trying to make sense.

"His family?" I say stupidly. I take a seat in a nearby rickety stool, a move that Storm doesn't like. He begins to whimper again, so I stand up for his comfort. "Of course, of course," I stammer.

I've always wanted Jal to return to his family. From the start, it's what I wanted for all these babies. That was the goal – to get them back into the arms of the people who love them most. But my insides crawl with a scream I can't scream.

"Chen is currently working to update the code on our data transmission system to delay the uploading of medical information on our subjects until after we are able to produce the documented benefits of our research findings. We can't risk leaking too much to Common Good without them guessing that we've initiated a study without their approval, not until we can prove its success. I don't plan on getting arrested, at least until the rest of my little people are cured."

Undertech Pascal takes Storm from me. He tries not to stare at the tattoo spanning my chest. He motions to the door with his head and whispers, "Go."

I touch his arm in thanks.

"I am on my way there, Maven. Please wait for me." I need to say good-bye to my boy.

"J'Mave," Ringol starts.

"Don't move him yet!" I deactivate my chip before he can argue.

I head for the door, and then stop. Turning back, I rush to get my painted rock out of the pocket of my soiled labjacket. I almost forgot it.

A chipchat message pops up from Kleo: *Mayday. Camcall me, ASAP.*

I ignore it, because there's no time, and she want to tell me the same thing: baby Jal is leaving us.

By the time I decontaminate and make it to our original quarantine room, Kriz is preparing Jal for his journey. She gently slides his feet into thermosocks.

"Hello baby boy," I say. He squeals with joy when he recognizes me, pumping his arms and legs. I rush over to him. "I will sit with him in pre-travel decontamination before–" But I can't say it. Letting go of Jal is like letting go of a piece of my own body.

I take Jal from Kriz and walk into the decontamination chamber closest to the magnetran platform. The door closes behind us, and the chamber begins to hum with cleansing gusts of air. Jal grabs my cheeks with his little hands as I speak into his ear. "What is your real name, little one? Your mother will love seeing that smile of yours. You won't even miss me, and you'll grow to be very old."

I sing him lullabies a little too slowly, squeezing his body into me. He laughs, and I fight my tears with everything I have. I don't want him to see me cry because today should be a happy day for him. I rub his back, and the rock that Jal Cayan gave me falls onto the bench. I stare at it for a moment. It's beautiful, really. *May good health find you always.*

I've held onto this rock because it means so much it to me. I'd cherish it until the day I die, except now – today of all days – it feels right to pass it on, so I tuck it into the baby's sock.

My chip beeps with a quick note from Undertech Pascal. Four more infants were delivered to the sick lab. They need me as soon as I can get back.

I exit the decontamination chamber and hand my beautiful baby boy over to Kriz, who is waiting outside. My body feels heavier without him.

Ringol stands alongside her, and has changed from a

medsmock into his official uniform. For people who don't know him, who don't realize his eyes are normally clear and his posture is usually a bit more formidable, he looks passable.

"You're to be congratulated," he whispers. "You did this – you are responsible for sending him back to his parents. Thanks to you, he'll live a perfectly normal life."

I smile even though tears now stream down my face. How can I argue? This was my goal, the happy ending. I just wasn't ready for it.

"You're conquering Drake's plague, I'm sure you'll break Sterling's next," he says. "You're the best decision I've made in years."

"I couldn't have come up with a theory for Drake's plague without studying Sterling's so closely," I mumble. So many things I hated at the time needed to happen for everything else to fall into place, so we could help the Omnit infants. "Or without Kleo."

He tries not to stare at my tattoo, but I can tell it's bothering him. "I'm going to have a DermaTech come to help you with – that."

I glance down at the writing. *I am but a dullard.* "Don't."

Somehow, it's become a part of who I am now. Just a few weeks ago, I'd have jumped at his offer. But after watching almost everything fall apart, and holding it together without breaking apart myself, in some crazy way this tattoo is a symbol of my success. Besides, in Allund's mind, all Omnits are dullards – including baby Jal. That's what Allund meant by the tattoo, to lump me in with people he despises. He couldn't have guessed that I'm happy to be considered part of these children.

"Are you coming to dispatch with us?" Ringol asks.

"Undertech Pascal urgently needs me." Besides, if I stay, I'll never let them take Jal away. So I kiss my baby boy one more time. "I love you. But now, I have to help your friends get ready to see their families too."

Kriz begins to weep quietly, and I can't look at her.

"Goodbye, baby," I say. "You are my heart."

I turn away and try to force myself to walk. All I want to do is to grab the baby and flee. Instead, I will my feet to move and bolt down the closest corridor, turning at the first bend. I run down another hallway, crashing into the wall, then turn down the next hall and continue to run until I can't catch my breath and my legs have gone numb. Slamming into a wall, a jolt of pain shoots through my ribs from the impact, and I slide down to the cold, marble floor, remembering Jalaz Cayan's brittle bones.

Oh, his broken bones, his broken dreams – my poor, poor Jalaz. He was too brilliant to keep buried underground, and I would do anything to have him back. I used to tease him for his science-y quirks, but Jalaz was so right to choose the very worthy profession of genomics. I hug myself and shiver. I'll do everything I can to solve Sterling's Plague after we're done with Drake's. For Jalaz. I'll do my best, and hope it's enough, for all good.

My baby Jal is probably strapped into the magnetran by now, and I worry about who'll watch him on his trip. My stomach pulls and twists, imagining him crying for me, or any familiar face. He knows no one. I wipe my face, wet with nonstop tears, with the sleeve of my smock. Because of the efforts of so many of my brave Subter co-workers, he'll be reunited with his family, thank everything that has ever been good. In all honesty, every Subterranean dreams of a family reunion, so it's almost like it's happening for all of us.

With Jalaz's painted rock tucked inside baby Jal's sock, I can't help thinking that Jalaz Cayan, in some infinitesimal way, gets to go home too.

My ChiPro beeps again, and I want to ignore it, but it's Kleo so I answer.

"Thanks for returning my message, Newness," she says sharply as she walks down a corridor. "Oh, wait. You didn't. And put a blasted labcoat on, for all good. Has everything gone to pot since I've left?"

I blink. "I thought you were going to warn me about baby Jal having to leave GCE."

"No." She stops walking and drops her head. "I'm sorry. I didn't know."

"He's better off," I cut her off. "What did you need?"

"It's what *you* need J'Mave. A heads-up." She smirks in the way only Kleo can. "I'm on my way to GCE – with Allund Woynauld."

"For all good!" My muscles tighten remembering Allund's fingers on my skin. "Does Ringol know?"

Kleo hesitates a moment too long. "He can't know, J'Mave. I never told you how much I admire you for your honesty, so I realize not-telling-Ringol falls outside your comfort zone, but this condition is a strict part of the cease-bomb deal."

"Kleo–" I start.

"Wait," she says, putting her hand up, her brows squeezing together. "There's more." She swallows hard. "He has a recording of your medera, Julia-something-or-other. A holographic video he says you need to see."

"Gelia?" I gasp. Invoking her name sends goosebumps up my arms. I would do almost anything to see her again. Does that mean he knows where she is? Does he have her? "Gelia Cayan?"

"That's the one," she replies slowly, like she doesn't want to say more. "Allund insinuated that there is information on it about you too, and he'll only let you have it if you meet his terms."

My voice turns hoarse, and I can barely ask my next question. "Is she… alive?"

A flash of sorrow crosses her eyes, and my heart drops. "He won't say anything else about it, at least not to me." She knows how I feel about my former burrow family, and I know she'd do anything to give me the answers.

"I hate this," I say through my teeth.

She shakes her head. "You're not hearing me. Whatever's on there about you might not be good."

I rub away the sweat that's started to bead on my forehead. I'm so tired of this man's demands. I'm so tired of how he seeks to control me. I'm so tired of how good he is at inflicting me pain. But how can I just give in to Allund's demands? "It's blackmail," I say finally. "I don't want that tyrant anywhere near –"

I stop because Kleo is shaking her head.

She inhales deeply through her nose. "Blackmail or not, we must help him in order to finish our trial," she interrupts. "For the babies," she says firmly. "You also need to know if Allund is still a threat to you, or to anyone else you care about, no? We'll be there in thirty-four hours." And before I can respond she signs off.

In the ensuing silence, my drumming heartbeat echoes in my ears along with her words.

I'm tormented by the knowledge that she's right.

CHAPTER 32

No More Secrets

Ringol has been recovering in a private infirmary in the undertunnels with Kriz, his constant caretaker. I didn't know there was yet another secret room in those tunnels, but at the same time I'm not surprised. I've been monitoring his health stats remotely because I cannot allow any more public professions of love from him, no matter how much I miss his banter, his eyes, and – for all good – his touch.

After Kleo's camcall yesterday and a restless night, the hours before she'll arrive with Allund seem to fly by. I've stationed myself at Ringol's desk during the last of them in an attempt to respond to each of his external messages from his personal tablet in my best impersonation of Ringol-esque logic and language. We can't let anyone outside of GCE know about his illness for many reasons, but most of all, because we've used him as one of our own subjects in an unsanctioned experiment. Still, it feels wrong to sign off with his name. Luckily, I have his permission.

I shift ever so slightly in his chair and breathe deeply. He's spent many hours in this space, and I can smell him as if he were sitting here with me, which just makes me want to go to him more. Maddelyn used to describe the dancing colors of a flame to me because I was never able to look directly into its light; the oranges, reds, yellows, and the hottest indigos. That's what Ringol is for me, the bluish flame beckoning to me, the center of everything. I want to go to it. To him. I want the danger.

But I've got plenty of that right now, don't I? Sparring brothers, infectious diseases, missing mederas, threats upon threats upon more threats.

While Kleo and I have a plan to keep Ringol and Allund separated, I'm questioning everything right this minute. How am I behaving any better than Ringol when he kept things from me? Besides, what could Allund do if I've already told Ringol by the time he gets here? He can't refuse the treatment and risk his own death.

I laugh, because how silly it is for me to think Allund's got the upper hand. He doesn't.

After I finish responding to the external messages, I clear off his desk and ready myself to go down into the depths of the undertunnels to speak with Ringol about Allund. To tell him the truth. Yet when I raise my eyes to the doorway of his office, he's already standing there, dressed in travel clothes.

"No," I say. My face warming at the mere sight of him. "You're not leaving?"

He holds up his hand. "Zuzan," he starts.

"Allele," I remind him through my teeth.

Ringol pauses before he speaks again, as if he's in pain. But not the pain he's been battling since his migraines hit. This runs more deeply. I can see it in his eyes. A wearied expression of helplessness flashes across his brow and he drops his head. "My father has died."

I'm confused for a moment. His biological paternal code came from a blend of several men, but when I search the sadness in his countenance my thoughts quiet, and I realize exactly what he's saying. "You mean the Omnit man who raised you?" I forget Ringol grew up with a family. "Drake's plague?" I assume.

He nods. "I'm going to attend his funeral."

"You're only just recovering yourself," I interject. "You're too weak to work. How can you even think you're fit for travel?"

"I don't have full medical clearance, but I'm monitoring my stats." He starts to walk towards me, disarming me with his sad smile. "I'll take all the necessary medpatches with me. But Zu – my family – they've all been exposed to Drake's plague, my mother, my extended family, my friends." He paces as he speaks, his voice growing louder like he might burst, and then he turns and looks directly at me pleadingly. "They're going to die without my help. Your help, really, because you're the only one who can be credited with our sole solution."

I fight the urge to beg him to stay, because I know in my bones he must go. And yet, how can he just leave me here? Numerous terrible scenarios run through my mind, all of which end in my never seeing him again. "There's no way to induce Indigo Flu upon your whole Omnit group without word getting out, Ringol. Outbreaks are rare, except in some very specific regions."

Before I can resist any further, he's in front of me, embracing me so tightly I can hardly catch my next breath.

"You are going to be the reason my loved ones live. I'm so grateful you're here. My mother worried I was following orders blindly, but I wasn't. I sincerely thought you could help, and now my mother sees it too. I can't get to her fast enough. Her debilitating headaches began three days ago."

He releases me, and it's only then that I feel his trembling. Tears glisten his cheeks, and I know that he's leaving no matter what.

"We'll talk when I return," he continues. "You've always wanted a medership, and with the correction to your vision and your extended LE, there's no reason you can't be one. If you can believe it, I want you to be a medera almost as much as you want it for yourself. I can see now that you have so much to give your future students. With you guiding our next generation, maybe we can right some of the wrongs happening. Maybe there are many ways to end the fighting."

"A medera?" I say stupidly, and my heart quickens. Although I wouldn't change my work at GCE, I can't deny that the absence of teaching young minds hasn't haunted me. "Wait. Then... we could be together? Together, together. No hiding?"

"We could have a legitimate relationship," he smiles. "As equals. If that's what you want."

I laugh, and pull him closer to me. "As if you've ever been my equal," I tease.

I'm quieted again when he reaches for my face and glides his fingers down my jaw. I pull his collar until he leans forward, and our lips meet for a slow, soft kiss.

"No more crazy secrets," he says as my heart sinks, not because I disagree, but because of the giant secret I, myself, carry at the moment. "Only truth from now on."

Someone clears their throat at his office door. "It's time," Kriz says, as we spin towards her like we've been caught sneaking the last sugar cube. "Your hover jet is prepped on the tarmac."

Ringol smirks and kisses me again in a way that makes the blood pulsate through my body at full speed.

"Ringol," Kriz warns. "We only have a few minutes of clearance for your takeoff."

"Wait! Ringol," I say. How can I let him leave with such a big 'truth' to be shared? "It's about A–"

"It'll have to wait until he returns," Kriz says as she hastens him with a mere look, much like Gelia would do for me. Ringol looks on apologetically.

"No, you don't under–"

"I love you," he calls from the hallway, and I scurry to the door to watch him go. "We can't communicate through electronic messages or calls until I return. No one can know I'm gone." When he and Kriz turn a corner, I lean against the wall, feeling alone. Left behind. Guilty.

I swallow these emotions because there's only one thing I want to feel right now, and I need him to know it.

"I love you, too, Ringol!" I yell, hoping he can hear me.

I've never been so happy, and yet so incredibly sad. But I know he needs to help his family, to save them from certain death. I know I would do the same.

Seven hours after Ringol left, I'm riding in the same hydraulic elevator as he did. It clanks and glides for a half mile to ground level. I'm wearing full hazmat gear and carrying a taser baton, but no one can protect me from the person I'm about to greet – the man who has stripped more from my soul than anyone living above or below the earth.

My ears pop as the elevator's pressure changes. During the final few meters, the cabin slows like a dying heartbeat. The door unlocks with the sound of a vacuum, sliding open to the vastness of the omniterranean world. Out of habit, I close my eyes to the impending sunlight even though my protective contacts will adjust automatically to the level of light exposure.

"You there, Newness?" Kleo asks over my ChipPro.

I smile at the sound of her voice and blink away the bright haze coating the horizon. The scenery reminds me of overexposed, antique pictures. The heat of the sun nearly cooks me, and a damp sweat starts to form across the surface of my entire body, although I haven't even stepped from the elevator yet. There's a flurry of howling sounds in the distance, most likely a pack of wild dogs on the hunt. The taser baton is more for them, since they are very common in this region. It's not like a simple electric shock could help me fight off any militant-minded people.

"Do you need me to count to three for you?" Kleo jokes, her way of encouraging me. "I'm turning to ash out here!"

"Let's do this." Holding onto the trim of the open cylindrical elevator vestibule, I place one foot on the cement platform outside. Then the other. I can hardly catch my breath as I enter the world full of skies, enormous space and light. Endless light. It's more gorgeous than anything I've seen in books or pictures. But then I catch a glimpse of a crater, which could only be there because of the bombing. I nearly drop the baton as I steady myself.

"Use your hand to shade your eyes," Kleo says over the sounds of the dogs in the distance. "And make sure you watch where you're walking."

A shadow crosses over my feet, and I duck before I realize it's a crow flying overhead.

"You've got this," she says.

She stands about two hundred yards away in her own hazmat suit, next to the tarmac and a hoverjet from Woynauld's Academy. "You're looking hotter than hot, if you don't mind my saying so," she says in all her... Kleocity.

A giggle starts in my throat and pops through my loneliness. She's here, but because she isn't adequately immune to the Indigo Flu we can't risk coming in contact. "I miss you, Kleo."

I fully expect some satirical, mocking reply, but instead she nods. "Same, my sister."

And then I see it. Movement twenty feet to my right near the longer grass. She must have walked him over there before returning to the tarmac. It's really him: Medero Allund Woynauld.

My body tenses as if I'm watching a venomous snake, though he's on his back almost as helpless as the Omnit babies we are working to cure below ground.

"He's pretty pathetic and weak, J'Mave Allele," Kleo says with a solemn air. I begin my trek over as he struggles to sit up. "I mean, he's a pathetic and weak excuse for a human specimen, but he's very sick, too."

"Check," I say.

"Just be on your guard, Allele. My internal danger alarm is ringing in the worst way around this guy, and I don't think I've ever despised anyone more. Maybe Drake." She sighs. "No. It's a close tie. I loathe them both."

My body fights me as I walk over to Allund. My muscles

jump and twist, ready to run if I have to. But I don't – he's writhing on the ground and my shadow is exaggeratedly tall as it looms over him. "Get up."

He startles like he didn't expect me. "My head. Painful. I can't."

I glance in Kleo's direction.

"I know we have to do this," she says, "but I hate leaving you with him. Still, we never promised to be civil. Make him feel the pain he's caused. Make him breathe every reverberation of the bombshells we've experienced. Let him feel the injustice that Horizon and all the other children suffered."

My heart jumps and tears form in my eyes at her mention of her beloved Horizon.

I turn to Allund and grab him by the shoulders of his hazmat suit, yanking him with what might be double my normal strength. I will never call him 'Lord' again. "I said, get up."

Somehow, he rises with my help. "J'Maven Allele." His voice is muffled under his travelmask – he hasn't camcalled into my chip. "Or Zuzan – whomever you are – I have aggrieved you." His eyes are half open, and he flinches as his migraine pounds with his changing body position. "Thank you for helping me. What should I call you – Zuzan, or J'Mave Allele?"

"I want the Gelia Cayan video," I say in as controlled a voice as I've ever had in his presence.

"You will have it," he says. "I promise, as soon as you've injected me with the cure."

Nukleo turns and boards the jet that awaits her. "Burn that provirus into him if you must."

I set my jaw on Medero Allund. Instead of speaking to him directly, I chipchat his earpiece and speak loudly. "Why don't you call me the name you bestowed upon me, Miss Dullard. Now, walk."

He grips my shoulder, and I cringe. I can't help but think about the day he held onto my collar, dragging me to the tattoo chamber at the academy, ripping my blouse open with no dignity. I want to scream and knock his hand off me.

The grass brushes against our shins as we walk, and he makes it about five feet before he tumbles to the ground.

He reaches up to me. "Slower, please."

And then everything he's done to me washes through my being. The ridicule, the physical abuse. The tattoo.

"I am but a dullard." I reply and turn toward the elevator, leaving him to follow me. While it feels wrong to refuse help to someone in his condition, it's the bigotry that his PoSSE group preaches, a burning hatred which brought Drake's plague into this world in the first place.

He crawls a few more feet. "You can't leave me here with the wild animals."

"I am but a dullard."

"You aren't, though!" he pleads. "I didn't know who you were. I am sorry."

But I keep walking, refusing to help. I step inside the elevator, turn to face him, and wait. He half crawls, half walks his way over.

"I will call you J'Mave Allele. That's what your staff is used to, and it speaks to your brilliance." He stumbles a bit when the ground changes to the concrete platform around the elevator. "I can't begin to express my humility or my repentance."

"I am but a dullard," I say.

He stumbles into the elevator and I press the buttons to descend. Every time he begins to speak, I cut him off. I am but a dullard. I say it just as I did that day at his academy, over and over again as he forced me to in front of his students. He wraps his arms over his head and slides to the floor. "Please stop saying that. My brain will explode."

But I continue. All the way down into the depths of the earth, I tell him what he so wanted to hear a short while ago. The wicked-most part of me hopes the change in altitude affects his migraine as much as it does for all the Omnit babies.

By the time we reach the bottom, he has frustrated tears in his eyes as he begs me to stop.

I ignore him, reciting the security code to Ms. Kriz so she knows it's safe to open the hatch. I couldn't do this without Kriz's help – I told her about Allund as soon as she was done seeing Ringol off. She was, as I expected, wholly unhappy with the situation but at least we both agreed that Ringol must be informed as soon as he returns.

In a weird way, she is almost eager to see Allund. After all, he was her pupil for years. "Allund," she had said, "really went through a lot. I did what I could for him to no avail. He always seemed to gravitate towards hate and retribution."

The mechanical locks release and the elevator door slides open. I remove my suffocating headgear, rubbing my head through my sweat-dampened hair. Kriz helps me drag her former pupil into the decontamination chamber. We each take him by one foot and yank with all our might until he's inside. She's only a wick taller than I am, so it takes all of our combined strength.

She presses the controls to engage the decontamination and cleansing process, and I collapse onto a shiny metal bench. A week ago, I sat here and sang lullabies to baby Jal.

"I am but a dullard," I say again.

Kriz turns to me questioningly, and then finally looks into the face of my enemy. "It was he who did that to you?" I thought she might have guessed before now.

He releases the bottom of his mask so we can hear him more clearly. "Hello, Medera Krizia Woynauld." Goosebumps prickle my arms to hear her entire name. She's registered as a Crypt in our GCE database. "I never did believe you when you told me that mederas don't have favorite students. As a medero myself, I don't even pretend to hide mine. Admit it. You always liked Ringol more."

"And I never believed the therapist who said you were completely rehabilitated after the intensive psychotherapy. Ringol gave me more reason to like him." She narrows her eyes. "Now, I'll ask you to admit it. How dare you permanently ink such a hateful phrase on our J'Mave Allele?"

"Is it any wonder why I turned out the way I did?" Allund cries with renewed vigor. "With such a medera as you? You should have seen our family. The only one who cared for me at all was father."

Kriz stands as if she can't take it anymore, and her muscles quake. "Your father, as wonderful as he was, would only be ashamed of you now. Be grateful he's not alive to see it."

Allund startles. "He's... He's not dead?" He turns to me to settle the matter, as if he can't trust his own medera.

"Ringol," I say, as I take out the longest needle I could find for the injection, "is off to his funeral." I jab Allund as roughly as he did me, only I'm giving him a provirus to save his life, not a paralyzing agent to control him. "Your 'cure' is complete. You will develop Indigo Flu symptoms anywhere from a few minutes from now to a few hours. If you're able to survive that, you will recover normally. Hear me now: tired as I am, you will send me that video of Gelia or I will personally drag you back up to the surface and let the wild dogs enjoy an easy meal."

"I can't believe he's dead," Allund mumbles weakly.

"The video," I snap. "Now."

He nods slowly and presses his chip. "Lieutenant Crick, you may release the video."

"Crick?" both Kriz and I say simultaneously.

My chip dings with a new message; I don't have to look to know what it is.

"You're welcome," he says. As if I'd ever thank him. "Just don't forget our arrangement. That silly burrowmate of yours is safe for now but make no mistake, she is in as much peril as I am. It's an eye-for-eye type of arrangement, if you will," Allund says gruffly. "She may be in love with Crick, but his loyalty lies with me."

Jet.

"He's got Maddy," I say, as Kriz grimaces.

Allund smirks through his pain, a smile so devious and

twisted it sets my teeth on edge. "You must always think five steps ahead," he says in a mock-female voice: a poor imitation of Kriz. Then he changes back to his own. "Zuzan Cayan, you may be brilliant, but you will never outsmart me. I have too many connections, and you have too much to lose. That makes you vulnerable."

His eyes turn glassy, and as the motorized cycle of the decontamination chamber whirs to a stop, Allund begins to gag like he's about to vomit. The virus has already taken hold.

When the chamber control panel buzzes to signify the decontamination is complete, Kriz presses her thumb into the bioscanner to open the door. We flank each side of Allund and lift his elbows to exit the chamber.

We're able to flop him clumsily onto a gurney before taking him to the undertunnels.

Kriz and I agreed that no one else at GCE should know that we have Allund Woynauld here for treatment. They all have enough to worry about. We get him settled into the same room in the undertunnels where Kriz had Ringol recover. She agrees to keep watch over him while I keep everything else afloat within GCE.

I turn before I leave her alone with him, and realize she's quietly crying, like she's grieving the boy who Allund used to be. I don't want to, but I glance at him. The shininess of his skin makes me wonder what he went through when he was set on fire, and I shiver. His adoptive father had loved him, and I suspect Ringol and Kriz did, too. I suppose it's like the love I had for Maddy during her mold exposure. I never gave up hope that she could come back to us.

Soon, Allund will develop dark circles under his eyes like Ringol. For now, he shifts uncomfortably in the infirmary bed. A fever has set in. According to Ringol's account, it intensifies the headaches and nausea.

Good, I think, as I turn away. I tap my ChipPro to check the file that was sent, and I'm surprised that it's a full holographic video. It pops out in front of me – it's Gelia, looking frail and confused. I freeze. She's sitting at a student desk in what looks to be a lessons gallery, but it's not at the Cayan Burrow. What the jet?

"Oh my medera," I whisper. "I'm so sorry I left you the way I did."

I'm about to press "play," my heart beating triple speed, when I receive a call from an undertech on duty with the newest infants that had arrived. "J'Mave, we need you," he says.

So, I swipe the image of Gelia to close it, and frown when she's gone, feeling a longing as intense as ever. "I'm on my way."

CHAPTER 33

Immense Personal Strength

The emergency with the infants turns out not to be so dire. Some of the undertechs are still easing into their new roles as temporary parents to the infants, and therefore, they need as much encouragement as the children at times. This particular undertech couldn't get their child to sleep, so I showed them a few techniques and then handed the quieted infant back to them.

All five of the new arrivals are now deep into their proviral treatment, and the original babies are each in different stages of recovery, according to their bloodlabs and tests. In fact, seven or eight of these precious babes are nearing full health.

We won't be able to keep them here much longer.

We shouldn't.

They all have families, and any child who has the ability to grow up with their family should do so.

After I finish my rounds, I steal away to Ringol's office and close the door so I can watch the hologram of Gelia. Somehow, I feel more secure sitting at Ringol's desk. For a moment, I consider checking in with Kriz beforehand, but she would call me if she needed anything.

I take a breath and open the Gelia file again. There she is,

looking entirely out of place at a burrow that isn't hers. My
stomach churns as I swipe "play."

The holographic video comes to life as Gelia pounds her cane
into the floor. "I demand to see Medera Zamption immediately!
You cannot keep me here. Hello?" Gelia appears to be looking
directly into the camera as if she knows she's being watched.
I shiver.

And then a door opens in the rear of the room. The silhouette
of a tall figure appears. At first, I hope it's Ringol, but that
wouldn't make sense.

"Hello, Medera," he says just as his face comes into the light.
My jaw tightens at the sight of Allund. "Do you know who I
am?"

"Certainly, Medero." She swivels in her chair to face him.
"Good health."

"No," he says to my medera. "Let's skip the civilities. My
friend, Medera Zamption, called me when you showed up
on her doorstep begging for a spot for one of your former
students."

Medera Gelia's shoulders fall.

"I see you didn't realize we were connected, Zamption and
I," he says. "Now, this wouldn't be the same 'student' that was
sent to me with false FFR data, would it?"

"I don't know what you mean," Medera Gelia retorts.

"I'm sure you don't," he says in a derisive tone. "Well, this
green burrowmaid has mentioned you to my staffmembers
and subsequently has created an awful fuss for my academy.
Do you know who I'm talking about now?"

Gelia's eyes close slowly, and her lips move in a silent "pah."
An overwhelming wave of shame washes over me, much
the way I felt when I came to Cayan Burrow as a small child,
knowing that my new medera had read the unfair report from
my nurserymaid. When I left Cayan, Gelia urged me to get
along with people, and I just couldn't. I caused an upheaval,

but I'd argue that Allund deserved it. Arguing has always been a problem for me.

When she opens her eyes, she smiles. It's not Gelia's friendly smile, though. It's her all-knowing expression, her show of immense personal strength that I miss every single day.

"It is my opinion," she says slowly, annunciating each word, "that your new staffmember may like to suggest some improvements. She is unfairly limited by her Life Expectancy, though her brilliance surpasses any student I have ever taught, as does her capacity for empathy. You might try some of that yourself."

I smile at my medera's words. She is not angry with me. She knows me, and I love her for it.

"Unfortunately, since you altered her records and neglected to tell me she was previously called to another position, she was whisked away to her formerly accepted undertech job," he says. "What, exactly, are you trying to hide about her?"

He watches for Gelia's reaction, but she remains stoic. She's not giving him an inch.

"We know that you attended school at the same burrow as Izodora Camu." Allund holds his fist up as if he's angered by the very thought of Maven Camu for some reason. "Do you deny it?"

"Why should I deny attending school?" Gelia asks innocently. But I didn't know this. Gelia and Izodora were linked long ago, like me and Maddy? A million questions race through my mind.

"And here," Allund continues, "we find you at Zamption's door still attempting to outplace her. Tsk, tsk, teacher. I'm having you taken into custody and charged with falsifying the official FFR records, and I'm suing you for the cost and subsequent disruption to my academy."

Gelia laughs. "Thank all good."

"All good?" Allund says incredulously. "Didn't you hear? You're getting arrested."

"Perhaps," Gelia says. "But you've solved the last thing I was trying to accomplish as a medera. I know now that my girl is safe and in a position that better fits her abilities."

"She corrupted a very good b'arm of mine! And I also need to let go of my head burrowmaid! Heed my words, I will find out what is going on with this girl." Allund cries. "And all you can do is sit there smiling like you've succeeded in something important?"

"I'm an old woman," she replies, using her cane to help her up to a standing position; her beads, the symbol of all the students she has loved and taught and sent on to a fulfilling life, clack together in her thick locks. She faces the camera once again. "I could die happy today. I spent hours alone after all my students had transferred, going through old textbooks and paging through novels, hoping that what I did I did made a difference. And then I realized I had one more thing to do. Now you tell me it is complete."

Paging through? She must be talking about my books. All other Cayan students had their tabs. If she only knew how much I missed her!

"Officer!" Allund calls, and a man appears at the door.

Gelia bangs her cane twice. "Hear me now. I am ready." She smiles at the camera – her real smile – and turns to leave just before the video ends.

Gelia is alive, and I couldn't reach her because she's been arrested. Jet.

I watch the video again, and then use Ringol's tablet to research recent arrest stories until I find hers. It's new. It was only posted two days ago.

Longtime, respected medera found to have altered student records, taken into custody and released to a treatment center for dementia, it read. It's not an ideal situation for her but at least she's safe for now. Still, I will get her out if it's the last thing I do. It looks like Gelia was several steps ahead of both me and Allund.

My stomach flips. I told Allund exactly where Ringol is. What if Allund still has "connections" out that way, where they used to live?

I call Kriz on my chip, but she doesn't pick up. Jet, jet, jet!

Running out of Ringol's office, I head off to the entrance of the undertunnels, deep inside GCE's intestines. I can't believe I willingly told Allund where his brother has gone. Ringol is out there alone and exposed! How could I be so stupid?

I call Kriz again, but she still doesn't pick up. For all good, where is she? He couldn't possibly have done something to her. He was too weak!

I round the corner to the secret entrance, and I'm out of breath. There's no way Allund could be so many steps ahead of me. I can't let myself even think it.

I dart through the side of the tunnels I hadn't been to before today, and head to the room where we're treating Allund.

"Kriz!" I shout from the hallway.

"In here!" she calls just as I enter the room. She's holding Allund steady over the side of the bed as he vomits into a receptacle.

I blow out a deep breath and hold my stomach, cramping from the unnecessary sprint I just put myself through.

"What is it?" she asks.

"His ChipPro," I say. "Where is it?"

She points to a console on the far side of the room. "I've put all his things over there."

I quickly rifle through his belongings and find his chip.

"What's the matter?" she says. "You can't tamper with that, you know. It's government issued. There are regulations."

"He knows where Ringol is," I remind her and Kriz gasps. "If anything happens to Ringol, it's my fault."

"Trusting Allund has always turned out poorly for me." Kriz takes his chip from my hand, tosses it to the ground, and crunches it under her heel. So much for regulations. "Five steps ahead, indeed. Don't worry. I've stayed many steps ahead of this one before."

"But we can't keep Allund here forever. His 'people' will be looking for him. We have to warn Ringol somehow." I say.

"We will, J'Mave. Ringol and I have a system worked out. Now, go and rest," she says comfortingly, in a way that reveals how good a medera she once was. Now she's something entirely different. "You have babies to save."

I shake my head, watching her clean up after Allund's mess, as if she's perfectly fine with where she is in the world.

I pause. "How do you do that?" I ask her. "You're a medera. You could be teaching children, and doing a much better job than Allund."

She covers Allund's forehead with a damp cloth in the gentlest manner and then turns to me. "I suppose we're a lot alike then, aren't we? As a former medera, I'd have to answer you with a question. Haven't you made sacrifices along your journey? And would you be the person you are today without those?"

I blink at her. "I've come a long way, yes. But I still want to teach."

"Ah," Kriz says. "But being a medera and teaching people are two different things, no?"

I shake my head in confusion. Does she mean she's teaching me now?

"Who else could have instructed the GCE undertechs in the care and development of infants? J'Mave Nukleo never even considered it, and I daresay neither did Ringol. No. It was you who has not only saved the lives of the infants, but has impacted so many of your undertechs. You are already an amazing teacher, Zuzan. Not because you're a genius, but because you love." And then Kriz does something I would never expect. She hugs me. "And I am grateful to you beyond words."

"Thank you," I say, holding her embrace.

I suppose you have to value love to benefit from its power.

I look closely at this woman as she returns to Allund's side.

She gave each of her two charges everything she could out of her love for them. One became my brave Ringol, who is kind, loving, and moral, even if he refuses to wear a hat. And then there's Allund, who for whatever reason chose anger, vengeance, and hate. He values it, spreading it to everyone around him, fueled by his fear. Fueled by focusing on what makes us different, instead of what makes us the same. Hate is a mighty powerful force, too, and can spread like a plague.

He can get to Maddy. He can get to Gelia. And for all good, it's possible for him to get to Ringol. But it's also possible for him to change, and I hope he does. Maybe the time Allund spends convalescing with Kriz will revive the more human parts of him.

Even the great Maven Izodora Camu couldn't have postulated such an experiment.

Perhaps a mederaship is still in my future, I think. And I hope hard-as-diamonds for a long-term relationship with Ringol to be as well. But whatever happens, I will be guided by love. It's what Gelia would have wanted for me, and what I want for myself.

I smile at Kriz, thankful for her lesson, and turn toward my chamberroom to chase some rest.

Kleo, Kriz, and I will figure everything else out tomorrow.

ACKNOWLEDGMENTS

When my youngest son was born with a congenital brain malformation and later diagnosed with autism and developmental delays, my husband and I were devastated, knowing the struggles our child would deal with his whole life. We halved our income so I could stay at home to focus on his development. I appreciate my husband Tom, and my older kids, Tommy and Sarah, who had to give up so much as a result. While we have hundreds of prickly memories during the tougher times, we have even more memories of the pure love and joy we've experienced because of Drew.

For years we thought Drew would never speak, so we did our best to teach him letters and words. By the time he went to kindergarten, he was able to recognize practiced words. He wasn't, however, capable of spontaneously using words to communicate until he was five or six years old. The day he said "I love you" to me was glorious. Although he still can't hold a sustained conversation, he can now successfully get his point across when he needs to. He's changed my perspective on life in monumental ways, for which I am humbled and grateful.

I need to thank my sister Cecilia (the real writer), because when I needed to use my brain again about a year after Drew was born, she introduced me to an online writers' critique forum. I soon made friends and was introduced to a second online writing forum, Write Stuff Extreme, where Zuzan's story was born. My forum friends read and critiqued chapter-length installments at a time, and contributed to my growth as a writer by pointing out plot holes, providing humorous encouragement, and reminding me about characterization and emotion. Thank you, Antonio Diggs, Krisztina Fehervari, Mary Frame, Katharina Gerlach, William Hahn, and Jennifer Thorne, for spending countless hours reading my words when they were in rough form. I also need to thank Cindy Baldwin, Christie Buckner and Rick Wheeler, my good friends who have been wonderfully supportive of me for years.

After about a decade of writing with four manuscripts and no publishing contracts, I was about to give up. It was around this time that Ali Herring, who read Zuzan's story several years prior, surprised me with an email after she took a job as a literary agent. Her undying faith in this story and belief in my writing amazes me to this day. Thank you, Ali, my fantastic agent, for being such a caring soul. Thank you to Gemma Creffield, my terrific editor, who recognized our vision for *Burrowed* and brought Zuzan to life.

Sincere thanks to my parents, Bob and Geraldine, who as high school teachers allowed me to witness dedication and love for a job which impacts so many young people. And finally, thank you to all the teachers, therapists, and school aides in Drew's life who have brought him farther than we ever dreamed possible.

CHAPTER ONE

Hypovolemia
A state of decreased intravascular volume, including as a result of blood loss.

The sun was barely up, but the hour didn't keep folks from scrambling in to sell their blood. Early bird donors packed into lines that stretched to the entrance, their collective anxiety like a vapor that flooded Willa's nostrils when she walked in behind them. After so many decades on the job, she could almost discern the iron tang of it. That they were a mixture of types was obvious by their dress, with some low- and midbloods sprinkled in among the usual O-negs. Willa double-checked the time in case she'd somehow arrived late and glanced around for the station manager. "Claude?"

"Over here," he called, rounding the corner from the big freezer.

Willa held her arms open toward the growing mob.

"Price boost," said Claude.

"Again?"

"Check your PatrioCast," hollered Gena from down at Stall D. "Came down thirty minutes ago."

Willa slipped on her reading glasses and brought up the alert screen on her handheld touchstone:

▽ **PATRIOCAST 10.19.67** ▽

Residual ionizing radiation since Goliath causes latent spike in chronic diseases

To answer demand, Patriot offers the following incentives for units donated above the Draw. Valid through 10.21.67:

ONEG: +40.75

OPOS: +34.64

ANEG: +18.75

APOS: +16.67

BNEG: +5.7

BPOS: +5.13

ABNEG: +1.71

ABPOS: +1.45

▽ *Patriot thanks ALL DONORS. Your gift matters!* ▽

Patriot called it the Draw, but the people called it the Harvest. It came every forty-five days, a reaping of blood from every person sixteen and up. But it wasn't the Harvest that had Donor Station Eight packed to the gills. It was the chance to sell. For those feeling blooded enough to give beyond the minimum, Patriot was a willing buyer – that was the Trade.

Willa hung her jacket and donned her black lab cloak, then brought Stall A online. She buttoned the cloak and pulled its hood snug to her head as the various scanners and probes hummed to life. Each stall had two lanes, corral like, so phlebotomists could handle a pair of donors simultaneously if they were dexterous enough to manage. Willa was.

All of Patriot's collectors carried the title of "Phlebotomist," a point of unvoiced contention for Willa, since she was the only one who'd ever actually been a genuine phlebotomist. Sure, the others could pull a blood bag, spot-check it for authenticity, and drop it in the preservation vaults, but they wouldn't know the cubital vein from the cephalic. Especially Gena. Decades before the world went sideways, Willa had been trained in the old ways of venipuncture. Not that it mattered. True phlebotomy was an antiquated practice, irrelevant, like driving a car, another thing she used to be good at. The new ways were undoubtedly more efficient. It was for the best, after all. People in the Gray Zones needed the blood.

Willa's first two donors, a man and a woman, stepped into the lanes and lowered their shoulder-zips, exposing ports in their skin onto which blood bags were connected through a small siphon and needle junction. She quickly removed and processed the man's bag, then turned to the woman.

The man interrupted, "I got extra," and presented a second full bag from a satchel.

"Where'd you get this one, Tillman?" Willa asked. He was in so often that his sourcing had to be black-market. Most likely blood muggings. The cash-for-blood trade had created an unseemly underground economy, and it was booming.

"It's mine, *reaper*," he answered with a devious grin.

He knew that she had to take the blood if it scanned clear. It was company policy to accept any blood offered, so long as the phenotype, or blood type, matched the donor's profile. That didn't guarantee it was actually the donor's blood – far from it – but it gave Patriot a veneer of deniability if they were ever accused of being a market for questionably-sourced product. She ran it over the needle probe, which analyzed for phenotype, as well as other immunoreactive antigens and antibodies, the organism of origin, diseases, and the percentage of red blood cells in eryptosis, or cell death. If the readings were off, the bag would be rejected.

The probe cleared the unit and she dropped it curtly into her booth's cooling vault. Tillman smirked and scanned his touchstone for credit. "See you tomorrow," he said.

"You'd better not," said Willa.

She rotated to the woman. "Sorry about that, ma'am."

The woman was rough, wearing her thirty or so years like fifty. She held her sleeve open loosely, eyes drooping. Willa sighed and reluctantly removed the blood bag from her port. "Ma'am?"

The woman's eyelids fluttered as she struggled to say something. Her head flopped forward and she collapsed against the stall, her thin legs and arms in a tangle.

"Claude! Gelpack!" Willa rounded her station into the narrow corral. "Ma'am?" She tapped the woman's cheeks.

When Claude arrived, Willa traded the woman's blood bag for the gelpack, a small syrette filled with carbs and epinephrine used to jumpstart folks who sold more than their bodies could give. She broke its cap, pushed the two tiny needles into the skin on the inside of the woman's arm, and squeezed the contents into her basilic vein.

Claude looked at the woman, shaking his head. "Crazy. An A-neg in here trading like a lowblood."

Willa applied a small bandage over the wound and gave a touch of pressure. "How do you know she's A-neg?"

"Just a hunch." He leaned into the stall and scanned the bag on Willa's console. "Mmhmm. A-neg."

"The incentives are too high, Claude."

"I hear you, Willa Mae, but…" he dropped the bag into her vault and took the chance to whisper "…what can you do? Rules are rules." He gave a helpless shrug.

Willa helped the woman to a bench along the wall opposite a screen tuned to the Channel. She let her eyes blur over it while the stranger went in and out of consciousness on her shoulder. Back before the war, before Patriot, the medically recommended wait between donations was fifty-six days. This was to ensure that people fully recovered between donations. The absolute earliest that the human body could replenish a unit of blood was twenty-eight days, with many people taking up to three times that. The Harvest had lopped eleven days from the interval, mandating one donated pint every forty-five. If you wanted your government food rations, you showed up. If you didn't, you starved.

The Harvest alone was enough of a strain. But Patriot had gone a step further, offering cash to people willing to sell even more than the Harvest minimum. Of course, people were drawn in. Robots had taken most of the jobs and the Trade was regarded as something like basic income. Except folks were paying for it with the fruit of their veins. It never ceased to amaze Willa how much people could adapt, walking around in a constant state of hypovolemia just to get a little more coin, wearing symptoms so long that they eventually became character traits. Weakness, fatigue, confusion, clammy skin. Eventually anemia or shock ended the cycle. To Willa it was like state sanctioned Russian roulette, and folks were just spinning the cylinder.

Claude looked at her sideways. She was violating company policy by vacating her stall, but Claude tended to give her wider berth than the others. She had quickly worked her way up to Stall A – the equivalent of first chair in an orchestra – and had never relinquished it. Her gaudy production numbers brought her a certain amount of leniency.

The woman's hands lay folded against the bench like possum claws; skeletal and dirty, the dwindling meat beneath the skin a ticking clock. Willa had seen it all before, a cycle of destruction that churned through the districts to touch every family.

The woman straightened as if she'd been suddenly plugged back in.

"Ma'am?" Willa asked with a gentle touch to her wrist.

"What do you want?"

"You passed out. You've given too much."

The woman's pupils tightened on the screen, where a scrolling chyron flashed yet another incentive bump and she sprang from the bench. Willa latched to her arm instinctively. "There's no need. You're A-neg. The price will be the same tomorrow. Please, don't."

"Get off me," she growled. Willa knew it wasn't who the woman really was, but the Trade had a way of exposing the nerves. Ripping her arm away, she returned to the back of the line.

Willa stepped into her stall and got her line moving. She processed bags, checked for fakes, but her eyes stayed on the woman. In short order, she was next in line, a new bag on her port, filling red pulse-by-pulse. "I'm feel good," she mumbled in anticipation of Willa's objection.

"No, you don't," said Willa. "That's the gelpack talking. It's just adrenaline. Please don't do this."

The woman leaned heavily on the side of the stall. "You haffto I got kids."

She was technically correct. Willa did have to. Grudgingly, she removed the half-full bag and processed it. It was a brutal thing, the blood trade, but here she was stuck on the receiving end of it; a cog in a runaway machine.

Just before close, a notification glowed orange on her display. She deactivated her stall, sending glass barricades across the lanes and flagged Claude in Stall B. "Coolant."

Claude summoned Willa's donors to his line and they grumbled their way over.

Willa angled a panel open and dipped her hand into her cooling vault. Her toes curled anxiously inside her orthotics. It was warming. "How much room do we have in the big cooler?"

"Topped out after lunch."

She had almost fifty liters. Blood couldn't be transfused after four hours in warm conditions due to bacterial proliferation. It would go bad long before morning if she couldn't get it cooled and her pay would be docked. "I'll call a technician."

"Good luck with that."

Willa tapped the support button and sat helplessly as donors side-eyed her from the long lines in front of Claude. *Sorry* she mouthed.

Closing time came with no technician responding. Normally, all of the vaults would be taken to the distribution hub after hours, but with no way to cool hers, it had to go now. She wheeled the vault, about the size of an old hotel refrigerator, from under the console and unhooked the cables from the processing interface. Having taken all of the extra donors, Claude's line was still out the door.

"I'm taking this to SCS," said Willa.

"Sorry, Willa, I'd do it, but..." The station supervisor couldn't leave with donors present and Patriot didn't turn away willing supply.

"I know," she said. "When you're done... do you mind... can you fetch Isaiah from school?"

"Sure. He's at the same spot?"

"He is. Thank you, sweetheart."

"My pleasure," answered Claude, swiping blood bags from the donors nearly as fast as she.

Outside Station Eight the sky was purple on one side and orange on the other, with clouds like gray icing layered between. The type of weather Willa described as *soon-to-be*. Mid October cool, soon-to-be cold. She shivered preemptively and hailed a taxi drone.

Drone rides were an absolute luxury in the blood districts and Willa felt guilty in summoning one, even if it was necessary to help her ferry the vault. After half a minute, a taxi drone in mustard yellow broke from the low-hanging clouds.

The sight of a drone descending from the sky to land right in front of you was something Willa would never get used to, even though they'd been around for decades. They seemed alien. Aside from helicopters, things that could fly were supposed to have wings. And drones were *not* helicopters.

To Willa they looked like flying gumdrops. Aside from some aerodynamic ridges that pinched out from the sides, they were rounded at the edges and slightly narrower near the roof. The motors were mounted in an array around the top rim, giving them a crownlike appearance. They were called "ducted fans," though the term meant little to Willa. They resembled giant rolls of toilet paper with propeller blades tucked snuggly against the inner walls. Independent articulation allowed them to control not only lift, but direction and altitude. With small alterations to the blade shape over the years, they were hummingbird quiet. Another eerie feature.

The taxi landed and the door swept open from the bottom. *Welcome aboard CROW FLIES*, it said.

"Patriot Distribution, SCS," said Willa. "Quickly please."

We will arrive at Patriot Distribution, Southern City Segment, in two and a half minutes.

Once she'd buckled into the bench and secured the vault to the cargo clip against the wall, the drone lifted off. A screen around the inner perimeter created a false three-hundred and sixty degree window, interrupted only by an actual window, set like a porthole in the door. She'd flown in plenty of drones but, much like their appearance, she had never gotten used to them – how they felt, how they took away all control. She longed for the solid predictability of a steering wheel and the responsiveness of an accelerator. Before the war, before the Harvest, before Patriot, when the asphalt was still good and cars could be afforded, Willa owned the roads, collecting tickets like blue ribbons. Speeding – her one real vice. But that was then. Nowadays, a car would appear every so often near the business district, but only the rich had money for such extravagances.

The drone traveled through the early evening glow in electric silence, toward the rough geographical center of the Southern City Segment. This was one of four such segments that made up the city, along with North-by, Crosstown, and Eastern. Each had a distribution center that collected the day's take from the donor stations in that segment. Totals from each were then shipped by transport drone to Central City Collection – CCC – downtown. Set in the middle of an urban forest, Triple-C was a sprawling complex that Patriot media proudly termed "the Heart" because it was the central hub for the circulation of blood to the Gray Zones. *From our heart to yours*, so it went.

Willa put her hand to the side of the vault, anxious over the precious cargo warming inside. Her anxiety was double since she didn't know when the coolant had actually gone out. It was possible the entire load was bad, and a single day of lost pay could break her.

The drone settled and Willa quickly unclipped the vault. *You have arrived at Patriot Distribution, SCS,* said the drone. *Will you be needing continued service?*

"No, thank you," she said, her heart already pounding like a countdown.

Have a most pleasant evening, then.

"You too." She rolled the vault onto the concrete apron in front of the building. The drone sped away.

Set off from the more densely populated residential areas, SCS Distribution stood alone at the center of a magnificent hexagonal concrete expanse, surrounded by a wall with trees stretching up behind it. A single road led out and into the blood districts. As far as she could tell, the place was empty. No people or other drones. Just a speedloop tube descending from the building's outer wall and into the ground at the far side.

The transports had not yet taken to the sky, and until they'd all departed, she had time to deposit the vault. She wheeled it heavily to one side of the huge polygonal building where a cutout in the thick concrete had a processing interface that looked like an old automated teller machine.

Willa's orthopedics slipped on the moist concrete as she struggled to roll the cooling vault to the connection point at the far end of a ramp.

Her bangs wicked away beads of sweat as she wrangled the vault. *You're too old for this.* Finally, with her legs about to give, a loud click signaled the vault's successful connection to the interface and it absorbed into the building. She rested against the wall for a moment, letting the cool cement sooth her nerves. Above, the blood transport drones began to filter from the building. They were wider and shorter than human transport drones, more utilitarian, and less refined – shaped like giant cigar boxes with ducted fans powerful enough to carry up to six cooling vaults apiece. Their only embellishment was the phrase BE A PATRIOT illuminated on their bellies.

She felt for her touchstone at the end of its lanyard and navigated to the screen that would register if the blood had gone through. It still read 00.00. She'd gotten the blood to distribution but wouldn't receive credit if it had spoiled. Holding her breath, she watched the numbers and willed them to change. They had to change. They had to. Afraid to blink, her eyes started to burn.

… 47.52 liters

Relief. A stay of execution. Only two and a half liters rejected.

She exhaled and stood up. Aside from the exiting parade of blood drones, she was alone. The air smelled like rain. She pulled up the hood on her reaper's black and began walking. Maybe she'd get home before it really came down.

She stopped after only a few steps, thinking that she'd heard something like a distant mosquito. It became more pronounced, a high-pitched whining that seemed to emanate from the squadron. One of the drones had fallen below formation. Even if it cleared the wall, she could see it wouldn't make it over the trees. A tick of panic came at the loss of such a large amount of blood, especially after she'd exerted so much effort to save a single vault. She briefly envisioned herself running underneath to try and catch it. Much as she disliked the Harvest, the Gray Zones needed every drop. Willa drew up her touchstone and alerted Patriot Emergency.

The motors on the drone struggled as it sank, with one exploding in a torus of glowing shrapnel. It hit the compound's outer wall and smashed to the ground, sending prop blades into the hull and gashing the steel. Vaults tumbled onto the pavement as the twisted carcass came to rest. Willa felt herself drawn through the debris field, but stopped short of the drone, still showering sparks. Calm down, she thought, there's no one in there.

A metal ring rolled lazily to her foot where it toppled over, and silence returned. She took stock of the scene and began toward the wreckage, careful to avoid the red slick of donor blood that would soon coat the asphalt. But as she neared the drone, her stomach twisted.

There wasn't any.

She triggered her touchstone's light and flashed it over the ground. Not so much as a drop of red, and no bags whatsoever. Had they remained inside the vaults through the crash? Had they all somehow held? Their poly construction was strong, sure, but those fan blades... it seemed impossible. Nearby, a dented vault laid open on its side, one wheel still spinning. She knelt to look inside.

Suddenly a white light blanched her vision. Willa turned into the beam eyes closed, her touchstone held aloft. "Willa Mae Wallace!" she yelled. "Station Eight, SCS."

The light descended from the sky and settled nearby. She cracked an eye just enough to make out the shape of a Patriot security drone silhouetted against the backdrop of the outer wall.

"Step inside, please," came a voice.

Willa took a final glance at the carnage and headed for the drone. When she was clear of the glare, the door opened to reveal a nice-looking man standing inside. He was in his early forties with a tanned face and a full head of brassy hair. His beige suit set off a bright pink tie and matching pocket square that immediately made Willa think of country clubs – if those still existed someplace. Her eyes were drawn to a gold pin in the shape of the letter "P" with the stem plunged through an anatomical heart that rested against his lapel.

"Yes, well, the newer insignias are terribly bland, are they not?" He spoke as if already in mid-conversation. "I suppose I flout the corporate message by remaining loyal to the original logo after a rebrand."

"I've seen you at our station before, I think," Willa said, "but I'm afraid I don't recall your name."

"Jesper Olden." His voice had the velvety timbre of wealth. "Patriot security. Please, step in from the cold." He took her hand and helped her inside.

"You don't look like security," she said, forgetting herself, then quickly added, "I mean – my apologies, it's been a long day. You just don't see people dressed like you many times in the year. Especially not out in the districts."

"No offense taken, Ms Wallace." He tapped the control screen. "We should have you home in fewer than two minutes."

"Oh, you don't have to do that, sir, I'm OK walking." But just like that, Willa felt the drone lifting off.

"Nonsense. We don't need you getting hit on the head by a defective drone." He gave a tepid chuckle. "Think of the liability."

Willa smiled weakly. Liability? The court system had long ago been largely dismantled, now used only to settle financial disputes among corporations and wealthy individuals. Regular people didn't meet the net worth threshold to utilize the system. His choice of words was perplexing. Maybe he was just using outdated vernacular as a matter of habit. Perhaps he was so out of touch that he didn't even consider how ridiculous the reference had been. He stared blithely out the window and Willa decided that must be it.

"Well," she said, "thank you for the ride." She stepped to the opposite side of the passenger compartment and took a seat. Relief was immediate. She'd always stored anxiety in her feet.

Olden considered the viewscreen. "Ah, there they are. The diagnostics on the crashed drone, see?" He gestured to some figures that Willa couldn't make out and gave the rest a cursory review. "Did you hear or see anything odd? Did you note anybody in the area before it went down?"

"I didn't see anyone else," she affirmed. "It just fell, that's all." There had been at least one empty vault in the wreckage but she had a gut feeling she wasn't supposed to have seen that.

"No one saw you there?"

"Not anyone other than you, Mr Olden."

"Wonderful. I appreciate the effort you made to get your take processed, especially this close to our Patrioteer conference." Willa knew about the conference, an annual two-day meeting for upper management to do whatever it was upper management did. Jesper played with the screen. "Let me credit you, let's say, five hundred as bonus for your effort. Is that fair?"

"Oh, Mr Olden, you shouldn't do that," she protested, uncomfortable accepting unearned lucre.

"Don't be foolish, Ms Wallace." He tapped in the amount. "That drone could have killed you."

"It was nowhere near–"

"Willa. May I call you Willa?" he said without really asking. "I insist on it. Patriot insists on it." He brightened. "You could buy Halloween candy this year. Five hundred would cover the entire segment, I'd bet. You'd be royalty."

"It's too much, Mr Olden, I'd prefer you didn't give me any money." The amount was more than a week's pay, and easy money came with strings. Aside from that, Halloween hadn't been observed for at least twenty years.

"And I'd prefer our drones not endanger top performers." He tapped the display. "Now let's not have any further discussion of the matter. *With anyone*."

"I'm just happy to do my job."

"I assure you, Willa, we appreciate it." He flattened his suit jacket. "Ah, here we are at your stack. Do you feel well enough to return to work or will you need some days off?"

"I'm fine," she said as the door opened. "I'll be there tomorrow."

"Lovely, then. A good evening to you and to Isaiah."

She shivered at the mention of Isaiah. It always surprised her when Patriot managers voiced little details about her life that she considered private. She halfway assumed that the executives received prompts from their implants whenever they spoke with low level workers to make them seem more relatable or friendly. But she never got used to hearing strangers mention her family members out of turn.

The drone lifted away and her touchstone signaled the arrival of the money. An influx of five hundred would have had her rejoicing and thanking God out loud if she'd actually earned it. Entering her apartment stack, it felt like a chain.

She greeted Isaiah with a suffocating embrace that made him lose whatever game he was playing on his old viewer and he grumbled an objection.

Claude, who had come over to keep an eye on Isaiah, politely passed on a dinner invitation. She couldn't blame him. He was a station supervisor and didn't have to eat from The Box like everyone else. The Box – a literal box of prepackaged food – was provided by Patriot to residents of the blood districts who maintained one-hundred percent participation in the Harvest. The idea had been sold as a way to streamline subsistence programs. Instead of going to the store and picking out groceries for yourself and your family, the government picked them for you. Processed mystery meats and condensed dairy, sickly sweet canned fruit cocktails, powdered grains. On lucky weeks, a handful of oat cubes or tea. Many lowblood families relied on The Box completely. With her job, Willa leaned on it as a supplement, but few were able to live entirely Box free. She'd pass on it too if she could.

She and Isaiah ate genmod pasta prepared with a splash of black-market vinegar, topped with the last of some dehydrated poultry cubes that she'd managed to stretch over a full week. She stirred her bowl until they puffed into something that resembled the meat they had once been, and took small bites, chewing deliberately to make it all last. Isaiah devoured without ceremony.

A thought occurred to her, curiosity in the wake of her encounter at SCS, that she might tune to *The Patriot Report*. The show, which aired in place of the local news, touted Patriot's blood collection statistics and good deeds. Willa considered it a painfully tacky program, tortuously drawn out to thirty minutes in length, and cast in the mold of an old lottery-drawing segment complete with a shiny host yammering on through billboard teeth. The company served a vital role but bragging about it in such an ostentatious fashion left a bad taste. The fringes of the country were at war. People were suffering.

Swallowing her disgust, she turned it on, drawing Isaiah to the screen like a moth to a porchlight. Another reason she rarely watched anything.

"Isaiah, please," she said, yanking him back a reasonable distance. "It's nothing good."

Tanned darker than a roast turkey, the host was flanked by two scantily-clad assistants who held up digital posters announcing the statistics for every precinct within each of the four city segments. Willa did a double take. Setting her dinner to the side, she paused the screen and quickly added the figures. Southern City Segment was reporting a full take, highest in the city.

Impossible. With a crashed drone – carrying what were most likely empty vaults – SCS should have been dead last. They were either mistaken or they were lying. She reached for something to write with and jotted down the numbers, thinking she'd discuss it with Claude, but her pen scratched to a halt. Jesper had been clear. She couldn't tell Claude, couldn't tell anyone.

For more great title recommendations,
check out the Angry Robot website and
social channels

www.angryrobotbooks.com
@angryrobotbooks

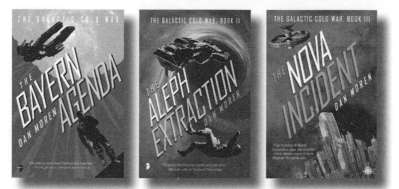

Science Fiction, Fantasy and WTF?!

@angryrobotbooks